THE SITUATION HAD GONE MUCH TOO FAR

Though everything in her revolted against it, she knew that the time had come to reveal her name. "You should know that I am no common doxy," she said. "I am a highborn lady."

He laughed in that way of his that she was coming to thoroughly detest. "Sweetheart, those games are all very well in their place. But the time for games is over. I want a real woman in my arms tonight, a willing one and not some character from a fantasy."

What a fool she had been to think she could use this man for her own purposes. She had badly miscalculated and now she was paying the price.

Bought and paid for—that was what was in his mind. She was aware of something else. He didn't really want to hurt or humiliate her. He wanted to have his way with her. He thought he had that right.

He wasn't forcing his caresses on her. He was simply holding her, watching her with an unfathomable expression. "Julian," she whispered, "Victoria Noble is not my real name."

"I didn't think it was," he said, and kissed her.

The sudden flood of pleasure was so shocking that Serena's whole body went slack. She could not get command of her breathing.

There was worse to follow. . . .

Dangerous to Love

Elizabeth Thornton

BANTAM BOOKS
NEW YORK • TORONTO • LONDON • SYDNEY • AUCKLAND

DANGEROUS TO LOVE

A Bantam Book / July 1994

Bantam reissue / April 1997

ISBN 0-553-56787-X

Published simultaneously in the United States and Canada

Bantam Books are published by Bantam Books, a division of Bantam Doubleday Dell Publishing Group, Inc. Its trademark, consisting of the words "Bantam Books" and the portrayal of a rooster, is Registered in U.S. Patent and Trademark Office and in other countries. Marca Registrada. Bantam Books, 1540 Broadway, New York, New York 10036.

PRINTED IN THE UNITED STATES OF AMERICA

RAD   0 9 8 7 6 5 4

This one is for my
editor, Wendy McCurdy,
and she knows why

Dangerous to Love

Chapter One

❦

The first time Serena saw him, she knew there was going to be trouble. He had that look. It was the sudden stillness that alerted her to his presence. She looked up from the cards Flynn had just dealt her and became aware of a silent, menacing figure in the open doorway. One hand rested casually on the hilt of his smallsword, and even in that dim light, she could see the distinct challenge in his eyes as they scanned the various tables in the tavern's crowded, smoke-filled common room.

Dangerous. Reckless. Wild. Those were the words that passed through Serena's mind. When his glance fell on her, taking in her filmy costume, lingering on her artfully painted face framed with soot-black curls, and the wide expanse of white bosom, especially the wide expanse of white bosom, her fingers itched to reach for her cape to cover herself. She had no idea why his interest should fix on her. In relation to some of the other "ladies" who were present that evening, she was hardly worth a second stare. Nothing too much, nothing too obvious—that was the rule she and Flynn followed.

Remembering the role she was playing, she smiled at him vaguely and drew Flynn's attention to the stranger by fingering the black silk patch at the corner of her mouth, her signal to be on the alert. Then the stranger's eyes passed over her, and calling for a tankard of ale, he found a place for himself at a table against the wall. Only then did the hum of conversation resume.

Serena darted a quick, questioning look at Flynn. It

was one of the other players, however, a resident performer at Drury Lane, who answered Serena's pointed look. Cassie, in Serena's opinion, *was* worth a second stare. The girl's looks were dramatic, and her tightly laced hooped gown of crimson damask set off her supple curves to admiration. Serena had left off her hoops this evening, knowing that they would only get in the way once she and Flynn embarked on their mission.

"Julian Raynor," whispered Cassie, her eyes fairly devouring the gentleman in question, "you know, the gamester. Oh Lud, he's looking our way," and she slanted Raynor a flirtatious look that was half challenging, half mischievous.

Cassie's partner, a young actor, let out an impatient sigh. "Ladies, may I remind you that a card game is in progress? I suggest you mind your cards."

"And I second that suggestion," said Flynn, giving Serena a very straight look.

It was hard to concentrate on the game of whist that was in progress when the name of London's most notorious gamester was reverberating inside her head. Somehow Serena managed to contribute to the lively conversation that went on about her, as well as play her cards without drawing attention to herself. But behind her smiles and carefully untroubled expression, her mind was hard at work.

What she could not fathom was why Raynor would deign to visit a ramshackle place like this one. The Thatched Tavern was not, by any means, a hovel, but it was no palace either. Its patrons were a motley lot, ranging from the upper echelons of household servants to the odd student as well as a plethora of theater people from nearby Drury Lane. As for the gambling, it was desultory, and rarely for high stakes.

For their purposes, the tavern was an ideal rendezvous.

There was much coming and going. Neither Flynn's untutored tongue nor her cultured accents would rouse anyone's suspicions. Flynn was, in actual fact, a footman. She was passing herself off as an actress, or an aspiring actress to be precise. The most compelling reason for choosing The Thatched Tavern for their rendezvous, however, was because it sat above a secret Roman drain which led to a labyrinth of underground passages. Flynn knew these underground passages like the back of his hand.

Raynor's setting was far different from this. He was a professional gambler, and kept a gaming house, a magnificent place just off Fleet Street where, it was rumored, fortunes were won and lost every night on the turn of a card. The patrons of his establishment, among them her own brothers, were drawn from the wealthy upper classes.

Raynor was so out of place here that Serena's mind worried at it like a dog with a bone. She had good reason to be worried. At any moment, their "passenger" would be delivered, and it was their job to transport him to a safe house, close to the docks, where her younger brother, Clive, was waiting for them. At first light, weather permitting, their "passenger" would be aboard ship taking sail for France and freedom.

That thought put her in mind of something else she remembered about Julian Raynor, or Major Raynor as he was generally known. The man was credited with being something of a war hero. His daring exploits at Prestonpans were almost legendary. Some said that if there had been more like him on the field that day, government forces would have crushed the Rebellion that much sooner, and there never would have been a Culloden.

He was an enemy of the Rebellion, and that made him her enemy too. If he once got wind of their real purpose in being here this evening, it could prove catastrophic not only for their "passenger," but for Clive, Flynn, and her self also. Aiding and abetting Jacobite fugitives was still a capital offense.

For a fleeting moment, Stephen's face swam before her eyes. The thought of Prestonpans, where Raynor had won such glory for himself, never failed to revive the old memories, the old ache. At Prestonpans, Stephen had cruelly perished, and all her dreams with him. It was entirely possible that it was Raynor's hand that had cut down her betrothed.

No good could be served by perpetuating the old hatreds. She understood this. She accepted that the Cause was lost. But so long as the authorities hunted down Jacobite fugitives as if they were vermin, there was still something to fight for. Her own father was one of the lucky ones. When the Rebellion failed, he had managed to escape to France, where he now languished. Until amnesty was offered to all Jacobites with a price on their heads, their escape route must remain open.

From the corner of her eye, she saw Raynor adjust the angle of his chair, as though to get a better view of her table. Why was he here? What was he doing watching their table? She fervently hoped that it was Cassie who had caught his eye, and not herself or Flynn. Cassie might have been playing to the gallery, so animated were her expressions and gestures. Evidently, she was playing up to Raynor, hoping to attract his interest. Flynn, on the other hand, looked perfectly unremarkable. In his powdered toupee and wire-rimmed spectacles, he had aged ten years. No one would have taken him for the flamboyant young chairman who was forever getting into fisticuffs with other chairmen when their sedans got in his way. Her own getup was equally deceiving. According to Flynn, the black wash in her hair and the powder and paint had completely transformed her.

If they were ever caught, their safest course lay in stick-

ing as closely to the truth as they dared. It was not unknown for ladies of fashion to risk their reputations in
their search for novelty and amusement. Her presence
here might cause a brief scandal, nothing more. The real
danger lay when she and Flynn were in possession of their
"passenger." The sooner he was delivered, the better it
would be for all concerned.

Apart from Raynor's presence, things were going according to plan. With a quick, meaningful glance in
Flynn's direction, touching her little finger to the curl on
her brow, she signaled that it was time to move on. The
next hand must be their last.

It was her turn to deal. There was a time when she
would have invented any pretext to avoid this chore.
She'd had a year of nights in places like this one to hone
her skills. Flexing her fingers, she skillfully sliced and cut
the cards, then quickly dealt each player a hand. Her eyes
lifted without volition, and were caught and held by Raynor's inflexible stare.

The fine hairs on the back of Serena's neck rose in
foreboding. Oh God, she knew when she first saw him
that there was going to be trouble. Swallowing, dragging
her eyes away, she threw out her first card.

She played as if her life depended on it, not because she
wanted to win, but because she couldn't help herself, not
when Raynor's gaze was fixed on her, and she was sure,
now, that she was the one he had singled out. Winning,
in this company, was easy. It was losing that took all her
powers of concentration. When she took every trick,
Flynn slanted her a warning frown. She knew what that
signified. The last thing they wanted was to draw attention to themselves, and there would be plenty of attention
if she was suspected of being a cardsharp. Win a few, lose
a few, that was the strategy they followed. It wasn't as
though the card-playing were essential. It was a means of

fitting in with the crowd until their "passenger" should arrive. By sheer force of will, she managed to lose the last two tricks. Then the game was over, and as Cassie and her young actor became involved in a heated lovers' tiff, she and Flynn pocketed their winnings.

By this time, alarm was pumping blood to every pulse point in her body. Flynn recognized her tension and managed a quiet, "What is it?"

It was nothing. It was everything. It was Julian Raynor. She shook her head.

She was aware of the door opening to admit a newcomer, aware of the leather-bound volume the young man clutched to his bosom; she was aware of Flynn idling his way to the door to engage the newcomer in conversation; but most of all she was excruciatingly aware of Julian Raynor rising and beckoning with one finger, summoning her to his table.

Though her temper flared at the arrogant gesture, she was in no position to antagonize him. She picked up her feathered cape and slowly sauntered over.

"Sit down." He indicated the empty chair he was holding. His voice carried a note of amused interest. His look was one he might have bestowed on a piece of prime horseflesh he was intending to purchase.

Through the sweep of her blackened lashes, Serena made her own appraisal. He was tall, too tall for her comfort. His dark hair was lightly powdered and tied in back with a ribbon. The lace at his throat and wrists, though of the best quality, was not lavish. His blue silk coat, embroidered at the edges and on the great turn-back cuffs with silver thread, hugged his broad shoulders. He wasn't handsome as her brothers, Jeremy and Clive, were handsome. This man's looks were too harsh. Some might have called him the epitome of elegance. Serena could find no fault with his appearance. What she mistrusted was the glitter of some nameless masculine emotion in those silver-gray eyes. It made her skin prickle. As for his manners, they verged on the insolent. More than ever, she was convinced that her first impression of Julian Raynor was correct.

It was then that Serena remembered something else she had heard about Julian Raynor. There were rumors of duels, and women, scores of women, and debauchery on a scale she could not imagine. She could well believe it. This man was dangerous.

This was not the time to put him in his place. The situation called for tact and caution, though neither were her strong points.

"Major Raynor, is it not?" she said, and smiled pleasantly. "You do me too much honor, sir."

She glanced idly over her shoulder, hoping to summon Cassie to her. One quick look told her that her newfound "friend" was leaving the tavern in high dudgeon. Swallowing a sigh, Serena turned to face the enemy.

One dark brow was lifted in cynical mockery. "You had me fooled for a time there, ma'am, but now I am on to you," he said.

Her mind reeling with the shock of his words, Serena slowly sank into the chair he held for her.

"First, allow me to say that you play remarkably well for an amateur." He bowed over her hand, then seated himself on the other side of the table.

"Thank you," she answered numbly.

"But cards are not precisely your game, are they?"

She dropped her lashes to conceal the stark terror his words had evoked. "I don't know what you mean."

"I think you do. I think you knew, or guessed, that I wouldn't be able to take my eyes off you if I suspected you were a cheat. And it worked."

"Cheat?" repeated Serena carefully. The word she was in terror of hearing was *traitor*.

He leaned forward, and she caught the gleam of laughter in his eyes. "Your ploy succeeded, as you can see. Shall we drink to the occasion?" Signaling to one of the serving wenches, he ordered a bottle of claret.

It was becoming clear to Serena that Julian Raynor had no idea of her real reason for being here. Her alarm abating a little, she steered her eyes casually in Flynn's direction and noted that he had drawn their "passenger" into the shadows while he waited for her to join them.

She could well imagine what was going through Flynn's mind. He would be cursing her for endangering herself by even being here this evening. They never could see eye to eye on this. Flynn regarded Serena's part in their mission as unnecessary, and he would have preferred to handle things by himself. This Serena would not allow since she knew Flynn's heart wasn't in it. He was involved because she was involved. It would be unscrupulous to let him take all the risks.

Her eyes returned to Raynor. Though he was relaxed and smiling, her first impression of him lingered, and she decided on instinct not to provoke him by refusing to drink the wine he was pouring out for her. "I wasn't cheating," she said.

"Oh, I know that now. Haven't I just said so?"

"But . . . what made you think that I was?"

"The beauty patch, the little curl on your brow, and the way you fingered them. These are the props and methods of the rank novice."

Flynn would have said that she was indulging a vulgar taste for melodrama. He had no use for the signals she had invented, and so he had told her.

In spite of her uneasiness, she managed an arch smile. "Perhaps I was distracted?"

"And perhaps you are a very clever woman."

His eyes smiled into hers as if, thought Serena, they shared a secret joke. Not wanting to pursue this dangerous subject, promising herself that from now on she would listen to Flynn, she raised her glass to her lips. "What is the occasion we are drinking to?" she asked.

His eyes teased her wickedly. "To our better acquaintance," he said, "Miss . . . what is your name, by the by?"

She had her answer ready. "Victoria," she said at once. It was a name she had always liked, even as a child, and one that she thought was more appropriate to her nature than the insipid *Serena*. "Victoria Noble. An actress by profession," she threw in casually, trying to establish the role she had adopted.

"An actress? Where are you playing?"

She was prepared for this question. Her little mouth trembled, and her eyes slid away before lifting to look deeply into his. "An actress of sorts is what I should have said. You know how it is." Her shrug was eloquent. "There are more actresses than there are parts to be had."

"Say no more, Miss Noble. I understand your position perfectly."

A ripple of unease ran up her spine. She knew an innuendo when she heard one. Did he perhaps know more than she suspected? Then why was he smiling at her and not calling for a magistrate?

Under cover of drinking her wine, she sent her gaze in search of Flynn. There was no sign of him or their "passenger." This was serious. Flynn would not leave her unprotected unless an emergency forced him to. In spite of her fear of Raynor, it was time to decamp.

She set down her glass and made a move to rise. "The hour grows late," she said, "and"—she stifled a yawn behind her hand—"alas, I am excessively fatigued."

Laughing, with the swiftness of a striking cobra, he had her by the wrist. "I like an eager wench. But sweet, allow me a little time to set the stage." To her blank look, he elaborated. "I have yet to bespeak a room for us. Drink your wine. This won't take a moment."

"A . . . bespeak a room for us?"

"If not here, somewhere else. Oh, did you think that I would take you to my gaming house? Hardly. I have to live there, and I should prefer a little more privacy."

When his meaning finally became clear to her, she did not know whether she wanted to stamp her foot and spit on him, or dissolve in a fit of the giggles. That Julian Raynor, a rake of the first magnitude, should have mistaken the daughter of Sir Robert Ward for a common doxy! It was hilarious. It was outrageous. She must be a better actress than she knew.

She watched him go with supreme complacency. As soon as the doors had closed upon him, she was on her feet, reaching for her feathered cape. Disregarding the protests of the waiters and serving girls, Serena entered the kitchens. As she advanced toward the door she took to be the back exit, it opened, and several uniformed militiamen pushed into the tavern. She heard the word *Jacobite* and did an about-turn.

Her heart was beating so furiously, she could hardly catch her breath. In all the confusion of thoughts that raced through her brain, one stood out starkly. They had been betrayed.

Forcing the hysteria to recede, she tried to take stock of the situation. Flynn must have heard or seen something while she was in conversation with Julian Raynor. They had always known that the most perilous part of their mission was when they collected their "passenger." Once they went underground, as Flynn would have it, no one would find them in that labyrinth. Praying that Flynn had not delayed on her account, she pushed through the door to the front entrance.

From here, she could see the lanterns outside, and beneath them, a detail of militia assembling on the pavement. Her eyes flicked to the staircase. When an arm circled her waist, she cried out in panic.

"It's only me. Who were you expecting?"

It was Raynor's voice, laced, as always, with that intolerable masculine amusement. From the corner of her eye, she saw someone try to leave the tavern only to be turned back by one of the militia. She could take her chances with the militia, or she could take her chances with Julian Raynor.

She looked up at him, her eyes wide and unfaltering. He was a gamester, but that did not mean he was an unprincipled rogue. According to her brother Jeremy, Raynor was one of the best. Stifling her misgivings, with one eye on His Majesty's militia, she allowed Raynor to lead her to the staircase.

Chapter Two

❦

D alliance, reflected Julian, had been the farthest thing from his mind when he had given in to the impulse to visit The Thatched Tavern that evening. He had been standing on the gallery of his gaming house, sipping a glass of champagne, idly watching the comings and goings of his fashionable patrons, when he'd been struck with the notion that he did not much care for the society he kept. Their affectations, their pursuit of novelty, their fatuous conversation, even the smell of them had ceased to amuse him. He was bored, and for a young man who had just turned thirty, and who, moreover, was at the pinnacle of his profession, this was an odd state of affairs.

Boredom, he had quickly reminded himself, was a small price to pay for the wealth he was accumulating. And it wasn't as though the sum total of his ambition was to spend his life in a gaming house. He was sinking every spare penny into a plantation he had acquired in the Carolinas. A new life in the New World—that was his life's ambition, and he would begin it just as soon as he had taken care of a long-standing matter of honor.

The inevitable thoughts of Sir Robert Ward rushed in to plague him, followed by the inevitable memories of his own family and the bitter, bitter end they had all come to. Soon, he promised himself, very soon, Sir Robert would meet with the fate he deserved. He would make sure of it.

In quick succession, he'd downed several glasses of champagne, trying to dislodge the murderous rage that the thought of Sir Robert Ward never failed to raise in him. It was the waiting that was the source of his frustration, this restlessness that possessed him. Once he had dealt with Sir Robert, he would be free to go on with his own life.

At this point in his reflections, his eyes had strayed to Lord Percy and his cohorts, a set of mincing fops with painted faces and rouged lips. Julian tolerated them for only one reason. They were inveterate gamblers and money burned holes in their pockets.

It was then that the impulse had struck him. What he needed was a taste of real life, where men knew how to be men, and so-called gentlemen with their fine clothes and effeminate manners would be given short shrift, not at the point of a sword, not with dueling pistols at ten paces, but with a grueling bout of fisticuffs.

He was spoiling for a fight and knew just the place where he could find one. Within minutes, he had turned the management of his club into the capable hands of his second-in-command, and he was hailing a sedan to convey him to The Thatched Tavern.

To his surprise The Thatched Tavern had come up in the world since he had last haunted its precincts. No longer were there rough rivermen and quick-witted cardsharps who would turn on a man if he chanced to look at them the wrong way.

He hadn't found the fight he had been spoiling for, but just the same, he'd found sport of sorts. He had taken one look at Victoria Noble, and the oh-so-casual way she had fingered her beauty patch, and he'd put her down as a cardsharp. He, none better, knew all the little tricks of her profession. He should. In his time, he had unmasked many a cheat who had employed much the same methods as she.

From that moment on, it had amused him to watch

her, trying to discover which of the gentlemen was her secret partner in crime. It had taken him a good half hour to reach the conclusion that the girl was not a cheat, but a very clever baggage who knew how to fix a gentleman's interest.

It was all deliberately done, but very effective for all that. Her companion, a far more striking girl, had failed to elicit more than a passing glance. She was too obvious. She flaunted her wares. Miss Noble had used her wits. Evidently recognizing him, she had played out her little charade, knowing that any gamester worth his salt would not be able to tear his eyes away, hoping to catch her out. The clever baggage had caught *him* out! By the time he was on to her, he wasn't seeing her as a cardsharp. He was seeing her as an interesting and provocative specimen whom he would like to know better. Much better.

An actress of sorts was how she had described herself, and everyone knew what that euphemism signified. Not that he had any quarrel with women of that class. With his history, he would be a hypocrite to condemn her. Whores and prostitutes had been the companions of his youth, not so much as objects of pleasure, but as friends and counselors. Truth to tell, the highborn ladies of easy virtue with whom he took his pleasure were not so very different from the whores of his youth, and he liked them the better for it.

Victoria Noble, if that was her real name, did not precisely remind him of the whores of his youth. She had style, he would give her that. In point of fact, from his not inconsiderable experience, he would have to say that Victoria Noble was probably the best that money could buy, and it was his opinion that before long she would be the mistress of some wealthy gentleman of fashion. Hard on that thought came the notion that the wealthy gentleman in question might well turn out to be himself.

It wasn't that she was a raving beauty, or that her figure was exceptional. Her features were refined and dominated by a pair of lively blue eyes. Her form was pleasingly feminine, not too thin, but not overripe either. He supposed that her dark hair was her best feature, though it was hardly *à la mode.* It was long and lustrous, and fell to her shoulders in waves. Without hesitation, however, he could have reeled off the names of a dozen women who could put her in the shade, except in one particular. They did not possess one tenth of this girl's allure.

When he looked at her, he had the uncanny feeling that he was seeing many women. At present, in her white embroidered dimity, she had the look of a virgin about to be sacrificed on Aphrodite's altar. Earlier, when he had caught the pulse of passion in her eyes, she had put him in mind of an Eastern slave girl whose sole object in life was to pleasure her lord and master. Then she had tilted her chin, staring him down, and he had an impression of a *grande dame,* presiding at her fashionable salon. It set a man's mind to wondering what ravishing creature she would turn into next.

He knew one thing. He had never met anyone like her before. He knew something else. He had to have her, and he did not care what price she put on herself. Grinning, he reached for the claret bottle and held it out to her.

Serena accepted the offer of wine. Her one thought was to use any means at her disposal to delay the moment when he would suggest that they retire to the adjoining bedchamber. At the moment, they occupied a small private parlor and were seated before a blazing fire. At his suggestion, she had removed her cape. Having already exhausted the subject of his gaming house, she was wracking her brains for some other neutral topic of conversation.

"Tell me about yourself," he said.

Oh God, how she wished she could oblige him, then this farce would be brought to an end. But that wasn't what she wanted either, for then he would dismiss her, and she would have to go downstairs and face the militia. Besides, how could she reveal her true identity now? How could she explain her presence here tonight without the escort of her footman? The truth would not save her, not with this man, not with the hero who had fought with government forces at Prestonpans. He was an anti-Jacobite. If he knew the truth about her, in all likelihood, he would hand her over to the militia without a qualm.

"There's not much to tell." Delaying while her mind grappled to invent a background for herself, she sipped her wine.

"Family?"

"No. I'm an orphan." This seemed to be far easier than inventing a fictitious family whose names and attributes she was sure to muddle.

"Ah, then you have no resources to draw on except those with which nature endowed you. By the looks of you, I'd say you've done very well for yourself."

She wanted to hit him. "Thank you," she said.

From the floor above came the sound of a door slamming, followed by the muted tramp of boots. Another door slammed.

"What do you suppose is going on?" she asked. Her eyes were fixed on the ceiling.

"Mmm? Oh, the tavern has a full house. I was fortunate to find accommodations for us."

Serena's eyes flitted nervously to the door that gave onto the bedchamber, and a trembling began in the pit of her stomach. It would never come to that, she promised herself. She wasn't a complete simpleton. She knew that before a woman of the street bestowed her favors, she made sure the gentleman could meet her price. That wasn't going to happen in her case for the simple reason that she was going to set her price at something astronomical. When negotiations broke down, as they must, she would make a dignified exit. But not before time, she cautioned herself, not before the threat of the militia had been removed. Once they were gone, she would order the landlord to call a hackney and she would return to her home none the worse for her adventure.

Could it really be that simple? It could, she told herself sternly, as long as she kept her head. She mustn't panic. As long as they remained in this little parlor and Raynor made no move to get her into that bedchamber, she had nothing to fear.

"Shall we make ourselves comfortable?" he said, and under her startled gaze, he unfastened his smallsword and set it aside. He slipped off his coat, and began on the buttons of his waistcoat. That, too, went the way of his coat.

"Help me?" he said, his fingers on the top button of his shirt.

Serena moistened her lips. It was time to introduce the subject of her fee. Another door slammed, only this time it was on the same floor. The tramp of boots drew nearer. The militia, it seemed, were making a thorough search of the building. Were they looking for her? Did they have a description of her? Wide-eyed, she rose to her feet.

The girl's eyes, thought Julian, were fathomless, enticing a man to plumb her secrets. She was a siren, with arts as old as time, against which a mere mortal man had no defense. She came to him in small, halting steps. Her shy reluctance was a sham, of course, but it did not feel like a sham. She was, he acknowledged, a consummate actress. Slave girl, siren, virgin, *grande dame*—she would be whatever a man wished her to be.

"Kneel down," he said, and she knelt at his feet, the picture of womanly submission. He drew her between his thighs. "Unbutton my shirt."

God, she was good at what she did! No simpering, no coyness. She was a woman who knew the value of silence. She knew a lot more than that. There was no haste to her movements, but rather a slow sensuality that edged his passion to crisis point. Breathing was becoming difficult. His shaft was so hard he thought his breeches would burst.

When the rap came on the door, Julian closed his eyes and cursed vehemently. "If that damned landlord—"

"Open in 'Is Majesty's name!" came the strident command, and the doorknob rattled.

With eyebrows raised, Julian reluctantly stood and went to answer it. Over his shoulder, he said, "Don't move from that spot."

He opened the door just as the young militiaman on the other side was about to kick it in. "State your business, man," said Julian without ceremony.

Ned Maseby took in the state of undress of the finest gentleman he had ever seen in his life. A quick look over the gentleman's shoulder revealed the reason for the dishabille.

His Adam's apple bobbing, young Ned said, "Begging your pardon, yer honor, but we 'as reason to believe that one of them there Jacobites is 'iding out in the tavern."

Julian forbore comment, though there was much that he might have said. He might have said that this was not the kind of peace he had fought to procure, where the defeated enemy, all men of honor, were mercilessly flushed out to be hunted down as though they were foxes. In all civilized countries, the killing stopped on the battlefield. The treatment of Jacobites by those in authority was a scandal to all right-thinking Englishmen. He had fought on the winning side, and he took no pride in it.

"A Jacobite?" he said pleasantly. "And do I fit his description?"

"Eh." Ned grinned sheepishly and tried to make a joke of it. "Not if ye're not a Scot. The lad we are looking for is one o' them 'ighland chieftains."

In his flawless cultured accent, Julian said, "Then you should have no difficulty finding him."

The hand holding the door had relaxed a little, and as it opened wider, Ned's eyes bulged. The girl on the floor was unpicking the laces that held the edges of her bodice together.

The lecherous grin on the young militiaman's face swiftly vanished when he encountered the storm in Julian's eyes. Swallowing, saluting smartly, Ned mumbled an apology and moved off.

Having shut the door and locked it, Julian hesitated a moment, his brows pulled together in a frown.

Serena was half turned away from him, tightening the strings of her bodice with fingers that shook alarmingly, not knowing whether to be pleased or dismayed that the harlot's role she played was so convincing that it had taken in both a rank libertine and a lecherous member of His Majesty's militia.

"What is it?" asked Serena. "Why are you frowning?"

Julian pushed his gloomy thoughts to the back of his mind. "No need to be frightened," he said. "You know our brave militia lads. They must invent traitors where none exist."

Traitors, that's how he thought of Jacobites. She had been right not to trust this man. He would never have aided a Jacobite fugitive. Not that they needed his help now. From what the militiaman had said, it was obvious that Flynn and their "passenger" had got clean away. Now she had to do the same.

"Let's start over, shall we?" said Julian. He returned to the chair he had vacated. "And this time, I shall try to keep myself well in check. No, don't move. I rather like you kneeling at my feet in an attitude of submission."

He raised his wine glass and imbibed slowly. "Now you," he said. When she made to take it from him, he shook his head. "No, I shall hold it. Come closer."

Once again she found herself between his thighs. She didn't know what to do with her hands, but he knew.

"Place them on my thighs," he said, and Serena obeyed. Beneath her fingers, she could feel the hard masculine muscles bunch and strain. She was also acutely aware of the movements of the militia as they combed the building for Jacobites.

"Drink," he said, holding the rim of the glass to her lips, tipping it slightly.

Wine flooded her mouth and spilled over. Choking, she swallowed it.

"Allow me," he murmured. As one hand cupped her neck, his head descended and his tongue plunged into her mouth.

Shock held her rigid as his tongue thrust, and thrust again, circling, licking at the dregs of wine in her mouth, lapping it up with avid enjoyment. When she began to struggle, his powerful thighs tightened against her, holding her effortlessly. Her hands went to his chest to push him away, and slipped between the parted edges of his shirt. Warm masculine flesh quivered beneath the pads of her fingertips. Splaying her hands wide, with every ounce of strength, she shoved at him, trying to free herself.

He released her so abruptly that she tumbled to the floor. Scrambling away from him, she came up on her knees. They were both breathing heavily.

Frowning, he rose to his feet and came to tower over her. "What game are you playing now?"

"No game," she quickly got out. "You are going too fast for me." She carefully rose to her feet and began to inch away from him. "We have yet to settle on my . . . my remuneration."

"Remuneration?" He laughed softly. "Sweetheart, I have already made up my mind that for a woman of your unquestionable talents, no price is too high."

These were not the words that Serena wanted to hear, nor did she believe him. Men did not like greedy women. Though she wasn't supposed to know it, long before his marriage, her brother Jeremy had given his mistress her congé because the girl was too demanding. What was it the girl had wanted?

Her back came up against the door to the bedchamber. One hand curved around the doorknob in a reflexive movement, the other clutched the doorjamb for support.

Licking her lips, she said, "I . . . I shall want my own house."

He cocked his head to one side. As though musing to himself, he said, "I've never had a woman in my keeping. Do you know, for the first time, I can see the merit in it? Fine, you shall have your house."

He took a step closer, and she flattened herself against the door. "And . . . and my own carriage?" She could hardly breathe with him standing so close to her.

"Done." His eyes were glittering.

When he lunged for her, she cried out and flung herself into the bedchamber, slamming the door quickly, bracing her shoulder against it as her fingers fumbled for the key.

One kick sent both door and Serena hurtling back. He stood framed in the doorway, the light behind him, and every sensible thought went out of her head. Dangerous. Reckless. Wild. This was all a game to him!

He feinted to the left, and she made a dash for the door, twisting away as his hands reached for her. His fingers caught on the back of her gown, ripping it to the waist. One hand curved around her arm, sending her sprawling against the bed.

There was no candle in the bedchamber, but the lights from the tavern's courtyard filtered through the window, casting a luminous glow. He was shedding the last of his clothes. Though everything in her revolted against it, she knew that the time had come to reveal her name.

Summoning the remnants of her dignity, she said, "You should know that I am no common doxy. I am a highborn lady."

He laughed in that way of his that she was coming to thoroughly detest. "I know," he said, "and I am to play the conqueror. Sweetheart, those games are all very well in their place. But the time for games is over. I want a real woman in my arms tonight, a willing one and not some character from a fantasy."

She turned his words over in her mind and could make no sense of them. Seriously doubting the man's sanity, she cried out, "Touch me and you will regret it to your dying day. Don't you understand anything? I am a lady. I—"

He fell on her and rolled with her on the bed. Subduing her easily with the press of his body, he rose above her. "Have done with your games. I am Julian. You are Victoria. I am your protector. You are my mistress. Yield to me, sweeting."

Bought and paid for—that was what was in his mind. She was aware of something else. He didn't want to hurt or humiliate her. He wanted to have his way with her. He thought he had that right.

He wasn't moving, or forcing his caresses on her. He was simply holding her, watching her with an unfathomable expression. "Julian," she whispered, giving him his name in an attempt to soften him. "Victoria Noble is not my real name."

"I didn't think it was," he said, and kissed her.

His mouth was gentle; his tongue caressing, slipping between her teeth, not deeply, not threateningly, but inviting her to participate in the kiss. For a moment, curiosity held her spellbound. She had never been kissed like this before. It was like sinking into a bath of spiced wine. It was sweet and intoxicating, just like the taste of him.

Shivering, she pulled out of the embrace and stared up at him. His brows were raised, questioning her. All she need do was tell him her name and he would let her go. She never doubted it for a moment.

Something else was at work in her, something that made her hesitate. She was twenty-three years old and no man had held her like this before, kissed her like this, looked at her as he looked at her. Love and marriage had passed her by. Though she'd had suitors in plenty, when they discovered she had no dowry, they melted away. She would never know a lover's embrace, never share a lover's kisses. She was a maiden aunt, and that was all she could ever hope to be. What harm could there be in a few stolen kisses? He was an attractive, virile male. Any woman would be proud to have him for her lover. She didn't want a lover, only a few stolen kisses.

"Kiss me, Victoria," he said.

Victoria. How easy it would be if only she really were Victoria. Victoria could do whatever she wanted, be whatever she wanted. There were no restraints on Victoria. If only . . . oh, if only.

Her head was buzzing with all the wine she had drunk, and she closed her eyes trying to get a grip on herself.

When his mouth settled on hers, she splayed her hands over his arms, restraining him. Beneath the sensitive pads of her fingertips, powerful masculine muscles bunched and clenched. For an instant, only an instant, she gave in to the temptation to run her hands along that warm, smooth skin. As the kiss lingered, her fingers glided over his broad shoulders, along the strong column of his neck, and became lost in the rich texture of his hair. Deep inside her, she felt the stir of something sweet and wanton.

His lips traced over her face; his teeth nibbled, then nipped. She knew she was smiling. She hadn't known kisses could be like this. He was playing with her. Not to be outdone, she ran her lips over his shoulders, absorbing his scent and flavor. He tasted of fresh air and windswept nights, and something dark and forbidden.

She closed her eyes as whisper-soft kisses drifted from the corner of her mouth to the tips of her breasts. When his lips closed around one tender nipple, she made a small inarticulate sound. He groaned, and brought his head up, kissing her fiercely, possessively, demanding she surrender everything to him.

The sudden flood of pleasure was so shocking that Serena's whole body went slack. Her hands clenched and unclenched around his shoulders, trying to convey her distress. She could not get command of her breathing. Her head was spinning. She was sure she was going to faint. There was something hovering at the edge of her consciousness, but she could not hold on to it, did not want to hold on to it. In the space of a few seconds, every sensible thought dissolved and slipped away.

She was beyond caring when his hands drifted over her, divesting her of her garments one by one. She lay on the mattress, twisting restlessly, trying to get closer to him. Shivering with pleasure, she wound her arms around his neck and pressed abandoned kisses to his face and shoulders.

When she felt his fingers probing her there, between

her thighs, she cried out, and her head came off the pillow.

"What is it, Victoria?"

His breath was warm upon her skin. His hands soothed, pressing her back into the mattress. She felt the rigid thrust of his shaft on her thigh, and she looked about her, bewildered, as though she were awakening from a dream.

"What is it, Victoria?" he repeated. His lips brushed her eyes, then her mouth.

"I . . ." She wasn't Victoria. She was Serena. *Serena!* Chilled and shocked, she stared at him.

"Come back to me," he murmured, and winding his hand around her hair, he gently tugged her down.

"I am not Victoria." Her voice was no more than a shaken whisper. She was still shuddering in the aftermath of the sensual onslaught, still trying to come to herself. Tears squeezed from beneath her lashes as guilt and shame rushed in to scourge her. How could she, Serena Ward, have allowed things to come so far? How could a few stolen kisses have led to this? She was naked, in a strange bed, with a strange man. He touched her again, intimately, and panic rose in her.

Her hands moved to his shoulders, restraining him. "Julian, please," she implored, "please?"

"So soon, my love?" There was a smile in his voice.

"I can't . . ." She shook her head.

For a moment, she thought her words had made an impression on him. He levered himself up, relieving her of some of his weight. She heard the hiss of his breath as he inhaled deeply, then rational thought shattered as his body imposed itself upon hers.

Her hoarse cry of pain was lost beneath his smothering kiss. She bucked and kicked out, trying to dislodge him; her nails raked his shoulders. Her pathetic attempt at resistance was to no purpose, but seemed only to increase his ardor. Locking her to him in an inflexible embrace, he quickened his movements, driving into her, submerging her in an unfamiliar world where the senses held sway, and though she remained unmoved by it, she knew in her own self it was because she had willed it so.

Some time was to pass before Julian released her. "I've never had your like before," he said. "No woman has ever made me want to master her."

Shivering, aching, Serena closed her eyes, shutting out the sight of him. What a fool she had been to think she could use him for her own purposes. What folly to think she could be Victoria and do whatever she wanted. She wasn't anything like Victoria. She was a product of her upbringing. She was a Ward, a *Ward,* and if her poor mother could see her now, she would turn in her grave.

It was so unjust. She had not wanted things to go this far. She had tried to tell him, but he wouldn't listen. She might as well have tried to turn back the tide as restrain Julian Raynor in the throes of passion. That was the trouble, of course. She had not known the first thing about a man's passion, had not known that a few stolen kisses could lead so quickly to mindless delight. She had left it too late, and she had paid the price for her folly.

He kissed her softly. "You don't regret it?"

She wanted to lash out at him but had not the will nor the energy. What would be the use? The worst had already happened. All she wanted was to find some quiet sanctuary where she could sort out her thoughts on the catastrophe that had overtaken her.

"No," she said tonelessly.

Pressing a kiss to her bare shoulder, he said, "Go to sleep. We'll talk later."

Silently, she rolled to her side, away from him, listening to the sound of his breathing, waiting for sleep to claim him so that she could slip away.

She moved fretfully, brushing at the hand that was kneading the underswell of one sensitive breast. The hand persisted. Opening her eyes, Serena looked down. With a gasping cry of horror, she hauled herself up. His back was propped against the pillows, a lazy, wicked smile tugged at his lips. Light streamed through the window, but it was the feeble light of early dawn.

Gritting her teeth, she flung herself from the bed, and went in search of her discarded garments. Ignoring the damage that had been inflicted by uncaring masculine hands, she quickly donned them, keeping a wary eye on the man in the bed.

Julian yawned, stretching his arms wide. Muscles bunched and rippled across his powerful torso as he laced his fingers behind his neck. The threat that Serena had sensed in him from the first moment she had set eyes on him was no longer there. With the foolish grin on his face and the relaxed posture, he put her in mind of a well-fed feline.

"You were a virgin," he said, pleasure evident in every syllable he uttered.

Serena fumbled with the tapes of her petticoat, and her head came up. "And that pleases you?" she asked incredulously. Even the rakes and roués in her set were known to be scrupulous in their treatment of virgins.

"Naturally, it pleases me, though I hardly expected it. You are no green girl, are you? Oh, not that I am complaining, you understand. I count myself lucky that I was the one you chose when you decided to embark on your profession."

"Chose *you*? I never chose you! You were a lightning bolt that struck me when I least expected it."

She bit down on her lip to stem the rising tide of fury. Her wicked tongue, Flynn had often told her, would be the death of her. The prudent thing to do was to leave this place quickly and without fuss, before she gave in to the very understandable temptation to shriek obscenities at him.

"I see what it is," said Julian, regarding her steadily and shrewdly. "In the cold light of day, you are beginning to have second thoughts. My advice to you is *don't*. It's too late to turn back. You made your decision. You have no reason to change it, and many good reasons to go on with it."

Hatred filled her so completely that she could not find the words to answer him. He knew that he had taken a virgin. He should be on his knees, begging her forgiveness. He should be offering her marriage. And she would throw his offer back in his teeth and walk away laughing.

Misreading her silence, Julian went on gently, "I have more experience of the world than you. I know what your future would have been like, and I think you know it too. Virtuous girls of your class eventually find themselves married to dancing masters or shopkeepers. It's a hand-to-mouth existence. It would do for some women, but it would not do for you, else you would not be here with me now. This day would have come for you sooner or later.

"It has its compensations. As my mistress, you will live in the lap of luxury. Sweetheart, I intend to pay very handsomely for the privilege of having taken your maidenhead. Besides, you have a natural aptitude for the position I am offering." He cocked one brow suggestively. "Now come back to bed, and let me teach you about the pleasures to be had between a man and his mistress."

She had a temper. It was a shortcoming she had tried to master by sheer force of will, and when that failed, by applying to her religion. Appearances to the contrary, Serena was devoutly religious.

When she could unlock her jaw, she inhaled several long calming breaths. To give her more time to subdue her temper, she turned her back on him, and began to wrench at the strings of her bodice, trying to fit the thing to cover her bosom in spite of the rent that bared her back. When the strings of her bodice snapped, and he chuckled, she spun on him like an avenging fury.

"You great oaf!" she lashed out, circling the bed with her long strides. "I am no doxy! Did I not tell you last night that I was a highborn lady?"

"That is what I like in you," he said. "You have the manners of a lady and the morals of . . . well, shall we just say that in bed, you are no lady, and that is how it should be?"

"The morals of a whore!" she shrilled. "That's what you were going to say!"

"Sweeting, don't get your hackles up. I mean that as a compliment. For my purposes, you will suit admirably."

"How can I have the morals of a whore when I was a virgin? It's impossible!"

"An attitude of mind, is what I meant. Believe me, I'm not finding fault. We are two of a kind."

She wanted to see him suffer as she had been made to suffer. She wanted to see him shaking in his boots, and he would shake in his boots if he knew that she had two brothers to avenge her honor. Most of all, she wanted to see him grovel. Her every instinct cried out to see this man humbled. The frustration of knowing that there was nothing she could do was unbearable.

She would go insane if she did not express her anger. "Julian Raynor," she scoffed, "a gamester and a libertine! I would no more think of taking up with your kind than I would with thieves and murderers. If you knew my name, you would be shaking in your boots. I am not some poor, unprotected doxy. I am a baronet's daughter. Live in the lap of luxury with you?" She laughed derisively, convincingly. "My father and brothers would see me dead first."

Her angry outburst acted on him as she hoped it would. His smile faded; his face paled; the arms that were pillowing his neck fell to his sides.

"A baronet's daughter?" he said.

The pleasure of wiping the smile from his face was not so great as the growing conviction that her temper had led her into committing a horrible blunder. Refusing to think of possible consequences, pressing her lips together, she looked around for her feathered cape. When he surged from the bed, she was so taken by surprise that she stumbled and fell against the dresser. It occurred to her then that he had a temper to match her own, but where hers was flash-fire hot, his was ice-cold, more controlled and much more lethal.

Catching her by the shoulders, he dragged her to the window. His eyes studied her face. "Who are you?" he demanded.

When she stared at him with her head flung back, blue defiance shimmering in her eyes, his fingers tightened and he shook her with enough violence to rattle her teeth. "I'll have your name," he said, "or I swear I shall make you my prisoner until I get to the bottom of this."

It was no idle threat. She knew it was no idle threat. Then the authorities would be called in to search for her, and everything would come to light.

"Serena Ward," she got out quickly, when he would have shaken her again. "My name is Serena Ward."

The silence that greeted her words was long and profoundly chilling.

"Sir Robert Ward's daughter?"

She nodded in the affirmative, her mind frantically at work as she waited for the spate of questions that was bound to follow. What was she doing here? Why had she allowed him to think that she was a woman of easy virtue? Why had she not put a stop to it sooner?

She saw the fury in his eyes. She heard the sharp intake of breath, then he released her and began to dress himself with swift competence. His silence made her so uneasy that she stood there like a petrified rabbit, afraid to make any move that might draw attention to herself.

Once dressed, he strode through the door to the little parlor. As he shrugged into his coat and belted on his smallsword, Serena, as wordless as he, picked up her cape and arranged it over her shoulders.

Events moved quickly after this. He hustled her down the stairs and out of the tavern. At the first blast of cold air, her skin came out in goose pimples. There were no trees in this stretch of road, no flower boxes, no birds singing, nothing to show that summer was just around the corner. It was April, but to Serena, it felt like the dead of winter.

Not a militiaman was in sight. After summoning a chair, he opened the door and practically flung her inside. When she turned on him, ready to do battle, he captured her hand and bowed over it with exaggerated, insulting gallantry.

"Never say that Julian Raynor does not pay his debts," he said, and to the chairman, "The lady will give you her direction." With that, he turned on his heel and returned to the tavern.

Serena unclenched her hand and gazed down at the object Julian Raynor had pressed into it. It was a note, drawn on the Bank of England, made out to the bearer in the sum of fifty pounds. She looked up and caught one of the chairmen grinning at her. Glaring at him, she returned her attention to Raynor's note. This, she thought, was the final humiliation, and her eyes narrowed to fiery slits as she stared at it.

Chapter Three

❧

Serena's fury with Julian Raynor was momentarily forgotten when her sedan turned the corner of the Strand into Buckingham Street. A new thought had taken possession of her mind. If anyone were to see her arriving home in such a state and at such an hour, it would be extremely awkward. As far as her elder brother, Jeremy, knew, she had gone with friends to Ranelagh pleasure gardens with the very proper escort of Clive.

If Jeremy were to see her now, not only would she be in trouble, but Flynn and Clive also. Jeremy knew nothing of their clandestine activities, and Serena hoped he never would. He would feel betrayed, and accuse them of jeopardizing the security of the whole family for the sake of a dead cause. But it wasn't like that, not really. They were only trying to help a few men who had lost everything, men whose only crime was that they had fought for the wrong side. They would do as much for anyone.

It was something they had drifted into. Clive was the one who had reluctantly recruited Serena when she had surprised him in his rooms in Charles Street when he was sheltering a young Jacobite, a friend from Oxford, whose departure for France had been delayed because of the fog. There were more like him, Clive's friend had told them, many more who could be saved if only there was someone willing to brave the risks. He had given Clive the name of a connection in Oxford, and that had been the start of it.

Over time, they had developed an almost infallible strategy. After their connection, whose identity was known only to Clive, delivered their "passenger," it was up to them to shelter him until he could be got safely away. Last night, while she and Flynn were in The Thatched Tavern taking delivery, Clive had waited for them in a safe house close to the docks. The docks were well patrolled. When the coast was clear, Clive would signal that it was safe for them to proceed. After delivering their "passenger," they would enjoy a glass of wine. Then she and Flynn would return to Buckingham Street under cover of darkness.

It was not dark now.

When her chair approached the last house on the street, a corner house that was closest to the riverbank, she called out to the chairmen to let her out at the side gate. There were no windows looking out on this stretch of road.

The moment she stepped down Flynn pounced on her. He had discarded the disguise, and the sparks in his green eyes matched the glitter of the tiny emerald attached to his left ear.

"I'll pay off the chairmen," he said, giving her a look that said far more than she wanted to hear. Then in a carrying voice to the chairmen, "When I get 'er inside, I shall box 'er ears. Where did you find 'er?"

"Who is she?" asked one of the chairmen.

"The girl I thought I wanted to marry," said Flynn, glancing in Serena's direction, noting with approval that she had slipped inside the wrought-iron gate and was hovering on the other side of the garden wall.

The chairmen exchanged a look, then one of them let out a bellow of laughter. "If I was you," he said, "I'd ask 'er where she got that fifty-pound note," and with a cheery wave, he motioned his partner to move on.

"What was that all about?" asked Serena when Flynn caught up to her.

He grasped her by the elbow and hurried her round the side of the house. " 'Ave you lost your senses? You should 'ave sent someone to fetch me. What's the world going to think when they see Serena Ward arriving 'ome at this time of the morning without a proper escort? You don't look as though you 'ave been out to a fancy do. If you wants my opinion, you looks as though you'd taken a tumble in the 'ay. Let's just 'ope that anyone who caught that little scene out there took you for one of the maids."

In an effort to head him off, Serena said, "Where is Jeremy . . . and Catherine and Letty?" The night before, Jeremy had escorted his wife, Catherine, and his young sister, Letty, to Lady Noyes's rout. These affairs were in the habit of breaking up in the wee hours of the morning.

"Where do you think? In their beds where all decent aristocrats ought to be after gallivanting all night."

"They . . . they didn't miss me?"

"Not as far as I know. When I got in late last night, they was all sleeping like babies. Do you know, can you imagine what I went through when I discovered you was not in your bed? I've spent 'alf the night looking for you. If you 'adn't come 'ome when you did, I was going to wake Mr. Jeremy and confess all."

"I'm glad it didn't come to that."

"I'm not so sure it wouldn't 'ave been the best thing that could 'ave 'appened. The master wouldn't take too kindly to a member of 'is 'ousehold aiding and abetting Jacobites. He'd soon make you fall into line, my girl."

Serena was silent. Flynn's words had pricked her conscience, not only because she was deceiving her family, but also because Flynn was a reluctant accomplice. It was only his devotion to her that had persuaded Flynn to help them. Oh, he was sympathetic enough to any man who found himself a fugitive and on the wrong side of the law, but he would never have committed a treasonable offense if it were not for her. Though she knew that Flynn, with his knowledge of London and its labyrinth of underground passages, was far more essential to the escape route than she was, she had tried to leave him out of it. But Flynn would not hear of it, not so long as she was involved. She did not know what she had ever done to inspire such devotion. At one and the same time, it humbled her, and made her feel horribly, horribly guilty.

It could not be for much longer, she consoled herself. The flow of fugitives was inevitably drying up. A year had come and gone since Culloden, and it had been more than three months since the last Jacobite had passed through their hands. They had done their part and she did not regret it. At the same time, she never, *never* wanted to endure another night like the one she had just lived through.

They had come to a small brick building, the washhouse, which adjoined the coal cellar at the back of the house. Flynn motioned her inside, then went to check on the whereabouts of the other servants. Within minutes, he had returned and was beckoning her to follow him. After entering the house, Flynn led the way along a short dark corridor to the door to the servants' staircase.

"I take it," said Serena as soon as they had entered her bedchamber, "that everything went off well?"

"You take it correctly, if you calls 'well' evading the militia by the skin of our teeth, not to mention going 'alf out of my mind when I arrived 'ome to find your bed empty. I was under the missapre'ension, you see, that you'd found a chair or an 'ackney to take you 'ome."

"What made you think that?"

"Because I went back to fetch you, just as soon as I deposited our mutual friend in the underground drain. You wasn't in the tavern, so where the devil was you?"

"You went back to the tavern when the militia were still there?"

"Why shouldn't I? They wasn't looking for me or you. They was looking for Jacobites. Now, I'll 'ave the 'ole story, and mind you, no evasions or 'alf-truths. Where 'ave you been? And what's all this about a fifty-pound note?"

Serena's relationship with her footman was an odd one, to say the least. Though Flynn was only twenty, he had the longest tenure of any of the Wards' servants. He was indulged to a degree. At the same time, he was Serena's most ardent protector, having attached himself to her from the first day he had joined Sir Robert's household, at six years old, as a page.

At twenty, Flynn had matured into a broad-shouldered, strong-limbed, good-looking young man. His features were refined. His fair hair had a tendency to curl. A smile was forever lurking at the back of his intelligent green eyes. Though he was a footman, and wore the plain gray livery of the Ward household, with his powdered hair, and the emerald winking in his ear, he had the look of a dandy. Clive Ward, who was younger than Flynn by a year, tended to follow Flynn's modes rather than those of his own set.

As Flynn plumped himself down on the bed, Serena sank onto her dressing-table stool, and folded her hands together. She really wasn't up to this. What she wanted was to rant and rave and break dishes and annihilate the character of Julian Raynor. Then, after a bout of weeping, she would start on herself.

She was twenty-three years old, and not once since she had entered society had any man succeeded in taking advantage of her, though some had tried. Putting men in their places was one of the things she did really well. Last night and this morning she had not put Julian Raynor in his place. In thinking that she could control him, she had committed a fatal error. He had used her and then abased her, and he had earned her undying hatred.

"Well?" said Flynn at length. "Shall we begin with the fifty-pound note? 'Ow did you come by it?"

She dared not tell him the whole truth. That was the trouble with ardent protectors. They could not be relied upon to keep a cool head. If Flynn were to discover what she had suffered at Raynor's hands, there was no saying what he would do. She didn't care what happened to Julian Raynor, but she had no wish to see Flynn hanged for murder. As for her brothers, if they got to hear of it, they would challenge Raynor to a duel, and from what she had heard of Raynor's skill with smallsword and pistol, that idea was not to be entertained either.

"It was like this," she said, and began on a carefully expurgated account of the night's events. When she came to the conclusion of her tale, she looked at Flynn hopefully.

Arms akimbo, he stared at her. "Are you saying," he asked with insulting incredulity, "that the major fell asleep without laying a 'and on you?"

"It was the wine. I told you he had too much to drink. And I encouraged it."

"And that when you both wakened in the morning, you told 'im your name, just like that, and 'e gave you a fifty-pound note to pay off the chairmen?"

"I think he recognized me, that's why I told him my name."

"Serena, your cheeks are bloomin' and we both know what that means."

Serena had a trick of composing her features that would have done credit to the queen of England. "Flynn," she said gently, "it is not for you to question your employer."

"So, there *is* more to it than you are telling me."

Serena pressed her lips together.

Murder kindled in his eyes. "Never say that Raynor ravished you!"

This was intolerable. She wasn't ready to think, much less speak about Julian Raynor and what had happened between them. "Of course he didn't ravish me!" she snapped. "I told you what happened."

"Yes, well, that may do very well for a judge and jury, but it won't wash with me. Serena, this is Flynn you are talking to." He flung his arms wide. "And I knows you." Head cocked to one side, he said musingly, "So, 'e didn't ravish you. That means 'e seduced you. Am I right?"

Her smile was tight and not very encouraging.

Flynn scratched his chin, taking in her crumpled frock, and the ruffled feathers on her cape. "If you played your cards right, my girl, you could snare the major," he said.

"What?"

"You know, marry 'im."

Serena's jaw dropped. Gasping, she started to her feet. "Marry him? Marry *him*? I wouldn't marry that . . . that Philistine if my life depended on it!"

"What 'ave you got against the major?"

"What have I . . . ? I don't believe I'm hearing this."

"So 'e 'ad 'is way with you. But you can't blame 'im for that, or so you told me. He mistook you for a doxy, and you played along with 'im."

Serena gritted her teeth together and closed her eyes. "You have no conception of what it was like. Furthermore"—she glared at Flynn—"I don't wish to discuss it."

"It's always like that the first time for a woman," said Flynn. "With practice, it gets better."

She gazed at him in utter confusion and hurt. "Flynn," she whispered, "I thought you were my protector. I thought that if you knew the truth you would . . . you know . . . do something drastic. I thought you would want to tear Raynor limb from limb."

He edged forward, elbows on thighs, chin cupped with both hands. "And so I would, if I thought the major 'ad taken advantage of you. But don't you see, it was the other way round? You took advantage of 'im. The thing to do now is to press your advantage before some other lady snatches 'im. If I knows the major, and I do, when 'e 'as a chance to think about it, 'e will want to do the 'onorable thing."

Once again, Serena lowered herself to her dressing-table stool. "I think," she said faintly, "that you have taken leave of your senses. Julian Raynor is no fit husband for the daughter of Sir Robert Ward."

It was Flynn's turn to glare. " 'Oity toity! When did you get so 'igh an opinion of yourself?"

"But I don't—"

"The major, let me tell you, my girl, is one of the finest gentlemen I knows. 'E 'as got a library in that 'ouse of 'is that casts the one 'ere into the deepest gloom, yes, and 'e invited me to make use of it whenever I please. You wants to know what separates a real gentleman from those painted fribbles what are always 'anging on your skirts? A real gentleman knows 'ow to treat 'is inferiors. Ask the major's croupiers. Ask 'is operators. They'll tell you if the major is a real gentleman or not."

"How he treats women is more to the point," retorted Serena. "Flynn, I don't want to argue with you. What I should have said was that Raynor is no fit husband for the daughter of Sir Robert Ward because he is an anti-Jacobite. My father would never allow it."

"You are three-and-twenty," said Flynn, slowly, distinctly, his elocution suddenly as cultured as Serena's. "You don't need your father's permission to marry, and Sir Robert is not here. What would you have me believe —that you are a dutiful daughter? I know better than that!"

She smiled at this, and shook her head. "No, I know better than to try and fool you. But Jeremy believes that Papa may yet be given a pardon. What a terrible thing to greet my father on his first night home with the news that I'd married one of the enemy."

"A pardon? Is it settled, then?"

"Jeremy is hopeful that it will be arranged by the end of the month."

They both fell silent as each became lost in thoughts of Sir Robert. Serena's reflections were tender. Flynn's were cynical.

Pardon for Sir Robert Ward was a costly business. There were "presents" to be made to officials to ease the way, and fines to be paid off, and God knew what all. The Wards were fortunate that they had not lost everything when the Rebellion failed. They could thank Mr. Jeremy for that. He'd had the good sense to stand aloof from his father's politics and remain loyal to the Crown. In the harsh retribution that had fallen on Jacobite families following the Rebellion, the Wards had remained relatively unscathed. Until now.

If he were Mr. Jeremy, Flynn reflected, he would tell Sir Robert to go to hell. Appearances to the contrary, the Wards were close to ruin, and Flynn blamed Sir Robert for it. He'd emptied the family's coffers when he'd thrown in his lot with Charles Edward Stuart, and then he'd unscrupulously commandeered the legacy that Serena had inherited from her mother. Letty and Clive were fortunate that they were underage and their legacies were still in trust, or Sir Robert would have commandeered those as well.

Also to be pitied was Mr. Jeremy's wife. Catherine Ward had brought a respectable portion to her marriage, and what a wife brought to her husband belonged to him outright. It was Flynn's opinion that that money would soon go the way of all the rest, if it had not done so already.

Charity begins at home, that was Flynn's motto, and a father who did not put the welfare of his own children first wasn't much of a father. Because of Sir Robert, the Wards were mortgaging themselves to the hilt. Financial ruin was only a step away.

"Your father don't regard Mr. Jeremy as one of the enemy," he offered cautiously, "and he ain't no Jacobite."

"Jeremy did not take up arms against the Cause," Serena replied with so little hesitation that Flynn surmised this was not the first time this question had teased her mind. "You might say that Jeremy was neutral. Papa understands this. Besides, have you forgotten that the man to whom I was betrothed lost his life at Prestonpans? If I ever wed, it will not be to someone who would dishonor Stephen's memory. There is one thing more. Julian Raynor has no more wish to wed me than I do him, so this is a useless conversation."

"But—"

"Leave be, Flynn! Now, if you please, tell me how things went off last night."

This was soon done, for aside from the close call at The Thatched Tavern, everything had gone smoothly.

"And Clive knows that the militia were there?"

"You may be sure that it was the first thing I told 'im. We're to lie low, that's what Clive thinks, and I agree with 'im. 'E is going off this morning to tell 'is connection in Oxford that we are no longer accepting lodgers, leastways not for some time to come."

Her brow was knit in a frown. "Does Clive suspect an informer, or what?"

"Serena, 'e is being cautious, 'tis all."

She nodded at this, and the frown gradually lifted. "If

the authorities were on to us, they would have arrested us by now."

"Very true. Now, to get back to Raynor——"

Rising in a swish of skirts, she glared down at him. "If I hear that man's name one more time, I swear I shall scream."

"But——"

Moving quickly to a silk screen against the wall, she said over her shoulder, "If you would be good enough to draw a bath for me, Flynn, I should like to bathe and change my clothes," and slipping behind the screen, she began to disrobe.

It was an effective way to bring the conversation to a close. Not to be outdone, Flynn stalked to the screen. "And don't be forgetting to soap your fool 'ead," he said through gritted teeth. "Not that that will make a jot of difference to what's inside it."

"What?" asked Serena, poking her head around the side of the screen.

"Your 'air, don't forget to wash your 'air." And inwardly berating himself for worrying about a baggage who was well able to take care of herself, Flynn went to do her bidding.

It was always like this, he told himself philosophically, from his first day at Ward House, when he'd pissed his breeches because he'd been too afraid to ask where the privy was, and Serena, without fuss or embarrassment, had found him a change of clothes. Sometimes, when Serena was at her most stubborn—like now—he thought he must have been mad to sell his soul at six years old for a pair of pissed breeches.

In all fairness, he had to admit there was more to it than that. In the intervening years, Serena had stood in the role of mentor to him. She had taught him to read and write. His cultured speech, which he could employ when the notion struck him, was the result of her patient tutoring. She had instructed him in manners and deportment so that when he broke the rules, it was from choice and not through ignorance. He had ambitions for his life which he had shared with no one but Serena, knowing that he would be laughed at by anyone else. One day, he was going to make something of himself. Serena believed it too.

More and more, however, the conviction had grown in Flynn lately that the burden of Serena was becoming too much for him, and that it was time to relinquish it into older, more experienced hands. The political climate, Sir Robert's imminent return, the threat of bankruptcy hanging over the family, and not least Serena's involvement with Jacobite fugitives—all these things pressed heavily upon him. Moreover, it was more than time for him to cut the tie that bound him to the Ward household. If he was going to make something of himself, he must strike out on his own. He was reluctant to do so until he saw Serena settled.

Julian Raynor was just the sort of man Flynn would have chosen for Serena if he had been her fairy godmother instead of her self-appointed guardian. All the chairmen knew of the major and his splendid house on St. Dunstan's Court, just off Fleet Street.

Raynor was a regular nob, a gentleman who treated lackeys and lords indiscriminately, that is to say, on their merits. Basing his opinion on below-stairs gossip, Flynn surmised that the major's odd position on the fringes of society had something to do with it. A man who frequently met with prejudice was more likely to judge with an open mind. Having met with condescension and snubs most of his short life, Flynn heartily approved this trait in his betters. That the major never failed to tip generously for a job well done did not hurt his case with Flynn either.

There were other things Flynn liked about the major, things he had observed when he waited patiently in the vestibule, in the wee hours of the morning, while Mr. Jeremy lingered at the green baize tables. Julian Raynor knew his way around women, be they whores or duchesses. Such a man would know how to tame a sharp-tongued, irrepressible female who was used to going her own way.

He was exaggerating, of course. There was more to Serena than a sharp tongue and a strong will. She was also warmhearted, generous, and loyal to a fault. Perversely, these virtues only added to his worries. Serena gave herself far too freely and not often wisely. She doted on her miserable father, and took the most appalling risks for a set of people who were as close to fanatics as Flynn ever hoped to meet.

What he wanted was for Serena to take all that misplaced devotion and give it into the safekeeping of a man who was a worthy mate for her, a man who would appreciate all her fine qualities, as well as temper her failings; in short, a man she could respect or be made to respect. Such gentlemen did not grow on trees.

This thought turned his mind to Captain Horatio Allardyce, the scoundrel who had come sniffing around Serena's skirts when she was barely out of the schoolroom. It wasn't Serena Allardyce had been interested in, but her dowry. One look at Allardyce and Flynn had known he was up to no good. Serena wouldn't listen. Poor Serena. She'd had a rude awakening. Allardyce's fancy woman, the worldly Lady Amelia Lawrence, had soon put her wise to what was going on behind her back. After that, Serena gave men of Allardyce's stamp a wide berth.

Her next suitor, Stephen Howard, was a gentleman of

unquestionable virtue. Flynn had had no quarrel with Mr. Howard, except that he had known he wasn't the man for Serena. He was too tame, too biddable. Another thought occurring to him, Flynn frowned. Surely Serena did not lump Major Raynor with Allardyce? Anyone with sense could see they were as different as a silk purse was from a sow's ear.

He wondered about The Thatched Tavern and what exactly had taken place between Serena and the major. Almost as soon as he had thought of it, his mind had rejected the idea of rape. Flynn considered himself a shrewd judge of character, and unlike some gentlemen he could name, the major did not strike him as the type to force himself on a woman, not even if he believed that woman to be a harlot. He'd seen Raynor, once, in a chilling rage when one of his operators, a beautiful girl by the name of Emerald, had been waylaid and almost ravished by one of Raynor's own patrons. His views on men who preyed on defenseless females were well reported at the time, and the duel that had followed, in which the major had deliberately blown his adversary's powdered toupee from his bald head, had not only added to the major's popularity among his peers, but had also taught them a lesson. From that day to this, the girls who worked for Raynor went unmolested.

Flynn could not see such a man going against his own principles. Besides, Serena did not have the look of a woman who had been mishandled. There wasn't a mark on her. Then again, she did not have the look of a woman who had been well and truly pleasured. It was no great feat to put two and two together. Not a rape, decided Flynn, but a seduction which his intrepid mistress had begun, confident that she would be the one to call the shots. Being the innocent she was, it would not have occurred to her that there would come a point when nature would insist on taking its course. He couldn't stop grinning. Evidently, the experience was not one Serena cared to repeat. Finally, a man had come out on top, and she didn't like it, not one jot.

He knew well enough that her brothers would not be as complacent as he if they ever got to hear of it. Oh no, they would get all worked up, and belt on their small-swords, and go after the major demanding satisfaction. Flynn might have done the same if Serena were younger and less worldly. But she was three-and-twenty with no dowry to attract suitors, and, by far the most tragic to Flynn's way of thinking, fast becoming reconciled to her single state. This chance encounter with Raynor was on a par with answered prayer, if only she could be made to see it.

It wasn't only Serena who needed to be persuaded of her good fortune. Though Mr. Jeremy was not the stiff-necked prig his father was, Flynn did not think that he would welcome an alliance between his sister and a man who owned a gaming house. That was the trouble with the gentry. They put stock in the wrong things. Well, he was bound and determined that Serena was not going to let Julian Raynor slip through her fingers, not if he had anything to do with it.

That Julian would not do the honorable thing never once seriously crossed Flynn's mind.

Chapter Four

❧

She was the daughter of Sir Robert Ward. Julian cursed long and fluently under his breath. He would rather it had been any woman than she. No doubt the jade anticipated that he would come crawling on his hands and knees, begging her to marry him. She would wait till hell froze over before that happened.

Having tasted almost nothing of the breakfast he had ordered, he threw down his napkin and left the dining room. His look was so forbidding that when he paid his shot, the landlord decided not to mention his own troubles, which were considerable. Since the militia had not found the Jacobite they were hunting the night before, they had marched off instead with two harmless residents who could not give an adequate account for the money in their purses. Such goings-on were not only un-English, but frightened away customers.

Preoccupied, abruptly turning on his heel, Julian strode toward the stairs. There was something he should have done before he had rid himself of the girl, something that would soothe the small ripple of conscience that was contributing to his murderous temper. She could not possibly have been a virgin. He must have been mistaken in that, which was not inconceivable, since he had never tampered with a virgin before. How would he recognize the breed? No, not a virgin, he assured himself, but one of those bored ladies of fashion who would dare all just for the thrill of it. He knew her type. It was not he who had been the seducer, but she. He was the victim, for if he had known her identity, he would not have given her the time of day.

When he came to the rooms they had occupied, he strode through the small parlor without looking to left or right, into the bedchamber and straight to the rumpled bed. Grasping the covers, he dragged them back.

Hell and damnation! Streaks of dried blood stood out starkly against the white sheet. So she had been a virgin. She had told him the truth about that. But that did not mean that she was an innocent. She had known what she was doing when she'd entered these rooms with him. Hell, they had made a bargain—she would become his mistress if he would set her up in style. The daughter of Sir Robert Ward would never become any man's mistress. Then what game was she playing?

As he had told her, she was no green girl. He judged her to be in her mid-twenties. Was it possible that she saw herself as a confirmed spinster, with no hope of marriage? Had she made up her mind that if only for one solitary night she would know what it was to be a woman? And in the cold light of day was it shame and remorse that had made her lash out at him?

He slammed out of the room and out of the tavern in a far worse temper than when he had entered it. He did not know which angered him more—the knowledge that she was Serena Ward or the growing conviction that she had chosen him at random to make a woman of her. Striking out toward the Strand, he damned Serena Ward to all eternity for making him the victim of her schemes, and he double-damned himself for not recognizing her before things had gone this far.

Though he had never been introduced to her, he had seen her often enough from a distance—a tall, graceful girl who gave every appearance of knowing her own worth. She was proud and dignified, and as cold as a block of marble—that was the impression he got. She was also fair-haired. He remembered this particularly because the other members of her family were all as dark as ravens.

Last night, her hair had been ink-black, dyed, no doubt, and her costume anything but dignified. As cold as a block of marble? He almost laughed aloud. Serena Ward, baronet's daughter, was as hot as a blacksmith's furnace with the bellows going full blast. Not that she would admit to it. Oh no, she had to make him out the villain of the piece if only to salve her own conscience. Five minutes, less than five, that was all he needed to prove that behind that demure, ladylike exterior beat the heart of a harlot.

Damnation! What was he thinking? He already had proved it and now he was paying for it. He wasn't a complete scoundrel. He knew what a gentleman generally offered when he found himself in this predicament. His parents had instilled in him the principles by which they had lived out their lives. But this case was different. This was Serena Ward. He could never shackle himself to the daughter of the man who had viciously brought his own family to complete and utter destruction.

Besides which, Serena Ward was no more eager to receive his addresses than he was to offer them. *I would no more think of taking up with your kind than I would with thieves and murderers.*

He was a gamester, and as aware as she of the great gulf that separated them. In his own setting, men of rank treated him as an equal. He was a fine fellow who could be counted on to extend their credit when they bet heavily at his tables. Out of his own setting, he was given a mixed reception. There were some, mostly those of a military background, who judged him on his merits. There were others who might welcome him into their homes but only through the door that gave onto the back staircase, and only to all-male affairs from which the daughters of the house were excluded.

He entered his gaming house by a side door that gave onto a staircase. One floor up, he came to his private suite of rooms. At this time of day, the only people he was likely to meet were members of his domestic staff. None of his operators or croupiers lived on the premises, and his apartments, which were on two floors, were completely private. There was a door to the gaming house on the top landing, and no one entered that door except by invitation.

Julian's manservant, who was part valet, part butler, came forward to greet him. It was not unusual for Julian to return home as dawn was breaking, or even later. Tibbets never passed comment on his master's nocturnal habits when a woman's perfume clung to his garments. This morning, Tibbets's infallible nose caught no whiff of perfume.

About to offer the major one of his rare smiles, Tibbets checked himself. "If I may suggest, sir," he said circumspectly, "a spot of breakfast and a pot of coffee?"

"No, you may not suggest," snapped Julian. Brushing by the startled valet, he entered his bedchamber and locked the door. A moment later, he flung the door wide and roared for his manservant. "A bath," he said, "with plenty of hot water. See to it, Tibbets."

Unclean. He felt unclean, and that had never happened to him before. She had used him as if he were a stud, and she the mare that was in need of servicing. Restlessly, he paced back and forth as lackeys came and went, readying his bath for him.

Having dismissed the lackeys, Julian peeled out of his clothes and thrust them at Tibbets. "Burn them," he said.

Tibbets opened his mouth, and quickly shut it. "Certainly, sir," he replied, making a mental note to clean and press the costly garments and set them at the back of the clothes press until his master was in a better frame of mind.

As the door closed upon Tibbets, Julian immersed himself in the near scalding water. With soap and washcloth, he went at himself, trying to dislodge the tantalizing scent of her. It wasn't perfume. That was easily got rid of. This was something darker, and unique to the girl. After a prolonged scrubbing, he paused, resting his arms along the rim of the tub.

Now that he had time to think about it, there were things about Miss Serena Ward that did not add up. He knew of many ladies of fashion who made excursions to dens of vice for the sheer titillation of the experience, but never unescorted. Where, in all of this, was the girl's escort of last night? He remembered something else. Serena Ward was reputed to be virtually in mourning for a lover, her betrothed to be exact, who had perished at Prestonpans. Many men since had tried to woo her but the lady, as rumor had it, was not to be won. He was glad he had remembered that.

His anger seemed to have cooled along with the temperature of his bath water. Surging from the copper tub, he reached for a towel and proceeded to dry himself vigorously. Having donned a brocade robe, he sprawled on top of the bed and gazed at the intricate plaster ceiling, his eyes tracing the designs on the cornices, over and over, as if to memorize them.

What was there about his family, he wondered, that they should attract the notice of a viperish brood like the Wards? Was it something in themselves, some fatal flaw that marked them out as victims? Was it blind chance, or was it the machinations of a capricious, malevolent fate bent on their destruction? And where would it all end?

It had started in 1715, at the beginning of the first

Rebellion, when Sir Robert Ward had taken one look at Lady Harriet Egremont and had promptly offered for her. Lady Harriet was Julian's mother. The girl's father, Lord Kirkland, had accepted Sir Robert's offer against his daughter's wishes. Sir Robert was everything he wished for in a son-in-law. Their families were both of the Jacobite persuasion. The earl's heir, Lord Hugo, and Sir Robert were inseparable friends. The only problem with all of this was the lady's infatuation for a most unsuitable gentleman. This was Julian's father. William Renney, as he was then known, was tutor to Lady Harriet's younger brother, James. When Renney was dismissed from his post, the young couple eloped, in defiance of Lord Kirkland, and went into hiding.

As a young boy growing up in Bristol, Julian had known nothing of this. His life was as happy and carefree as any child had a right to expect. His father, with the help of his mother, had opened a school for the sons of the local gentry. As Julian remembered, when he wasn't at his books, he was off playing with the other boys, reenacting every skirmish and battle of the past Rebellion. Those were the golden years of his life.

He could never quite remember when the turning point had come. What he did remember was that the school failed and within a year or two, after several moves, they were in Manchester, and the only source of the family's income was the private tutoring his father did at home. By this time, the little family had grown. There were two more mouths to feed, for the twins had arrived when Julian was eight years old.

Mark and Mary were delicate children, and a constant source of worry to their parents. For all their worries, all their shortage of funds, the family was affectionate and close-knit. And when the twins turned three, their circumstances changed for the better, or so it seemed at the time.

William Renney had procured a position as tutor to Lord Hornsby's sons, and Lord Hornsby was a generous employer. There was money enough to send Julian as a boarder to the grammar school in Oxford which his father had attended as a boy. Against all these material advantages, however, was the sad fact that the family was to be scattered. A tutor was not allowed to have a private life, but was required to reside where his charges resided. The Renneys were never to be reunited.

There was one other thing that had troubled Julian. They were to change their name from Renney to Wright. He remembered his mother holding his hand tightly as his father explained the reason for the change. For the first time, Julian learned of his parents' elopement, and was given to understand that this act was regarded as so reprehensible by the nobility that his father could never find employment as long as he kept his own name.

It was the truth, and yet it was a distortion of the truth, and so his parents, with the best will in the world, had deceived him. What seemed incomprehensible to him now was that he had never sensed the depths of their worries, he had never questioned the life they led nor thought of the future with anything less than supreme confidence. He was a clever boy with all the advantages of his father's private tutoring. It was expected that he would one day find a position in some government ministry or perhaps at the university. But not under the name of Julian Renney.

He hated to remember those few years he had spent at school in Oxford, not because they were unhappy, but because they were bought with money his parents could ill afford. It was worse than that. His father had gone into debt to procure an education for him that befitted the son of a gentleman.

He groaned softly, shutting his eyes as though he could avert the memories that were rushing in to claim him.

Summoned from school, he discovered that his father had been dismissed from his position and thrown in debtors' prison. His mother was in deep despondency. He was thirteen years old and hardly able to cope with the burdens that had fallen on his shoulders—the twins, household chores, dread for his father's fate, and worst of all, fear for his mother's sanity. It was very evident to him that his mother feared someone was out for their blood and that they must go into hiding.

Bailiffs came. He remembered going for them when they put their hands on his mother to evict her from their rooms. The next thing he knew, he had taken a blow that sent him staggering to his knees. When he recovered from the blow, they were in the parish workhouse, but he had no recollection of how they had got there. Hell could not have terrified him more. Hollow-eyed children, brutal, gaunt-faced women, and few males to speak of. There were three hundred people housed in that barracks of a building, and in the space of two months, twenty-seven of them left it as corpses. Three of those corpses were his mother and his young brother and sister.

A groan broke from him, and he twisted to his side, one arm flung over his eyes as he tried to shut out the harrowing memories. He remembered the cold, little doll-like faces of his brother and sister, and the frenzied resistance he had put up when the orderly had tried to take the twins away from him. "They're not dead! They're not!" he cried out helplessly. "They are sleeping. Why won't you believe me?" Later, he'd heard that the parish officers never intended that young children should survive the appalling conditions. It was too costly to keep them.

He had escaped from the workhouse and had tried to find his father. Another blow awaited him. While he had been incarcerated in the workhouse, his father had died of jail-fever and had been buried in a pauper's grave.

God knew what would have become of him, a boy of thirteen, if he had not fallen in with a whore, a madam of a brothel. Billie McGuire was her name, and for some inexplicable reason, she had taken to the waif who lived and slept rough in the alley outside her door. By this time, fearing that the authorities might be after him, Julian had changed his name yet again. From that day to this, he had been known as Julian Raynor.

At this point in his reflections, Julian got off the bed and went to stand by the long sash window, staring out at the scene below. Barrow boys were patrolling the streets, selling their wares, and footmen and maids from nearby houses were purchasing succulent baked pies and fresh fish and other delicacies for the noon meal.

A year ago, when he had opened his club in this fashionable neighborhood, it had seemed that he could go no higher. He'd owned other gaming establishments in his time, and though he had done remarkably well from them, those had been in the provinces.

In London, he discovered, gaming houses flourished in spite of the laws against them, and the authorities turned a blind eye to what was going forward under their very noses. They could hardly do otherwise when the chief offenders were gentlemen in the upper echelons of both government and court circles. So long as one was circumspect, no questions were asked. For this reason, his gaming house was officially known as a gentleman's club.

He still felt as he had always felt since he had left his schooldays behind. He did not belong; he was a foreigner in a strange land; he had nothing in common with the people he met and mixed with. When a patron once paid his gaming debts with a plantation in the distant Carolinas, a new dream had captured his imagination. He wasn't looking for security or riches. He was looking for something worthwhile to give his life to. And just as soon as he had dealt with Sir Robert Ward, he would shake the dust of England from his feet and begin a new life in the New World.

That restlessness was upon him again. He strode to a large oak wardrobe, pulled out his riding gear, and began to dress.

It was one of his usual rides, and Saladin, his roan, would have known the route without direction. On a rise overlooking the hamlet of Chelsea, Julian dismounted. On one side, there were boats drawn up on the mud flats, and stands of plane trees and beeches shaded the foreshore. On the other side were the blackened ruins of Kirkland Hall. It was here that his mother had been born, here that his parents had met and fallen in love.

After mounting up, he descended the hill at a canter, then slowed to a walk as he approached the ruins. The gardens were a wilderness, and the once stately house, seat of generations of the earls of Kirkland, was now home to a flock of crows. They rose as one at his approach and croaked furiously before finding perches in the nearby avenue of oaks.

This was where it had all started, the night Lady Harriet Egremont had eloped with her brother's tutor, but there was far, far more to the story than Julian had been told by his parents. What they had not told him was that same night, Lord Hugo and his friend, Sir Robert Ward, who were both Jacobite fugitives, both hiding in the house, were betrayed to the authorities and government troops had swooped down on them. Lord Hugo was shot dead in the melee; the old earl was taken into custody. His destination would be the Tower. Only Sir Robert escaped. The last thing the soldiers did was put their torches to the Hall, burning it to the ground.

It was only in the last year that Julian had been able to piece the story together, only in the last year that he had discovered that Sir Robert Ward was the nameless, faceless monster who had stalked his father in revenge for what had happened that night. There had been some sort of proof, in the form of a letter, that William Renney was the informer, and when Sir Robert returned to England after the Jacobites received amnesty, he had made it his life's work to discredit William Renney and bring him to ruin.

Not for one moment did Julian accept that his father had been an informer. He knew him too well. Both his father and mother had passed on a set of precepts that had become the plumb line by which he measured his life. He might not be able to live up to those precepts, but he knew what they were. William Renney had lived his principles. He could never have committed so base an act.

Sir Robert Ward had set himself up as judge and jury and the verdict had been to bring William Renney to ruin and despair. And he had succeeded. But not well enough. Renney had left behind a legacy—a son with a debt to discharge.

Serena Ward was a complication he had not foreseen.

Chapter Five

James, Earl of Kirkland, shook his head. "The chances of Sir Robert Ward receiving a p-pardon for his p-part in the Rebellion are not very high."

This was not what Julian wanted to hear. Nevertheless, he treated Lord Kirkland's words with the respect they merited. As deputy minister at the War Office, the earl was in a position to know. He was reputed to be a tireless gatherer of information, with spy networks all over England and Scotland. Kirkland had good reason to be cautious. If there were another Jacobite uprising, he was the one who would be called to account.

They were in the reading room of Julian's gaming club, a very masculine haven done in shades of beige and brown, and not a flimsy, gilt-edged chair or mirror in sight. Sturdy oak tables and straight-backed armless chairs were set around the room in informal groups. This was the quietest room in the house, where patrons could amuse themselves by reading the latest copy of the *Daily Courant* and other periodicals, or, like his lordship and Julian, engage in quiet conversation. There were several gentlemen in the room, but none of them would have dreamed of imposing himself on a private conversation unless invited, and they expected the same courtesy to be extended to themselves.

"Others have received pardons," said Julian. "Why not Sir Robert?"

"Because," said the earl, "Sir Robert has defected to the S-Stuarts twice in his lifetime. That makes him a traitor twice over. He is not one to learn from his m-mistakes. He will never give up. He will always plot insurrection."

Julian thought about this for a moment. "Jeremy Ward was never of the Jacobite persuasion, was he?"

"No. Jeremy is not unlike m-me. Whatever we may think of the H-House of Hanover, we know that the Stuarts w-will only lead our country into anarchy. B-better the devil you know than one you don't know, if you see what I mean."

Julian laughed. "That's a strange thing for one of His Majesty's ministers to say."

Lord Kirkland looked slightly abashed. "What I m-mean to say is that I am for peace and stability."

"Yes, and like most Englishmen, you don't care if a monkey sits on the throne of England?"

"Quite." Lord Kirkland signaled to one of the waiters. "Bring us a bottle of Madeira, if you please," he said.

Of all Julian's patrons, Lord Kirkland always received the best attention from the waiters, not only because he tipped generously, but because he was unfailingly polite. Within minutes, the waiter was setting down a bottle of Madeira and two glasses.

As Lord Kirkland measured out the wine, Julian took a moment or two to study the older man and reflect on their friendship. The earl had made himself known to Julian shortly after he had opened his gaming house. He was half persuaded, the earl had told him in his diffident way, that Julian must be related to him, perhaps a distant cousin on the Egremont side of the family? It turned out that Julian's likeness to Lord Hugo was uncanny.

From that remark, Julian deduced that the earl and Lord Hugo had been as different from each other as chalk from cheese, for there was certainly no resemblance between himself and the earl. Kirkland had a thin, ascetic face, and his almost Puritan disdain for ornamentation gave him a monklike appearance.

A distant cousin on the Egremont side of the family? Julian had replied vaguely, revealing nothing. Nevertheless his lordship had convinced himself that Julian was the bastard child of his brother, Hugo. It's what the earl wanted to believe, was pathetically eager to believe, as if Hugo lived on in Julian. As for his mother, Lady Harriet, she was never mentioned. Julian could not bring himself to raise her name, not trusting himself to speak of her without breaking down like a baby.

Blinking rapidly, Julian accepted the glass of Madeira his lordship held out to him. He coughed to clear his throat. "I was in Chelsea the other day and took the opportunity, I hope you don't mind, of looking over Kirkland Hall. You never thought to restore the house to its former glory?"

"No, n-never. I leave that to my son, H-Harry. If it were not entailed, I m-might be tempted to sell the Hall. For me, it will always have too many tragic m-memories. And of course I don't mind, my boy. I'm only sorry that the fire destroyed all the p-portraits of our ancestors. Hugo isn't the only one you take after, you know, and it's more than looks. You are very like Hugo in other ways too. He was always the adventurous one, very confident, yes, and sometimes, alas, foolhardy."

"Lord Kirkland, I'm not convinced that—"

"I know, I know. F-forget I said that. It's only, well, it would be comforting to think that we were related, you know?"

Julian nodded sympathetically, and sipped his Madeira. When government troops had descended on Kirkland Hall, the earl had been no more than a boy of twelve. At a single stroke, he had lost his whole family. His sister had eloped, never to be seen again, his older brother had been shot to death before his eyes, and shortly after, the old earl had died a broken man in the Tower. The earl's life and his own had many parallels. They had both become orphans at approximately the same age. He understood the earl's sentiments only too well. Orphans never got over the feeling that they were alone in the world.

Though there were some similarities in their early lives, there was one major difference. He had been maddened by grief at the loss of his father. No one had mourned the old earl's death. By all accounts, he had been a brutal, unfeeling father. His son, James, had succeeded to the title at twelve years. Unfortunately, he had also succeeded to a guardian who, it was reported, was every bit as ferocious as the old earl. He'd led a terrible life until he had reached his majority.

After that, the earl's luck had changed. He'd married one of the richest heiresses in the whole of England, and if that were not enough, it was a love match to boot. There was a house in Hanover Square, and a palace of a place in the country near Seven Oaks. In spite of his wealth and position of eminence at the War Office, however, Kirkland was a very unassuming gentleman. It was said that he lived in fear of his own servants. This was an exaggeration, of course, but there was a germ of truth in it. Julian deduced that his lordship had had all the spirit beaten out of him as a young boy. He felt sorry for him, and at the same time, he liked him immensely.

He hadn't forgotten his real purpose in seeking Lord Kirkland out. Turning the conversation back to the Wards, he said, "I have recently come into possession of some bills and mortgages belonging to Jeremy Ward." This was not an unusual event for a gambler. Patrons frequently paid their gaming debts with vowels they held from others. "Is it possible, do you suppose, that he is trying to raise money to buy a pardon for his father?"

Lord Kirkland gave Julian a keen look. "I take it you would be in favor of such a m-move?"

Julian understood what was behind the question. Sir Robert and Lord Hugo had been fast friends. It was only natural that a son of Hugo's would be sympathetic to the baronet. "Why not?" said Julian. "He is a beaten man. What can he do? At the first hint of trouble, the authorities would haul him off to the Tower."

"What can he do?" Lord Kirkland snorted. "What c-can he do? If you only knew Sir Robert Ward, you w-would not ask that question."

"What manner of man is he?" asked Julian, settling himself more comfortably in his chair.

"You never met him?"

"No. I didn't come to London much until I sold out after Prestonpans. By that time, Sir Robert was in Scotland, fighting with the Prince. Later, of course, he was a fugitive and had made his way to France."

"You joined the army at sixteen, I believe you told me, and did a stint in India?"

Lord Kirkland was doing it again, probing into his past, trying to find a connection to his brother, Hugo. They had been through all this before.

"I spent five years in India," said Julian, and to hasten things along, he told the earl what he wanted to know before he could put his questions to him. "When I returned to England, I took up the only thing that I knew, the only thing of any worth I had learned with my stint in the army—gambling. I had a gaming house in Manchester, did I tell you?" He knew that he had. "But the Gaming Act of Forty-five shut me down. I was at a loose end and went back to being a soldier. After Prestonpans, I tried my luck in London. And the rest you know."

"Whatever happened to Mrs. McGuire?"

Julian almost choked on a swallow of wine. Mrs. Mc-

Guire was Billie McGuire, the harlot who had adopted him when he had escaped from the workhouse. For three years, he had lived in a brothel, and though it was strange at first, it was not as terrifying as the workhouse. He had liked the girls well enough, and had soon ceased to be shocked by how they earned their living. Like him, their ambitions were reduced to immediate survival, and morals and scruples did not enter into it. When he could, he paid his way with the winnings he made playing cards in inns and taverns in the area.

"Mrs. McGuire?" he said, looking puzzled. "Oh, the widow who adopted me when I ran away from school? She died and left me a legacy." This was no lie. "It was because of her generosity that I was able to buy my commission."

Lord Kirkland nodded. "You were very fortunate to find a home with her after you ran away from school. She sounds like a most generous-hearted lady."

Billie had certainly been all of that.

"And you never knew who your parents were or who paid for your schooling?" asked the earl.

"No, never. Good Lord! How did we get on to this? I beg your pardon. I had not meant to monopolize the conversation. We were talking about Sir Robert, were we not, and you were about to tell me what kind of man he is." He could be as persistent as the earl when it suited him, and he wondered idly if persistence was a family trait.

"Stern. Nasty. Single-minded," said the earl emphatically. "He h-hates weakness of any description."

"And yet, he was Lord Hugo's friend, was he not?"

"Yes, well, my b-brother didn't have a s-stutter." Realizing that he had inadvertently betrayed himself, Lord Kirkland gave an embarrassed laugh. "You will think I am being p-petty, but when I was a boy, I would rather be silent than talk in Sir Robert's presence. My stutter

irritated him, you see. As though I s-stuttered on purpose!"

"Not a very likable gentleman by the sound of things?"

"No."

"And since then?"

"I have rarely exchanged m-more than a few words
with him. Why are you so interested in Sir Robert, Julian?"

"Mmm? Oh, those bills and mortgages of Jeremy
Ward's? I was merely wondering if he will ever be in a
position to redeem them?"

"I shouldn't count on it, not if he is set on buying a
p-pardon for his father. They don't come cheap."

Julian's tone was carefully neutral. "Do you think the
Crown will grant him a pardon if he pays for it?"

"Oh yes. Money can buy a lot of f-forgiveness."

It was exactly what Julian wanted to hear.

He was one step closer to achieving his objective. Julian savored that thought as he went over his ledgers later
that same evening. He had amassed quite a number of
bills and mortgages belonging to Jeremy Ward. When Sir
Robert finally received his pardon and set foot in England, it would be in Julian's power to bring him to ruin.
Lord, if they only knew it! He was the one who was
footing the bill for this pardon, yes, and he never expected
to see a penny of his money again. He considered it
money well spent.

Hearing a sound from the wall behind his desk, Julian
put down his pen and went to open the doors of the
dumbwaiter that connected his private office to the pantry
on the floor below. He took the tray on which sat a jug of
coffee and a cup and saucer, and returned to his desk. In
his private suite of rooms there was no kitchen. When he

ate at home, all his meals were sent up to him from the kitchens in his gaming house by way of the small lift.

His thoughts did not dwell for long on Sir Robert Ward. Any thought of the Wards always brought to mind Serena Ward in particular.

If only she had been the girl she pretended to be. As he drank his coffee, he let that thought turn in his mind. If she had been Victoria Noble and not Serena Ward, he knew he would be in hot pursuit by now. He had never met a woman like her. It wasn't only that she appealed to his senses. She appealed to something else in him as well, something he could not quite identify.

This was a fruitless train of thought. She wasn't Victoria Noble. Victoria was the name of a character she had been playing. She was Serena Ward, and that was that.

She had been a virgin. A man of conscience did not dishonor an innocent young woman without making amends. Albeit unwittingly, he had taken her innocence, and now he was planning to compound the harm he had done by ruining her father. That did not sit well with him.

A man of conscience did not shrug off his responsibilities. This was one of the tenets by which he had been raised. Staring morosely into space, he drank his coffee.

Come what may, he had to do right by her. The thought drummed inside his head like a dirge.

Dark had settled over the city when Lord Kirkland came out of Julian's gaming house and summoned a sedan to convey him to a coffeehouse in St. James. He did not linger in the coffeehouse, but after a suitable interval, slipped unobserved through a side door. From there, he made the short walk to the exclusive Temple of Venus in King's Place.

It was his conversation with Julian that had brought on

his melancholy. *What manner of man is Sir Robert Ward?* More to the point, what manner of man was *he,* James, Earl of Kirkland? He had a wife who loved him, three children on whom he doted, and money enough to do whatever he liked. And now there was Julian, Hugo's son. And he deserved none of it. On Judgment Day, he would surely get what he deserved. Hadn't his guardian told him so?

His visit was not expected, and there was a delay as the proprietress of the establishment rearranged things so that he could be accommodated. It was, after all, a Thursday night, and he was a creature of habit. He was not expected till Saturday.

Here, naked, manacled to chains on the wall, his sins were beaten out of him by two stalwart, birch-wielding Amazons who had been well warned in advance to disregard his pleas for clemency. After his humiliating ordeal, he was allowed to rest until he had come to himself. He required no other services from these Vestal Virgins. Purified, purged of sin, he was ready to go home to his wife.

Chapter Six

When Serena next encountered Julian Raynor, it was two o'clock in the afternoon, and she was entering her sister-in-law's boudoir unannounced to return a fan she had borrowed from Catherine the night before. As Serena parted the crimson damask curtains that gave onto the little dressing room, she came to an abrupt halt. Catherine was dressed in a filmy negligee, at her dressing table, her face turned up to the gallant who was in the act of lowering his head to hers.

There could be no mistaking that handsomely chiseled profile nor the cut of the claret frock coat that perfectly molded his broad shoulders. Speechless with shock, Serena watched as the gentleman's fingers brushed Catherine's cheek in a voluptuous caress. When his head dipped, she was torn from her paralysis.

"Sirrah!" she cried out. She had given the servants explicit instructions respecting Major Raynor. Under no circumstances was he to be admitted to the house. That he should turn up here, in Catherine's boudoir, was insupportable.

Eyes flashing murder, she advanced upon him. "How dare you! How dare you!"

Two steps into the boudoir, and she became excruciatingly aware that she had made a royal ass of herself. There were several other ladies and gentlemen lounging around the room, and footmen were dispensing glasses of chocolate or coffee, and freshly baked pastries. This was no amorous assignation, but an informal levee, where a married lady of fashion, having just risen from her bed, might entertain members of both sexes while her maids prepared her for the day's round of pleasure.

At Serena's precipitous entrance, the gentlemen made a valiant effort to rise to their feet, no mean task when both hands were occupied with beverages and delicacies and their dangling smallswords were inclined to catch in the voluminous skirts of their richly embroidered coats. Julian Raynor slowly straightened and turned slightly to meet Serena's mortified stare. The twinkle in his eyes betrayed a complete knowledge of her gaffe, a gaffe which, happily, seemed to have escaped the notice of the other members of Catherine's little court.

"No?" he said whimsically. "Then where do you suggest I position it?"

Serena's eyes fell to the small enamel box in his open palm, and everything became clear to her. Raynor was advising Catherine on her toilette, and in particular, on where to place a black silk patch to dramatize her best feature.

"Where do you suggest I position it?" he repeated.

She longed to tell him. Oh, how she longed to tell him. Gritting her teeth, she tapped her borrowed fan in the middle of her own cheek. "Here," she said indifferently.

In faint amusement, he raised the eyeglass which dangled from a ribbon on his neck, and his bold gaze wandered over her, from the frilled lace cap atop her knot of unpowdered blond curls to her dainty slippered feet, taking in the blue silk overdress with its white hooped petticoat, and the white gauze scarf tucked decorously around her throat. When his eyes finally lifted to meet hers, they were laughing openly.

Serena rarely blushed. It wasn't in her nature. In that moment, however, she distinctly felt her skin begin to heat. His lingering inspection of her person was meant to press home the point that he knew her as something quite different from the refined lady of taste who now stood before him.

"Not here?" he murmured suggestively, and touched one finger to the corner of her mouth, reminding her vividly of the patch she had worn the night she had met him at The Thatched Tavern.

When she flinched from that touch, anger blazed momentarily in his eyes, then was swiftly suppressed.

His voice altered. "Catherine," he said, "pray present me to this charming child."

Catherine, who had been watching the pair with lively interest, readily complied. "Julian," she said, "you must know that this is Sir Robert's daughter, Serena. Serena, I have the honor to present Major Julian Raynor."

To Serena's credit, she managed to utter a polite commonplace and did not betray her relief when she was saved, by Letty's artless intervention, from further conversation with a man she had good reason to hate.

Flouncing to her feet, Letty quickly interposed herself between Serena and Julian. "Julian," she said, her smile bewitching, "may I suggest that a patch should always draw attention to a lady's eyes?" Her own lashes fluttered flirtatiously.

Seizing the opportunity to escape, Serena turned aside and seated herself beside a young gentleman who moved over to make room for her on a pink brocade sofa. She smiled and nodded at the several persons present, but her attention never wavered from the little tableau by Catherine's dressing table.

"Only if the lady's eyes are as strikingly beautiful as your own, Miss Letty," replied Julian. "Would you be kind enough to hold the box for me?"

Flirtation and frivolity, Serena reminded herself, were the hallmarks of a lady's levee, and no one, least of all a lady's husband, would raise an eyebrow at what was going forward in Catherine's boudoir. At this moment, all over London, scenes like this one were taking place. Ladies, married ladies, whose wardrobes were bulging with fine clothes, would be entertaining their guests in little more than their shifts. It was the mode, but it was also naughty, which, she supposed, explained why gentlemen attended levees in droves.

Julian Raynor's purpose in being here was a puzzle to her, but she knew that it was not innocent. Was he trying to humiliate her, or frighten her? Did it give him some kind of perverse pleasure to hound her like this? Why wouldn't he leave her alone?

For a whole week, she had hardly ventured outside the door, knowing that if she chanced to come face-to-face with him, it would be beyond her powers to keep a civil tongue in her head. Raynor had made his presence felt nonetheless, for his name was forever being mentioned by Catherine or Letty. They came home from every drive or rout, with their conversation, especially Letty's, full of Major Raynor. He was so handsome, so manly, so much the hero that Serena was hard-pressed not to box her sister's ears.

To her knowledge, Raynor had never bothered with Catherine or Letty before now. They were hardly his style. Within a week of seducing one sister, he was assiduously courting the other two. Damn the man! What was he up to?

Serena's fears were not for Catherine, but for Letty. She was a green, impressionable girl. Naturally the attentions of a man like Raynor would bowl her over, if only because he stood out from the crowd. A quick comprehensive glance around the room confirmed Serena in her opinion.

For the most part, the gentlemen were fops and far more taken with themselves than they were in getting up a flirtation with the ladies. Their wigs were powdered in every shade of the rainbow. The lace at their throats and cuffs was so profuse as to be ostentatious. Their painted faces and rouged lips put Serena in mind of a collection of china dolls. But it was the affected lisps and mincing manners that offended her the most. She had been acquainted with most of these gentlemen since they were rowdy schoolboys bent on deviltry. She knew for a fact there wasn't a genuine lisp among the lot of them. By and large, they were a set of harmless fribbles, and when they forgot themselves, which they sometimes did, they were even likable.

Julian Raynor was not an empty-headed fribble, nor was he a fop. Though she was loath to admit it, she had to say that in present company he cut a glamorous figure. Not that any of this weighed with her. In her mind, he would always be the man who had sent her home with a fifty-pound note in her hand.

Watching Raynor now as he deftly played the gallant with two women at one time, Serena became convinced that his notorious reputation did not do him justice. Gamester, rake, libertine—she would not allow such a person to trifle with her innocent sister.

To masculine sighs and exclamations and murmurs of delight, Julian deftly affixed the black patch high on Catherine's left cheekbone. As he turned away to hunt among the pots and bottles which littered the top of the dressing table, Serena was silent, watching him speculatively.

Unstoppering one, he sniffed delicately. "Lavender!" he disparaged, and pulled a long face. He tried another, then another, until he found one to his liking. "Tuberose," he said, grinning wickedly, "full-bodied and alluring, for a lady who has the style to flaunt her femininity."

In the mirror, Catherine's eyes flirted with him outrageously. Serena could not see Raynor's face, so she concentrated on what he was doing. Evidently, Julian Raynor was no stranger to a lady's boudoir.

When he began to apply the perfume to Catherine's bare skin with the tips of his fingers, an odd sensation fluttered in the pit of Serena's stomach, and her breathing slowed. To a stream of advice and encouragement from the onlookers, he stroked the heady fragrance along Catherine's eyebrows, her wrists, behind her earlobes, to the hollow of her throat. At each brush of his fingers, Serena felt as though her own skin were taking fire. There was an impression of suppressed sensuality in each mesmerizing stroke. The scent of roses permeated the air like some powerful, voluptuous aphrodisiac. She fought against its power.

Slowly, deliberately, he parted the edges of Catherine's negligee and Serena's breath became shallower, more audible. Above Catherine's lace-edged nightshift, the creamy swell of her breasts was visible. A hush descended. One gentleman snickered. Letty giggled. Serena could not have moved if someone had shouted that the house was on fire.

"And here," he said in a voice that was not quite hoarse, not quite a whisper, "for a lover, and only a lover to discover," and he brazenly dipped his rose-fragrant fingers beneath the shift, caressing the valley between Catherine's quivering breasts.

Serena could feel those strong fingers as if they had caressed her own breasts. Her nipples hardened and she stifled an involuntary groan.

"Wretched rake!" exclaimed Catherine playfully, and slapped his hands away. "Is no woman safe from you?"

"No," he said simply.

Everyone was laughing and applauding, as if the curtain had fallen on a stage performance. Serena was locked in memory. Powerful masculine hands were molding her to his hard length. There was pleasure there for the taking, if only she would allow herself to share in it.

His head suddenly lifted and his eyes met and held Serena's across the width of that small room. Awareness, exclusive, frightening in its violence, flashed between them, and she knew that he, too, had been locked in memories of that night.

By sheer force of will, she dragged her eyes from his. It was a while before she had collected herself enough to participate in what was going on around her. As maids displayed several gowns for Catherine's inspection, Serena threw out suggestions, trying to enter into the spirit of the thing.

"Not panniers?" said Catherine regretfully. She was fingering her latest acquisition, a flowered muslin with a pale green satin underdress. "But panniers are all the rage."

"Not," said Serena emphatically, "when one is engaged to attend one of Mr. Handel's concerts. Even the gentlemen have been requested to leave off their smallswords." She was referring to the awkwardness in a crush of people of ladies' voluminous hooped skirts and the ubiquitous smallsword which every gentleman sported.

Her idle observation brought a torrent of protests from Catherine's enraged beaux. Lord Percy spoke for them all when he lisped, " 'Pon my honor, I'll allow no man to dictate my conduct. Leave my thmallthword at home? And pray tell, what if I am thet upon by footpads and highwaymen, or thome knave inthults me? Devil fly away with Mr. Handel is what I thay."

Under cover of the heated conversation that followed, Julian Raynor relinquished his position at the dressing table and idled his way over to Serena, eventually stationing himself to one side of the sofa where she was seated.

When he leaned both arms along the back of the sofa, so that his breath warmed her nape, Serena went as taut as a bowstring. For her ears only, he murmured theatrically, "You may rest easy now, Victoria. Your little secret is safe with me."

"I am heartily relieved to hear it!" she retorted with more haste than caution. "And my name is Serena. Miss Ward to you."

They exchanged sober glances, then he smiled, a teasing grin, which only increased Serena's wariness. The rake looked almost harmless, which, she supposed, was a good trick for a rake. She had seen him when he looked quite different.

Reaching in the depths of his coat pocket, he withdrew a snuffbox. With an elegant snap of one wrist, he opened it and proceeded to take snuff. "You are not so old as I thought you were," he said. "Powder and paint will do that to a woman."

Serena's eyes darted about her. "I don't wish to discuss it," she hissed, her lips barely moving.

"Frankly, neither do I. However, I fear we must."

Catching Letty's suspicious eye upon them, Serena smiled and said through her teeth, "Major Raynor, there is nothing more to say. Please leave this house at once and never darken its doors again. If you persist in making a nuisance of yourself, I shall be forced to call one of the footmen to escort you out."

"You are," he said, stifling a yawn, "the most melodramatic female of my acquaintance. I have not endured the tedium of this past hour merely to have you turn me away now. I give you two choices, Victoria. We either discuss what needs to be said between us in front of all these witnesses, or we discuss it in private. Which is it to be?"

"There is no privacy to be had here!"

"Fine. Then you may begin by telling me—"

"Wait!"

"Yes?"

Conscious of the notice they were attracting, she gave way, but not very graciously. "The bookroom," she snapped. "With my brother not at home, it should be free. Ask one of the footmen to direct you to it. I shall give you a few minutes then follow you down."

Letty, coming up at that moment, threw Serena a vexed look before turning her considerable charm upon Raynor. Serena observed her with a careful eye. Since Letty had blossomed, at seventeen, into a young woman of rare beauty, she had begun to attract beaux like moths to a flame. The attraction was mutual. Men was all she ever thought about. Serena, who loved her sister dearly, was inclined to treat this affliction as a malady that time would cure. Watching Letty now as she practiced her newfound woman's wiles on Julian Raynor, Serena sincerely wished that she had taken the malady a mite more seriously.

Dimpling smiles from the aspiring Jezebel. Lazy grins from the rampant rogue. Serena felt something move inside her, something she neither wanted nor liked. Excusing herself, she moved to the empty chair beside Miriam Porter, old Judge Porter's dashing young wife, and listened with feigned absorption to a conversation in progress on the merits of David Garrick's performance as King Lear, which had been performed the night before at Drury Lane. But when Julian Raynor said his adieux to Catherine and slipped from the room, she was burningly aware of it.

In the corridor, Julian was met by a young footman with an emerald winking at his left ear. At sight of Julian, he gave a start, then a slow, foolish grin spread across his face.

"Miss Ward will see me in the bookroom, if you would direct me to it," said Julian.

"I should deem it an 'onor, Major Raynor, sir," replied Flynn with so much enthusiasm that Julian's brows rose.

This was not the welcome he had met with the first time he had tried to gain admittance to the house. On that occasion, the door had been shut firmly against him by a decrepit butler who looked as though his face had been cast in marble. Miss Ward was not at home nor ever would be to Julian Raynor, he was given to understand. It was regrettable that his scruples would not allow him to accept that answer.

"Flynn, is it not?" said Julian conversationally, as they descended the stairs.

"Fancy you remembering me," said Flynn.

It was no great feat, thought Julian, for Flynn was the most colorful footman to appear on the London scene for some time, and that was saying something. His lack of decorum, not to mention his amorous adventures with highborn ladies, had made him a person of some celebrity. What Julian could not understand was Flynn's attachment to the Wards. It was reported that the young footman had received many advantageous offers to lure him away and had refused every one of them.

On entering the bookroom, Julian paused, his eyes instantly drawn to the portrait on the fireplace wall. Elsewhere he had noted large empty spaces on the walls where it was evident pictures had once hung. By the looks of things, Jeremy Ward was reduced to selling off his picture collection in his efforts to raise money.

Julian's smile was tainted with scorn. There were still servants in plenty, and the ladies of the house did not look to him as though they were practicing economies.

Their conversation was all of new gowns, and the lavish entertainments where they might show them off. When he remembered the workhouse, and what his own family had been reduced to, his throat tightened painfully.

For a long moment, he struggled with his feelings, trying to master them. He should be glad that the Wards were living beyond their means, for it put them more securely in his power.

He crossed to the fireplace. With an arm resting on the mantel, he studied the portrait intently. It was a moment before it came to him that the young woman who gazed down at him was not Serena Ward. This lady, whom he assumed was the girl's mother, was the picture of well-bred docility. Unlike her daughter, the name *Serena* would have suited her. As for the girl, there were many names he would like to call her, but *serene* was the furthest from his mind.

The thought made him smile. It was impossible not to remember that Serena Ward had given him the sweetest pleasure he had ever found with a woman. Yet it rankled to know that he wanted her still. No man in his right mind wanted a woman who had tricked and deceived him, and who, subsequently, had displayed her utter contempt for him by barring him from her house. But beyond all this remained the unpalatable fact that she was the daughter of Sir Robert Ward.

He supposed he should have left well enough alone, should never have applied the perfume to Catherine's bare skin. It wasn't Catherine who had filled his mind as his fingers sought out all her pulse points, but the tantalizing image of bringing the haughty Serena Ward to her knees. At each bold touch, across the width of the room, he could almost feel her icy dignity begin to melt, and the thought had electrified him. One look had told him all he wished to know. He had accomplished his goal, he had shaken the girl to her very foundations, but in doing so, he had also shaken himself.

At the click of the doorlatch, he turned from the portrait.

Chapter Seven

~❧~

Serena entered the room in a flurry of skirts. After closing the door quietly, stealthily, she slumped against it. Her breathing was quick and audible; her cheeks were flushed. Her eyes were brilliant with emotion. When she spoke, no one could doubt that it was anger that moved her.

"I might have known," she said, "what to expect from you."

"Yes, I think you might," he answered reasonably.

"You had no business to force your way into my house."

"I didn't force my way in. I was invited."

Advancing a step or two, she stabbed the air with one hand. "You played upon my sister-in-law's good nature so that I would be compelled to speak with you."

In contrast to her impassioned tones, his were calm and faintly amused. "True," he said. "In the normal way of things, there would have been many opportunities to approach you. In your determination to avoid me, however, not only did you bar your house to me, but you also made yourself a recluse. I was obliged to use subterfuge to gain my ends."

"I'm warning you, I won't be threatened in my own home. I have two brothers, both of whom are experienced duelists. You will answer to them if you try to harm me in any way."

He folded his arms across his chest. "Perhaps we should invite your brothers to join us? They might be interested to know that their sister is not the innocent she pretends to be."

Her eyes flashed at the threat. "I was innocent, once, before I met you."

He shrugged and pulled out a chair. "That is what I wish to discuss with you. Sit, Victoria, or I shall be forced to make you sit."

In pent-up silence, she stalked to the chair he held for her. With one disdainful glare, she seated herself. Calm and dignity, she belatedly decided, those were her best weapons. The silence lengthened. Finally, she looked up at him.

When he saw that he had her attention, he smiled. "I have been exercising my mind," he said, "to try and discover what Serena Ward, baronet's daughter, was doing at The Thatched Tavern, and why she would surrender her virtue to the first man she chanced upon."

His words kindled a spark of alarm. She had more to fear than the loss of her reputation. A moment's reflection steadied her. He was curious, but he could not prove anything.

"Answer me."

She bristled at the command. "I did not surrender my virtue. It was stolen from me."

His sigh was exaggerated. "Somehow, I just knew you were going to take this tack. That is not how I remember it."

Her dignity was unshakable. "I can only repeat, I did not surrender. I fought you tooth and nail."

"Come now, Victoria. We both know that is a blatant untruth."

There was acid in the sweet smile she bestowed on him. "And we both know that you are an unconscionable libertine with a penchant for innocent young girls. Well, I give you fair warning, Julian Raynor. You had better stay away from my young sister or I shall lay charges against you."

He stared at her, an eloquent tension gripping his features. "Now what maggot have you got in your brain? I am not a libertine, nor do I have a penchant for innocent young girls, least of all your sister."

"Why should I believe you when I distinctly remember that you tried to steer *me* into a life of debauchery? And I was an innocent, was I not?"

"Hardly debauchery. I asked you to be my mistress."

"An honorable offer, I'm sure," she said, and sniffed.

"At the time, I did not know who you were. I took you for an actress."

She pounced on this. "Hah! Your own words condemn you, sir, for you are admitting that you prey on weak, defenseless women."

His eyes lightened with reluctant laughter. "Now that is where you are wrong, Victoria. It never once entered my head that you were a weak, defenseless woman. But we are digressing. Why me? That is what I want to know. And where was your escort?"

Her hands curled into fists. His indolent manner, his mockery, and his careless and totally erroneous assumptions touched her to the quick. Calm and dignity, she reminded herself.

"What are you implying? That I was overtaken with a sudden infatuation the moment I set eyes on you? That I find you irresistible? If you must know, you have the opposite effect on me."

"What effect is that?" he asked politely.

She searched for words to express herself. "You make me so uncomfortable that I can never be in the same room with you but I am overcome with the strongest urge to take to my heels."

She had heaped abuse on him, and he stood there

laughing at her. Calm and dignity were forgotten as she sprang to her feet. Burning with indignation, she made to stalk past him only to be forcibly restrained when his hands cupped her shoulders, wrenching her round.

Unsmiling, he said, "I would advise you to curb that temper of yours. Now, answer my questions. What were you doing at The Thatched Tavern? Where was your escort, and why did you play out that little charade for me?"

Once, when she was learning to ride, her mount had got the bit between its teeth and had bolted with her. The experience of conversing with Julian Raynor reminded her of that harrowing ride. There was no restraining him once he got an idea in his head.

Shrugging out of his grasp, she took a careful step backward. "It is not so unusual a thing for ladies of fashion to amuse themselves by visiting such places."

"Very true, but not unescorted."

"As to that, I became separated from my escort. Oh, I don't blame him. He didn't desert me. I was supposed to wait for him."

"Your escort deserves to be horsewhipped for leaving you unprotected. Do I know him?"

She smiled at his vehemence. "Oh no, Major Raynor. My escort that night is no concern of yours. I refuse to divulge his name."

"It might be my concern if he chooses to avenge your honor. An enraged beau—"

"He was not my beau—"

"—or brother."

She opened her mouth and quickly changed direction when she perceived his trap. "There is not the least likelihood of anyone avenging my honor."

He lifted a dark brow cynically. "I see. Go on."

She took a moment to arrange her thoughts in order

before saying, "I panicked. It's as simple as that. When the militia arrived, I panicked, fearing that they would learn my identity and escort me home in disgrace. You see how it was. You were there and, as I thought, offering a way out of my dilemma. It never entered my head that things would go so far."

"So the presence of the militia did have something to do with it," he said, as though thinking aloud. He had braced one hip on the edge of a long library table, and seemed to be mulling over what Serena had just told him.

She didn't want him to think too closely about the presence of the militia that night. Her clear blue eyes unflinching, she said, "Now that you understand all the circumstances, you must see that any reference to that night, any memory of it, fills me with loathing and disgust. We can have nothing more to say to each other, Major Raynor. Please leave this house and in future, if we should happen to meet, do me the kindness of refusing to acknowledge the acquaintance."

He stared at her long and hard, then shook his head, mocking the pose she had adopted. "I think I prefer Victoria to Serena," he said. "So, you are determined to make me the villain of the piece? Loathing? Disgust? That is not how I remember it, but we have already had this argument."

He paused, then inhaled sharply as if steeling himself to perform an unpleasant duty. "I am at your service, Miss Ward, willing to make amends for my unknowing villainy. Tell me what you wish me to do."

Marriage was implicit in his offer. Reluctance was evident in the insulting way the offer was made. Pride, as well as her own inclinations, dictated only one answer. "I have told you what I require of you, Major Raynor. I never want to see you again, nor ever wish to speak with you again."

Nothing registered on his face but polite interest. "Have you considered that there may be consequences from our night together?"

She couldn't prevent the flush that stole from throat to hairline. It was pride, again, that kept her eyes on his. "There is nothing to fear on that score," she said, and immediately began to count off days in her head.

"Good God! Surely it occurred to you before now? When last did you have your woman's courses?"

She gasped. "Even if I were with child, I would never lower myself to accept you for my protector or my husband."

A muscle tightened at the corner of his mouth. "It is, I know, a woman's prerogative to change her mind. If that day should ever come for you, I wish you to know that I would still honor the obligation my conduct has unwittingly incurred."

"That day will never come," she said scathingly. "I would as soon take up a life of debauchery as trust myself again to your honor."

His eyes darkened to slate. He bowed stiffly and retreated a step. "You have made your sentiments clear. Your obedient servant, ma'am."

His hand was on the doorknob when she called out to him. "I have been meaning to return this to you," she said, holding out his fifty-pound note as though she had laid hold of a dead rat.

He looked at the note, then glanced at the pained expression on her face. "Ah," he said, "that rankled, did it?"

She did not deign to reply to this, but merely lifted her hand a fraction, waiting for him to take the note from her.

"Give it to Victoria," he said flippantly, viciously. "She was worth every penny of it." He opened the door, then said over his shoulder, "Oh, and if you should happen to see her, you may tell her that my original offer still stands."

She waited till she heard the sound of the front door close upon him before venting her spleen. With one sweep of her hand, she sent books and papers flying from her brother's desk. She was tempted to rip the note into tiny shreds, but instead stuffed it in her pocket, promising herself that one day she would make Julian Raynor eat it.

Flynn entered a moment later. "Well?"

"Well what?" she said brusquely, and brushed by him.

He followed her into the hall and up the stairs. "Did the major offer marriage?"

"In a manner of speaking," she replied coolly.

"What does that mean? Either 'e did or 'e did not."

"His reluctance was insulting—not that it matters. I would not marry that man if—"

"Yes, yes, I know. If your life depended on it. If 'e was the last man on earth. And what does reluctance 'ave to say to anything? You surely did not think 'e would be overjoyed to find 'imself caught in the parson's mousetrap?"

She halted on the stairs and turned to face him. "Flynn," she said sweetly, making him wince, "the major has promised to give me the one thing I desire above all others."

"Which is?" he asked cautiously.

"His everlasting absence," she retorted and continued on up the stairs.

Flynn watched her progress in simmering silence. Not for the first time, he reminded himself savagely that Serena was her own worst enemy. After a moment's inward debate, he turned on his heel and quickly left the house. His destination was Julian's gaming house in St. Dunstan's Court.

As Serena approached the door to Catherine's boudoir, it opened, and a gentleman came through it. Serena frowned. "Lord Charles?" she said. "I did not know that you were present at Catherine's levee."

"Didn't you?" he said. "Oh yes, I was there, in the background. Good day to you, Miss Ward." He left her so abruptly it was almost uncivil.

Serena's eyes trailed him as he descended the stairs. She did not like Lord Charles Tremayne. Now that she thought about it, he put her in mind of Julian Raynor. But whereas Raynor reminded her of an alert black panther, Lord Charles had the look of a tawny, sleepy-eyed lion. The difference was superficial. They were both predators.

When she entered the boudoir, she saw that Letty and their guests had all taken their leave.

"Serena, help me?" Catherine had donned her long chemise and was being helped into her corset by one of the maids. Serena went to assist her. The maid was happy to relinquish the strings of the corsets into Serena's capable hands and moved about the room, tidying and straightening cushions.

"He's very handsome, wouldn't you say?" Catherine peeped provocatively over one shoulder, then faced the mirror.

"Who?"

Shaking her head, Catherine laughed softly.

The strings of the corsets suddenly tightened and the laughter turned into an agonized squeal. Aware that her sister-in-law was in one of her capricious humors, Serena dismissed the maids.

"Say when," said Serena without much sympathy and hauled vigorously till, by degrees, Catherine's tiny waist was whittled down to a man's handspan. When her victim croaked a hoarse protest, Serena eased back on the strings and deftly tied them in a bow.

It was some time before Catherine was able to chance movement. After slipping into the discarded negligee, she gingerly reseated herself at her dressing table and waved Serena into a chair.

Catherine's lips were twitching. "Who?" she said and laughed in open mockery.

"All right, he's handsome," admitted Serena with obvious reluctance. "He's also dangerous. I could tell that just by looking at him." And she never spoke a truer word.

Catherine's dark eyes danced wickedly. "As I remember, that's exactly how I thought of your brother when I first set eyes on him."

"You can't compare Jeremy to the likes of Raynor."

"Why can't I?"

"Well . . . think of Raynor's reputation. He is a notorious rake."

"And brothers can't be rakes? Oh dear, I think I've shocked you."

Smiling, Serena shook her head. "I know you are teasing me, Catherine. Jeremy is above that sort of thing. Oh, I don't say—"

Catherine's laughter drowned out Serena's words. "The reason you never got to hear of Jeremy's adventures, my dear Serena, was because you were his little sister. Who would dare to tell you? But I knew of them, and I don't mind telling you, now, that for the longest time it spoiled your brother's chances with me."

Serena's delicate eyebrows winged upward. Though she and Catherine were genuinely fond of each other, and they were close in age, the nature of their relationship had prevented shared confidences. This was something new.

Shrugging off this unsavory picture of her brother, which she was sure was exaggerated, she said casually, "I met Lord Charles in the corridor." When there was no response to this, she went on more boldly, "He looked like thunder."

At these words, Catherine giggled. "I think he was jealous of Julian, you know, when he doused me with the perfume. If looks could kill . . ." She shook her head, and laughed.

Bristling with indignation, Serena demanded, "What right has Lord Charles to be jealous? He is not your husband. I . . . I wish he would not make a nuisance of himself by intruding where he is not wanted."

Catherine's face registered astonishment. "Poor Charles! You *have* taken him in dislike. Serena, it is the fashion for eligible young gentlemen to attach themselves to a particular married lady. It means nothing. Charles and I have known each other since infancy, and your brother Jeremy knows it. Charles is as much Jeremy's friend as he is mine. He is not intruding."

Serena was not convinced that Lord Charles was as much her brother's friend as he was Catherine's. She half suspected that he was in love with Catherine, and that made her feel uneasy. Lord Charles was a notorious rake, and therefore she did not trust him to behave honorably.

She kept these misgivings to herself, and merely replied, "I don't consider Lord Charles particularly young or eligible. He must be thirty if he is a day! And his reputation with ladies of a certain class is equal to that of Raynor's."

This sent Catherine into hoots of laughter. "My dear Serena," she said, trying to control her mirth, "what has that to say to anything? Charles is independently wealthy, is he not? He is heir to his father, the marquess? You may take my word for it, he is a matrimonial prize, and when his interest fixes on some eligible girl, both I and what you are pleased to call 'ladies of a certain class' will sink into oblivion. Now, tell me what you think of Julian. And before you say anything, let me tell *you* that I was watching you both, and I recognized the signs."

There was an interval of silence, then Serena laughed. "What a fanciful imagination you have, to be sure! A professional gamester and the daughter of Sir Robert Ward? My father would never entertain such an idea."

"I can't argue with that," said Catherine, chuckling. "However, what fathers want and what fathers are made to accept are two different things, as I should know."

"How is your father?" asked Serena, seizing on any pretext to change the subject. "Shall we see him at Riverview?"

Her ploy was successful, and the remainder of the conversation was of Riverview, the property which Catherine had brought to her husband on their marriage. Riverview was near Gravesend on the Thames estuary, and a favorite of Catherine and Jeremy's two young sons, Robert and Francis. There were boats there, and fishing, and interesting walks, and a hundred things to occupy young boys. When not in London, the Wards often retreated there, and were always in residence during the summer months. Robert and Francis were already there with their nurse, and the rest of the family were due to join them by the end of the following week.

Once in her own chamber, Serena permitted her smile to fade. The ordeal of having to listen to the praises of Julian Raynor made her want to tear her hair out. Was Flynn right? Was Catherine right? Had she misjudged the man? In an effort to be fair, she set aside hearsay and prejudice and concentrated on her own feelings toward Julian Raynor.

In all honesty, she would have to admit that she was largely responsible for what had occurred between them at The Thatched Tavern. Yet, the knowledge that she had brought it on herself did not lessen her dislike of the man by one iota.

She sank to her knees before a large mahogany dresser and pulled out the bottom drawer. Beneath a neat pile of embroidered silk stockings, she found what she was looking for. It was a miniature of a young man. His fair hair was neatly tied back. He gazed out of his portrait with the clear-eyed expression she remembered so well. A lump swelled in her throat.

She had not loved Stephen, and he had not loved her, but there had been affection there, and chaste kisses with the promise of something sweeter to come. Their life together would have been safe and predictable.

Julian Raynor was neither safe nor predictable. She usually gave such men a wide berth. She had good reason to. Once, a long time ago, she had made a complete and utter fool of herself over an unprincipled rake. When she made a mistake, she learned from it. It was her misfortune that on the night she had met Raynor, circumstances had worked against her. She sighed. Rake or no rake, he was not to blame for everything that had happened that night.

With one last look, she replaced the miniature and shut the drawer softly.

Her expression altered when she pulled from her pocket the banknote Raynor had given her. His signature on the bottom was as big and bold as the man himself. One day, she would take great delight in stuffing Julian Raynor up his own nose.

Chapter Eight

It was settled. The pardon for Sir Robert Ward was granted on May 21, 1747.

The Wards had gathered in the bookroom and were sitting informally around a tea table. The servants had been dismissed on the understanding that they would be called when their services were required.

"We are very fortunate," said Jeremy Ward, his eyes touching in turn upon each person present. "Not only were we able to raise the necessary funds, but we also had a powerful ally working on our behalf."

Clive reached for a bonbon and popped it in his mouth. "There is one other circumstance which you omitted to mention, Jeremy."

"Which is?"

"Don't forget, Papa is English. My God, if he were a Scot, he would not stand a chance. Just look at the lists of the Scots Jacobites who have been declared outlaws. They will never come under a general amnesty. It's unjust, that's what it is. One law for us, and one law for them."

"You seem remarkably well informed."

Clive sat up a little straighter. Jeremy always had this effect on him. There was ten years difference in their ages, and it told. Even more significant was Jeremy's position as head of the house. In his father's absence, he had assumed burdens which had matured him beyond his years. He had his share of the Ward good looks, but those other traits which distinguished all the Wards—their impetuosity, their passions, their haughtiness, and their sometimes careless charm—had been checked by the weight of his responsibilities.

"I'm not saying anything that is not general knowledge," said Clive, retreating behind a wall of sullenness.

"I hope for all our sakes, that's all it is."

"And what might you mean by that?"

Hackles were rising. In an attempt to divert the threatening storm, Catherine rattled her cup and saucer and invited Letty to help her replenish empty teacups. Serena, recognizing the ploy, assisted by handing round the tray of buttered bread.

Jeremy pressed a hand to his temple. "I'm not accusing you of anything, Clive. I hope, that is, I know you would do nothing to jeopardize the pardon we have worked so hard to procure." He tempered his harsh tone with a smile. "Forgive me if I sound a trifle overanxious. I've been closeted too long with Lord Kirkland. He is a fund of information on the secret societies that are proliferating all over England, Jacobite societies I should say. Nothing will come of them, of course, except that a few hotheads are likely to end up on the gallows."

"And Kirkland told you all this?" asked Clive incredulously.

"He wasn't betraying his position as deputy minister if that is what you think. You must have heard of these societies also. In the clubs and coffeehouses, there's talk of little else."

When Clive said nothing, Jeremy pinned him with a penetrating stare. "Clive, I know where your sympathies lie, but I also rely on your good sense. You would not be so foolish as to plot treason and insurrection?"

"No! Of course not," Clive answered at once. "I swear it, Jeremy."

Visibly relaxing, Jeremy accepted the cup and saucer Letty held out to him.

Serena entered the conversation at this point. "You mentioned a powerful ally. Who is this person?"

"The deputy minister, Lord Kirkland."

"Why should Lord Kirkland wish to help Papa?" asked Letty.

"Because Father was once friend to Kirkland's older brother," answered Jeremy. His tone became drier. "After the Rebellion of '15, Father found refuge with Kirkland's people for a time before he was smuggled out of the country. Lord Kirkland helped him because of the close ties that once existed between Father and Lord Hugo, you see. Leastways, that's what he says."

"What other reason could there be?" asked Serena.

Jeremy smiled. "I'm probably doing the old boy an injustice, but it occurred to me that he might prefer to have Father here, where he can keep an eye on him, rather than in France."

"Who is Lord Hugo?" said Letty.

"Letty!" began Clive impatiently. "We have more to discuss than this slice of ancient history."

With equal passion, Letty exclaimed, "And I suppose you and everyone else here knows all there is to know about Papa and Lord Hugo? It's so unfair! Nobody tells me anything! I hate being the youngest."

Jeremy and Catherine exchanged an amused glance, then Jeremy explained to Letty in as few words as possible the circumstances that had led to Lord Hugo's death.

Having heard it all before, Serena wasn't paying attention to her brother's words. She was looking at Clive. His face was flushed and there was a restlessness about him. It looked to her as if he were suffering the pangs of a guilty conscience, and she wondered what he was thinking. The escape route was no longer in operation, and as for his sworn declaration to Jeremy—that he was not plotting insurrection—she knew this was true. They were not Jacobites; they wanted only to help fugitives escape a barbaric fate. This was not exactly plotting insurrection, but the difference was a fine one. Clive must know it too.

"And Lady Harriet eloped with the tutor?" exclaimed Letty. "Poor Papa! But how romantic! I wonder what became of them?"

"Romantic!" Clive made a grimace of scorn. "Did you not hear what Jeremy said? That same tutor betrayed Papa and Lord Hugo, yes, and Lord Hugo lost his life because of it."

"How can you be so sure that Mr. Renney was the informer? It could have been anyone."

"That's as may be," said Jeremy in the voice that never failed to bring order when family discussions degenerated into vulgar squabbling. "The present is what should concern us. In a few days, I shall leave for France to see Father, to explain the terms of his pardon. He will be required to swear allegiance to His Majesty, King George, and his descendants. This pardon did not come cheaply. Suffice it to say that for some time to come, we must all practice the most stringent economies. This house, for example, will have to be let or sold. There is no sense maintaining two houses, and Riverview is close to London."

There was more, much more in this vein, so that by the time Jeremy finished, a distinct pall hung over the company.

Letty was the first to excuse herself. When Clive began to follow her out, Jeremy said, "Clive, I would be glad of your company when I go to France."

There was a moment of silence, then Clive stuttered, "Yes, of course. It's the least I can do. When do we leave?"

"Saturday at the latest."

Clive nodded and went out.

Serena, noticing the slump of Clive's shoulders, was eager to go after him. But before she left, on impulse, she crossed to where Jeremy was seated. Putting both hands on his shoulders, she leaned down and planted a kiss on his cheek.

"What is that all about?" asked Jeremy, laughing up at her.

"That," said Serena, smiling through tears, "is because I have not always appreciated you as I ought."

After Serena had gone, Catherine looked over at her husband. "Is it very bad, my love?" she asked quietly.

"I do not think it could be much worse." The harshness in his voice, grown suddenly bitter, brought her to his side.

She went down on her knees before him. "Tell me," she said, and reached for his hand, bringing it to her bosom.

"What more can I say? Creditors, mortgages, an estate that is heavily encumbered." He made an effort to shake off his gloom. "My work is certainly cut out for me. But we shall contrive."

She spoke quietly. "This is going to be very hard on the girls, Letty especially."

"It won't be forever," he said, squeezing her hand comfortingly. "In a year or two, I think our fortunes will be on the rise."

She smiled at this, and after a moment's thought, went on, "Jeremy, what was all that about with Clive? Why are you taking him to France with you?"

He grinned. "You don't miss much, do you? I don't want him getting up to mischief in my absence. I'm almost certain he belongs to one of those secret Jacobite societies."

"But Jeremy, from what I hear, just about every young man is a member of those societies. It doesn't mean anything. It's just the fashion and will soon pass."

"Yes, my dear, but those other young men are not Wards, are they? We have a reputation to live down. And with Father's pardon . . ."

"I see what you mean," she said. "Poor Jeremy, we are all such a trial to you." She broke off and laughed softly. "Jeremy," she said, "would you have any objection to having Julian Raynor as a brother-in-law?"

"Raynor? Don't say he's taken a fancy to Letty?"

"Letty? Now why should you think it was Letty? It's Serena I'm referring to."

She was quizzing him, teasing him out of his black humor, and he responded in kind. "Serena and a gamester? I just can't see it."

"Answer the question. Would you have any objection to Julian Raynor as a brother-in-law?"

"What? Object to having a Croesus in the family? I should say not! But, my dear, my opinion counts for nothing. My father would never permit it."

"Yes, well, we both know there are ways of getting round fathers. And don't forget, Serena is her own mistress. She is accountable to no one but herself."

His brows drew together in a frown. "Catherine, you're not serious?"

"Oh, my dear, but I am. Well, you must have noticed in the last little while how Major Raynor is present at all the assemblies and parties Serena attends?"

"But so is half of London," he protested. "That doesn't mean anything."

Catherine slanted him a superior smile. "Furthermore," she said, "Serena and I cannot go out in the carriage, or do a little shopping, but we 'accidently' run across Major Raynor."

He thought about this for a moment. "And Serena encourages him?"

"Hardly. That is not Serena's way. But anyone with eyes in his head can see that they are taken with each other."

His look was skeptical.

Catherine nodded. "If I were you, Jeremy, I would start getting used to the idea of Serena and Julian Raynor."

Serena went immediately in search of Clive. She did not have far to look. He was in the front hall, on the point of taking his leave.

"Clive, I should like a word with you," she said.

"Can't it wait? I have an appointment—"

"It can't wait," said Serena, and held the door to the morning room for him.

As soon as he had crossed the threshold, she shut the door, and said, "What is it, Clive? What's wrong?"

"Nothing! That is, everything! Well, you heard what Jeremy said. I had no idea things were so bad with us."

She studied him closely. "Yes, but that's not it. Something was bothering you before Jeremy told us about our financial troubles. What is it, Clive?"

He stammered, and looked away, then finally blurted out, "The last thing I wanted was to involve you! Truth to tell, I was glad you were out of it. This is a dangerous business, a man's business, and women should have no part in it."

She laid her hand on his sleeve and looked up at him in appeal. "Let me be the judge of that. Now tell me what scrape you have got yourself into."

For a moment, he hesitated, then plunged into speech. "The thing is, I agreed to take delivery of another 'passenger.' There's no way of putting it off, and I don't know who to trust or turn to. I must go to France with Jeremy. Oh God, Serena, what am I going to do?"

When the constable came to call at Ward House, with the exception of the servants, Serena was all alone. Summoned from the small sitting room which was reserved for the ladies of the house, she took a few moments to tidy herself before entering the downstairs blue saloon where the constable awaited her.

Constables calling at the house was not so unusual an event. Their most common complaint was that the Wards' chairmen had become embroiled in a bout of fisticuffs with other chairmen whose sedans had got in their way. London chairmen were colorful characters and notoriously ill-tempered. Serena prayed that this call was no more than that.

She greeted Mr. Loukas with all her usual composure. After inviting him to be seated, she explained why it was she who had answered his call.

"As you may know," she said, "my brothers have gone to France to make arrangements for my father's return."

"Yes, I had heard that Sir Robert had received his pardon. When did they go?"

"Two days since."

"And when do you expect them to return?"

Serena studied the constable covertly. He seemed a genial sort of a fellow—merry blue eyes in a florid face. His powdered wig was slightly askew, and that made him seem all the more likable.

Relaxing a little, she replied, "Now that I cannot tell you with any certainty. Before they left, my brother received word that my father was not in the best of health. Oh, nothing serious, you understand. Sir Robert suffers from gout. As soon as he is fit to travel, they will escort him home."

"And Mrs. Ward? Did she go with them?"

"Oh no. Catherine, that is, Mrs. Ward and my younger sister have gone to Riverview to be with the children. I, myself, would have gone with them if my little mare had not come down with a fever. Goldie is so indulged," confided Serena, "that she would rather go into a decline than allow anyone to doctor her but I."

It was all so distasteful, this subterfuge and misleading people, but there was no way around it. She had promised Clive that she and Flynn would see that his "passenger" got safely away, and that meant, of course, that she must remain in London until the thing was done. What made everything worse was that people accepted her explanations so easily. They trusted her, and that hurt. If only Catherine had made some protest, she did not think she would feel so guilty. But Catherine had merely said that though the children would be disappointed, they would know that Serena's little mare must come first.

"I trust your ministrations were successful?" observed the constable politely.

The last Serena had seen of Goldie, she was in her stall, eating her head off. "It's too soon to say," she said, managing to look anxious. "Her constitution is very delicate, you know. These thoroughbreds are all the same."

Having dealt with the amenities, Serena was not quite sure how to proceed and Mr. Loukas seemed to be in no hurry to state his business. Reflecting on the last time a constable had called at the house, she said in a conciliatory way, "I presume Flynn has been involved in another brawl? You may believe I shall deal very severely with him. Now, if you would be so good as to tell me what the damages amount to, I shall pay them at once."

As it turned out, the constable's visit had nothing to do with Flynn. It was Clive whom Loukas had been in hopes of finding. This is what Serena feared most.

"Clive? Why should you wish to see Clive?"

"My dear lady, let me set your mind at rest. My business with your brother has to do with another gentleman, an acquaintance of his. Perhaps you have heard of him? Lord Alistair Cumming?"

Not only had Serena heard of Lord Alistair, she knew exactly where he was. This was the "passenger" she had promised Clive she and Flynn would look out for. He had been delivered into their care in the wee hours of that very morning. At this moment, he was lodged in a room in a house in Whitefriars Street. Before the night was out, they were due to return and convey him to his ship.

"An acquaintance of my brother, you say? The name has a familiar ring to it. But . . ." She shook her head. "I regret, I cannot help you, Mr. Loukas."

Little more was said after this, and before long, the constable had taken a very civil leave of her.

Serena was mulling over this conversation, when Flynn entered the room. "What did 'e want?" asked Flynn without preamble.

In very few words, Serena told him of the reason for the constable's visit.

"I don't like the sound of this," said Flynn.

Neither did Serena. "Pooh!" she said. "What can go wrong? The constable isn't likely to suspect a mere female. And we can't just leave poor Lord Alistair in the lurch."

"Why can't we? 'E's a man, ain't 'e? Let 'im take 'is chances, that's what I say."

"Flynn, you know you don't mean that. Besides, he's only a boy."

" 'E's a soldier, and the same age as me, for God's sake. What do you think they wants 'im for—peeking under ladies' skirts?"

She wasn't listening to him. "Give me five minutes to dispense with these hoops, then we shall be on our way."

"Oh no! Not this time, Serena. I ain't putting my 'ead on no block for no traitor, not even if he is your brother's friend."

She showed him a perfect set of pearly white teeth. "Don't worry, Flynn. Your head is safe from the block. They hang commoners."

He watched her go with a smile on his face, a smile that Serena would have deeply distrusted if she had been there to see it.

In the carriage that conveyed them to Fleet Street, Flynn carried on from where he had left off. Serena let him run on without interruption. Her attention was given to adjusting the white feathered demimask she had borrowed from Catherine's plethora of accessories. Ladies of fashion were often to be seen around town at night wearing masks to hide their identity.

From his corner in the coach, he said glumly, "I tell you, I'm at my wits' end. I don't know what I'm going to do with you."

Serena gave him a dry look. "I might say the same to you. Honestly, Flynn, if you go on the way you've been doing, you are going to come to a bad end."

He grinned hugely, aware that she was referring to his amorous adventures with several ladies who moved in her own circles. "What 'ave I been doing?" he needled.

"You've been dropping your aspirates," she retorted nastily.

"Them's not all I've been dropping," he riposted. "And you're a fine one to speak!" When her lips set in a prim line, his grin intensified. Laughing, he sprang up and rapped his knuckles sharply on the roof, signaling the coachman to stop.

"This isn't Whitefriars Street," said Serena. "Why are we stopping?"

"Use your 'ead." He reached in his coat pocket and pulled out a fat purse. "I don't like the looks of that constable. 'E's a fly one."

"You think he may be following us?"

"Let's just say I didn't reach the ripe old age of twenty by forgetting to look over m' shoulder."

Once on the pavement, a change came over Flynn. When paying off the coachman and addressing Serena, he was the picture of deference, a well-bred lackey who knew his place. It was all show, of course, but it preserved the proprieties in public.

At one end of Bouverie Street, there was an alley, an airless, unsavory place with rows of washing stretched limply from window to window above their heads. One step into it, and Serena put her perfumed handkerchief to her nose to smother the smell of rotting refuse. They weren't alone. Huddled in corners were the shapeless forms of men and women in various stages of inebriation. From lighted windows one floor up, naked girls brazenly postured, while their pimps accosted passersby in the street below. Business seemed to be brisk.

Serena was not so sheltered that she had not observed similar scenes around Covent Garden and in Drury Lane when she attended the theater. Closer to home, in the Strand, where a century before the private palaces of great noblemen had proliferated, prostitutes and their well-breeched patrons could be observed taking the air as soon as dusk settled over the city. There was an elegance to the Strand, however, that was not present here. This was squalor and on a scale she had never witnessed before.

They delayed until Flynn was satisfied that the coast was clear, then, using a labyrinth of connecting alleys, they finally came out on Whitefriars Street. Only then did Serena dispense with the perfumed handkerchief.

"You are certainly no stranger to these parts," she commented, her brows lifting meaningfully.

He answered her with a grin.

The house where they had lodged Lord Alistair appeared to be quite respectable, relatively speaking. Hackneys and sedans came and went in the street, and the patrons in the coffeehouse on the corner were more in the style Serena was used to. At the head of the stairs, Flynn halted and knocked on a door, not in a desultory way, but rhythmically, as if he were rapping out a signal.

"Who's there?"

"Your little white rose," whispered Serena, giving the password she, herself, had invented.

Flynn rolled his eyes. "This is better than the theater," he said. "Look, while you entertains young Romeo 'ere, I'll check on things downstairs."

The door opened to reveal a remarkably handsome young blade dressed in the height of fashion. His garments had been supplied by Serena, courtesy of Clive.

"Mistress Ward," he said, a smile lighting his eyes, and he ushered Serena inside.

Lord Alistair's manners, his unwavering loyalty to a lost cause, everything about this young man found favor with Serena. Even the cultured Scottish brogue caught her fancy.

He pulled out a chair and dusted it off with his handkerchief. "You'll share a glass of wine with me, milady?"

The wine, too, had been supplied by Serena, courtesy of Sir Robert's fine wine cellar. "Thank you kindly, sir," she said.

There was only one glass. Serena took a sip, and offered it to Lord Alistair. He fairly blushed at the implied intimacy. This, very naturally, put her in mind of the last time she had shared a glass of wine with a gentleman.

Gentleman? She remembered the thrust of his tongue and the way he had lapped at her, practically devouring her, and she, too, blushed rosily. If Julian Raynor had ever blushed in his life, she would eat the fifty-pound note she kept in the top drawer of her dresser.

"I shall remember you to my dying day," said Lord Alistair. "I never thought to find such kindness among the English. You are the bravest lady I have ever been privileged to meet."

You have the manners of a lady and the morals of a whore. That was the kind of compliment Julian Raynor passed out, and in the weeks following the night of The Thatched Tavern, his manners had scarcely improved. She'd thought they had an understanding, that in future they would give each other a wide berth. He was doing it on purpose, flaunting her wishes, turning up where she least expected him. Catherine's levee had been the start of it. Now, she could not drive out in the park, or go shopping, or attend a musical evening or whatever, but he was there, trying to fluster her with those knowing looks of his, whispering "Victoria" in her ear when no one was listening. It was impossible to avoid him, impossible to deflate him without rousing everyone's suspicions. She was forced to nod and smile and make conversation when what she really wanted to do was spit on him. Victoria, indeed! Victoria Noble was only a figment of her imagination and the sooner he understood that, the sooner his interest would wane.

Determined to banish Julian Raynor from her mind, she embarked on a flow of small talk, introducing the subject of St. Andrew's University. This was where Lord Alistair had met her brother, when Clive went there for a year as an undergraduate. When they heard feet taking the stairs, they both fell silent, and their eyes went to the door. A moment later, Flynn burst into the room.

"Militia," he hissed, "with that there constable! We'd best get the 'ell out of 'ere."

After dousing the lone candle, Flynn led the way, having previously ensured that they had another exit.

As they climbed the stairs to the roof, Flynn propelling Serena with a hand on her elbow, he whispered encouragingly, "Would I allow anything to 'appen to m' darlin? 'Ave no fear, princess! I shall get us out of 'ere."

They halted at a half-landing with a window giving onto the back of the house. From below came the sound of doors slamming, and the thundering of feet, as though an army had been given the order to charge. Serena's eyes widened in horrified comprehension as Flynn removed a ladder from a small closet. With Lord Alistair's help, he maneuvered it out the window, till they heard it thunk on something solid on the other side.

"I'll go first," said Flynn, and leapt onto the ladder, balancing like an acrobat.

"Hold!" said Lord Alistair. "If you are caught with me, you won't stand a chance. This is where we separate."

Flynn laughed, and to Serena's ears it seemed that he was enjoying the whole thing immensely. "We won't get caught," he said. "Soon's we get out of 'ere, I'm going to show you *my* London. We are going down, below ground, to the warren of drains and sewers them Romans left behind."

"But we are miles from the docks, man."

"True. But we are very close to Raynor's place. 'E'll shelter us, 'cos he owes Miss Serena, 'ere, a favor, see?"

Serena gasped. "Flynn, I'm warning you now, I won't go anywhere near Raynor's place, and that is final."

"Fine," said Flynn. "Then you best tell us what's to be done."

"There they are!" came the shout from below.

Serena swallowed hard.

"Well?" said Flynn.

"You win," she said, and grasped the hand he held out to her.

Chapter Nine

❧

Julian sat at his large leather-topped desk in the office of his gaming establishment, scanning the contents of a letter which he had found waiting for him when he had entered his office a short time before. The perfumed notepaper was too sweet and cloying for his taste, but the message titillated his interest. It seemed that Lady Amelia Lawrence had given her present lover his marching orders, and to prove it, she had enclosed the key to the side door of her house in Whitehall. It was an invitation Julian must regretfully decline.

Whistling the refrain of some bawdy ditty he'd picked up around army camp fires, he contemplated the author of the letter for a moment. Lady Amelia was all satin-soft curves and voluptuous, flash-fire heat, the way he liked his women to be. She wasn't popular with her own sex, but that was to be expected. The lady attracted gentlemen like flies to sugared water. She was, Julian admitted, a born predator, not that he cared one whit about that. Their former liaison had been unabashedly carnal, and that had suited him just fine. *Former liaison,* Julian reminded himself. That was all in the past, and the sooner the lady understood it, the better it would be for all.

A picture of a different kind of woman drifted into his brain. He had an impression of something cool and distant, something tantalizingly just out of reach. Serena Ward. Remote, unattainable, cool as a mint julep. But that was only a first impression. The image became sharper—thick-lashed, wide-set eyes flashing blue fire; a lush ripe mouth begging to be kissed into silence; fireworks, Catherine wheels, rockets exploding overhead with all the velocity of a sudden summer thunderstorm.

It was sheer lunacy to pursue his present course. He'd done his bit; he'd gone hat in hand to try to make restitution for what, in his mind, she had invited on herself with her outrageous conduct. And what had he received for his pains? Exactly what he had expected to receive. She had given him his character, spat on him, and had sent him off with a flea in his ear. And even in the weeks following that interview, after Flynn had come to him and had persuaded him to continue, he had tried to make himself agreeable to her. And still she fought him at every turn. A sane man would let it go at that. His conscience should be clear. He should forget her.

Flynn would not let him forget, and Flynn was more tenacious that his own conscience. But Flynn had not been there when she had refused his offer of marriage in no uncertain terms.

Libertine. He could feel his hackles rising as he remembered how her nose had turned up when she had flung the word at him. Actually, she hadn't flung the word at him. It had dripped from her beautiful mouth like poison. Libertine! He was no libertine. He did nothing to excess. He wasn't a saint, by any means. He was a male, not one of those rouged, simpering milksops, who danced attendance on her, and who wouldn't know what to do with a woman if their lives depended on it. But he had known, and he was never to be forgiven for it.

Suddenly conscious that his lips were twitching, he frowned. *Lunacy,* he warned himself, and sighed. In an effort to banish the provoking image of Serena Ward, at least for the next few minutes, he flipped through the documents which he had been perusing before he had come upon Lady Amelia's letter. They were all here, all the mortgages and notes he had surreptitiously acquired in the last year, the combined worldly wealth of the Ward family. To his knowledge, there was nothing left to mortgage or sell. All he need do was wait out the few months until they fell due and he would have Sir Robert Ward exactly where he wanted him.

It was unfortunate that in ruining Sir Robert, the other members of his family would not come out of it unscathed. Unfortunate, but unavoidable. Sir Robert was the one who had set this inexorable chain of events in motion and Julian refused to feel even a twinge of remorse for what he was about to do. The Wards were grown men and women and well able to take care of themselves. They would survive. Whereas his family . . .

He touched his fingers to his brow as his thoughts lost focus, and he fought memories that were so painful that sometimes only the oblivion from a bottle of brandy could gain him respite.

For a long, long time, he sat motionless, staring into space. Coming to himself by degrees, he picked up the mortgages and notes he had been perusing. He rose and moved to the dumbwaiter behind his desk. Feeling with one hand, he moved a lever. There was a click, and a panel fell open. He tossed the documents inside, closed the panel, and shut the doors to the lift with a snap.

For the next several minutes, he worked on his ledgers, studying columns of figures, making notations from a sheaf of promissory notes he held in his hand. Gaming, his books told him, was a very profitable business indeed. And that was all it was to him—a business. He was not an inveterate gambler. He had a flair for it and could calculate the odds and probabilities with lightning speed. He never bet when the odds were against him. He never overreached himself. His flair and patience had brought him more wealth than he knew what to do with, perhaps more wealth than was good for him.

For the most part, gentlemen paid their debts with hard cash. There were times, however, when cash was in short supply, when Julian had to make do with other forms of security. There was the property in South Carolina, as well as a fine house on the outskirts of London and a hunting box in Scotland. Fine plate, costly jewels, thoroughbred horses, shares in thriving business ventures —Julian had amassed them all without a ripple of conscience. He reasoned that if it were not he it would be somebody else. Gambling was so ingrained among the English upper classes as to be almost second nature to them. Moreover, the pigeons whom he fleeced were well feathered. They could afford their losses. He knew this because the membership committee of his club was very careful to screen prospective members.

His thoughts were interrupted by someone rapping on the door. Julian went immediately to answer it.

A gentleman who was attired in much the same manner as Julian—fashionable but not to the point of foppishness—entered the room. Like Julian, he wore no smallsword, which immediately identified him as belonging to the house. Instead of Julian's restrained elegance, however, he gave the impression of a soldier out of uniform, which is exactly what he was. His hair was unpowdered and his broad, craggy face was wreathed in a smile. David Black, more commonly known as Blackie, advanced into the room. Julian returned to his desk.

"Well?" asked Julian. "Has the parson arrived?"

"He has, and as instructed, we fitted him out and he is presently sitting at your board, eating the best dinner he has ever had in his life. Julian, what are you up to?"

"One of our patrons wishes to get married. You know the house's policy. Whatever a gentleman wants a gentleman gets."

"But that policy only applies to the dining room, you

know, for out-of-season tomatoes or strawberries and suchlike. And who would be so foolhardy as to enter into a Fleet marriage? That is no marriage at all."

Julian leaned back in his chair, grinning unrepentantly. "Now that is where you are wrong, Blackie. I'm not saying that Fleet marriages are regular. I'm not saying that they are irregular. It all depends on what the couple wishes to make of it."

Blackie shook his head, recognizing that Julian was not in a confiding humor. "At any rate, that's not why I interrupted you. There is someone downstairs who wishes to speak with you."

"Yes?" said Julian negligently. He was tidying papers on top of his desk, looking for Lady Amelia's note.

"A young lady. Quite frankly, my first inclination was to show her the door. Her dress, her hair." He shook his head. "I mistook her for a woman of the street. As soon as she opened her mouth, I could tell I'd grossly mistaken the matter. Haughty," said Blackie, nodding his head sagely.

Julian's dark head came up. "Go on," he said.

"What? Oh, appearances to the contrary, it would not surprise me to learn that she is a duchess or very close to it. 'Course, I did not recognize her because she is wearing a mask. But that's not all, Julian. It seems that she and her two escorts entered by the secret passage, the one that comes out on Billing's cockpit."

"Serena," breathed Julian, so softly that Blackie did not catch it. "Where are they now?"

"In the crimson drawing room. Am I to understand that you know the lady?"

An unholy light glittered brilliantly in Julian's eyes. "Oh yes, I know her. Serena or Victoria. She must be one or the other," and with that cryptic remark, he left the room.

* * *

She had never felt more humiliated in her life, or more frightened, or put upon, or enraged. She wanted to tear her hair out. No. She wanted to tear Flynn's hair out. He was playing Cupid—the traitor!—and nothing could convince her otherwise.

They could have made a run for it, and now it was too late, or so Flynn insisted. She was not sure that she believed him. It seemed to her as if he had deliberately delayed, giving the militia time to catch up with them at every corner. She shuddered in reaction, thinking of that awful chase through the sewers. Surely it had not been necessary to come to Raynor's place? How could she tell? She didn't know her way around that horrid labyrinth, and Flynn had held off telling her what was on his mind until they had burst into that fiendish cockpit.

It was so humiliating. They were to throw themselves upon Raynor's mercy, Flynn told her, and beg him to support their story of an elopement that had gone wrong when Flynn, catching sight of their pursuers, had panicked. Who was she supposed to be eloping with? she had wanted to know. *Raynor,* Flynn had brazenly flung at her, robbing her of speech for the next several minutes.

Raynor? She would rather it was anyone but Julian Raynor! Only her dread for Lord Alistair could make her go through with it. Poor boy, he was very subdued. It had turned out that he had a phobia of small, confined spaces. Underground passages made him almost swoon away in terror. It was perfectly true that they could not have gone on much longer.

She flashed him a kindly smile as he mopped at his brow with a white linen handkerchief. Her eye was not nearly so kind when she turned it on Flynn.

"Nice place Raynor's got, ain't it?" said Flynn, breaking the long silence.

Halting in her pacing, Serena glared at him. "Nice place?" Her tongue dripped venom. "You should be ashamed to bring me to this den of vice."

At this, Lord Alistair pocketed his handkerchief and looked about him with interest.

"Den of vice? Nothing of the sort! This is a respectable establishment, I'll 'ave you know, and not like some I could name."

"You call this respectable?" She made a motion with one hand, encompassing the luxurious interior. All the furnishings were done in a color that put her in mind of juicy, overripe plums. But her mind was burning with far more than the decadence of her present surroundings. She was thinking of the scene that had met her when she had come out of that horrid, horrid cockpit and had stumbled into the entrance hall, her eyes momentarily blinded from the glare of a thousand candles in the chandeliers overhead. When her vision had cleared, she had gaped at the white marble and gilt-edged Ionic columns, and the murals on every available surface depicting lascivious nymphs and satyrs in every conceivable depravity.

No less decadent than the house was the crush of noisy fashionables who jostled her—gentlemen with powdered wigs, attired in richly embroidered coats in every hue of the rainbow, and masked "ladies"—hah!—in waist-hugging hooped skirts with little more than a wisp of gauze to cover their bared breasts. And champagne, naturally, flowing like water.

She might have borne it. After all, she was the suppliant here. Then she had come face-to-face with the woman she despised most in all the world. Lady Amelia Lawrence, dark, statuesque, and well favored if not well endowed, drew her skirts away from her as though she, Serena, were a foul-smelling beggar. All the ladies were masked, but Serena would have recognized Lady Amelia if she had met her on the river Styx. She had her own distinctive perfume, a mixture of cloves and rose, and she never changed it.

Now Serena's indignation knew no bounds. And her brothers were members *here*? It was no wonder that she and Catherine had never been able to persuade Jeremy to take them to Raynor's place on those nights when suitably escorted females were permitted on the premises.

"This is no better than a bawdy house," she declared, voicing her thoughts aloud.

At this, Lord Alistair made a halfhearted attempt to turn the conversation. "I think we have managed to throw them off the scent," he said.

Flynn glanced up at the ceiling, as though seeking inspiration, before returning Serena's glare. "You 'as a nasty mind, my girl, that's what you 'as. This is a gaming 'ouse, don't you know? What did you expect? So it's not as demure as taking tea in your dainty little parlor. If it was, Raynor wouldn't 'ave no patrons, now would 'e?"

"I might have known you would take his part," was all she would allow herself to say before she resumed pacing the floor.

Ignoring her ignoring him, Flynn said, "You'd best get a civil tongue in your 'ead if you wants the major to 'elp us out of the fix we are in. If I'm not mistaken"—he flicked aside a crimson curtain, and glanced out the window—"the militia will soon be closing in for the kill, and you knows as well as I do that our retreat 'as been cut off."

At the mention of the militia, Lord Alistair stumbled to his feet. Unsheathing his sword, he stood, rather shakily, at the ready. He still looked to be suffering the effects of his nerve-wracking experience in the underground passages.

Flynn let out an impatient oath. "Put up, man, for God's sake, before you do yourself an injury."

What Lord Alistair might have said was forestalled as the door opened and Julian Raynor strode into the room. Serena's humiliation was complete. He had the appearance of a man who had risen late from his bed to enjoy a leisurely bath before donning his freshly laundered garments. He was immaculately turned out in a gray velvet coat and white satin breeches. The lace at his throat and cuffs was as pure as the driven snow. Even the smell of him irritated her. It was a pleasant blend of starched linen and cologne, and was discernible, but only just, over the stench of her own tattered and mud-spattered gown. She stank of the sewer she had just crawled out of, and the knowledge both shamed her and set her temper to simmering.

"Victoria," he said, laughing at her, "does this mean that you have had a change of mind?"

The barb, a reference to the position of mistress he had once offered her, fell wide of its mark. She was too aware that unless she could persuade this man to help them, would be all over for them. "Julian," she said meekly, "you know that my name is Serena."

His face fell in an attitude of mock sorrow. "Then, Serena, my question still stands. Does this mean you have had a change of mind?"

This reference, of course, was to his humiliating offer of marriage and her insulting refusal of it. A sideways glance at Flynn showed him nodding his head vigorously. She moistened her lips and tried to look properly beseeching. "The thing is, Julian . . ."

"Good God!" he said. "What is that stench? And what happened to your gown?" Without waiting for her to reply, he acknowledged Flynn, then looked with interest at the young man with the drawn sword. "Good evening," he said. "Serena has forgotten her manners yet again. I am Julian Raynor, and you might be . . . ?"

"Lord Alistair Cumming," said the young Scot in his unmistakable brogue. He bowed.

Julian stood there, staring at that drawn sword. Then his eyes swept over Flynn and Serena, taking in their filthy, disheveled appearance. "Don't say . . ." he began, then his gaze suddenly sliced to Serena, searing her with the intensity of that look. "The Thatched Tavern?" he said. "The militia? The Jacobite fugitive? That's why . . . ?" The silence fairly blazed with his dawning comprehension of past and present events. "Now what are you trying to involve me in?" he yelled.

Wringing her hands, she turned to Flynn. "I told you how it would be. You got us into this, Flynn. Now what do we do?"

His eyes on Julian, Flynn said, "The militia are on our trail. They must know we are 'ere, or they will soon work it out. We left some of them in Billing's cockpit. I reckon we 'as five minutes, ten at the most, before they gets 'ere. Where can we go? Who can we turn to? I knew you would not refuse to 'elp us, Major Raynor, sir, because you owes Miss Serena 'ere your protection. Is that not so?"

"She doesn't want my protection. She told me so."

"That was then. This is now. If you chooses not to 'elp us, Major Raynor, sir, it's the gallows for us."

They stood staring at each other for a long, long interval, then both gentlemen suddenly broke into broad grins.

Serena could not believe that they would stand around joking when every second brought them closer to discovery and the gallows. "Julian," she said desperately, "this is no laughing matter. There is a horrid constable pursuing us, and at any moment he and his militia are going to come storming through your doors, demanding that you hand us over to them."

Julian looked to Flynn. "Flynn?" he invited.

Flynn inhaled sharply, then took the plunge. "Lord Alistair, 'ere, is the least of our worries, as I see it. That's if 'e can be persuaded to keep 'is mouth shut and 'is sword sheathed. 'E could easily pass 'imself off as one of your patrons. Mind you, there's still the problem of getting 'im to 'is ship, but we shall cross that bridge when we comes to it."

"He'll never pass himself off as one of my patrons with that stench on him," Julian pointed out.

"Yes, well, we could all do with a bath and a change of clothes." Sniffing his sleeve, Flynn grinned then went on carefully, "It's Miss Serena who stands in the most danger. That constable fellow was following 'er, you see. 'Im and 'is soldiers chased us through the sewers. They knows we are up to something." He gave Julian a man-to-man look. "It won't be easy to convince them of 'er innocence."

"Innocence of what? That's what I should like to know," said Julian, his eyes boring into Serena's.

She gritted her teeth, meeting that look with all the fervor of her passionate nature. "If it is treasonable to help Jacobite fugitives escape to safety, then convict me. But nothing will convince me that I am a traitor!"

The hard look in Julian's eyes gradually softened. Crossing to the door, he opened it and yelled, "Tibbets!" The summons was answered almost immediately by a very superior-looking servant.

"Ah, Tibbets," said Julian, "this young gentleman"— he indicated Lord Alistair—"is in need of a change of clothes. See to it. And Tibbets, use the back stairs. And I'd be obliged if you would send Mr. Blackie to me. At once, Tibbets, at once."

He turned to Flynn. "Go with him, Flynn."

"No!" This came from Serena. "That is, they know we were together. They don't know about Lord Alistair. Flynn must stay with me." She looked at Flynn imploringly, but his eyes were on Julian.

"Yes, I get your drift," said Julian. "But I wish to speak with you in private. Flynn will return in a few minutes."

No one was more surprised than Serena when Lord Alistair fell on his knees before her. For one awful moment, she thought that the boy had swooned, then she was wishing that he *had* swooned. Lifting the hem of her filthy skirt, he pressed his lips to it. "You are the loveliest, bravest lady I have ever known," he said, and with one fond look, he was gone, and she and Julian were alone.

"You need not look like that," she said, shifting uncomfortably. "It is only a mark of respect. The boy meant nothing by it."

"Oh, you need not tell me that. I know it means nothing."

She bristled. "And I suppose you would never dream of according a lady such an honor?"

He smirked. "My dear Serena, the day I meet the lady *worthy* of such an honor is the day I shall admit myself to an insane asylum. In short, no such woman exists."

She had been feeling somewhat kinder toward him, but at this insulting remark, she drew herself up.

"Serena, I—"

"You need not wonder why we thought we could count on your support. Julian Raynor always pays his debts, or so you once told me. I'm calling in the debt."

A muscle jerked at the corner of his mouth, and the softness went out of his expression. "My protection, I believe, Flynn mentioned? How may I serve you?"

Serena looked away. "All you need do," she said in a

subdued way, "is support our story—that is, that Flynn was bringing me to you so that we could . . . elope."

Julian folded his arms across his chest and regarded her steadily. "You do realize that by helping you, I may be putting my own head on the block?"

Her eyes were unfaltering on his. "I realize it."

"Victoria," he said gently, "this time your price is exorbitant."

A trembling began deep in her body. "You won't help us?"

"I didn't say that. All I am saying is that the exchange is unequal. I shall expect you to make up the difference."

"And how may I do that?"

His brows rose. Her color heightened.

The door was flung open, and a young woman, one of the house's crack card players, rushed into the room. "Julian," she got out breathlessly, "there is a constable demanding to see you, and . . . and he says that militia have surrounded the house. You must come at once."

Serena stared at him with huge stricken eyes.

His whole posture was unbending. "Well, Victoria, is it to be yes or no?"

In her mind's eye, she saw herself poised on the brink of a bottomless precipice. "Yes," she whispered.

"I want your word on it."

"You have it! But what are you going to do?"

His eyes mocked her. "Marry you, my dear Victoria. I'm going to marry you."

Chapter Ten

❧

It was not at all as Serena had imagined her wedding would be. It didn't feel like a wedding. She didn't feel like a bride. There was no church, no organ music, and no flowers, only Julian's private little office, cluttered with books and ledgers. Her gown was borrowed from one of the gaming-house wenches, and looked it. The band on the fourth finger of her left hand had been hastily fashioned from a curtain ring. A curtain ring of all things! In lieu of family and friends to toast the "happy" couple, she had the benefit of one footman, who was grinning like a Cheshire cat, and an officer of the law whose coat pockets bulged with pistols and hand irons. Worse by far was the minister who had conducted the service. Mr. Hargraves was an inmate of the Fleet, a debtor on day parole who was obliged to return to the prison before the night was over. Oddly enough, it was Mr. Hargrave's presence in the house (and she still did not know how Julian had managed it) that had finally convinced the constable that they were telling the truth.

A Fleet marriage, a trumped-up affair—she might have known what to expect of Julian Raynor.

At that moment, Constable Loukas caught her eye and he raised his glass of champagne in silent tribute. This benevolent, bewigged old gentleman scarcely resembled the ferocious officer of the law who had cross-examined them all, less than an hour ago, in this very room. At that time, Constable Loukas had seemed a formidable adversary, and an irate one to boot. He had not appreciated the mad chase through the sewers any more than Lord Alistair had.

Julian, naturally, had done most of the talking, having previously warned her to keep her mouth shut and her eyes downcast in the manner of a blushing bride. He need not have bothered to warn her. His recitation of events would have shamed the most brazen harridan. Not only did he support the story they had concocted, namely that their flight through the sewers was nothing more sinister than an elopement that had gone seriously awry when the bride's footman had panicked, but he had also embellished the tale, giving the distinct impression that the marriage was a matter of urgency since the bride might or might not be in what was politely referred to as "a delicate condition."

After this, the constable had become all solicitation. He meant to see, so he told her, that the major did right by her. His signature would be on their marriage certificate as witness to their union. Let Raynor try to get out of it, Fleet marriage or no, and she had only to call on him, and he would vouch for her. He really was a dear, sweet man.

She wouldn't call on him, of course. The first chance she got, she was going to burn that certificate, and it would be as if the marriage had never taken place. That was the reason Julian had felt safe in going on with it, and that was the reason Fleet marriages were so notorious. They were easily invalidated. Many a gullible woman, thinking that she was a wife, had lost her virtue to some unprincipled scoundrel who had decamped with the marriage certificate safely in his pocket. Without it or unimpeachable witnesses, nothing could be proved.

Her eyes drifted to her "husband" as he moved aside to have a few words with Flynn. Julian was angry with her, and he had every right to be. By involving him in the affair, she had put his life in jeopardy. Without his intervention, reluctant though it might be, there was no saying how things would have turned out. If their positions had been reversed, she was not sure that she could have acted as generously as he. He knew the risks, and in spite of them, he had helped her. When she went to join him, there was a smile on her lips, and her manner was conciliatory.

Julian saw that smile and it did not sit well with him. Everything had turned out just as she wished it. If he hadn't fallen in with her wishes, he had no doubt that beautiful mouth would be twisted with temper, hurling abuse at him.

The trouble with Serena, Julian reflected, was that she was too used to getting her own way. Her life had been too easy. There were too many people who doted on her—her brothers, Flynn, and from what he could gather, the man to whom she had once been betrothed. Even that boy whom she had met for the first time today!

How could she have allowed him to lay his hands on her and abase himself in such a manner—kissing the hem of her gown? She had blushed, *blushed* like a young silly schoolgirl. If it had been he who had dared to do such a thing, he could well imagine the upshot. She would have planted her foot in his face, and he would have thought the better of her for it.

He never would kiss the hem of her gown, of course. Not only was abasement not in his style, but the last woman he would humble himself for was someone like Serena. Proud. Defiant. Shrewish. She would pounce on any show of weakness and use it against him. She couldn't win against him, of course, but that wouldn't stop her trying. It was something to bear in mind.

Reaching for her hand, he raised it to his lips. "Happy, my love?"

She let the sarcasm pass. "More happy than I have a right to be," she said, striving to sound as if she meant it.

Flynn's eyes flicked from one to the other. Setting down his glass of champagne, he said, "Well then, I reckon you two lovebirds wishes to be alone."

The smile on Serena's face faded. She slanted a glance at Constable Loukas, noting that he was enjoying a quiet tête-à-tête with the parson. "You can't leave yet, Flynn," she said, giving him a look that she hoped spoke volumes.

Flynn's answer was to yawn hugely. "Once you and the major gets settled," he said, "send for me. In the meantime, I've got other fish to fry."

Thinking of Lord Alistair, she nodded and whispered, "Be careful."

Flynn was not sure what was going through her mind, but he knew that she hadn't thought any further ahead than the next hour. Well, he'd wished, no, he'd prayed, for older and more experienced hands to take on the burden of Serena, and he wasn't going to turn craven now. Raynor had married her, and whatever lay in her future was between the two of them. Still, he had not known how hard it would be to relinquish her, and relinquish her he must, if only for her own good.

The break, he knew, must be clean and absolute, with no half measures, or Serena would use him as a shield. She was Raynor's now, and he was not about to come between man and wife. His eyes were burning when he slipped from the room.

Serena caught Julian's sleeve as he made to move away. "Julian," she said, her voice low and convincing. "Please?"

Though his expression was not very encouraging, she braced herself to go on. Turning slightly to keep her words from reaching the two elderly gentlemen on the sofa by the fire, she moistened her lips. "There has been something I have been meaning to say to you, but there has not been the opportunity."

He wasn't going to make this easy for her. Looking deeply into his eyes, trying to convey everything in that look, an apology, gratitude, and remorse, she went on softly, "I have been wanting to thank you for what you did tonight. 'Thank you' sounds so inadequate, but I don't know what more I can say." She lifted her shoulders and let them drop. "I do thank you, Julian, from the bottom of my heart. I mean that sincerely."

He smiled without warmth. "I'll wager that almost choked you."

She was ready to snap at him. He always had this effect on her, but the parson and constable coming up at that moment, she fell silent.

"There's more to marriage than fine clothes and a fine setting. Remember your vows, my child," were the parson's parting words to Serena.

The constable was more forthright. "I'm a witness to your marriage, my dear. Remember, you may rely on me."

"I'll see you out," said Julian. "Serena, I have a few things to see to. Why don't you sample the culinary delights my chef provided for us? This won't take a moment. All right?"

Serena wandered around the little office, her thoughts occupied with the parting words of both parson and constable. Though she and Julian had yet to discuss what their next step would be, naturally Julian would have no desire to let the marriage stand. As for witnesses and vows, a marriage that was not consummated was no marriage at all, not even in the eyes of the church.

The lump in her throat seemed to expand, constricting her next breath. Reaction was setting in, she assured herself. It was hours since she had last eaten. Remembering

Julian's words to her, she went to the small gate-leg table which had been set with the best the house had to offer. Julian's French chef was one of the drawing cards of the house, and she could see why.

There were soft roes of mackerel baked in butter, and truffles stuffed with herbs; oyster patties, and lobster rissoles; and a host of delicacies she could not begin to identify. The smell was tantalizing, if one had the appetite to enjoy it. She couldn't eat a thing. She reached for a plain biscuit to nibble on. As she moved to the fire to warm her cold hands, her eye was caught by a paper, a letter or a note, which had slipped under Julian's desk. She retrieved it and was about to lay it on the desk when the unmistakable scent of rose and cloves filled her nostrils. This was Lady Amelia Lawrence's fragrance.

She could not tear her eyes away from that one-page epistle which seemed to have stuck itself to the tips of her fingers. As she scanned the lines, her cheeks burned hot. This was no billet-doux in the manner of her own innocent letters to Stephen. This was lewdness on a scale she could never have imagined.

She shouldn't be surprised, not really. She had known what Lady Amelia was. It was all of five or six years since they had taken to avoiding each other, and when they inadvertently came face-to-face, they barely acknowledged the other's presence. Captain Horatio Allardyce was the cause of their estrangement. She hardly gave Allardyce a thought these days. But remembering her own gullibility at the time still had the power to hurt her. He was her first love, and she had loved him with all the pent-up longing, all the desperation that only an adolescent girl could know. He had told her he loved her too. He wanted to marry her, and since her father would never consent to the marriage, they were going to elope.

Lady Amelia had put her wise to Allardyce. It seemed

that while he was courting Serena, he had been bedding the delectable and much more worldly Amelia. It was Serena's dowry Allardyce wanted, so Amelia had told her. In those days, before the Cause had taken every penny they had, her dowry had been substantial.

No wonder Julian had behaved all evening like a lion with a thorn in his paw. He had an assignation to keep with Lady Amelia. He must have been straining at the bit to be done with her so that he could enjoy the carnal delights Amelia Lawrence described so graphically in her salacious letter.

Well, far be it from her to stand in his way. As though the letter scorched her fingers, she dropped it on the desk. Her eyes were sizzling when she quit the room.

This part of the house was not open to the public, and she saw no one as she quickly traversed the corridor to the staircase. She meant to retrieve her belongings from the little chamber where she had donned her borrowed finery, then she would find Tibbets and have him summon a hackney to take her home. At the very last, with all the dignity she could command, she would wish her "husband" long life and happiness and bid him a civil farewell.

As she was descending the narrow, dimly lit staircase, Tibbets appeared below her, bearing a silver tray and two pewter tankards. Just as she was about to call out to him, he disappeared through a door, leaving it open. Flynn's voice came to her through that open door.

"She'll be as mad as an 'ornet if she ever discovers my part in this."

"Why should she discover it?" asked Julian. "As far as Serena knows, she has engineered everything to suit herself."

This brought muffled masculine laughter.

"Ah, Tibbets, those are for my friends here," said Julian.

Serena couldn't begin to understand what was going on, but her suspicions were aroused. When Tibbets next appeared, she flattened herself against the wall. Damnation! Julian's manservant had closed the door. *Now* what was she going to do? Her first act was to extinguish the candle in the wall sconce, plunging her part of the staircase into semidarkness. Then, with slow, cautious steps, she descended the stairs. When the door suddenly opened, and Constable Loukas and Flynn came out together, she froze.

"What happened to the real Lord Alistair?" asked Constable Loukas. "That's what I want to know."

"We got 'im clean away two days since, and that, my friend, is all you needs to know." Then laughing together, they descended the stairs, leaving the door slightly ajar.

A horrible, unspeakable suspicion was beginning to take possession of Serena's mind. When she reached the door, she touched it with her hand, and it moved inward a few inches. Julian and Lord Alistair were rising to their feet, having evidently shared a drink together.

"You overplayed your hand there," said Julian.

"What? By kissing the hem of her gown?" There was not a trace of a Scottish brogue in Lord Alistair's amused accents. "I thought it was a nice touch, myself. And your wife really is the loveliest, bravest lady that I have ever met. She could not know that we stood in no danger."

Julian said something low and violent.

His companion laughed. "Now that I am here, I might as well try my luck at your tables."

"No," said Julian, "I'd rather you waited until Serena is safely away. There's no sense taking unnecessary risks. And if she were to see you in a different role, she would know that things are not as they seem to be."

Serena's clenched fist connected with the door, slamming it hard against the wall. Both gentlemen swung to face her. "I'm afraid it's too late for that," she said, and she stormed into the room. Her first target was the man she knew as "Lord Alistair."

"Why?" she said. "Why would you do such a thing?" Tears of mingled outrage and torment glazed her eyes. "I risked my life to help you, or so I thought. And all the time you were nothing more than a paid lackey of this scoundrel. God, and to think I liked and trusted you!"

"Leave us, Harry," said Julian.

"No," she cried out, her eyes never leaving the young man's face. "Who are you? You owe me that much at least."

"My name is Harry Loukas." He glanced at Julian, and that hard look silenced him. He bowed and stepped past Serena, then went through the open door and shut it.

Drawing a long, tear-choked breath, Serena swung to face Julian. "They are related, I presume?"

"Constable Loukas is Harry's grandfather," he replied quietly. "I've known them both these many years."

"Everything was a mockery, wasn't it? Constable Loukas? The militia? The chase through the sewers? Damn you! Look at me when I talk to you!"

He had turned aside to pour a measure of brandy into a glass which he now thrust into her hand, curling her fingers around it. "Drink it," he said.

She made no move to obey him, but stared at him with huge, anguished eyes. "The militia? How could you have managed the militia? It's impossible."

His expression was inscrutable. "There was no militia involved."

"I saw them! I heard them!"

"No. You only imagined you did. Or perhaps Loukas arranged something. I don't know."

"Loukas!" she spat at him. "He is no constable, is he? He is another of your paid agents?"

He answered her without inflection. "He is, or was, a constable, now retired."

He had raised the glass to her lips, forcing her to swallow some of the liquid. She slapped his hand away, and stood there staring at him, almost staring through him, as if he did not exist.

"Serena—"

"And Flynn? How could you have persuaded Flynn to deceive me? What hold do you have over him?"

He answered her gently, as though he were addressing a hurt child. "I didn't persuade Flynn. He came to me, reminding me that I had an obligation to you."

"What obligation?"

"To give you the protection of my name; to make restitution for my sins."

She began to laugh, then checked herself when she heard the hysteria in her voice. "You're not saying that you engineered the whole thing merely to make me your wife?"

"That's exactly what I am saying."

"I don't believe you!"

"Nevertheless, it's the truth."

"Do you think I am a simpleton? There is something else behind this, something you are keeping to yourself."

"What, for instance?"

"I don't know, but I know a barefaced lie when I hear it." She laughed. "What a stupid thing to say! You were all deceiving me, and I never tumbled to it." Her voice cracked.

"I'm not lying to you now. Serena, don't be too hard on Flynn. He acted from the best motives in the world. He is devoted to you."

"A fine way he shows his devotion!" Pressing her fist to

her mouth, swallowing audibly, she moved away from him. She began pacing restlessly as her mind was deluged with a flood of conflicting impressions.

"But Flynn did not want to help Lord Alistair. After Loukas came to call? He tried to persuade me that it was too dangerous. And you"—she looked at Julian with loathing—"you had no knowledge of what we were doing. God, I had to remind you of the debt you owed me before you would agree to support our story."

He regarded her steadily, but made no attempt to reply to her accusations.

"I arranged everything, I know I did!"

"No, Serena. You only thought you did."

"It couldn't have been an elaborate plot! We were doing it for my brother Clive. Don't say he is part of this too!"

"No. He merely provided the means and we used them."

Closing her eyes against the threatening tears, she curled her fingers around the back of a chair for support. It was so devious that she could hardly follow all the twists and turns. Two nights ago, she and Flynn had been set to take delivery of Lord Alistair when word had reached them that his arrival would be delayed. And she had not thought to question any of it. "What happened to Lord Alistair, the real Lord Alistair, I mean?" There was a break in her voice.

"Drink the brandy and I shall tell you."

She glared at him in tempestuous scorn, but she raised the glass in spite of her loathing, and obediently sipped from it. "Well?"

"I decided not to involve you in Lord Alistair's escape. Frankly, your presence wasn't necessary. Flynn and I took care of the matter two nights ago without your being aware of it. Set your mind at rest. Lord Alistair should have reached a safe harbor in France long since."

"*You* decided! *You* decided! And who gave you the right to meddle in my affairs?"

"I think you know the answer to that question as well as I do. Serena, you brought it on yourself."

Her chest was so tight that she could hardly breathe. She had trusted them, and they had all betrayed her. She couldn't believe it of Flynn, wouldn't believe it of Flynn. Yet, none of it could have come about without his connivance. She remembered something else—Flynn's conviction that it was Raynor's duty to marry her.

The picture of Flynn coming to Raynor and begging him to do right by her made her feel nauseous. But Raynor hadn't done right by her. "It was a Fleet marriage," she said, "and that is no marriage at all."

He folded his arms across his chest in that indolent way she thoroughly detested. "Come now, Serena. You would never have accepted a church wedding. Don't you think we knew it? And I think you must not have been listening when I explained the nature of Fleet marriages to you. As I said, they are whatever the couples in question wish to make of them. You are my wife, Serena, and I have the marriage certificate and the witnesses to prove it." His voice gentled. "It wasn't a marriage that perhaps either of us wanted, but it will suit. You will be under my protection. My wealth will be at your disposal. You will be safe, Serena. I owe you that much at least."

A cold, trembling paralysis held her in its grip. She heard his words, but her mind flatly rejected his logic. There was a more devious reason behind it all, if she could only discover it. No man went to such lengths to make restitution to a lady who neither desired nor asked for it. Knowing that she would never get a straight answer from him, she spun on her heel and stalked to the door.

As she reached for the doorknob, he said in a hard, authoritative voice. "Where do you think you are going?"

She answered him with all the contempt she could summon. "To hire a clever barrister. I believe you mentioned that also when you explained the nature of Fleet marriages."

Laughing, he reached for her. Her hand came up like lightning, and she dashed the contents of her glass in his face.

The brandy dripped from his chin to the fine Michelin lace at his throat. Her head was thrown back defiantly, daring him to retaliate. He found his handkerchief and dried his face.

"Serena," he said, and gave a long sigh of barely contained frustration. "I will allow that in this instance your anger is justified, up to a point." He pocketed his handkerchief. "Frankly, my sweet, you are beginning to overstep that point. In the morning, after a good night's rest, you will begin to see things differently."

The amused tolerance in his voice acted on her temper like powdered sugar on an open blaze. "If it's the last thing I do, I shall punish you for this. You think this is amusing! Ask Flynn, ask anyone! A Ward never forgets or forgives an insult."

It was only temper speaking, but she took a savage delight in seeing that her words had some effect, then the look was gone from his eyes, and the amusement had returned.

"Then I look forward to our future battles."

"You are . . ." She had run out of words to describe his villainy.

"Yes, I know. I think you will like my house in Twickenham. It's on the Thames, did you know? You have"— he glanced at the clock on the mantel—"ten minutes to make yourself ready before we leave. Oh, don't give a thought to what you are to wear. I took the liberty of having Flynn pack a few things for you. Serena, don't argue. For once in your life, give in gracefully, or I shall be tempted to resort to brute force."

The ground seemed to be moving beneath her feet. He said her name, but she was no more ready to accept his concern than she was his high-handed commands.

"Don't touch me!" she said fiercely, and his hand fell away. For a moment, she leaned against the door, battling the rage that choked her. Coming to herself, she flung the door wide, and went quickly to the small chamber which had been reserved for her use.

Serena had been hurt before, but never like this. It was so violent, so overwhelming, that her whole body was shaking in reaction. She had to clamp her teeth together to stop them from chattering. The sense of betrayal by people she had liked and trusted almost sent her to her knees. It was all an act! They had all been playing a part, and how easily they had duped her! Flynn, the constable, Lord Alistair! Even Julian! How he must have laughed when she had humbled her pride and thanked him for all that he had done for her. Thank him? She ought to have murdered him!

Calling herself every kind of a fool, snatching up the feathered mask she had worn earlier, with trembling fingers, she slipped it in place, adjusting the ties in the combs in her hair. She wasn't ready to give up yet. Instinct had taken over. She moved like lightning, mounting the stairs to the landing with the door that connected Julian's suite of rooms to the gaming house. Once she was through the door, she felt safer. There were plenty of people about who were either coming or going, or moving between the various apartments. Stumbling in her haste, she began to descend the great, cantilevered staircase. When she reached the spacious hall, and no outcry had been given, she slowed her pace. Attaching herself casually to a noisy group who were on the point of leaving the premises, she made her escape.

Outside, hackneys and sedans seemed to choke the street, and linkboys with their torches held aloft were calling out their prices, offering to light their customers' steps on their way home. She did not know how she was going to pay for a sedan, but she had a footman summon one for her just the same. She entered it quickly, gave the chairmen her direction, and slumped down so that only the top of her head could be seen through the windows.

She knew, as soon as they had turned the corner, that they were going the wrong way. Before she could make up her mind whether or not it was an innocent mistake on the chairmen's part, the sedan was set down and the door was opened.

"Our carriage awaits," said Julian. Reaching into the sedan, he grasped her by the wrist. "I would advise you to come quietly, Serena. My patience is almost at an end."

So taken by surprise was she that she allowed him to help her from the sedan.

"Serena," he said gently, "you did no more than I expected. Did you really suppose that I would let you out of my sight? I had footmen posted at all the doors with orders to watch for you."

She saw that they were at the corner of Fleet Street. A coach was drawn up, close to the pavement. At Julian's signal, one of the coachmen jumped down and went quickly to open the door. Serena pulled back sharply.

"No," she said, struggling with him. "You'll not abduct me!"

"Get in," he commanded fiercely, and he gave her a shove.

She looked around wildly. The chairmen, she knew, would not lift a finger to save her, in spite of their pained expressions. There were other people about, however, decent people she could appeal to who were coming and going from a coffeehouse farther down the street. From close at hand came the reassuring cry of the watchman as he called out the hour. She had to act quickly before it was too late.

Drawing a quick breath, she opened her mouth and screamed at the top of her lungs. Julian's hand clamped around her mouth, shutting off her next breath. She lashed out at him, giving him a glancing blow on the cheek. In spite of her resistance, he was maneuvering her toward the open door of the coach.

"Help me," he said through gritted teeth to the coachman who held the door.

Two sets of hands were laid on her. She might have given up the struggle if she had not heard shouts of alarm and the thud of approaching feet. She tore out of Julian's grasp just as he swung her in an arc toward the waiting carriage.

She lost her balance and went sprawling. She heard Julian shout her name. In the next instant, pain exploded through her as her head connected with the edge of the carriage door. Staggering to her knees, she made a feeble attempt to regain her balance, then the pain receded as a merciful darkness engulfed her.

Her last conscious thought was not that she hated Julian Raynor, but that he hated her.

Chapter Eleven

er brain was reeling. Every bone in her body ached. She wished that they would have done with their questions so that she could lose herself in sleep.

"What is your name, my dear?"

Why did he persist in asking the same question, over and over? "Victoria," she said. "Victoria Noble. Who are you?"

She was aware that the stranger had relinquished his place to someone else. "Drink this," said a voice she recognized. Supporting her with one arm around her shoulders, he raised her from the pillows.

She forced herself to open her eyes. "Julian?" His face was very grave; his eyes shadowed with concern. When he put the cup to her lips, she sipped from it carefully, but the pain in her jaw was more than she could bear. She whimpered, and he gently set her back against the pillows.

The sound of voices whispering indistinctly drew her eyes to a man and woman silhouetted against the bright glare at one of the windows. She recognized neither of them, nor did the room look familiar to her.

"Julian, where are we?"

"Hush," he said. "Don't excite yourself. We are at my house in Twickenham."

Reassured by his answer, she let her eyelids droop. She knew that her memory was hazy, but he was here, and for the present that was all that mattered. "Don't leave me," she murmured, and felt around on top of the covers until she had found his hand. His fingers closed around hers in a comforting clasp. Sighing, she allowed the sweet oblivion of sleep to claim her once more.

When he was satisfied that she was comfortable and settled, Julian carefully removed his hand from her clasp. He gestured to the physician, then exited the room. Both men were silent as they descended the stairs. Julian led the way to his bookroom.

"Concussion," said Dr. Ames, as soon as they had crossed the threshold. He was a short rather stout gentleman in his early fifties. His manner was respectful and at the same time confident. Dr. Ames had long since discovered that confidence begat confidence, especially when dealing with the upper classes.

"Your wife has taken quite a knock," he said.

Julian poured out two glasses of sherry and handed one to Ames. Motioning the doctor to a chair, he seated himself. "She did," he agreed, "but she seemed to recover from it, or I would never have brought her out here. In the coach, she was subdued, certainly, but there was no evidence that she had lost her memory, not until this morning when I tried to wake her. How serious is it?"

"In this instance, not very serious, I should think. I've seen cases like this before. She knows you, and she remembers her name, her maiden name, and that is very encouraging. In a few days, with rest and care, I'd say her memory will be fully restored. The thing is not to force it, but to allow nature to take its course."

Since these words brought no change to his companion's bleak expression, Dr. Ames went on more bracingly. "Come now, Major, you yourself must have some knowledge of concussion and its effects. In the aftermath of battle, there are always soldiers who don't know who they are or how they got there, or even which side they are supposed to be fighting for."

"And I also know that some of them never recover the full use of their wits."

"That's just my point. Mrs. Raynor is well on the road to recovery. She knows what is important to her."

"Meaning?"

"As I already told you, she knows her name and she recognizes you. If it will set your mind at rest, I shall look in every afternoon to see how our patient is progressing."

"I'm obliged to you," said Julian.

Very little more was said after this, and the doctor was soon making his excuses. At the front door, he halted. "Victoria Noble," he said. "Would your wife be a connection of the Nobles of Arden Park?"

"No," answered Julian and his expression did not invite further comment.

As soon as the front door had closed upon the doctor, Julian returned to his wife's bedside.

"I'll take over now, Mrs. Forrest," he told his housekeeper. "Oh, and perhaps you'll make up a bed for me in the little dressing room? I want to be close by in the event that my wife wakes during the night."

As the housekeeper went to do his bidding, Julian pulled a chair close to the bed. When Serena moaned, he was instantly on his feet, bending over her, murmuring indistinctly as he smoothed back her halo of gold hair. One side of her face was badly bruised, and there was a lump the size of a goose egg on her right temple. There were other bruises and scratches marring her beautiful skin, but those were on her body, and were, according to the doctor, only superficial.

By and large, he accepted Dr. Ames's diagnosis. He'd seen many a soldier who had taken a far more severe blow to the head than Serena, and who had come out of it unscathed. Serena was disoriented, but she was reasonably lucid. She had recognized him. That was something, he supposed. As for giving her name as Victoria Noble, he wasn't quite sure what to make of that. More strange by far, however, was her manner toward him. That had undergone a complete reversal. It was too bad it wouldn't last.

He was responsible for this, he thought savagely, and flung himself down on a chair. He had brought her to this pass! Had anyone ever told him that he was capable of such bestial conduct, he would have challenged that person to a duel. He couldn't understand why this girl could provoke him to such lengths. Looking at her now, his throat tightened. She didn't look like the spitfire who opposed him at every turn. She looked like a defenseless child who had taken a beating from a callous and uncaring monster.

He had meant it all for the best. He didn't want to hurt her. He wanted to protect her. A man of honor did not simply take an innocent young woman and discard her like so much refuse. She was the marrying kind of girl. He had ruined her, albeit unwittingly. If he did not do the right thing by her, his conscience would forever hold it against him. Whether he wanted to or not, he felt responsible for her.

There was another, equally compelling reason for making her his wife. Serena's fate was tied to her father's fate. He had racked his brains for a way of keeping her out of it. He owed her that much at least. Only one solution presented itself, the same solution. If she were his wife, he would have some say in the ordering of her life. He could provide for her, and at the same time make sure that not a penny of his money went to support her father. The problem was, Serena would never willingly become his wife.

When Flynn, understanding his dilemma though not all the reasons behind it, had approached him, he had been more than willing to give him a hearing. By this time, his own thoughts were becoming more fanciful, on the lines of abducting her and incarcerating her in his hunting box in Scotland, with or without benefit of marriage. With Flynn's connivance, he had tried to court her, and when that had failed, they had concocted their elaborate plot. Serena, Flynn had suggested, could be tricked into doing something when no power on earth could force her into it. It seemed incredible now, with everything that had happened, that he had entered into the thing in an almost humorous frame of mind. Stealing a march on Serena was something he could not resist.

It was then that Flynn had staggered him by revealing that Serena was the mastermind behind a Jacobite escape route. After that, there was no holding him back. If ever a woman was in need of a husband's guiding hand, that woman was Serena. For her to run such risks! For her to gallivant through sewers and underground passages, the known haunt of London's criminal element! Anything could happen to her.

Something had happened to her. She had fallen in his way, and he had taken advantage of her. Now, more than ever, he was determined to protect her. And so, with the help of his good friends, Loukas and young Harry, they had concocted their scheme.

Everything had worked in their favor—Catherine Ward's removal to the country, Lord Alistair's arrival on the scene, Serena's determination to participate in his escape, and the absence of Jeremy and Clive Ward at the crucial time. And he did not expect any insurmountable difficulties when the marriage was made public.

Very soon now, he would finally come face-to-face with the man who had been his family's nemesis. Flynn was to send word to him the moment Sir Robert arrived in London. He had warned Flynn to say nothing of his marriage to Serena. As far as anyone knew, Serena was now at Riverview with her young nephews and Catherine. Besides, it would be his duty, his pleasure to tell Sir Robert of their marriage in person. Serena had a husband now, and though Sir Robert might not approve of him, he would accept the connection with dignity rather than stir up a monumental scandal. He would not want to lose face. He, Julian, had a fair idea of what to expect from the man.

From various sources, he had pieced together a sketch of the man's character—proud, haughty, highly conscious of his own worth, and fanatical in both his loyalties and his hatreds. Few people looked forward to his return. Whatever the terms of the pardon, Sir Robert was not the sort to change course once he had embarked on it. He, Julian, could vouch for that.

Fragments of memories drifted in and out of his mind. A cold gray barracks of a building, gaunt-faced women, hungry hollowed-eyed children, corpses in shrouds, and above all, a despair so deep, so choking that even death might be preferable.

He brushed a hand across his eyes, as if to brush away the harsh memories. When that failed, he rose and moved to the window, staring out at the great stretch of lawns that swept down toward the Thames. He did not know how long he had been standing there when a sound from the bed drew him back to the present.

He covered the distance to Serena in a few strides, leaned over, and touched a palm to her cheek. Satisfied that she was not feverish, he tucked the covers that she had dislodged more securely about her. At the brush of his hands, she sighed, and whispered his name. Julian stilled, looking down at her with an arrested expression.

Shaking his head, he returned to the chair by the bed to resume his vigil. "Serena," he said softly, "now what am I going to do with you?"

His negligence had cost him dearly, had cost them

both dearly, for if she had not discovered his duplicity, he was sure he could have persuaded her to spend a night or two in his house if only to allay the suspicions of Constable Loukas. And once he had her here, there would have been no going back. It had seemed to him, then, that when she was under his roof, everything would fall naturally into place between them, especially with Serena in a receptive frame of mind. She looked upon him as her savior. That had been borne out by the pretty speech she had made him, thanking him for all that he had done for her. He was not above using these softer feelings she had betrayed for his own purposes. He was no callow youth when it came to women. There were few who could long withstand his considerable power to charm. One green girl had not seemed so formidable a challenge. And a real marriage would simplify everything between them.

Whether due to the glass of brandy he had ingested earlier, or to his numbing anxiety for her, other thoughts rushed in to taunt him. *Conscience?* Was that really what was behind the elaborate plot to get her in his power? A prolonged attack of conscience? Or were there other reasons that he would not admit to, not even to himself?

He leaned his neck against the chair back and closed his eyes, laughing silently and without mirth. He could not come near her, think of her, without damning to hell the fashion for tight-fitting men's breeches. Oh yes, a real marriage would certainly simplify everything, he mocked himself. Not only would his conscience be clear, but he would also have access to that beautiful, supple body. Lately, it was all he could think about.

When she came to herself, she would be a flaming, fire-breathing dragon. His considerable power to charm would never come into it. Once again, he would be forced to act the tyrant. It was in Serena's nature to contend with a man until she had mastered him, or until the poor devil

(Flynn's words) had retired from the field in ignominy. It was not in his nature to be mastered or to retire from the field.

He closed his eyes on a smile. When he opened them the curtains were drawn and the candles were lit. Serena was moving restlessly, crying out in her sleep. Stretching his cramped muscles, he rose and moved to her side. When he brushed the back of his fingers to the bruise on her cheek, she fought him off and came awake with a cry.

She gazed up at him with huge, frightened eyes. He had never seen her wear this face before—confused, vulnerable, and so very pale and shaken. His arms went around her, pulling her into the shelter of his body.

"Julian?" she whispered tearfully, and pressed closer, tucking her head beneath his chin. "I thought . . ." Her voice shuddered to a halt.

"What did you think?"

"I thought you hated me. In my dream, you hated me."

He cupped her chin, tipping her head back. Her lips were slightly parted and trembled with the effort to catch back her sobs. Against the wall of his chest, he could feel the strong beat of her heart as it gradually slowed. His head dipped, and he pressed a chaste kiss to those softly parted lips. Then another. And another.

"I could never hate you," he said.

She relaxed against him. "Don't leave me," she whispered. "Lie with me, Julian. Lie with me."

When he stretched out beside her, she turned into him, nestling against him like a trusting child. By degrees, her breathing evened and he knew that she slept.

She awakened to the swish of drapes and the sudden, blinding glow of an afternoon sun. She lay there between wakefulness and sleep, trying to get her bearings. There was nothing to guide her, nothing solid to hold on to in the mists that were locked inside her head. As the panic rose in her throat, one name came to her. *Julian.*

"Mrs. Raynor? I've brought ye a bite o' breakfast."

The soft, west-country accent only added to Serena's sense of panic. Gritting her teeth against the pain in her head, she pulled herself up. The smiling lady in the brown spotted muslin with its high lace collar had the look of a plump mother hen watching over her new-hatched chick.

"I'm Mrs. Forrest, m'dear, the housekeeper," she said.

Serena's only thought was that Julian was not there. "Julian!" she cried out, and pushing back the covers she made a halfhearted attempt to rise.

Mrs. Forrest set down the tray she was carrying. Clicking her tongue, she went to help Serena. "Now lass, if ye must know, the major is with the doctor. They'll be coming in to examine ye in a minute or two. Ye'll want to pretty yerself up afore they get here."

When Serena rose to her feet, the walls of the room seemed to recede and spin away from her. Her legs buckled beneath her. "There's something wrong with me," she gasped.

"It's the concussion, from the accident. I heard Dr. Ames tell the master. There's nothing to fear, lass. Ye had a nasty fall, 'tis all."

Concussion. Accident. These words were vastly reassuring. She'd suffered a head injury. That would explain the confusion and the dizziness and nausea. She rubbed her fingers against the frown on her brow. "I want my husband," she said, sounding like a fractious child.

At these words, the housekeeper smiled. "And ye shall have him, just as soon as ye are ready to greet him."

The bribe was irresistible. More at ease now, Serena allowed the housekeeper to assist her with her toilette.

When Julian entered with the doctor, she was sitting

up in bed, drinking a glass of chocolate. At sight of Julian, the feeling of being utterly alone and lost receded a little. She set down the glass and put out a hand to him. He crossed to her at once, clasping it as he seated himself in a chair next to the bed.

She tried for a smile. "Julian," she said, "I can't seem to remember things."

He squeezed her hand encouragingly. "Don't worry about it, pet. Dr. Ames says that it's only a temporary loss of memory."

She looked at the doctor, but when Julian made to move away from her, her hand tightened, keeping him by her.

Dr. Ames smiled encouragingly. "It's not uncommon in such accidents."

"What accident?" she asked. "I don't remember, you see."

The doctor looked a question at Julian.

Julian cleared his throat and said carefully, "It was a carriage accident. You were thrown and you caught your head against the edge of the door."

She put a hand to her head, and said ruefully, "What a way to begin our honeymoon!"

Dr. Ames was not slow to follow up on this. "You see?" he said. "Already things are coming back to you. You knew that this was to be your honeymoon. We don't want to force it, but it would be helpful if you could tell us how much you do remember. For example, what is your name?"

She smiled at this. "What I do remember is your asking me that selfsame question over and over, till I wanted to scream in vexation."

The doctor beamed at her. Julian said quietly, "Answer the question, my love."

"My name is Victoria." She was very sure of this. She

had a clear recollection of Julian saying her name, not once, but many times. "Victoria," and she smiled shyly at Julian. "Victoria Raynor, now."

The doctor rubbed his hands together in evident glee. "And what about your family?"

"I'm an orphan." The words came to her lips automatically. *I'm an orphan*. She'd said those words before. "And I am or was an actress." She looked to Julian for confirmation, but he was staring intently at their clasped hands.

"An actress?" said the doctor, faltering a little. A quick look at Julian's forbidding expression soon restored his composure. "What more do you remember?"

"I don't remember anything else."

"Yet, you knew that you were coming to your husband's house. No, no. Don't look to your husband for help. Look at me, Mrs. Raynor, and tell me what you remember."

She frowned in concentration. When she looked up her eyes were fear-bright. Her voice came out a shaken whisper. "It's no use. I can't remember."

Julian glowered meaningfully at the doctor, then gathered his wife's trembling form in his arms. "It will all come back to you," he said. "Don't think about it now."

"Your husband is right." Dr. Ames smiled his professional, reassuring smile. "I have every confidence that your faculties will return in a matter of, oh, days if not hours. Don't concern yourself with either the past or future. Think only of the present moment. Enjoy this beautiful house and its tranquil setting. Do a little gardening. Go for long walks. Everything will come back to you in time."

And things did come back to her, in dribs and drabs. Her first recollection came on the following morning, when she was allowed out of bed for the first time. Julian was showing her over the house. It was built in the Palladian style, all marble and intricate plasterwork, and Ionic columns in the great entrance hall. Her steps slowed when her eyes fell on those columns.

"This reminds me of your gaming house," she said, then her eyes went wide. "Of course, you are a gamester, and a very successful one!"

Julian seemed to have taken root on the spot. "So, it's coming back to you?"

She was too enthralled with her power of recall to notice that anything was amiss. Her bright eyes were darting all over the place, taking in the paintings on the walls, all of them of pastoral settings. "I've been there, haven't I? At your gaming house, I mean? I distinctly remember murals of nymphs and satyrs. Very naughty nymphs and satyrs, I should say," and she turned her mischievous eyes upon him.

"And all of them depicting scenes from mythology," he was quick to point out.

She pulled a face. "I suppose you are going to tell me that gentlemen patronize your establishment to improve the tone of their minds?"

It was just the sort of remark that Serena might have made. His mouth drew down slightly, then he noticed the laughter lurking in her eyes, and his lips turned up. Something inside him seemed to unclench. She was going to be all right. The fear and uncertainty no longer shadowed her eyes. The bruise on her cheek had faded, as had the swelling on her temple. Even her memory was returning, and though it boded no good for him, for her sake he wanted her to become Serena again.

Interrupting his train of thought, she said gaily, "Oh, don't worry, Julian! I'm well aware that you would have no patrons if gaming was as demure as taking tea in my dainty little parlor." Her brows pulled together. "Now where did I hear that before?"

"Don't press yourself," he advised gently. "You heard the doctor. Everything will come back to you in time."

He was to repeat those words to her several times during the course of the day. He was amazed at her forbearance. If he had been the one to lose his memory, he knew he would have been beside himself with frustration, and the Serena he knew would have been in no better shape. But this was Victoria, a charming, vivacious creature who was determined to be pleased with her new husband and everything about him—his house, his servants, the way he earned his living—and she refused to allow a mere temporary loss of memory to spoil things for them.

It gave him food for thought. Mistrust and hostility had dogged their acquaintance almost from its inception. Is this how it might have been between them if they had met under different circumstances? Was Victoria merely a side of Serena that he had never been privileged to meet? His next thought followed naturally from that. If he could have one or the other, Serena or Victoria, which one would it be?

He was still humorously debating the question later that evening. They were in Julian's bookroom, lingering over coffee, having enjoyed an excellent dinner prepared by his housekeeper and her husband. The Forrests were really caretakers, and the only servants on the premises. On the grounds of the house, which had come to Julian by way of a gaming debt, there were many more servants, guards in fact, posing as gardeners and gamekeepers, to ensure that no one either entered or left his domain without his consent. It was for Serena that he'd taken these precautions. They were hardly necessary for Victoria.

"Tell me how we met," she invited as she replenished his coffee cup.

"You heard Dr. Ames," he temporized. "It's best not to force memories on you. All in good time, Victoria."

There was a flash in her eyes that reminded him of the old Serena, and he felt himself rising to the challenge. Then she was all sweetness and light again, and he was oddly disappointed.

"Oh, very well," she said. "Then tell me about yourself. How did you become a gambler? Surely there can be no objection to telling me that?"

He never talked about himself if he could help it. He was on the verge of changing the subject when he checked himself. The time would come when he would have to explain his actions toward her father. She might not accept those actions, but at the very least he wanted her to understand that right was on his side. The trouble was, Serena would never give him a hearing. This was a chance that might never come again.

"It was either gaming or a life of prostitution," he told her flatly. "Oh yes, Victoria, prostitution. Didn't you know that young boys are much in demand as prostitutes?"

She didn't know, as he could tell from her shocked expression. When the shock of his words had faded he said more gently, "It's not a pretty story. Are you sure you want me to go on?"

"I want to know everything about you," she said.

"Even if it gives you a thorough disgust of me?"

She smiled at this. "Nothing could ever give me a disgust of you."

If only she were Serena and not Victoria, those words would have counted for something. Smiling cynically, he began by relating the circumstances of his early years.

"Then, when I was thirteen," he said at one point, "I was sent to the parish workhouse with my family."

He told her nothing that could possibly connect him to her father, nothing about the vendetta which had brought his family to ruin. That could wait until later, after their marriage had become an incontrovertible fact, and not before retribution had finally caught up with Sir Robert. Time would work in his favor.

As his story progressed, his voice became less confident. Sometimes he hesitated before going on. There were several long stretches of silence when he had to search for words to explain himself. At last, the story was told. He stopped suddenly and stared at her with something like mockery in his expression.

She lifted her head, and gazed at him reflectively. He had spoken with a deep, moving bitterness, far different from anything she had ever heard in him before. Memories were skirting the edges of her mind, and though they did not materialize into anything substantial, she knew that he had never before confided so much to her. Judging, correctly, that though he had confided in her, he would scorn her pity, she said simply, "I told you that nothing could ever give me a disgust of you."

The cynical mockery in his expression faded, and his eyes bored into hers. She had a flash of recall; strong masculine hands were molding her soft curves to the hard planes of his body. Pleasure hovered as he locked her to him in an unyielding embrace. He was remembering it too. She could see it in his eyes. Then he was turning away, reaching for his cup, asking her in a matter-of-fact voice to refill it for him. With shaking fingers, she hastened to obey.

As time passed, Julian had less and less to say for himself. He had opened a door better left closed, not because he regretted her knowing about the life he had led, but because it wrapped the two of them in a warm cocoon of intimacy, making them susceptible to each other. She was Victoria, not Serena, and that made her the wrong woman.

His body did not know the difference. It had carnal

knowledge of her body, and would not let him forget it. He knew that his chest was rising and falling, and that his breath was coming more rapidly. He felt the fierce stir of his senses, his blood growing hot, his heart pounding. He was possessed by lust and there wasn't a damn thing he could do about it, not when he knew that he was having an effect on her too.

Those blue eyes that could sizzle with temper were meltingly soft, drawing him in. Her lips were slightly parted, and against the flimsy material of her bodice, the outline of her nipples was clearly evident. She was Victoria, and if he laid a finger on her, Serena would exact a terrible price for taking an unfair advantage.

But Serena was not here.

Losing patience with himself, he set down his cup and saucer and rose to his feet. "Go to bed," he told her harshly. "I have things to do. Don't wait up for me. I may not turn in for some hours."

In the hall, he grabbed his cloak and went out into the dark windswept night.

Chapter Twelve

❧❧❧

Julian awakened to the rattle of glass or china and the tread of feet padding about in the adjoining chamber, Serena's chamber. Every muscle in his body was tense. The short, narrow trundle bed which he occupied in the little dressing room was definitely not up to his usual standard. He shifted to his side and noted that it was still as black as pitch outside the window. Turning his head on the pillow, he glanced in the direction of the door. A crack of light from Serena's chamber spilled under it. Reaching for his robe to cover his nakedness, he went to investigate.

She was perched on the edge of the bed, drinking a glass of milk. Beneath the thin fabric of her nightshift, he could clearly distinguish the outline of her full breasts. His throat tightened as desire swept through him.

"What is it? What's wrong?" he asked.

She looked at him carefully, searchingly, then patted the bed, inviting him to sit close to her. "I wakened and could not get back to sleep," she said, "so I went down to the kitchen and fetched a biscuit and a glass of milk."

When he sat beside her, he was careful to leave a small space between them. In the silence, he heard his own breathing and odd little sounds of the house settling and what might have been rain outside the window. Not since he had taken his first woman had he felt so inept and ill at ease or, conversely, so dangerously close to disgracing himself. When she set aside the glass from which she had been drinking, his heart began to pound against his ribs.

For a moment, she seemed uncertain. Her eyes slipped

away from his. When she looked up, her stare was direct and steady. "I've remembered something," she said.

"What?" His voice was hoarse. Somehow or other, she had dispensed with the careful distance he had set between them. Her knee was grazing his.

"We were lovers before we came here." The pupils of her eyes grew large as she subjected him to another searching look. "I've been thinking about it since I wakened. That's why I can't sleep. It was good between us. I know it was good between us. But now it seems you don't want me. I wish you would tell me what I have done to displease you. Or better yet—tell me how to please you."

The silence was charged. He could sense her arousal. Like a summer heat haze, it clung to him, filling his mouth, his nostrils, entering his pores, his bloodstream. He was steeped in her arousal.

"You don't know what you're saying," he got out hoarsely. He could scarcely think coherently for the battle that was raging inside him. She was willing. He was eager. What was there to stop him?

It was dishonest. She would despise him. If only she were Serena.

She touched her fingers to the furrow on her brow, smoothing it away in a gesture he remembered, a Serena gesture. "I was so sure. I can't be imagining it. It's so real to me."

"What is it you think you remember?"

Another long, searching look. Whatever she thought she saw in his expression emboldened her. She pressed a hand to her abdomen. "Longing so intense, I think I shall die from it. I ache for want of you. You, me, and—" She broke off as horror welled in her. "Don't say it wasn't you!"

Ah . . . damn! He bent his head and brushed his lips against hers. "Of course it was me."

He kissed her with all the pent-up passion of a man who had been celibate too long. It was more than a kiss. He made love to her mouth, fusing their lips together, filling her with the thrust of his tongue the way he wanted to fill her with the thrust of his body. When she drooped against him, he groaned.

Just one kiss, he promised himself. One kiss, then he would remind himself of all the excellent reasons why this must go no further. But as the kiss lingered, mouth devouring mouth, rational thought deserted him. His body was aching with awareness of her body. He wanted his hands on her. His hunger was uncontrollable, responding to the hunger he felt in her.

She moved and he found himself lying alongside her, pushing her back into the pillows. When they pulled apart, they were both gulping for air.

This time, he wasn't going to take her with all the finesse of a rutting stag. This time, there would be cherishing and pleasuring. This time he would make sure that he brought her to completion.

He pulled back slightly, his hand dipping beneath the hem of her shift, wrenching it up, moving it over her thighs. She shifted, helping him to lift it over her shoulders and head. As her arms reached for him, he held her off. He was no stranger to Serena's body, but his memory of it was tactile. This time, he wasn't going to be cheated of a single thing.

Candlelight bathed her, touching her rounded curves in a satiny glow, veiling the womanly valleys in shadow, as if to protect her from his immodest masculine scrutiny. He would allow her no modesty. Eyes holding hers in an unyielding stare, he moved her, arranging her so that nothing was concealed from him.

Her breasts were full and firm, their aureoles like ripe crushed berries. Her waist was incredibly slender, no wider than a man's handspan. The flare of her soft thighs and the golden thatch at their junction were beautifully formed, perfect in their femininity. The one thing to mar so much perfection were odd scratches and abrasions on her ivory skin where she had scraped herself in her fall.

He touched her, brushing his fingertips lightly over her sleep-warmed skin, and the heat from her body seemed to enter him, constricting his breathing, tightening his loins. Dipping his head, he pressed little kisses to each scratch and abrasion that marred her beautiful skin. His lips brushed, his tongue stroked, tasting her, wallowing in her flavor and scent. When his hand cupped a breast, molding the fullness with his fingertips, she made a choked pleasure sound. He toyed with her, clamping with fingers and thumb over each rosy nipple, bringing them fully erect. She lifted herself into the caress, offering him more. Groaning, he replaced his fingers with his tongue, then his mouth, sucking gently, then hard. She was moving rhythmically beneath him, parting her legs in unknowing need. One hand slipped lower, his fingers brushing against the fleecy thatch between her thighs, not entering her, but enticing her, and she arched herself against the pressure of his hand. His fingers probed, entering her, becoming dewed with the essence of her body.

Serena mewed like a kitten as she felt those bold fingers parting and sliding, then delving into the quivering folds of her femininity. He stopped. Just like the last time, those exquisite sensations stopped. She would die if he stopped now.

"Please! Julian!" She was sobbing in her need.

He laughed softly, and the stroking began anew. It was hellish. It was heavenly. She knew she was panting, but she couldn't stop herself. Her world seemed to have diminished to the clever fingers that were moving in and out of her body, flexing, then withdrawing completely as he deliberately teased and tortured her. With the heel of one hand, he rubbed her delicately, revealing a pleasure point she had not known existed. His fingers delved deeper, became more rhythmic as he increased the pressure. Gasping, she clamped her legs together, trapping his hand. It was too intense, too much too . . .

"Ahh . . ." Head thrashing on the pillow, she twisted and turned as the convulsions stormed through her.

A long while later, she opened her eyes and looked up at him with something like awe.

Satisfied with what he read in her expression, Julian shrugged out of his robe and sat back on his heels. "Now you," he said. "I have ached to feel your hands on me."

She shuddered on the shallow breath she inhaled. Her eyes were wide and unflinching on his lap, as though she could not believe what she was seeing. His sex was so hard, so engorged that he was gritting his teeth in anticipation of the pleasure of her touch. She moistened her lips and looked up at him.

"Julian?" she said tremulously.

He gave a shaky laugh. "Oh yes, that too. But you can start by putting your hands on my shoulders."

At her first shy touch, he caught back a groan, but as her fingers descended, plowing through the mat of dark hair on his chest, pleasure became pain. He sucked in his breath. "What the . . . ?"

Somehow, her ring had caught in a whorl of springy chest hair. She worked it free, twisting the ring around her finger. When it came away, releasing him, she stared at her hand thoughtfully.

"Julian, I'm not your wife. I'm your mistress. That's it, isn't it? You need not be afraid to tell me."

"What?" His head jerked back.

"This ring. It's not a real wedding ring. Don't you think I know that?"

"But . . ." He didn't want to talk. He was aching for completion. She *owed* it to him.

"And there are other things. I have a distinct recollection of you offering me a house and a carriage if I would become your mistress. Darling, don't look so stricken. I think I always knew that you would never marry me. A man of your substance will look higher than a poor actress, no, an aspiring actress, for his wife. I don't mind. Really I don't."

All the excellent reasons for keeping his hands off her marched through his head, making a timely though unwelcome appearance. He didn't want to think of them. He ached with the pain of unfulfilled desire. He wanted to roar with the injustice of it. It was his resolve to make their coupling good for *her* that had brought him to this. If he had taken her the way he had wanted to, no, the way she had wanted him to, quickly, and with few preliminaries, by now they would be entwined, sleeping in sated bliss.

He felt outraged, and knowing he was being unreasonable did nothing to calm his sense of ill-usage. Jaw clenched, he hauled himself to the edge of the bed and got awkwardly to his feet. He kept his back to her as he donned his dressing robe, giving himself a moment or two, until his desire had ebbed to manageable proportions.

When he turned and saw the look on her face, his sense of ill-usage evaporated. She could not know that when the male of the species was sexually thwarted, he generally made an ass of himself. She was misreading his silence, blaming herself for the aggression that any fool could detect in him. There would be other nights like this one, he promised himself, other nights when nothing would save her, not even Serena.

Bending to her, he kissed her swiftly. "I thought you

understood that we were wed and coming to my house for our honeymoon?"

She shook her head. "I remember you saying something of the sort in the carriage that conveyed us here. Now that other things are coming back to me, I wondered if I might have been mistaken."

"You are my wife," he said, clearly and forcefully. "Believe it."

"But this ring?"

He couldn't tell her the truth, that it was a prop to deceive Serena into thinking that their marriage was a hastily contrived affair. Nevertheless, he told her no lie when he said, "Our marriage was sudden. That ring is only a temporary one. There is another that I meant to give you, but with the accident and everything, it slipped my mind. You have suffered a concussion. You are confused, you know you are. You were never my mistress, though it's true that we were lovers." He managed to smile ruefully. "I should be horsewhipped for forgetting myself. Dr. Ames warned me that you must have complete rest, and I aim to abide by his advice."

As he spoke, he retrieved the nightshift from the floor, and on returning to the bed, assisted her into it. "Close your eyes and try to get some sleep," he said, helping her beneath the covers. "I promise to abide by the doctor's orders until you are more yourself."

She caught his hand as he made to turn away. Tears magnified her eyes. "Julian, is this true?" she whispered. "Am I truly your wife?"

"Oh yes. I have the marriage certificate to prove it."

Bringing his hand to her lips, she kissed it passionately on the open palm. "I am the happiest woman in the world."

He felt the potent effects of that kiss all the way to his

loins. Before he could change his mind, he blew out the candle and strode from the room.

An hour later, he was still wakeful, moving restlessly in his cramped bed. In one part of his mind, he was regretting leaving—Victoria? Serena?—to her chaste bed. In another part of his mind, he was elated, remembering what she had told him.

Serena was going to be as mad as fire when she came to herself and discovered that Victoria had been betraying all her little secrets. Disgust and loathing? That's not how Victoria remembered it. Though she was confused, she knew that they had been lovers. *I ache for want of you.* Beneath Serena's demure exterior, she burned with a passion to match his own. He had sensed it, once, until she had denied it in no uncertain terms. "Little liar," he said, smiling smugly.

Her passion enthralled him, all the more so because it came in such an intriguing, complex baggage. Of the many passionate women he had known intimately, not one was memorable, though there wasn't one he regretted. With few exceptions, their faces and bodies all ran together in his mind, indistinguishable one from another. Those connections had been easy and casual, the way he preferred it. Nothing with Serena would ever be easy, nothing would ever be casual. His last thought before sleep claimed him was that it was entirely possible he had finally met his match.

Serena could not believe how shy she was with her husband when she met him at the breakfast table the following morning. She was an actress. Actresses she knew were bold, dashing creatures. Flirtation and dalliance came naturally to them. Surely she should have the confidence to make some teasing remark about what had taken place between them the night before? Julian was the one to tease her, and all she could do was start babbling about the weather. It was unseasonably hot. She was sure a storm was brewing. Then again, mayhap not. The twinkle in his eyes set her teeth on edge. An actress should not be so gauche. She assumed that the concussion she had sustained had something to do with it. There were times when she felt like two women, Victoria Noble, the actress, and . . . someone else. Even the clothes in her wardrobe added to her confusion. They hardly seemed flamboyant enough for an actress.

When she mentioned her odd flight of fancy to Dr. Ames on his next visit, he was able to reassure her.

"Concussion is an odd business. Your memory may be erratic for some time to come. However, every day I see an improvement in you. You mentioned actresses a moment ago. You see? It's all coming back to you, or how would you know what to expect from members of your profession?"

In his own mind, he was not nearly so confident. This was the third day after his patient had suffered a concussion, and though in all other respects he was well pleased with her progress, he could see no good reason for the selective loss of memory. He sensed brain damage, or a curious disturbance of the nervous system. He betrayed none of his uncertainties to Serena, but urged her in that hearty way of his to forget about the past and get out and about in the fresh air as much as possible. To Julian, in private, he cautioned patience.

Julian frowned at this. "I understood you to say that it was a mild concussion, and that my wife's memory would be fully restored to her in a matter of days?"

"And so I thought. I still think so." He shrugged helplessly. "It's almost as though she does not wish to remember."

"Are you suggesting that she is shamming?"

Dr. Ames was astonished. "Good God, no! What would be the point of it? All I am saying is that these are early days yet."

He did not mention that he had decided to confer with an eminent colleague in London if the effects of the concussion had not worn off in another day or two.

"It was in my mind," said Julian, "to post up to town to attend to some business matters. This would mean leaving my wife overnight."

"Do so, by all means," replied Dr. Ames at once. "Mrs. Raynor is in good hands here. I am close by—not that I anticipate anything untoward. As I said, Mrs. Raynor is the picture of health. The rest and quiet can only be beneficial."

Once alone, Julian took a few moments to reflect on his conversation with Dr. Ames. He smiled grimly when he remembered the suspicion that had crossed his mind when the doctor had suggested that Serena did not wish her memory to return. She was up to something!—that's what he'd thought. He'd dismissed that absurd notion almost as soon as it had occurred to him. As Ames had indicated, there would be no point in Serena trying to deceive him in this. In point of fact, the Serena he knew would not be able to sustain such a deception. She would burst if she could not tell Julian Raynor exactly what she thought of him for all that he had done to her.

Laughing softly to himself, he entered his bookroom. She would have her day soon enough. He had decided that the time had come to reveal everything to her. Perhaps it had been a mistake to keep her in ignorance of her true identity, but the doctor had assured him the effects of the concussion would quickly wear off and had advised him not to force things. The doctor had been too optimistic. She must be told, and soon. But not, he cautioned himself, before he had returned from town. Serena in her right mind would get up to all sorts of mischief if he were not here to restrain her.

When his thoughts turned to his business in town, his smile gave way to a frown. There had been no word from Flynn, not a whisper to indicate what was going forward with Sir Robert Ward. There had been a delay of some sort, that much was evident. He would look in at Ward House and confer with Flynn, as well as attend to a few other matters that he had put off until Serena was safely his wife.

He wasn't worried about his gaming house. Blackie had things well in hand. Every day a courier came from town with a full accounting of the night's takings. Julian liked to be kept abreast of things. All the same, perhaps a quick visit would be wise. He might hear something of Sir Robert there.

His thoughts drifted. He had a vision of lush rosy contours, and deeply shadowed valleys, and virgin forests that tempted a man to chart them or lose himself in the attempt. Lost in Serena land with no hope of rescue. It was a tantalizing thought.

Serena's first inkling that Julian was keeping her a prisoner on his estate came when she tried to put the doctor's advice into practice. A walk to the village of Twickenham, she decided, would help to while away an hour or two. But porters refused to let her through the gates, and no amount of arguing on her part could persuade them to let her pass.

"A safeguard, merely," Julian assured her when she reproached him about it at the noon meal. "You are still suffering from the effects of the accident. All in good time, Victoria, all in good time."

Something else occurred to her. "I never saw an estate with so many gamekeepers and gardeners." Now where did her knowledge of estates spring from? "On my walk this morning, it appeared to me that half of them were strolling about, trying to look busy."

The hand that was lifting a cup to his lips had become arrested in midair. Carefully setting the cup on its saucer, Julian voiced the same thought that had occurred to her. "What do you know of estates and gardeners and game-keepers? How much do you remember?"

"I don't remember anything of any significance."

"Yet you mentioned an estate. What am I to make of that?"

It was his accusing tone of voice that made her color up. He was looking at her as though she were a stranger and not his wife of a few days. There was something wrong here. No. It was all in her imagination. She was suffering from concussion, that's all it was.

She pressed a hand to her temples. "I beg your pardon, what did you say? These days, I can't seem to concentrate on any one thing for more than a few minutes at a time."

His expression instantly softened. "Forgive me. I shouldn't have pressed you like that." His eyes glinted wickedly. "I suppose I'm as eager as you for the effects of the concussion to wear off, and you know why."

He laughed when her color ran even hotter. "It's no bad thing that I have business which takes me to town. There is plenty to occupy you here in my absence. Don't—"

She didn't let him finish. "You are going to town?"

"It's not that far away."

"Take me with you," she said impulsively.

"That would not be wise."

"Why wouldn't it?"

"I'm only following the doctor's advice." After a slight hesitation, he went on casually, "I should mention that for your own protection my men have orders not to allow you to leave the grounds. No, don't look like that. I shall be gone for only one night. As I said, there's plenty to occupy you here for that length of time."

That was his final word on the subject, and nothing she said could move him.

An hour later, she was on the front steps, her eyes trailing horses and riders as they cantered down the tree-lined drive. Within moments, they had passed through the wrought-iron gates and were lost to view.

Without her husband, her doubts returned in full force. There was something far wrong here if only she could put her finger on it. She looked at the ring on her finger. It was a curtain ring, she was certain of it. He had promised her another ring, but he had not produced it. If she were not his wife, why would he lie to her about it? She was more than willing to be his mistress, as he well knew. And why was he keeping her a prisoner?

The result of so much useless, concentrated reflection was to bring a return of her chills and headaches. She wandered up to her chamber, slipped fully clothed beneath the covers, and dozed. When she wakened, not only were the chills and headaches gone, but she was seized with an electrifying thought. *You are my wife. Believe it. I have the marriage certificate to prove it.*

Marriage certificate! Now why hadn't she thought of that before now? When Julian returned, she would ask him to show her their marriage certificate, then all her doubts would be laid to rest. She need only contain her impatience until tomorrow. Tomorrow. . . . she could never live with this uncertainty for one more night. Damnation! Why hadn't she asked Julian to show her their marriage certificate?

She was smoothing the covers of the bed when the thought struck her. In all likelihood, it was somewhere in the house. It was no great feat of logic to deduce that if it was in the house, Julian would keep it in his desk. That thought quickened her footsteps as she made her way downstairs.

Her steps flagged when she came to the door to Julian's bookroom. She hated to pry into his possessions. It smacked too much of deceit and betrayal, especially if she were found out.

She would not be found out, she told herself, because the first chance she got, she would tell Julian what she had done. And really, there was no shame in it. A woman had a right to look at her own marriage certificate. Resolved, she turned the doorknob and pushed into the room.

The massive walnut desk was a splendid piece of furniture, though rather old-fashioned, a combined bureau and cabinet, and was positioned against the wall between two long windows. The key was in the lock of the cabinet doors, as if to proclaim that the master of the house had nothing to hide here. Serena unlocked the cabinet and gently set the doors back on their hinges. The same key opened the front of the bureau. When she had lowered the front, she stepped back and surveyed the multitude of partitions and drawers that were revealed to her.

She knew at once that this was not Julian's working desk. It was too neat, too much a showpiece. Everything was arranged in perfect symmetry. Her eyes touched on the decorative ivory quill with its matching pen cutter, the precisely placed silver-topped glass inkpots, with matching container for wafers, the ubiquitous china pounce pot. In this neat arrangement, she saw the hand of Julian's housekeeper.

Smiling, she raised her eyes to examine the cabinet above. Her eyes lit up when she observed the ornamental pilasters topped by tiny gilded statues of Greek deities. Every desk she had ever known had a secret compartment.

No one of any intelligence kept valuables or important papers in it. Those were deposited in bank vaults, or with one's solicitor. Marriage certificates and love letters and other things of that nature—things worthless to thieves and robbers—those one kept in the secret compartment of one's desk.

She had to stand on Julian's chair to reach the gilded figures at the top of the pilasters. She tried to twist and turn them every which way, but they were immovable. A decoy, she finally decided, and stepped down from the chair to rethink her strategy. It was then she noticed that on the bases of the pilasters were gilded initials, Julian's initials, a *J* and an *R*, only they were in the wrong order, the *R* on the left pilaster, and the *J* on the right.

Thoroughly engrossed by the puzzle of the desk, she fiddled with the initials. And then she had it! They were keys, only they were in the wrong locks. Working more confidently, she pried the *R* from its socket and gave a crow of triumph when her guess was proved correct. It took only a moment to set Julian's initials in the right order. There was a click, and the pilasters slid out to reveal the secret compartment behind a row of narrow drawers.

It was just as she had anticipated. There was nothing of interest there but her marriage certificate. Smoothing it open, she began to read. Her smile died as she scanned it over and over, unable to believe what she was reading. The names leapt out at her, and with the names came faces, and finally a complete recollection of events. One name drummed inside her head, her own name. Serena Ward. Serena Ward. Serena Ward.

She collapsed in Julian's leather armchair as if she had been knocked into it by a powerful blow to the abdomen. Thoughts were crowding into her head so fast that she could hardly keep pace with them. Julian had engineered the whole thing. Flynn had betrayed her. It was a Fleet marriage. Lord Alistair was an imposter. Julian hated her.

Those thoughts were easier to bear than the ones that followed. As Victoria Noble, she had conducted herself with all the aplomb of a half-witted moonling. Those long, flirtatious looks she had slanted him! Her eagerness for his kisses and caresses! What was the matter with her? True, she had lost her memory, but that was no reason to lose the wits she had been born with. Serena Ward would never have been taken in by a man of Julian Raynor's stamp.

Longing so intense I think I shall die from it. I ache for want of you. Dear God, that could not have been her speaking! The only ache Serena Ward had ever experienced for Julian Raynor was a strong compulsion to knock his head off. Victoria Noble should be locked up in an insane asylum for her own good.

Her face burned with shame. How could this have happened? How could she have tried to seduce him the night before? And she had tried to seduce him. She couldn't lie to herself about that. She had done everything that she could think of to wake him and bring him through that door from the dressing room. She'd opened her window wide and shut it with a snap; she'd cried out as though she had awakened from a vicious nightmare; she'd slammed drawers and thrown her comb and hairbrush against the wall. He'd slept through the whole of it. His snores had been ample proof of that. A fine night nurse he had turned out to be! She could have been overcome with apoplexy, and no one would have been the wiser. Finally, when she had given up in disgust and had stomped downstairs to fetch a glass of milk and a biscuit (when he was the one who was supposed to see to her comfort), the perverse man had come through the door. She groaned when she remembered the way she had acted, coyly inviting him to sit close to her, making sure that her leg brushed against his. And later. . . . No, she wasn't ready to think about later, or she would expire of mortification on the spot. What must he think of her? Oh God, what must he think of her?

"It wasn't me," she said, in the manner of a child caught out in some particularly nasty piece of work. "It was Victoria Noble. She and I are two entirely different people."

She had believed that she was an actress. Actresses did not suffer from prudishness or an excess of scruples. That's why she had not cared whether she was his wife or his mistress. That's why she had acted the coquette with Julian Raynor. Without knowing it, she had been playing a part. And that's why she had been impatient with herself when she could not live up to the role she had assumed. Serena Ward and Victoria Noble had not known of the other's existence, except in a pale shadowy form. Damn Victoria Noble for what she had done!

And damn Julian Raynor! He knew, and he could have stopped her. Instead, he had egged her on, taking advantage of the situation, making her feel things as Victoria Noble that to remember as Serena Ward filled her with d—

Heat. And hot and cold shivers. And an awareness of her body that was almost painful in its intensity. Just thinking about Julian and the way he had touched her, the way he had kissed her, made her ache to experience it all over again. *I ache for want of you.* She must be depraved to feel this way about him, a man who had deceived her and abducted her. She wasn't depraved. It was Victoria Noble who was depraved and so she would tell him if he dared to laugh at her. What did it matter what he thought of her? By the time he returned, she would be long gone.

That thought steadied her, and she was able to leave off her useless self-recriminations to take stock of her position. She was a prisoner here. There was no point in going to Julian's men with long, involved explanations of who she was and how she had been abducted, leastwise, she did not think so. At any rate, she could not take that chance. They were all under the misapprehension that she was his blushing, love-struck bride. They wouldn't be expecting her to creep away in the dead of night. Fine. She would creep away in the dead of night.

That was easier said than done. Even supposing she managed to slip away, she couldn't simply walk all the way to London in the dark. It must be all of nine or ten miles distant. The first thing she must do was reconnoiter, like a general going into battle. Only when she knew the lay of the land would she be in a position to make her plan of escape. She had learned that piece of wisdom from Flynn.

He had abducted her and made her his prisoner. What did he hope to gain by it? Only one thing occurred to her. It had something to do with the escape route. Nothing else made sense. Was he perhaps a government agent? Did he hope to lay a trap for some unsuspecting Jacobite fugitive? Is that why he had confined her here as his prisoner while he went off to do his dastardly work? Without some clue to guide her, she would never solve the puzzle.

Her eyes narrowed as she contemplated Julian's desk. Her conscience no longer bothered her. Drawer by drawer, she went through it systematically. When she found nothing there, she turned her attention to his books. An hour later, she was still none the wiser, except in one small particular. His library was as extensive as any she had ever encountered, especially in the classics section. Though this bore out what Flynn had once told her about Julian's love of books, it gave the lie to what Julian had told her about his early years. Only an educated man would have a library like this. He'd had no formal education beyond the age of thirteen—that's what he'd told her. His story had moved her to tears and to admiration, as he had meant it to. How well he had played her! Her one regret was that she would not be here to see the look on his face when he discovered that she had escaped his net.

A voice in the corridor pulled her from her reflections. Moving quickly, she set Julian's desk to rights. The last thing she did before quitting the room was to slip her marriage certificate into the inside pocket of her petticoat.

Chapter Thirteen

❧❀❧

Serena was lying fully dressed on top of the bed, listening to the storm that raged outside her window when she heard the sudden commotion of doors slamming and voices raised in anger and alarm. Then she heard Julian's voice above the rest, and she came off the bed like a panicked wild thing. Alert now to every sound, every danger, she stood there poised for flight.

Something was wrong. He wasn't due back till tomorrow. She had counted on him not returning until tomorrow. Her plans were set. As soon as the storm abated a little, she was going to slip away. There was a punt concealed in a thicket of bushes close to the river's edge. That punt was to take her downstream, out of Julian's domain, to the Seven Stars tavern, on the next bend in the river. Once there, she would find help.

She'd spent the day plotting and planning, verifying facts with unsuspecting caretakers and stableboys, as she devised a means of escape. Even now, she was fully dressed, her cloak folded over the back of a chair, waiting for the right moment to arrive to set her plan in motion. She had not anticipated this. More doors slammed, then Julian's voice issuing orders rose above the clamor. Moving to the door, she opened it a crack, then slipped through it. After listening for a moment, she edged closer to the balustrade so that she could see the entrance hall below. Men were milling about as two of their comrades used a blanket as a stretcher to carry an injured man through the front doors. The housekeeper, in dressing gown and papers in her hair, was in a flutter, asking questions of all and sundry. A few words of conversation reached Serena's ears. She heard the words *ambush* and *highwaymen,* then Julian's voice again, commanding someone to fetch Dr. Ames. When the hall emptied, Serena returned to her chamber.

She had scarcely closed the door when she heard feet taking the stairs. She gasped in alarm, doused the candles, and quickly threw herself into bed, pulling the covers up to her chin. When the door swung open, and he stood framed in the doorway with a candle in his hand, she blinked rapidly as though coming out of a deep sleep.

The candle cast grotesque shadows. His face was masklike, with huge black sockets where his eyes should have been. She had an impression of cruelty and thoughts so dark and barbarous that she flinched involuntarily.

"Julian?" Her voice was shaking. "What is it? What's happened?"

He was so still, so controlled that she thought her words had not registered. Then the tension across his shoulders relaxed and he said softly, "Nothing of any significance. I should not have disturbed you. Go back to sleep, all right?"

When the door closed and darkness blanketed her, she inhaled a shivery breath. Her thoughts circled and delved, trying to make sense of what was going on. There had been an armed confrontation of some sort. One man was injured. Naturally, they were not going to confide to the housekeeper the nature of that conflict. Highwaymen? She, for one, did not believe it.

Pictures flickered behind her eyes. She saw underground passages and unsuspecting Jacobites trying desperately to fight their way out of a trap. The connections that her mind made—Flynn, Lord Alistair, her own abduction, Julian's abortive trip to London—left her sick and shaken.

* * *

Julian descended the stairs in a meditative frame of mind. He thought it extraordinary that Serena would have slept through so much noise and commotion. He halted with one hand on the banister, half turned to look back over his shoulder, but the housekeeper coming up at that moment to ask where she should set up a bed for the injured man changed the direction of his thoughts.

In the kitchen, the injured groom had been set on a table in anticipation of the doctor's arrival. One of his mates was dosing him with brandy to help ease the pain. Thompson was the only one of the party to be injured in the attack, having taken a bullet in the shoulder almost with the first shot that had been fired. The other men who had made up the convoy had removed their hats and cloaks and were nursing tot glasses of brandy Mrs. Forrest had dispensed.

As was often the case after battle, when the threat of danger was removed, the survivors were making light of their hair-raising experiences.

"England must really be in a bad way," said one, "if our bleeding highwaymen can't make an honest living without having to work on nights like this one."

"Highwaymen? Who says they was highwaymen?" demanded another. "If you wants my opinion, I thinks they was well-breeched lordlings out for a bit of sport."

"What makes you say so?" asked Julian sharply.

"They didn't ask for no money, did they? No, they just came riding hell-bent out of the storm with pistols blazing. And when we returned their fire, they fell back like whipped dogs. Highwaymen has got more spunk."

"They wasn't to know that we were all troopers at one time," said the first voice. "They got more than they bargained for, that's for sure."

Another speaker entered the conversation. "Looks to

me, Joe, that you've been chasing the wrong skirt. Next time, do us all a favor, leave the married ones alone, else you'll get us all killed."

"What, me?" asked Joe innocently. He was a good-looking fellow, in his middle twenties, and was reputed to have a way with the ladies. "You're barking at the moon there, Davie m'boy. It's you married lads who should be looking over your shoulders. I ain't got no wife, see, so there'll be no widow to claim all my worldly goods."

"Yes, well, when you gets spliced you'll discover that your better 'alf spends your money before you gets it, and you still won't 'ave no worldly goods to leave when you kicks the bucket."

This sally brought forth muted guffaws of laughter. There was more in this vein, most of it an attempt to keep the injured man from dwelling on his troubles. Only with the doctor's arrival did the men make a move to return to their own quarters in the stable block.

Another hour was to pass before all was quiet in the house. A bed had been set up for Thompson in a small anteroom off the back parlor, close to the Forrests' quarters. Julian was the only person in the house who was still up and about. He was too wound up to seek his bed, his mind teeming with unanswered questions about the odd attack that had taken place when they were no more than a mile from home.

Highwaymen? Well-breeched lordlings? And if not, who else could it be? Ensconced in his favorite armchair in the library, he stretched out his long booted legs, resting them on the brass fender. In one hand, he held a glass of brandy from which he occasionally imbibed.

If they were highwaymen, why hadn't they commanded them to hand over their valuables? Coming up with no answer to this, he moved on to the next hypothesis. Well-heeled lordlings out for a bit of sport? He hardly thought so. This attack did not have the feel of mischief-making, not when firing pieces were involved. There had been something vicious about it, as though their object was . . . what? Murder? But who would wish to see him dead? Who would profit by it?

Leaving aside these fruitless conjectures for the moment, he retraced in his mind the day's events as if the answer was to be found there. On arriving in town, he'd made his first port of call his solicitor's office. He was now a married man, and he'd wanted to set his affairs in order. There were settlements to be arranged, and a will to be drawn up, and things of that nature. His next stop had been Ward House, to confer with Flynn. By Julian's reckoning, there had been more than enough time for Jeremy Ward to complete his business in France, and he meant to discover the reason for the delay.

Taking a long swallow from the glass in his hand, he rolled his neck on the backrest of his chair and closed his eyes as he contemplated the ambiguity of his position. On the one hand, he deemed it his duty to inform his wife's male relations of his marriage to Serena before they learned of it from another source. Whether or not they regarded him as a rogue and an upstart carried no weight with him. In his own mind, he had taken the only honorable course.

On the other hand, he was quietly plotting to bring his wife's father to ruin. That, too, was a matter of honor. He would not allow that his marriage to Serena was inconsistent with his purpose. It was mere chance that she happened to be the daughter of the man whom he was bound and determined would pay for his crimes. Not even for Serena's sake would he be deflected from bringing retribution down on Sir Robert's head. This was not revenge; this was justice.

For some few minutes, his thoughts dwelled on Serena.

Not liking his speculations, he turned them once more to his interview with Flynn.

There was no news of Sir Robert, Flynn had told him. In truth, Flynn was surprised to see him. As he pointed out, a scant fortnight had passed since Jeremy and Clive Ward had set off to fetch Sir Robert home. There could be any number of reasons for the delay, if delay it was. Sir Robert was known to be in poor health. Weather conditions in the English Channel were notoriously unpredictable, etc., etc., etc. And with that, Julian had to be satisfied.

"Now tell me 'ow Serena is going on," said Flynn at one point.

Julian did, making light of Serena's accident and subsequent concussion. The last thing he wanted was for Flynn to go chasing out to Twickenham to make sure she was well. Serena was now his responsibility, and he would allow no man to come between them.

Flynn's shrewd eyes held Julian's in a long stare. "Mmm," he'd said, "so she's giving you a spot of bother, is she? Well, that don't surprise me none. I told you 'ow it would be. If you wants my advice, you'll show 'er straight off that you means to be master in your own 'ouse. Just so long as I ain't there to see it, that is, else there's no saying what I might do."

And with those cheerful words ringing in his ears, Julian left him. His last order of business was a delicate one.

One by one, he'd called on several female acquaintances in order to end his connection to them, in case they had not already grasped that he was no longer interested. When he decided to set his affairs in order, he did not spare himself.

All the same, he was only human. It would have taken a better man than he not to suffer a few pangs of regret when confronted by those scantily clad temptresses in the privacy of their boudoirs. Cherry Marshall for one; Lady Amelia for another. His carefree bachelor life had never looked more alluring to him. Somehow he managed to extricate himself with nothing more serious than payment of the obligatory trinkets and a few enjoyable kisses. Very enjoyable kisses.

You degenerate! he chided himself. *What would Serena think if she knew about those kisses?* His unrepentant grin gradually faded as other thoughts intruded. Even now he knew of a score of beds with willing women in them, where he would receive a warm welcome. Victoria's bed was one of them. He wasn't sure about Serena's bed, and Serena's bed was the only bed he wanted to be in.

He drained his drink, then stared absently at the bottom of his empty glass. What the devil had induced him to attempt that long ride home in the dark with only grooms for protection? He'd made the decision on the spur of the moment. Once back in his gaming house, he had wandered restlessly from room to room until he had run across Lord Kirkland in the reading room.

The earl beckoned Julian over. "Well, you got your wish, and Sir Robert got his pardon."

Making light of it, Julian replied, "The report is that you put in a good word for him. But I understood you were not in favor of amnesty for Sir Robert."

A sly look crept into the earl's eyes. "I thought about what you said, and revised my opinion. Oh, we d-don't expect Sir Robert to turn coat, in spite of his oath of allegiance to the Crown. No. What we decided was we'd rather have him where we can k-keep an eye on him. He won't be able to blow his nose but we shall hear of it."

Laughing, Julian had turned away, and his eyes had locked with the hostile stare of Lord Charles Tremayne. Lord Charles looked away first. Julian didn't feel hostile. He was amused. Lord Charles was Catherine Ward's most devoted admirer. In his determination to approach Serena, Julian had paid court to Catherine, and Lord Charles had not liked it, not one bit. Julian could almost feel sorry for him. He would have no joy there. Catherine Ward was in love with her own husband.

This thought had made him restless again, and on impulse, he had decided to make for Twickenham. Since the ride home had been unpremeditated, why did he have the uncanny feeling that the attack on him tonight was a deliberate attempt on his life? His assailants could not have been lying in wait for him, since they could not have foreseen that he would return sooner than he had meant to. Had they followed him all the way out of town? And if they were not highwaymen, then who were they? Who had a motive to kill him?

Outside the window, a bolt of lightning streaked across the sky, followed almost instantaneously by an earth-shattering thunderclap. Rising leisurely, Julian ambled to the window and looked out. It was as black as pitch. He was on the point of turning aside when the landscape was illumined as though a thousand rockets had exploded overhead, affording him a clear view of the lawns and river. For the space of several seconds he saw it—a figure on the riverbank, a woman, he thought, attempting to launch a small boat. Then darkness blotted out the light.

He must be seeing things. No one, least of all a woman, would launch a boat on a night like this, unless that woman was desperate to escape something or someone. No sooner had the thought occurred to him than he had grabbed a candle and was sprinting for the stairs.

Though her bed was rumpled, the room was unoccupied. Without stopping his momentum, he flung into the dressing room. There was no sign of Serena. A plethora of thoughts burst through his mind, allowing free rein to every suspicion he had ever entertained. Like a statue, he stood there frozen, and then, with a muffled curse, he was off and running.

He descended the stairs two at a time. Though he could hear the Forrests stirring in the back of the house, he didn't wait. He grabbed his cloak from the chair in the vestibule and pushed through the front door.

"Serena!" The rain drowned the sound of his cry.

He dashed across the turf toward the river. "Serena!" He was bellowing at the top of his lungs, his heart pounding against his ribs. As his long strides covered the distance to the river, his thoughts scourged him, taunting him with his stupidity. He'd been too complacent, too sure of himself. He should have warned his men that behind his wife's artless looks and innocent smiles she was a scheming bitch. She was a Ward. He, of all people, should have known what to expect.

Fear and anger ripped through him, making him tremble. He had set a dozen guards to watch her. Where the devil were they? As for Serena, did she fear him so much that she would risk life and limb to escape him? She must think that she had good reason to fear him.

"Serena!" he roared. "For God's sake, answer me."

Providence rewarded that call with a flash of forked lightning. It streaked across the sky, and for one heart-wrenching moment, Julian had a clear view of her. She was in the boat, well downstream, and using a long pole to steer her small craft clear of rocks and river debris.

What the hell was she doing? Didn't she know that she was in a punt? She would never keep that small craft steady in this kind of weather.

Torn between rousing his men and going after her at once, he stood on the riverbank. Cursing the fates, cursing himself, and most of all, cursing Serena, he ran to the dock where the boats were moored.

Serena, oblivious of Julian's pursuit, peered into the

murky darkness, scanning the water ahead for obstacles. It was no use. She could hardly see her hand in front of her face. Even the shore had receded behind a screen of rain. This was not how she had imagined it would be; this was not the Thames she knew. There were no other boats on the river, no watermen calling out friendly greetings, no lights winking at her across the water to give her her bearings. She might have been traversing the river Styx in the Underworld.

Shuddering in spite of the humidity, pulling the hood of her cloak forward to protect her face from the sheet rain, she tried to beat back the panic that threatened to engulf her. When she had launched the punt, she'd almost had a change of heart. Only a fool would be out on the river in this kind of weather. The alternative was unthinkable. She could not, dare not face Julian, or at least, not the man who had entered her chamber with a candle in his hand. She had sensed that something wild and savage lurked just below the surface of that harshly handsome face, something cold and infinitely unpredictable. She couldn't explain her feelings. Instinct had taken over, warning her that she stood in the greatest peril of her life.

This was panic, she tried to tell herself. This was irrational. Julian was devious, but he was not dangerous. Or was he? If he were a government agent trying to infiltrate their little network, he was not merely dangerous, he was lethal.

She wasn't sure how long she had been moving downstream when she became conscious that hers was not the only boat on the river. There was someone behind her, someone following her, someone in hot pursuit. She could hear his oars dipping and rising as the boat gained on her, could hear the sound of a man's harsh breathing as he labored to overtake her. She closed her eyes momentarily as alarm shivered through her. He would never give up, never permit her to escape him now.

Luck was with her. In true Stygian fashion, vapor rising from the river, a sudden heat haze, closed around her, enveloping her like a shroud.

"Serena!"

Julian's voice. She checked the sudden sob that rose in her throat. Her breath was coming so hard and fast, she was sure he must hear it.

There was an ominous crack as her boat jolted and came to a shuddering halt. Heart pounding in alarm, Serena half rose to her feet. Edging her way forward, with hands outstretched, she reached out to feel the obstacle that was impeding her progress. She couldn't believe what her hands told her. Her boat had drifted to the riverbank where it had become lodged in the branches of an overhanging tree. She cried out as wet tendrils grazed her face, then subsided when she found herself clutching the drooping branches of a weeping willow.

"Now I've got you!" cried Julian.

As he reached out to grasp Serena's boat, she scrambled up and leapt for the bank. Her knees took the brunt of her fall, but she scarcely felt the pain. Hauling herself up, she spun quickly to ward off any attack.

Now that he didn't have to worry about her safety, a cold, murderous rage settled over him. "You little bitch!" he said. "You scheming, murderous little bitch!"

She backed away. "No," she said. "No."

At that moment electrifying fire ruptured the darkness. Ducking under his arm, Serena bolted.

Pausing for neither puddles nor the sting of rain on her cheeks, ignoring the squish of water in her boots, she hared along the riverbank. Once or twice, she changed direction, just to throw him off the scent. Whenever she stumbled, which she did frequently, she picked herself up and forced herself to go on. Soon, her breath was wheezing in and out of her lungs; there was a stitch in her side, and her wet garments were sticking to her like a coat of wet plaster.

When she came to a wooden footbridge, she stopped to catch her breath. The mist had thinned out at this point, and she looked around, trying to get her bearings. She'd thought she was following the river downstream. It came to her then that in her panicked, headlong flight, she had lost direction. She could be anywhere, and in that Stygian darkness, there were no landmarks to guide her.

Lifting her head, she listened intently. She heard nothing but the hiss of the rain. Though there was no sound of pursuit, it never once crossed her mind that he would give up the chase. She had to go on.

On either side of the path, dark stands of trees stood out like impenetrable prison walls. She had almost made up her mind to turn aside and find a thicket in which to hide, when she came out of the mist and caught the glow of a light way off in the distance. A great gasp of thankfulness shuddered through her. Throwing back her hood, unmindful of the sting of rain on her cheeks, she blinked as she tried to focus her eyes on that small welcoming gleam.

"Don't stop now," he said, right at her back. "We're almost there."

With a sob, she pivoted, swinging at him wildly with her balled fist. Her movement was anticipated. His hand caught that flailing arm and yanked on it, and she was lifted high off her feet to be hoisted over his shoulder. Her blows had no effect on him. Then her struggles ceased as she heard the crash of his boot against wood, and he maneuvered her through an open doorway.

When he set her roughly on her feet, she stumbled back against what appeared to be a table. As she stood there shivering, the dank air closed around her. The darkness was so profound that not even a shadow was discernible. No shadow was necessary. All her senses had come alive. She was aware of his presence, aware of the heat of his body and every breath he drew, but most of all, she was aware of the barely leashed violence.

There was a thunk as a bolt was shot home, then he was striking flint to tinder, and in short order, a lamp was lit. They were in a huge, dilapidated barn that seemed to be part workshop. Bits and pieces of machinery—axles, wheels, and things Serena could not name—were propped against the walls. Off to one side was a mound of straw. Her eyes absorbed everything in one lightning glance before fixing on the cold-eyed man who advanced to within a few steps of her. It wasn't courage that rooted her to the spot, but blind instinct. One hand curled around the hard edge of the table for support.

Wild. Dangerous. Reckless. She trembled as other more menacing impressions pressed in upon her. Something savage and primitive beyond knowing had been loosed in him. She didn't trust that cold mask of civility, that air of careful indifference. The man was like a sleeping volcano waiting to erupt.

"It would have been wiser," he said, "if I had made you my mistress and not my wife."

"I might have had something to say about that." Though her head was thrown back defiantly, inwardly she was quaking.

A bitter smile played across his face. "How did you arrange it—that's what I can't understand."

She moistened her lips. "What are you talking about?"

"Give it up, Serena. You know very well I'm talking about the attack on me tonight."

"Attack? I know nothing of an attack."

Her eyes darted to the barred door.

"Try to escape me," he said in a voice curiously devoid of the fury she knew consumed him, "and I shall make you sorry that you were ever born. Now, shall we begin at the beginning? How did you arrange it? Who was your accomplice? You will observe that my mind has not been idle. I know that there must have been an accomplice."

"How could I have arranged anything? There was no reason to. I thought I was Victoria Noble, or have you forgotten?"

He shook his head, laughing softly. "Now that was a brilliant ploy, and I freely admit it. You had us all duped and unsuspecting as sheep. What did you do—seduce one of my own men into becoming your messenger?"

More rash than wise, she shot back, "It's what I should have done, what I would have done if I had been in my right mind, you . . . you unprincipled spy!"

His smile terrified her. "Serena, you have gone your length. You shouldn't have run away. By that one injudicious act, you betrayed yourself."

She looked at him, at the hard, unyielding set of his features, the diabolical half-smile, and every muscle in her body contracted painfully. Her mind began to grapple with a way of escaping him.

Turning into the table she was leaning against, as though suddenly overcome with weariness, she said plaintively, "This is so unjust. I am the one who has been wronged. I was the one who was abducted and held against her will." As she spoke, she used the sodden folds of her cloak to conceal the movement of her hand as she felt around on the flat of the table for a tool, anything she could use as a weapon. Her fingers closed around a smooth length of iron, and she nestled it in her palm.

For a moment, uncertainty clouded his eyes, then the ice returned to them. "Enough of this," he said. "Tell me what I wish to know or I shall beat it out of you."

As his hands reached for her, she took a quick step back and struck out at him blindly. He tried to dodge the blow and it caught him squarely on the chest. She heard the thud of that blow, then his gasp as he sagged against the table. Glancing at the hammer in her hand, with a cry of horror, she threw it on the flagstoned floor. When he cursed her and made a move to straighten, she dashed for the door. It took only a moment to slide back the bolt. Without a second's thought, she burst through that door and took off like a fox with the hounds on her heels.

He immediately came after her. She had barely time to cry out before he had caught her and was lifting her high against his chest, with one arm curved under her knees.

Her head fell back against his shoulder, and his mouth seized hers in a brutal, punitive kiss. Head swimming, breath rasping painfully in her chest, she made a feeble effort to defend herself. Her resistance was met by a fiercer pressure on her lips, making it almost impossible for her to breathe.

When he lifted his head, his breathing was harsh and uneven. "You may yet succeed in your goal. But by God, if you are to become a widow, you'll know what it is to be a wife."

Turning on his heel, he strode for the barn and carried her over the threshold.

Chapter Fourteen

✤

All the fight had gone out of her. It was more than exhaustion. She feared him as she feared the storm. Neither reason nor resistance could prevail against him in this mood. Strangely, when that thought took hold, her panic ebbed and an odd anticipation shivered through her.

Feeling herself slip, she reached for his shoulders. He made a sound, something hoarse and guttural under his breath, and her eyes lifted to meet his. He took her lips again in another punishing kiss. This time, she did not try to fight him. From the deepest reaches of her feminine psyche came knowledge as old as time. Her lips softened, absorbing the fierce pressure of his.

When he raised his head, his voice was hard and unyielding. "That won't work with me either," he said. "Not now. You've left it too late."

There was a moment when it seemed as though he were waiting for her to answer him. When she said nothing, he adjusted her in his arms and, with a muffled oath, carried her to the pile of hay. Depositing her none too gently, he threw himself down beside her.

Rain and wind lashed the small windowpanes, making them rattle. Her own heart seemed to accelerate and beat in frantic counterpoint. When lightning and thunder suddenly erupted overhead, she cried out in terror and turned in to him.

Breath mingled with breath. For long, long minutes, they remained as they were, lips almost touching, skin heating, chests rising and falling as awareness grew in them. The genesis of the mad chase which had led them to this place and this point in time receded to the periphery of conscious thought, but the powerful emotions which had been loosed in them were still at work, seeking an outlet.

"I won't let you go," he said, "so don't ask me to."

"I . . ." She stared at him helplessly as she groped for words.

Whatever she was going to say, he didn't want to hear it. He couldn't stop now, wouldn't stop now. She'd kept him at bay for too long. He wasn't thinking only of the week she had spent under his roof as his wife. His frustration went further back than that, to the morning after he had first taken her, when he'd awakened in anticipation of only God knew what to find a virago in his bed.

From that day to this, he'd burned for her. He'd never denied it. And whatever scruples or curbs had held him in check no longer seemed to be there. The attack on his life, the chase, his fear for her safety, the violence of his emotions when she had turned on him—all these things had loosed the fragile controls of whatever it was that kept him civilized. Something dark and primitive moved in him, something that in his saner moments would have appalled him. He didn't want to hurt her. He wasn't going to force her against her will. What he was experiencing went deeper than lust to possess her woman's body. He wanted everything from her, and he couldn't explain what he meant, not even to himself.

"Julian, I—"

"No!" he said fiercely, cutting off her words. When he pressed down on her, Serena was driven back against the soft bed of hay. Her cry of alarm was caught by his lips and washed back into her throat. As his hold tightened, and his kiss consumed her, she clenched and unclenched her hands around the powerful corded muscles of his arms, trying to steady herself. It was some time before it was borne in on Julian that she wasn't fighting him and that his ardent attempts to kiss her into submission were unnecessary. Surrender. He could taste it on her lips, feel it in the soft and supple fit of her body against his.

When he released her mouth, he caught her to him, supporting her with one arm around her shoulders, and he buried his face in her hair. "I can't let you go," he said, repeating what he had told her earlier, only this time pleading with her. "If I can't have you now, I think I shall go insane. Serena, be generous, give in to me?"

As his words washed over her, her limbs gradually went lax. He wasn't the only one who would go insane. The events of that night had taken their toll on her too. She couldn't find the strength to fight him, didn't want to fight him. Something else was at work in her now, not passion, not desire, but some deep well of emotion that responded to everything that was masculine in his nature. *Julian,* she thought, half despairing, half in awe, *only Julian.*

He drew her closer, gathering her into the shelter of his body. "Don't say anything. I don't want to talk. I don't want to think. I want . . . I must . . . don't fight me. Please, don't fight me."

She didn't assist him when he removed her cloak, but neither did she resist him. He quickly dispensed with the rest of her garments, then began on his own. His hands were shaking.

Outside, the storm waxed wild and furious, as though a great battle raged around them. Lightning, thunderclaps, the hiss of the rain—Serena closed her eyes as the fury of the storm found an answering beat in the throb of her own body. Then she was aware only of Julian as he rose above her.

He was the only storm that counted—hadn't she always known it? Dangerous. Reckless. Wild. Only a fool would try to hold back the elements. The thought made her tremble, not in fear, but in excitement and anticipation. Her hands ran up his shoulders, locking behind his neck. He made a small sound, part pain, part protest. Raising her head, she crushed her mouth to his. His whole body jolted.

This is what he'd wanted from her, not submission, not acceptance, but passion as unbridled and desperate as his own. Beneath his hands, her body trembled. Her skin was hot and damp. His head swam with the scent of her, wild poppies and something dark and sensual that was uniquely her own. Lifting her to him, he began an intimate exploration with lips and tongue, claiming possession of what belonged to him. No one else had ever touched her like this. No one else ever would. She was his and his alone.

Her body was like molten wax. Her skin was on fire. She was drowning in sensation. Whatever he asked of her, she gave him without reserve. Modesty and shame no longer applied. Her movements became more rhythmic, more instinctive as she arched and writhed, enticing him to abandon his control.

Her small sobs of helpless need made him wild to take her. Savage. Potent. Primitive. It had never been like this before. He was a man of experience. He'd thought he had known everything there was to know about passion and pleasure. She was the first woman, the very first woman who had ever aroused him not merely to passion and a pleasuring of the senses, but to brand her irrevocably with the mark of his possession. When this was over, she would know to whom she belonged.

When his fingers slipped inside her and he felt the slickness of her tight sheath, he closed his eyes against the violent surge of lust that leapt in his blood. Though she was ready for him, he would hurt her if he took her the way he wanted to. He was too big, too strong.

"Easy," he said. He stilled her movements with the press of his weight.

She didn't want his restraint. She wanted his power and virility. Poised on ripple after ripple of suspended pleasure, she gasped his name, not once but several times. Pleading, begging with him, her voice throbbing with the force of her passion, she drove him to flash point.

Beyond reason, beyond thought, he thrust into her. Gasping, they both stilled. Arms bulging with strain, he slowly raised himself higher, relentlessly embedding himself deep in her body. His voice was low and harsh when he told her what he wanted from her. When she locked her limbs around him, he shook with the effort to tame the savage in him. She moved, and his control disintegrated. Rearing back, he plunged into her, taking her in hard violent thrusts, riding her in a frenzy of motion, emptying himself in a flood of pleasure.

She clung to him helplessly, glorying in the wildness in him. She wanted this, wanted him like this. She held the thought in that part of her brain that was still capable of reason, then she abandoned herself to the storm in all its primitive splendor.

When she awakened, she had an appalling sense of déjà vu. She opened her eyes slowly. From a few inches away, Julian's eyes glittered back at her. Inhaling sharply, she pulled herself up. She turned abruptly to look at the window. Though the storm had abated, it was still a long way from dawn.

She brushed back tangles of hair that fell across her face. The movement made her aware that she was naked. Pulling her knees up, she hugged them to her, covering her nakedness as best she might. Finally, steeling herself to look down at him, she said uneasily, "What is this place?"

Julian had been waiting for this moment to arrive, and had made up his mind that there would be no repetition of the first time she had awakened in his bed. At that time, he had been made to feel the villain of the piece and Serena, naturally, had made herself out to be his victim. This time he was not going to allow her to put him in the wrong.

"I thought that would be obvious. It's a disused barn that stands on my property." When she frowned, he nodded. "Yes, we are on my estate. Last night in the dark we came full circle, you see."

At the mention of last night, she made a movement to rise, but Julian was ready for her. His arm circled her waist, preventing her escape.

"You, Flynn, Lord Alistair," she railed, struggling in earnest to free herself, "you are all in this together."

He hauled himself up. "Last night, you didn't want to talk," he said, "and neither did I. There are things between us, I know, that must be settled, but not now, not at this precise moment. We shall talk later, a long time later. Give me one day, Serena, that's all I ask, one day before we allow the past to catch up with us. What difference can one day make? Will it change the attack on me that took place last night? Will it change the fact that our Fleet marriage is now a real one? You know it won't. What have we to lose by taking one day for ourselves?"

His voice was very low, very earnest, and very soothing. She couldn't think when his hands were brushing over her bare arms, sensitizing her skin. "But . . ." She mustn't give in to him. She had to find out what was happening with the escape route.

"We can't leave just yet, even if we wanted to. Our garments are soaked through. Besides, it will be hours before dawn. We can't traipse around the countryside in the dead of night."

He could sense her indecision. His lips took the place of his fingers, and warm, wet kisses dewed her throat, the slope of her shoulders, the rise of one breast. "Say yes, Serena," he said softly, "say yes to me. Say yes."

He tipped up her chin and breathed the word into her mouth, his lips moving on hers as though he were teaching a child to speak. "Yes," he said. "It's not hard to say. What is it, love? Why won't you give in to me? Didn't you find pleasure in my arms last night?"

"Last night," she began, meaning to say something of great import. The thought she wanted to hold slipped away from her as his words painted pictures inside her head. Last night in his arms, she'd found more pleasure than she'd ever dreamed of.

His tongue slipped between her lips and ran over the edges of her teeth. "Yes," he said. "I want to hear you say it."

"Yes," she said, closing her eyes. "Yes."

He shook her awake. "Why? Why did you say yes to me?"

"Because . . . because you make me feel things I don't want to feel."

He smiled enigmatically. "Do I, love?" He took one of her arms and draped it around his neck. He waited a moment. When she did not pull away from him, he let out a careful breath. "You have the same effect on me." But not this time, he cautioned himself. This time he was determined to restrain himself until she had conceded a few points. Major points.

The air froze in her lungs as he took the weight of one breast into his cupped palm. Everything in her melted with need.

"Julian," she got out on a shivery sigh. "Please."

He searched her face, absorbing the change in her. Her eyes were unfocused, her lips were parted. He could hear the little hiatus in her breathing as she strove to regulate it. As ever with Serena, when she could not quite grasp something, her brows were knit in a faint frown.

With infinite care, he squeezed one swollen nipple between thumb and forefinger. She gasped and brought her other arm up, draping it around his neck as her head lolled on his shoulder.

"This is awkward," he said. "Here, let me make you comfortable." He was very careful to keep her distracted with one hand caressing her breasts while he used his other hand to hint her into position. "That's better," he said. His back was propped against the wall of the barn. Her thighs were spread on either side of his flanks. Nothing protected her from the avid jut of his sex. It was some minutes before he was able to find his voice.

"Explain something to me," he said. "Why do you always fight me before you surrender, yes, and afterward too?"

He knew at once that he had said a bad word. Her head jerked back and her eyes widened then slowly narrowed as she tried to focus on him. "Surrender?" she said. "Surrender?"

He was nothing if he was not devious. He thought he had a right to be. She had put him through hell. As she made to get off him, he slid one finger inside the folds of her femininity, parting her, but not entering her deeply. Her hands convulsed around his neck and she reared up on her knees, head flung back.

"Julian," she gasped. "Ah . . . Julian."

He didn't stop what he was doing. "Yes, love, 'surrender.' I like it when you give in to me. Don't you like it when I give in to you?"

She sounded as though she were in agony. "And I detest . . . ah . . . Julian . . . don't."

He laughed softly. "You were saying? You detest?"

"I detest men who . . ." She went boneless and melted against him.

"Who . . . ? I really want to know."

He wasn't paying close attention to the conversation, such as it was. Triumph was rampant, making his blood sing. This wasn't the sweet and easy Victoria who was on fire for him. This was Serena, his haughty, prim-as-a-Puritan little prude who could cut a man down to size with one of her cool stares. And this time, he hadn't fallen on her with all the impetuosity of a rampaging bull. He was taking her slowly, building the hunger in her, in his determination to prove to himself if not to her that she was anything but indifferent to him.

He moved her slightly, so that he had access to her breasts. With tongue and teeth, he toyed with her nipples. His fingers were drenched with her woman's essence. He couldn't go on like this for much longer. He was ready to explode.

He pulled back to study her. Her skin was slick where his mouth had touched her. Her glorious blond hair fell in a veil around her face. Her limbs were sleek, and beautifully proportioned. Her full breasts were rising and falling as she labored to draw breath into her lungs. He had reduced her to a caldron of seething need. Good. It was about time that she experienced a little of what he had been made to suffer.

Her eyes opened and stared deeply into his. ". . . men who try to master me," she said.

"What?" He'd forgotten what they were talking about.

So had she, but the words came automatically. "I detest men who try to master me."

Her words reminded him that there was a purpose to

seducing her. Though talking was the last thing he wanted now, he fought the beast in him and managed to anchor his hands safely to her shoulders, urging her down on her haunches so that they were eye to eye. When she came to herself, he said sincerely though not quite truthfully, "I have never wanted to master you. As though I could! As though you would let me! That is not surrender."

"No?"

"No. Surrender is admitting that you want *this*"—his hands swept over her from breast to thigh—"as much as I do. You were made for this, made for me. You surrender to me. I surrender to you. In the act of love between a man and a woman, anything less is ugly and unacceptable."

He breathed deeply. "You told me once that you experienced only disgust and loathing when I made love to you. You implied that I had taken you by force. Does this feel like disgust and loathing, Serena?" He flexed his fingers deep inside her. "Does this feel as though I am forcing you?"

She blinked at him like a sleepy kitten coming awake. Though her body was in an agony of suspense for the completion that only he could give her, she sensed something behind the harsh words that roused her from her inertia. Those careless words she had uttered in anger had made a deep impression on him. They had done more than that. They had cut him to the quick.

Moving closer, she kissed him lingeringly. "I lied," she murmured against his lips. "You have never forced yourself on me. I never thought of you with disgust and loathing, *never*. I was ashamed of what you made me feel."

"But why should you be ashamed?"

"You were a stranger. I thought that no decent woman

would feel the way you made me feel. So I blamed you for it. Can you ever forgive me?"

A shudder passed over him then another. His eyes closed. "I have been in purgatory. I didn't know . . . I could not be sure." Teeth gritted, he said, "Your opinion of me could not have been lower than my own."

"Oh Julian, I'm so sorry. What can I say? If only there was something I could do to make it up to you."

His eyes opened wide. "Oh, there is," he said savagely, and reached for her.

Julian's men found them at first light. Having slept for only an hour or two, Serena was not at her radiant best. She slapped Julian's hands away when he tried to waken her. Those hands were ruthless, insistent, hauling her upright, dressing her when all she wanted was to sink into sleep. Those hands took liberties that in her saner moments would have outraged her modesty. She was aware that they had slipped beneath her bodice to knead her bare breasts. Those delicious feelings were beginning to steal over her again. It was lovely.

"Damn! I can't get enough of you."

She pouted when he withdrew his hands, but she made no verbal protest. With a little sigh, she cushioned her head on his broad chest. In the next instant, she was shaken rudely awake.

"I found this on the floor. Would you mind explaining how our marriage certificate came to be in your possession, and what you intended to do with it?"

It was his tone of voice that made her thoughts focus. Staring at the piece of paper he waved under her nose, she shrugged helplessly. "What does it matter now? Our marriage is a real one, isn't it, Julian?"

"It most certainly is." He folded the parchment and pocketed it. "I think it's wiser if I hold on to this."

"Fine," she said, and closed her eyes.

"Serena!" Laughter with a touch of impatience edged his voice. "It's time to be on our way. Now go and do whatever is necessary to make a lady comfortable before we embark in our waiting carriage."

When she came out of the privy he had led her to, she stood uncertainly, swaying on her feet. Julian's arms went about her, enveloping her in his warm cloak. Laughing, he kissed the pout from her lips then lifted her high against his chest.

In the coach, he watched her eyelids grow heavy the moment before her eyes lost focus and her eyelashes fluttered down, shutting him out. He had done this to her, worn her out with his voracious demands in a long night of loving. Far from chastening him, the thought made him smile.

It was the irony which amused him. He'd always thought of himself as a virile, passionate man, with a healthy sexual appetite. Serena had taught him a thing or two. He had learned that all these years he hadn't understood what passion was. With the right woman, with Serena, his sexual appetite was insatiable. He couldn't get enough of her, couldn't stop touching her, couldn't stop wanting her. It had never been like this before, and if there had only been more time, he was quite sure he would have taken her here, in the coach. And she would let him! That was the thought that kept his body hard with need. One touch from him and his little prude turned wanton.

He had asked for one day, just for themselves. He was bound and determined that one day would stretch into years. He'd made a beginning. It was entirely possible that he had fathered his child on her, and even if he had not, he knew how to get around Serena. He would chain her to him with the powerful sexual magnetism that he had proved existed between them. She might not like it; she might try to resist it; but he was more experienced than she. If it became necessary, he would not hesitate to use his experience against her.

It was inevitable that once she knew the truth about him, her trust would suffer a setback. Whether or not she would choose her own father over him was only of academic interest. She was his wife. His claims would be upheld in every court in the land. She would never escape him.

He wasn't a cold-blooded monster, Julian assured himself. He had almost made up his mind that Sir Robert's punishment would not be made to last forever. In due course, for Serena's sake, he would rescue him, but not before Sir Robert feared the worst, not before he'd had a taste of his own medicine. There could, of course, be no reconciliation. There could never be anything but hatred between Sir Robert and himself. Once the truth was out, he would carry Serena off to some far place where they could make a fresh start, out of her father's sphere of influence.

From there, his thoughts shifted to the attack that had taken place the night before. He didn't know what to make of it, but in the cold light of day, his conviction that Serena might have had something to do with it wavered.

He shifted her in his arms so that her head lolled back on his shoulder. She nestled against him trustingly, with the innocence of a child. He was still gazing at her reflectively when the coach pulled up outside the door of his house.

Julian left Serena sleeping like a babe while he went to check on his injured groom. Satisfied that he was progressing as well as could be expected, Julian had his housekeeper prepare breakfast for himself and serve it in the bookroom.

Not long after, the courier arrived from his gaming house with a full and detailed account from Blackie, Julian's second-in-command, of the night's takings. This time he had something for the courier to give to Blackie.

His marriage certificate was in a very sorry state. One corner was torn and there were several watermarks scattered over it. He grinned, thinking that it was too soon to say whether Serena would awaken in a temper and tear the house apart looking for this innocuous piece of parchment, or whether she would awaken reconciled to her fate.

Making an envelope of a page of vellum, he slipped the marriage certificate inside and closed the package with melted wax which he imprinted with his own seal.

"Give this to Mr. Black and tell him to deposit it in the safe," he told the courier. Morland, the courier, had undertaken many such commissions for Julian, and Julian had complete confidence in him. The same could be said for his confidence in Blackie. He would do exactly as Julian asked him to do and no questions asked.

Thinking of the attack of the night before, Julian sent two of his grooms with Morland as armed escorts. Not that he expected trouble in broad daylight. He had yet to report the attack to the local authorities. This he was reluctant to do until he had questioned Serena on her part in things.

Wandering upstairs some time later, he entered Serena's bedchamber. She was still sleeping like a babe. He traced a finger over her lips. Had she had something to do with the attack on him last night? What he refused to believe was that she had meant to do him serious injury.

There would be no plotting against him from now on. She was his wife, and her first loyalty was to him. Damn loyalty! He wanted more from her than that.

Serena awakened with the throb of desire beating hotly in her blood. She had a flash of awareness, then all her senses focused on Julian's hands as they roused her to passion. She sobbed his name, then gasped on a wave of pleasure as he entered her. Surging wildly, clinging to him, she went spinning into the void.

She jerked up from the pillows on a jolt of alarm. Some noise had startled her into wakefulness, something that made the fine hairs on her nape stand on end. Her eyes darted around the room, trying to get a grip on things. She was alone in her bed; darkness had fallen and the only light came from a lone candle on the mantelpiece.

There came a thud, and the sound of breaking glass followed by a shout that was abruptly cut off. Swiftly rising, she reached for her dressing robe and slipped into it, then, snatching up the silver candlestick, shielding the flame with one hand, she rushed from the room.

At the turn in the stairs, she halted. The great hall was ablaze with lights. Several soldiers in red coats were hustling a man out the door. Others were helping comrades who were sprawled on the floor, as though they had taken a beating. The Forrests were off to one side, Mrs. Forrest clasped in her husband's arms. The scene was ghastly and like something out of a stage performance or a nightmare.

The man who was flanked by two militiamen moaned and made a feeble attempt to shake them off. "Julian!" Serena cried out, and quickly depositing her candle on a table, she started forward.

At the sound of her voice, men turned to stare at her. It was then that she saw that Julian was manacled. His head was bowed, and one arm of his white lawn shirt had been practically torn off.

"Julian!"

She came to within a pace of him when one of the

militiamen raised his pistol and ordered her to stand back. Julian lifted his head and she flinched from what she saw there. Blood dripped from a cut on his lip. Murder was in his eyes.

"Bitch!" he snarled at her. "Scheming bitch!"

Serena fell back a step. Frozen in shock, she stood there staring as the soldiers turned to leave, dragging Julian with them. Then, panic-stricken, she went after them.

Outside, all was in shadow, but she could make out the shapes of horses and riders.

"Wait!" she called out as men mounted up. "What has he done? Where are you taking him?"

It was Julian's voice, malevolent and ghostly, that came to her out of the shadows. "I promise you, you haven't seen the last of me! And when we do meet up again, you'll rue—"

There was a soft thud, and his voice suddenly died. Terror-struck, she bolted forward, only to be dragged back by strong hands on her shoulders. Like a wild thing, she fought to free herself.

"There, there, lass!" Mr. Forrest's grip tightened. "It's a misunderstanding. It must be."

"But . . . what do they want with him?"

"They say he's a Jacobite conspirator. They say that someone informed against him, can you believe that? Time enough in the morning to get hold of a barrister and see what's to be done. No, don't make a scene. It will only go worse for the major. You know I speak the truth."

"Julian," she whispered brokenly as men and riders cantered into the gloom. "Oh Julian," and she fought to throw off the horrible intuition that the one day he had asked for was all that they would be allowed.

Chapter Fifteen

❧

There was no sleep for Serena that night. She was burning with impatience for dawn to break so that she could set things in motion to have Julian released. It was a misunderstanding or a case of mistaken identity. Over and over, she repeated those words, trying to take comfort from them.

The first thing to be done was to find out where the militia had taken him. Mr. Forrest's opinion was that they would have lodged him in one of the big London prisons, perhaps Newgate or the Fleet. His wife did not think so. There was a roundhouse in Twickenham. It was her opinion that they had lodged Julian there, and, as she pointed out, it would be foolish to make the long journey to town without first applying to the local authorities.

At the crack of dawn, Serena set off for Twickenham with only a groom for escort. All her hopes were to be disappointed. With the exception of the sergeant on duty, the roundhouse was deserted. The justice of the peace to whom the sergeant referred her, and who was not pleased to be roused from his bed at so ungodly an hour, knew nothing of Julian or any warrant for his arrest, nor did he care.

She made the return journey to the house in a daze, and was jerked rudely to her senses when her escort, swearing violently, reached for her reins and hustled her off the path.

"What—"

"Look!"

Concealed by a thicket of undergrowth, Serena peered

through the wrought-iron fence. What she saw made her inhale sharply. Swarms of soldiers in their red tunics were rousting grooms and stable boys from their quarters, and Mr. and Mrs. Forrest were on the front steps arguing with a gentleman who appeared to be the officer in charge.

"If I was you," said the groom, "I wouldn't go back in there. I would get myself a very clever barrister, then I'd lie low and wait it out."

Abruptly saluting her, the groom wheeled his mount and took off. Stunned, she watched him disappear around a bend in the path. It was obvious to her that he wasn't making for the house.

Torn by indecision, she debated with herself what to do. If only Flynn were here! That thought decided her. With one last look at Julian's house, she dug in her heels and followed the departing groom.

She arrived at Ward House dusty and disheveled but none the worse for her solitary ride. Flynn, mistaking her agitation for fury at his part in her Fleet marriage, hastily tried to placate her.

"I don't care about any of that," she said, leading him into a small anteroom. She abruptly told him about Julian's arrest the night before, and the subsequent events.

Like Serena, Flynn was sure that it was only a matter of time before Julian would be released.

The first thing to do, said Flynn, was find out where the major was incarcerated, and that could best be done by enlisting the support of Julian's friends at his gaming house. He went off full of optimism. When he returned some hours later, his face was very grave.

"You can't get near 'is place for bleeding soldiers. It's been shut down."

"What are the charges against him?"

"That's just it. No one seems to know anything, though the rumors are flying thick and fast. They say 'e escaped custody, and the soldiers are searching for 'im, but no one seems to know where he is or what 'e is supposed to have done. Now it looks as though 'e is as guilty as sin."

"Escaped custody?" Serena sat down as her legs buckled under her. "But . . . why would he do such a thing?"

"You tell me."

"Oh, Flynn! This is worse than a nightmare!"

Flynn took the chair opposite Serena's. "They're questioning all the major's friends, see? I was almost sure that I would arrive 'ome 'ere to find they 'ad taken *you* away."

Serena thought about this for a moment and shook her head. "They won't know where to look for me. If they are looking for anyone, it will be Victoria Noble, unless they go through my clothes and things and find something there to connect me to Julian." She shook her head. "No, there's nothing there. I'm sure of it."

"Victoria Noble?" said Flynn, looking at her as though she had lost her reason. "Who might Victoria Noble be?"

In as few words as possible, Serena explained about the circumstances surrounding her loss of memory and her subsequent confusion.

"God, what a muddle!" was Flynn's comment.

"Yes, but what's to be done?"

"What can we do but wait and see?"

This was not what Serena wanted to hear. "Perhaps if I go to the authorities and demand—"

"That won't 'elp the major! Don't you see, if they was to discover that you are Mrs. Raynor, they might use you to set a trap for 'im? God Almighty! They might start asking questions, then where would we be? Julian Raynor ain't no Jacobite, but *we* are. The last thing we wants is the authorities breathing down our necks."

The days that followed were like one long unrelenting

nightmare for Serena. It was easier for Flynn. He was actually doing something, nosing around coffeehouses and mixing with militia men and others in the know, ferreting things out before they became general knowledge.

In due course, he reported that the Forrests and the men who had been taken into custody had been set free with no charges pending against them. The militia, however, were still on the lookout for Julian and were to be seen patrolling the area of his gaming club as well as his house in Twickenham.

"They're saying the major is a Jacobite conspirator and that if 'e's caught, he'll—" Flynn quickly changed direction to avoid reminding Serena in her overwrought state of the horrible fate that awaited traitors. "At least they knows nothing of you," he said comfortingly. "That's something."

"They are bound to find out about me sooner or later. Don't forget, there were witnesses to our marriage."

Flynn made a derisory sound. "They won't say nothing. Those witnesses are the major's friends. The authorities will get nothing out of them."

That the authorities might use her to set a trap for Julian was the most compelling reason in Serena's mind for doing nothing. If Julian were to come looking for her, she did not want soldiers to be lying in wait for him.

I promise you, you haven't seen the last of me yet. He'd meant those words as a threat. One way or another, she would make him believe that she'd had nothing to do with his arrest.

When Catherine and Letty arrived posthaste from Riverview with a letter Catherine had received from France, Serena's apprehensions took a new direction. Jeremy had written to warn them that Sir Robert's health was very frail. It might be another week or two before he was fit to travel. Her sister-in-law's obvious concern touched a chord deep inside Serena. There was a moment of indecision when she might have confided in Catherine, but the older girl's response to her careful overture crushed the impulse.

"I presume," said Serena, "that you have heard about Julian Raynor and all the rumors that are circulating about him?"

"Raynor!" exclaimed Catherine, not troubling to hide her distaste. "And to think I once encouraged you to set your cap for him! That will teach me to meddle in things that don't concern me."

"Did you meddle? I don't remember."

"I hoped . . . well, it doesn't signify what I hoped. I'm only too happy that he has no connection to our family, not as things stand."

As the conversation went on, it became clear to Serena that no one, least of all a family with a history such as theirs, could afford to acknowledge friendship with a suspected Jacobite.

"Jeremy says," went on Catherine, "that we Wards must be like Caesar's wife. We must be above suspicion."

And with that, Serena withdrew into a cocoon of silence.

Within the fortnight, the furor over Julian's disappearance was superseded by other more titillating gossip. Lady Margaret Fairley eloped with her footman, and Lord Baringstoke decamped to the Continent after killing a man in a duel. It seemed that even the authorities had lost interest in Julian. And still, he made no attempt to approach her. She could accept that Julian was keeping his distance because he didn't trust her. What she could not accept was that an accident or some calamity had overtaken him. Her prayers had never been more fervent. She would accept anything, she promised, as if making a bargain with the Deity, if only Julian were alive and well.

She was brooding on that thought when she heard a carriage pull up outside the front doors. She raced to the window and looked out to see Jeremy stepping down from the coach. "Papa!" she said, then on a note of joy, "Papa!" and turning on her heel, she raced headlong to the front doors.

Catherine had got there before her. Serena had a glimpse of Clive with one arm around her sister-in-law's shoulders, then her eyes lifted as Jeremy stepped forward to meet her.

"Oh, my dear," he said, and reached out to steady her as she swayed toward him. "You must prepare yourself for the worst."

"Oh no," she said. "No!"

"Our father died a week since. He had a weak heart and nothing could be done to save him. He didn't suffer at the end. He simply slipped away from us."

She was shivering, and there was no reason for it. Warm air wafted in from the open windows, and her shoulders were covered by a silk stole. Lacing her fingers together to stop their shaking, she lifted her eyes and looked around the dinner table, touching briefly on each person present. Catherine, Jeremy, Clive, Letty—they were in no better shape than she. No one had done justice to the excellent dinner Cook had prepared.

This was a far cry from the homecoming they had anticipated. She saw now what she had not seen before. Jeremy's letter was meant to prepare her for the worst, and her mind had been so full of Julian that she had not realized it. She swallowed, thinking of all she had lost with her father's death. Whatever his faults, and she had never been blind to them, he was her father and she had loved him. In some respects, he'd been a hard man, quick to anger and slow to forgive. But he was also loyal, as his friendship for the Stuarts gave ample evidence. When everyone else had deserted the prince, Sir Robert Ward had stood by him, not counting the cost to himself or his family. It seemed fitting that he had died in exile in the service of that prince.

Sir Robert would not be interred beside her mother in St. Clement's churchyard, and that seemed fitting too. Charlotte Ward had lived in the shadow of her husband. A quiet, rather timid woman, the little animation she possessed seemed to drain out of her whenever her husband had walked into a room. Her gentle disposition was no match for his volatile and sometimes cruel outbursts. By the time of her death, Charlotte Ward had been a silent withdrawn woman. Sir Robert never respected those who did not stand up to him and her mother could not be other than she was.

No, thought Serena, she had never been blind to her father's faults, but in spite of them, she had loved him.

There was to be no funeral service, for her father had been buried in the cemetery of the small village where he had lived for the last year. There would be a notice of the death in the paper and that would be that.

"Father wanted it that way," said Jeremy, breaking the long silence. "He knew he was dying, and he gave me instructions about his burial and the kind of service he wanted."

"The prince was there, at Father's funeral service." There was a break in Clive's voice. "Disguised, of course. The French don't support him any more than his own subjects."

Jeremy's voice took on a hard edge. "Charles Edward Stuart has worn out his welcome in France is more like it, as he has everywhere else."

Clive stiffened. "I thought you liked the prince? You

dined with him, did you not? It seemed to me that you liked him well enough."

"I do like him. He is a charming companion, when he wants to be. But I know the risks of being friendly with such a man. His ambition to place his father on the throne of England is as fierce as ever it was. He hoped to enlist me to the Cause."

Lifting the sherry decanter, he rose from the table and went immediately to Serena to replenish her wine glass. "Your face is parchment-white," he said gently. "This has all been too much for you. Drink up. It will do you a world of good."

The solicitous words were almost more than she could bear. It was so like Jeremy to notice when something was amiss with any of them. She took a long swallow from her glass, if only to please him.

On returning to his place at the head of the table, he looked at each one in turn. Shaking his head, he passed a hand over his eyes. "Do I seem hard to you? I suppose I must. I wish it were not so. But the cost involved in obtaining a pardon for Father was so prohibitive . . ." He checked himself, paused, then went on in a more moderate tone, "I beg your pardon. I don't know what has brought this on. Grief, I presume. Father's death has been a great shock to us all."

Catherine said, "But Jeremy dear, you are not saying surely that we still have to pay for the pardon when it is no longer . . . I mean . . . there is no point in it now, is there?"

"No point whatsoever," he answered. "But the Crown has already accepted our money. We have seen the last of it, of that you may be sure."

"But that is so unfair!" cried Letty.

"Is it? I think you will find that His Majesty's ministers consider it a case of poetic justice. They are having the last laugh on a formidable enemy who caused them a deal of trouble in his lifetime."

Serena retired to her bedchamber in a state of utter exhaustion. Grief for her father was the easier part to bear for she was not alone in it.

It was Julian who weighed heavily on her mind. She longed to confide in Jeremy but feared to add to all his burdens. Moreover, she couldn't explain about Julian without revealing the escape route and her part in it. Besides, Jeremy wouldn't lift a finger to help Julian, not if he were suspected of Jacobite conspiracies. She did not blame Jeremy for this. She understood his position. He would do whatever was necessary to protect his family.

More than two weeks had passed since that awful night when Julian was arrested, and in that time he had made no attempt to get a message to her. Sometimes, it seemed that her time with Julian had been either a dream or a figment of her imagination. If it were not for the curtain ring she had hidden in a handkerchief in her dresser drawer, she would think she was losing her mind.

Moving to her dresser, she opened the top drawer and retrieved a lace handkerchief. Inside, she found not only her wedding ring but also the fifty-pound note, carefully folded, which Julian had once thrust at her. These were not the tokens a man gave a woman whom he admired and respected.

Thoughts circled inside her head, but the one that finally took hold was that she wished they had spent their last day together sorting out their differences.

"Oh Julian," she whispered into the silence, "I can bear anything if only you are alive and well," and covering her face with both hands, she wept in great shuddering sobs till there were no more tears to shed.

* * *

Pain shot through Julian's cramped muscles as he eased himself to a sitting position. The leg irons bit into the flesh of his ankles. His wrists were raw and bleeding and manacled to an iron ring low on the wall. The only light came from a crack under the door. There was the sound of scuttling and he kicked out with both legs, grimacing as the sudden movement sent pain to every muscle in his body. Squeals, then more scurrying as the rats got out of range. He didn't even know the name of the damned ship on which he was being transported, or for which colony the ship had set sail.

Transportation. He let the thought sink into his mind. There had been no trial, and no sentence. The so-called "militia" had beaten him senseless, then hustled him to the docks where he'd been thrown into this dark rat-infested pit in the bowels of a ship. What he could not understand was why they had not simply put a bullet in his brain and had done with it.

When he gritted his teeth, the pain came at him in waves. His jaw felt as if it were broken. He could put up with the pain. The beating had been worth it because it had been administered *after* he had left his mark, deliberately, on the leader of those cutthroats who had done this to him. It would take several stitches to close the gash he had inflicted on "Pretty's" face. The man would be scarred for life.

Pretty, that was what had impressed itself on Julian's mind. Long lashes, dimples, a slight build, and now a scar to disfigure the whole. One day, he promised himself, there would be a final reckoning. One day, he would come face-to-face with "Pretty," and then . . .

The image faded and Serena's face took possession of his mind. A coldness such as he'd never experienced before seemed to invade his soul, chilling his blood to ice. She had to be behind it all. Nothing else made sense.

In the weeks since he'd been incarcerated in this hell-hole, he'd retraced in his mind everything that had passed between them since their first encounter. By her lights, she'd had motive enough to send him to the colonies ten times over. She'd told him that she would find a way to punish him and he had not taken her seriously.

God, she had known how to play him. Those little throbbing cries of arousal, her uninhibited response to him, her sweet surrender—all of it was sham. Even her role as Victoria had fooled him. She was playing for time while she set things in motion. For all he knew, Flynn might have been her accomplice. If the pain in his jaw had not been so excruciating, he would have laughed at himself.

He had trusted her, wanted to protect her from the fate he had devised for her father. The irony was supreme. He was the one who was trussed up like a side of beef in a butcher's stall. Once again, a Ward had triumphed over a Renney.

"Pretty" had told him what his fate would be. Fourteen years as an indentured convict on a tobacco or sugar plantation. And if he ever returned to England, they would get rid of him permanently.

He would return, nothing was more certain, and he damn well refused to serve his term for whatever crime was on the trumped-up papers the captain of the ship had in his possession. He would find a way to return to her.

He flexed his hands in his manacles. He would find a way to return to her. He closed his eyes as the pleasurable images formed in his brain.

Chapter Sixteen

❧

As the weeks dragged by, Serena was afflicted with one complaint after another. She came down with the sniffles, then the ague, and was almost over it when she succumbed to the influenza. By the time she was on her feet again, she was a shade of her former self. Everyone, her family included, assumed that grief for her father's death was at the bottom of it. This was only partly true. It was the uncertainty over Julian that was taking its toll on her.

There had been a few flickers of hope from time to time. Rumors about Julian rose up and died away at regular intervals. Some said that he had escaped to the colonies to make a new life for himself; others had it from someone who could not be named that he had flown to the Continent and was last seen in Paris. One rumor soon substantiated as fact was that there were no charges pending against Julian and that the authorities were no longer looking for him.

Serena first heard this rumor from Flynn, but she had been afraid to give it much credence. When Jeremy repeated it over the tea tray on one of the few occasions he was able to tear himself away from his accounts and ledgers, her heart lurched against her ribs.

"This means, of course," said Jeremy, "that the way is clear for him to return."

"It could be a trap," Clive pointed out. "You know, once he shows his face, the powers that be will pounce on him."

Serena's hand shook so badly that her teacup rattled in

its saucer. Raising the cup to her lips, she pretended to drink from it.

"No," said Jeremy. "It's no trap, leastways, that's not how it appears to me. I had it from Lord Kirkland, and if anyone should know, it should be he."

"You know," said Letty, "I never could credit that Julian Raynor was a Jacobite."

"No more could I," responded Jeremy. "In point of fact, I rather suspected that he was a government agent."

"What makes you say so?" asked Clive sharply.

"What? Oh, it's just a rumor that is circulating in my club. They say that his arrest and escape from custody was a sham, a ploy to escape retribution from the members of some Jacobite sect he had infiltrated."

"If that is so," said Serena carefully, "then it were better for him if he stayed away, else his enemies may yet find a way to punish him."

"I hardly think so. It seems to me that if the way has been cleared for his return, his friends at Whitehall must be satisfied that he stands in no danger."

After this conversation, Serena's hopes took a gargantuan leap. Julian was a man of wealth and property. It was inconceivable that he would not return to resolve his financial affairs once the threat of arrest was gone. She must contain her impatience until that day arrived. Whether he was a Jacobite or a government agent no longer mattered to her. Her sufferings had taught her that the only thing that really mattered was that somewhere, somehow, Julian was alive and well.

In the months that followed, she forced herself to put a good face on things, though there were long stretches when she hardly had enough energy to rise from her bed and face one more dreary day. There was no escape route now to claim her attention. Either the trickle of fugitives had dried up or Clive and Flynn had decided between them that their little group had had its day. Even if they had decided to continue with it, she no longer had the heart for it.

For the first time, they began to put into practice what Jeremy had been preaching for so long. The staff was drastically reduced; when no tenant could be found for Ward House, Riverview was let; their finest thoroughbreds were sold off; gowns were refurbished or made over. It appeared to Serena that the period of mourning, when there were no parties or balls or entertainments of any note, was a foretaste of what was in store for them. For Letty's sake, something had to be done, and so she told Jeremy.

"I don't know where the money is to come from," she said, "but something must be done for her. She has a dowry, so there is every hope that she will make a good match. And to do that, she must go out in society and meet young people of her own age."

For the first time in a long while, Jeremy smiled. "Well, of course she must! And you also! Why do you suppose I have been such a tyrant these many months if not to secure the future for all of you? I am determined to see my two young sisters creditably established once this period of mourning is over. Don't despair. We are not paupers yet."

The conversation left Serena with plenty to think about. Jeremy was determined to see both sisters creditably established, not just Letty, but *her* also. Though Jeremy would not say so, once she and Letty were married, they would no longer be his financial responsibility. And, if either she or Letty made a brilliant match, they might be expected to bring money into the family to help settle their debts. Clearly, for the family's sake, it was their duty to marry.

This thought left her quite shaken. Even if she wanted

to do her duty (which she did not), she was already married. Or was she? True, she had no marriage certificate to prove it. The last she had seen of it was when Julian had pocketed it after the chase in the storm. She had no way of knowing what had happened to it.

In any case it was a Fleet marriage and easily invalidated—that was what Julian had told her. Had he dispensed with their marriage? Would he return for her? Dear God, where was he and why hadn't he come for her?

Some of these agonizing uncertainties were answered the day Flynn burst into the house with the incredible news that Raynor's gaming house had once again opened its doors. To a barrage of questions from Letty and Catherine, he replied that no, the major was not in residence, though it was his hand that was guiding the enterprise. He'd had it from no less a person than Mr. Black, the major's chief operator. It seemed that Raynor had fled to South Carolina where he owned a substantial property, a plantation. That's where he had been hiding out for the last year, and since the life there suited him very well, that's where he intended to remain for some time to come. In the meantime, letters had been crossing the Atlantic to his friends and agents in London with instructions on the deposition of his various holdings.

Over the next few weeks, Serena discovered that in addition to the plantation, there was also a house in Charles Town which was equal to anything to be found in England. Charles Town was reputed to be a perfect Georgian city with entertainments to rival those of London—innumerable clubs, assemblies, balls, concerts, and plays, not to mention the most beautiful and cultured women in the world.

These tidbits did not come to her all at once, but in dribs and drabs as the Wards began to resume their place in society. Julian, she learned, had been living the life of an aristocrat, hobnobbing with the cream of Charles Town society. His holdings in the Carolinas were almost the equal of what he had left behind in England.

She was glad for him, truly glad for him, and so she told Flynn when he warned her not to let her imagination run away with her. There could be any number of reasons for the major's delay in writing to give her an account of himself.

"All I ever wanted," she replied mildly, "was to know that he was alive and well. I'm satisfied, Flynn. Truly I am. You can't think I begrudge him the life he has made for himself in the colonies?"

This was pride speaking, and both she and Flynn knew it. In the privacy of her own secret thoughts, she veered between uncertainty and anguish. She did not want to believe that while she had been drowning in grief for him, not knowing whether he was alive or dead, he had scarcely spared her a thought.

The insidious thoughts dripped into her mind like a slow, corrosive poison. He wasn't like Allardyce. She refused to believe he was like Allardyce. Allardyce had only wanted her for her fortune. He had cared nothing for her. That last day with Julian, she could have sworn he felt something for her.

If there was one thing she had learned from her experience with Allardyce, it was that some men were dangerous to love. She had taken that lesson to heart. Stephen had been the opposite of Allardyce—comfortable, predictable, safe.

Was Julian dangerous to love? If she had not felt like weeping her heart out, she would have laughed at her own naïveté. Dangerous to love? She had known it from the moment she had set eyes on him.

Other more salacious rumors began to circulate about Julian, connecting his name to a string of beautiful women in Charles Town. These edifying morsels of gossip were conveyed across the Atlantic by diplomats and merchants who had visited the young colony in the course of their business. Serena absorbed it all in smiling silence.

"Now Serena," Flynn said placatingly, retreating a step as the familiar fire kindled in her eyes, "give the poor man a chance. You can't know that the major—"

As the china dish came flying at him, he ducked and it shattered harmlessly against the door. "Serena!" he said reproachfully. "Get a grip on yourself! So the major 'as the odd bit o' muslin in 'is keeping! What 'as that to say to anything? 'E's a man, ain't 'e? That don't mean nothing to men of the world."

"You knave!" Her teeth were gnashing together. "You liver-faced, toad-eating miscreant! Why must you always defend him?"

" 'Cos there might be a good reason for what 'e's done. For all we knows, the major could 'ave lost his memory. 'Ave you thought of that?"

He ducked again when the silver hairbrush came rocketing across the room, missing his nose by an inch.

"If it were not for you," railed Serena, her eyes darting around her bedchamber for another missile to launch at him, "I would not have come to this sorry pass! Do you know how I felt tonight, hearing those women's names coupled with his name?" Flynn did know, and was cautiously inching his way toward the door. Serena went on relentlessly, "It might have been *my* name they were making sport of! And you are the one who made it possible by duping me into that Fleet marriage!"

As she ducked under the bed and came up with the chamber pot, Flynn dived for the door. The chamber pot, empty, thankfully, caught him a glancing blow on the shoulder. "Serena," he reproved, staggering under the impact, then he took to his heels when she went for a candle-stick.

Bosom heaving, she stared at that closed door for a full minute. Throwing the candlestick from her, she turned away and flung herself across the bed. Remorse washed over her in a flood of tears. Poor Flynn! He had taken the blows that were meant for Julian Raynor. Great wrenching sobs shook her shoulders. While she had been wallowing in despair, he had been sunk in debauchery, living the life of an aristocrat. The rogue! The bastard! He'd written to his friends and agents in London, but not one word to her.

And why should there be? He had never cared for her. The fifty-pound note and the curtain ring in the drawer of her dresser gave ample evidence of his opinion of her. She'd been well and truly trounced by a master in the art of seduction. He'd even *told* her that their Fleet marriage was easily got out of. And like a half-witted moonling, she had let him have his way with her, *she,* Serena Ward, who thought she knew every trick ever invented by an unscrupulous rake to persuade a female to his bed. To such men, the chase was everything, and having caught their prey, they moved on to the next challenge. That's all she had ever been to him—a challenge that had touched his male pride.

He had cast her off not knowing whether or not she was with child. And to think she had wept bitter tears when her woman's courses had come to her. If Julian was lost to her, she had wanted his child to remember him by. Fool! It was only by the grace of God that she had been spared that final humiliation! She would have borne a bastard child and he would not have cared.

When the sobs died away, it seemed that all her dreams and hopes died with them. Even her rage was spent. When Flynn returned an hour later, looking anxious and unsure, he was met by a white-faced, somber-eyed stranger. The contrite apology he immediately accepted, but when Flynn tried to introduce the subject of Julian Raynor, the softness went from her and a mask of rigid composure tightened her features. The episode with Julian Raynor, Serena calmly informed him, would be forgotten as though it had never taken place. Even if he were to come for her now, she would not have him. His name was never to be mentioned between them again.

In spite of her best intentions, she broke down a time or two. Each time, she promised herself that it was the last time that she was going to cry for Julian Raynor. By sheer force of will, she drew on resources of strength she had not known she possessed. It was mainly pride that stiffened her backbone, pride that put a smile on her face when there was nothing in her life to smile about. It was entirely possible that one of Julian's friends might mention Miss Serena Ward in one of those letters that crossed the Atlantic at regular intervals. In that event, she wanted Julian Raynor to know that his effect on Serena Ward had been negligible.

Time passed, and the hurt and anguish became easier to bear. There came a day when she found, to her surprise, that she really was enjoying herself and that her smiles and laughter were no longer forced. She was finally cured of Julian Raynor. It was time to move on, time to do her duty and find some eligible gentleman with whom she could share her life.

Her experience with Julian had reinforced her opinion of men of his stamp. She'd had enough of men who were dangerous to love to last her a lifetime. Nor did she want that leap of the senses that had robbed her of logical thought whenever she was with him. Above all else, she wanted comfort and safety, and she found them in the quiet, unassuming person of Mr. Trevor Hadley.

Flynn, as ever, was the one who wouldn't allow her to forget about Julian Raynor. *Bigamy* was the alarming word he used to bring her to heel. In spite of her warnings never to speak to her of Julian Raynor again, he'd been trying to persuade her to write to Julian, merely, as Flynn put it, to clear the air between them. They were both too proud for their own good. Flynn could never be made to believe that Julian Raynor had played them both false.

Bigamy. It was something to think about. Finally relenting, she wrote a short letter couched in cordial terms to indicate that she was on the point of marriage. All she required from Julian was an assurance that he had destroyed all evidence of their Fleet marriage.

She was proud of that letter. Reading it over, she congratulated herself on striking just the right note. There was not a trace of acrimony in it, not a hint of the pain and anguish she had endured. It wasn't that she had forgiven him. He simply no longer mattered to her.

Captain Mosley was expounding to the passengers, who had the honor to sit at his table, on the vital importance of Charles Town as a seaport. It was all very interesting, but young Mrs. Jaffe could not prevent her eyes drifting to the gentleman who sat directly across the table. They would dock in a day or two, and it was highly unlikely that she would ever set eyes on Mr. Raynor again. He had business in London, whilst she and her husband had sold up and were returning to their home in Devon. Sighing regretfully, she raised her wine glass to her lips and tried to pay attention to the conversation. She would far rather hear of Mr. Raynor and his purpose in coming to England.

Her husband had told her the little he knew of the gentleman. It was not an unusual story. Mr. Raynor had come to the Carolinas two years before to escape some scandal in England. What he had seen of the flourishing young colony had intrigued him and he had immediately begun improving his plantation and using the profits from it to invest in other enterprises. He was a man of influence as well as a wealthy landowner. In Charles Town, he was an intimate of Governor Glen and there was speculation that soon he might be persuaded to let his name stand for the Commons House of Assembly.

Even without her husband's commentary, she would have known that Mr. Raynor was a man to be reckoned with. He had that look. It wasn't that he was forbidding. Indeed, his manner toward her had always been most gentlemanly, most respectful. Nevertheless, she sensed the steel in him. When this gentleman set his mind on something, nothing would stand in his way. It was, she supposed, the reason he had risen to prominence so quickly. Many gentlemen with his advantages let them slip through their fingers, gaming away their fortunes or wasting them on riotous living.

This thought reminded her of some of the gossip that circulated among the married ladies on board, ladies who moved in Mr. Raynor's circles in Charles Town. According to Mrs. Simmons, his *affaires* with a certain class of women were notoriously well-known the length and breadth of South Carolina. There were duels, and rumors of drunken orgies in the slave quarters, and debauchery too shocking to detail. When she had asked her husband about it, he had chastised her for being interested in things no gently bred lady should know about. That was the trouble with husbands. Their sense of propriety forced their wives to be devious in ferreting out information.

"I cannot credit," she had declared, with a fair show of indignation, "that the governor would welcome such a man into the ranks of his supporters."

Her husband had wavered for a moment, then carefully

explained that gentlemen did not set much store by how many mistresses a man kept, or how many duels he fought, so long as he was a man of honor. To her genuine indignation, he told her that such things rather added to a gentleman's credit among his peers.

Over the rim of her wine glass, she covertly studied Mr. Raynor, dimly aware that the conversation had moved on to the West Indies. He was in his mid-thirties, as near as she could judge, and had a certain something about him that excited feminine interest. It wasn't only that he was uncompromisingly male, or that he wore his fine clothes with a careless arrogance that drew all eyes to him. There was something more, something she could not put into words.

In that moment, Mr. Raynor lifted his eyes and caught her unwary stare, and like a creature of the wild that is cornered by a predator, she froze. Then his long lashes flicked down, veiling that look in his eyes, and she carefully expelled a breath before riveting her attention on the gentleman who was speaking, hoping that no one would notice the unbecoming flush on her cheeks.

Behind the polite mask of interest, Julian's frame of mind was anything but pleasant. In that moment, when he had caught Mrs. Jaffe's stare, he'd experienced a flash of déjà vu, as though it were Serena's stare he had captured, as he had once captured it at Catherine Ward's levee.

Damn Mrs. Jaffe and her resemblance to Serena! The girl's blond coloring, her lively blue eyes, and that air of breeding—all were so painfully familiar, and jogged memories he only wanted to forget. It made him wonder if, once he finally came face-to-face with his erstwhile wife, he would be able to keep from throttling her on the spot. It seemed that he was not so indifferent to Serena Ward as he had hoped he was.

When dinner was over and the ladies had withdrawn, he did not linger over the port and brandy, but excused himself and made his way on deck to the bow of the ship, where the strong sea breezes deterred all but the most hardy. Once there, he stood at the rail, looking out over the vast ocean toward England, remembering another time, seemingly a lifetime ago, when he had made the outward journey in far different circumstances.

Then, he had been John Adam, an indentured convict in chains, cooped up in a dark hole in solitary confinement. He'd been his own worst enemy then, attacking his captors in a frenzied dementia when they refused to listen to him. They had been well warned that he was a dangerous character and had subdued him, and kept him subdued with ferocious beatings. A prisoner who had broken ribs and was kept on starvation rations was a docile prisoner. In his mind, he'd never given up, but he had learned his lesson. If he were ever to escape, he must act as though the defiance had been beaten out of him.

Life on a tobacco plantation in Maryland had been infinitely preferable to life on the transportation ship, if only because the owner of the plantation saw him in much the same manner as he viewed a prime piece of horseflesh. He'd put down good money for him. It was in his best interest to see that his slave was cared for so that he could recoup every penny he had spent on his purchase and upkeep.

Only his hatred for Serena had given him the determination to survive. He would not be satisfied until he had settled the score with her. He'd made his plans carefully. In South Carolina, on the outskirts of Charles Town, he owned a plantation which was managed by a former comrade-in-arms who had served with him in India. If he could reach Charles Town, Dorsey would shelter him until he could return to England.

And he had escaped, just as he had known he would. It had taken him two months of near starvation and traveling mostly on foot to reach his plantation, and months after that to fully recover his health. In that time, his friend and overseer, Dorsey, had made discreet enquiries. What he learned was that there were no charges of any kind pending against Julian Raynor. He was free to come and go as he pleased.

Julian was skeptical. During his convalescence, he entered into a correspondence with his bankers, his solicitors, and his few friends in London. The information he received from them confirmed what Dorsey had told him. It also shed some light on Serena. Miss Serena Ward had conducted herself as if Julian Raynor had never existed. She had made no public outcry at his disappearance. It seemed to him that if she had been innocent, the first thing she would have done was let the world know that she was his wife. A wife had every right to call the authorities to account for what they had done to her husband. That she had not done so was more evidence that she had been the mastermind behind his abduction. Oh, she had grieved right enough, grieved over the untimely death of her father.

The report of Sir Robert's death had confirmed what Julian had always suspected. There was no justice in this world. His patience, his scheming, yes, even his soul-searching after he married Serena, had all been for nothing. Had he been possessed of a more fanciful turn of mind, he might have been persuaded that the gods, themselves, had ordained that the Wards were beyond the touch of a mere Renney, beyond retribution.

Sir Robert Ward had been the scourge of the Renneys, but he had not paid for his crimes. What then? Was he, Julian, to perpetuate the vendetta on the next generation of Wards, like some tragic hero from a Greek myth? Was this to be the pattern of his life? The idea did not appeal to him. With Sir Robert's death, even his hatred for Serena became muted. She was just another of life's ironic twists. Though he did not know it at the time, Sir Robert's death was a turning point for him.

During his convalescence, he had had a great deal of time to think. Returning to England no longer seemed so pressing. He'd always intended to make a life for himself in the New World. There would never be a better opportunity to discover whether life in the Carolinas was all he had hoped.

It was better than he'd hoped. In America, even for a man of his checkered past, the opportunities were limitless. All that mattered was his drive to make something of himself. He was still a gambler, but now he called himself an investor, and gambled on enterprises that profited not only himself but the colonists whose destiny he was proud to share. He felt a sense of belonging here that he had never felt in England.

There had been women, dozens of them, and he did not regret a single one. Over time, the memory of Serena Ward had become less and less distinct, and had finally faded into the blessed mists of forgetfulness.

Until he received her letter. It wasn't revenge or pique or curiosity on his part that prompted this tedious voyage to England. The past had lost its power to control him. America had done that for him. The future was what concerned him now, not the machinations of some scheming bitch in England. It had always been in his mind to return at some point to dispose of his gaming house and other properties in his possession. He wanted to be shot of everything that tied him to the old life, and that included a wife who was as eager as he to destroy any and all evidence of their misbegotten marriage.

He was the only one who knew where the marriage

certificate was. Of course he would destroy it. Serena Ward was nothing to him now, less than nothing.

He gazed off into the distance, lost in thought. Coming to himself, he scowled. A moment later, turning on his heel, he made his way below deck, to the privacy of his cabin.

Chapter Seventeen

✦

In the companionable silence, Blackie allowed his gaze to wander over the office which he had occupied during Julian's absence for the last two years. In his mind, it had always been Julian's office, stamped with Julian's personality, and now that Julian was sitting behind his desk again, it seemed as if the last two years had never been. The whole house was Julian's conception, and Blackie still could not believe that his friend meant to relinquish even a small part of it.

As Julian had pointed out, a man moved on, changed direction as events shaped his destiny. In a month, two at the most, he would be returning to the New World to the life that awaited him there. It went without saying that Julian would make a success of whatever he attempted. Blackie never doubted that for a moment.

"Why the glum look?" asked Julian.

Blackie shrugged, hesitated, then said sheepishly, "I never expected nor ever wanted to be the part proprietor of this place. Truth to tell, in the last little while, I've felt more like the caretaker waiting for his master's return. I shall miss your bark, Julian, if not your bite. And . . ."

"And?"

Blackie laughed. "I hope my luck is not about to turn."

"Luck has nothing to do with it," rejoined Julian, regarding his friend steadily. "You have proven your abilities to handle things in my absence, as the ledgers clearly demonstrate. You'll do fine, Blackie. You may take my word for it. And it's not as though I am making you a gift of the enterprise. I expect to be well paid from future profits."

Blackie glanced at the open ledgers on Julian's desk. "Well, there have certainly been plenty of those."

"Yes," said Julian, running one finger down a column of figures, stopping at a particular entry. "What surprises me is that in my absence our patrons could be persuaded to redeem their vowels. How did you manage it?"

Blackie bloomed with pleasure at this high praise. Laughing in a deprecating way, he said, "I took a leaf out of your own book, Julian, you know. I let it be known that if they did not pay off their gaming debts, I would make it public knowledge, and as you know, there is nothing to make an English gentleman lose face so much as the scandal of not redeeming his vowels. It's a matter of honor."

Julian smiled. "That was well done of you," he said, then went on casually, "What surprises me is that Jeremy Ward was in a position to clear his debts. As I understand, he practically beggared himself to obtain that pardon for his father."

Blackie glanced at the notation in the ledger that Julian was indicating. "Lord, yes!" he said, and looked reproachfully at Julian. "When I went through the promissory notes in the safe and came upon the bills and mortgages belonging to Jeremy Ward, I almost had an apoplexy. I could not believe that you would extend credit, and such an astronomical sum, to a man who was known to be tottering on the verge of ruin. I was sure the house would never see a penny of it."

"But I see from the ledgers that Sir Jeremy redeemed every last bill and mortgage."

"Not Sir Jeremy, no. Lord Charles Tremayne approached me and made me an offer for them. I sold them for half what they were worth." He looked doubtfully at

Julian. "Did I do wrong? I don't mind telling you, I jumped at Lord Charles's offer."

"You did the right thing," said Julian, and smiled. "What puzzles me is how Lord Charles knew that the bills were in my possession, and what he meant to do with them."

Blackie shrugged. "I never thought to ask. I was only too happy to be shot of them." He looked curiously at Julian.

Aware of that speculative look, Julian flicked open a silver snuffbox and offered it to Blackie. "What do you think of my mix?"

Taking a pinch, Blackie raised it to one nostril, then the other. "Very nice," he said. He did not know the first thing about snuff, nor ever wished to know. He left such things to connoisseurs such as Julian. Seeing that something more was required of him, he said emphatically, "Very nice indeed. Is it your own recipe?"

"No," said Julian, "it was a present from a lady."

"Ah," said Blackie, trying to sound noncommittal. In the week since Julian had taken up residence, Lady Amelia Lawrence had made an infernal nuisance of herself, sending round perfumed notes and gifts in an attempt to lure Julian into her net. For the most part, Julian had been preoccupied with business. If there was a woman in his life, Blackie wasn't aware of her. He hoped, for Julian's sake, that he wasn't going to take up with Amelia Lawrence. In Julian's absence, Lady Amelia had become a widow and Blackie feared that she had set her sights on Julian.

This thought had him grinning. If anyone could take care of himself, it was Julian, as his sojourn in the colonies had proved. In point of fact, it seemed to Blackie that Julian's arrest and subsequent flight to South Carolina had all worked out for the best. Julian was the same man he remembered, and yet he was different, less cynical, more at ease with himself. Except, Blackie mentally amended, when the subject of women crept into the conversation. That was when Julian was at his most satirical. Blackie divined that his friend had taken a mauling from one of those Charles Town beauties with whom his name had been linked in the last little while. No. Julian was in no danger of succumbing to Lady Amelia's lures.

"What put that grin on your face?" asked Julian.

Blackie shook his head. "You," he said. "Since your return, you have become a person of celebrity. Society matrons who once hid their unfledged chicks from your eyes are now outdoing themselves in trying to lure you to their parties. This is a far cry from those early days in the stews of Whitechapel!"

"Yes, we've both come a long way."

Blackie smiled to himself as the recollection of his first encounter with Julian came back to him. It had happened all of six years ago. He'd met Julian in a gaming den, and had propelled himself into the fracas which developed when Julian discovered that he was being cheated. There was no reason for Blackie to take Julian's part, except that a moment or two before, they'd exchanged a few words on their respective experiences serving in His Majesty's service. Julian was a military man. That was enough for Blackie.

Though they'd come out the worst in the melee, they'd managed to bloody a few noses before they were thrown unceremoniously out on the street. Afterward, they'd drowned their sorrows in the time-honored way and had become friends in the process. From that day to this, Blackie never ceased to be amazed that for once in his life, he had been in the right place at the right time. Julian Raynor never forgot a good turn.

"You know what they are saying about you, don't you?" said Blackie.

"What do they say?"

"Oh, some say that you were a Jacobite, and others that you were a government agent, and the reason you left England in such haste was to escape the wrath of whatever side you were working against."

"And what do you say, Blackie?"

"Why, I tell them what you told me, that it was always in your mind to go to America, and that your arrest merely hastened that day forward."

"And that's it in a nutshell."

Long after Blackie had returned to his duties, Julian sat at his desk, contemplating the ledgers. He cared little that Sir Jeremy Ward's bills and mortgages were no longer in his possession. He had acquired them for only one purpose and that was to ruin Sir Robert Ward. With the baronet's death, there was no point in going on with it. What puzzled him was Lord Charles's intervention. What good were they to him? If he was staving off ruin for the Wards, why not simply lend Sir Jeremy the money so that he could clear his debts in person? And how had Lord Charles known where to find them?

It hardly mattered to him. The Wards were no concern of his. He had more important things to occupy his mind. With a glance at the clock, he stowed the ledgers in the safe, an ingenious contraption in the shaft of the dumb-waiter that connected his private office to the pantry in the floor below. Only he and Blackie knew of the existence of this safe. A gambler could never be too careful with either his ledgers or the notes he had acquired.

His hand moved aside a stack of promissory notes, and touched upon a document that he had examined many times in the last week. Retrieving it, Julian examined it again. The seal was broken now, but that had been his doing. He had wanted to make quite sure that no one had tampered with the contents of the packet. His marriage certificate was not much to look at. It was torn and disfigured by several unsightly stains.

He stared at it for a long, long time before tossing it into the safe and depressing the lever that worked the secret panel. Having shut the doors to the dumbwaiter, he again glanced at the clock. It was time to keep his appointment with Lord Kirkland at the War Office.

"I c-came into the affair very late in the day, as I wrote you once I knew your direction."

Lord Kirkland topped up Julian's glass of sherry. "As I told you then, I called out the militia to look for you, but by then, of course, it was too late. You were already on your way to America."

"What I want to know," said Julian, "is who authorized my arrest?"

"That's just it. Your arrest was n-not authorized, at least, I can find no r-record of the magistrate who called the militia out to arrest you. I don't know what to m-make of it. It's an odd business, a v-very odd business indeed."

Julian could scarcely concentrate on the conversation for staring at the portrait on the wall behind the earl's desk. He felt as though he had been flung back in time, and he was a boy again, and his mother was laughing at something he had just said. His throat was so tight, he was drinking his sherry as if it were water.

Observing that Julian's interest was straying yet again, Lord Kirkland half turned in his chair to look at the portrait.

"She is very beautiful," said Julian. "Who is she?"

"That," said the earl, "is a p-portrait of my sister, Harriet, shortly before she eloped."

"I understood you to say that your picture gallery had been destroyed in the fire?"

"And so it was. This p-portrait was in a relative's possession. It came to me on his death."

This was the first time that the subject of Julian's mother had ever come up between the two men, and Julian seized on the opportunity to probe a little deeper, knowing that it might never come again. "It was a tragic story, as I have heard?"

"What have you heard?" The earl was fiddling with the stopper on the sherry decanter.

Julian hesitated, then plunged in. "I heard that Sir Robert Ward hounded the man your sister married, and that he died in debtors' prison."

"I'm surprised people remember the s-story. But yes, what you have related is the sum of what h-happened."

"And your sister? Whatever became of her?"

"I never found out. Well, I w-wouldn't, would I? She eloped when I was a m-mere boy. By the time I was in a position to look for her, ten years had passed, and the trail was cold. I knew she was d-dead, of course."

"How could you have known that?"

"Because, before his d-death, Renney took up a position with Lord Hornsby. He must have been a w-widower by that time. There was no s-sign of Harriet, no m-mention of her. And, if Harriet had been alive, she would have c-come for me. We were always very c-close."

Julian remembered well the straits that had led his father to take up a position with Lord Hornsby. Their little family had been scattered, never to be reunited. He couldn't stop now. "I believe," he said, "Sir Robert's hatred was motivated by a letter your tutor wrote to the authorities betraying him and Lord Hugo?"

"Was there a l-letter? Well, we have only Sir Robert's

w-word for that. He was to be m-married to my s-sister, did you know? He never forgave Renney, never f-forgot."

"Are you saying that Sir Robert hounded poor Renney because he was jilted?" asked Julian, frowning.

"It would not surprise m-me. Sir Robert was always a p-proud man. Anyway, it h-happened such a long time ago. We shall n-never know now."

There was a knock at the door, and the earl's secretary entered. After a short discussion of which Julian heard not one word, the secretary quit the room, and the earl returned to the subject of Julian's arrest.

"I c-called you to my office because this is in the nature of an apology for what you were m-made to suffer through our . . . well . . . you know what I mean."

"Incompetence?"

The earl shifted restlessly. "Who is to say what happened that night? At the time in question, riots were taking place in the city, and m-my hands were full putting them down. Didn't you know? Some naval men went on the rampage, setting fire to b-bawdy houses for whatever reason. When soldiers came out to subdue them, they went for them too. There were so many m-militia on the streets that night k-keeping the peace, that it was hard to k-keep track of them all.

"However, if you would give me some clue to the s-soldiers who arrested you, n-names, or even a description of the officer in charge, I would be p-prepared to pursue the matter until we discover who they are. One thing I can s-say for certain. They were acting on their own. No magistrate, no justice of the p-peace authorized your arrest that night."

Julian thought of "Pretty" and the scar he undoubtedly carried from their confrontation. It was the thought of Serena that made him hesitate. If it could be proved that she was behind his abduction, he didn't want the law to deal with her. He was quite capable of dealing with her himself.

"I regret to say that none of them stands out in my memory."

"Where did they t-take you? How did you escape them? You m-must remember something?"

With the exception of the perpetrators of the crime against him, no one knew that he had been transported to Maryland as an indentured convict. Everyone was under the impression that he had escaped from custody and had fled the country with the help of his friends. He debated taking the earl into his confidence, and decided against it. He was enough of a celebrity as it was. If it became known that he had served time as a convict, he would become an object of raging curiosity.

There was more to his reluctance than this. Once again, he was thinking of Serena. He did not wish for an investigation, fearing that she might be implicated. That he could still wish to protect her after what he had suffered at her hands filled him with bitter self-contempt.

Observing Julian's look, his lordship observed, "You know what people are saying about you?"

"That I'm either a Jacobite agitator or a government agent, and that my escape was engineered by my friends?" Julian's tone was amused. "Oh yes, I've heard."

Lord Kirkland was unsmiling. "I know for a f-fact," he said, "that you were not a government agent."

There was a pause, a silence that conveyed a faint threat. "Neither," said Julian, "am I now, nor ever was, a Jacobite agitator."

"I'm very g-glad to hear you say so, my boy, for if you were involved in p-plots against His Majesty, I would not h-hesitate to use the full force of my authority against you."

"It's no more, no less that I would expect," said Julian.

"As long as w-we understand each other."

"I thought," said Julian gently, "that I was summoned to your office to receive an official apology?"

The earl grinned. "Umm, more in the nature of an 'unofficial' apology. To be f-frank, the Crown never admits, you see, to making mistakes. We are not even sure that the soldiers who arrested you were g-genuine."

Julian was almost certain that they were not. "How did you hear about my arrest? You said you came into the affair late in the day, yet from what I have been told by my servants, you were quick off the mark. Your militia were out looking for me the following morning, only hours after my arrest."

His lordship replied vaguely. He could not remember the details. With the passage of time, events ran together in his mind and became blurred. And with this, Julian had to be content.

Lord Kirkland's last words to Julian were in the nature of a warning or a threat. "Have a care, my boy. We wouldn't w-want the same thing to happen to you again."

When Lord Kirkland arrived home, he found her ladyship in her dressing room, reclining on a sofa, reading a letter that had arrived by the afternoon post. The contents of the letter had obviously not found favor with the countess. Her lips were pressed in a thin line. Her pale blue eyes were narrowed in dislike.

"From Dorothea," she told her husband, holding her cheek up for his perfunctory kiss.

"Ah."

Dorothea, Countess of Trenton, was her ladyship's particular friend. Lord Kirkland had never been able to understand the bonds of this long-standing friendship which gave neither lady much pleasure. His countess and her friend seemed to him to be rivals, forever trying to outdo each other.

"She writes," said her ladyship in her precise way, "that Trenton has decided to completely refurbish their place in Hampshire. Isn't that just like Dorothea? In my last letter, I happened to mention that we were debating whether or not to do as much for Bagley. She has done this to spite me. There is no other explanation for it. Well, I have no intention of letting her steal a march on me."

She slanted her husband a considering look. "Do you know what I think, James?"

"What do you think, my d-dear?" The earl carefully disposed himself on a spindly, gilt-edged chair.

"I think I should like to invite that Mr. Raynor of yours to a house party at Bagley. He is all the rage at present, is he not? His name is on everyone's lips." She absently tapped a finger to her chin. "Yes, a house party with your Mr. Raynor as the guest of honor might be just the thing."

His lordship did not quite groan, but the sound he made was not far off it. "I have no objection to inviting Julian as the g-guest of honor to one of your parties, Esther, but couldn't we make it a small d-dinner party? You know how I l-loathe these g-grand affairs."

She came to him in a rustle of skirts, her finely drawn face close to his, one hand resting appealingly on his chest. He caught the faint scent of lemon and verbena from her graying brown hair. She had a look of delicacy that, he well knew, masked an unshakable resolve. Should he refuse her, the delicate air would vanish, and she would turn into a virago.

"What fustian, James. You are too modest for your own good. You must have more confidence in yourself. If you don't, no one else will."

Lord Kirkland loved his wife. He had often debated with himself why this should be so, and had come to the conclusion that his love was based on gratitude. Esther loved him. Though there was nothing worth loving in him, his wife loved him. She had become as necessary to him as his weekly visits to the Temple of Venus in King's Place.

He gave in gracefully. He always did. "A house party? I shall mention it to Julian. I can't promise more than that."

Chapter Eighteen

Refreshed from his bath and resplendent in burgundy velvet coat and white satin breeches, Julian made a leisurely descent of the main staircase in his gaming house. It was an hour before midnight, the hour when members of the fashionable set began their round of parties and dos. The rooms on the ground floor were therefore fairly quiet. Julian was glad of it, for in the week since he had taken up residence in his club, whenever he showed his face, which he did rarely, he was practically mobbed by the crush.

Blackie was right to say that he had become a person of celebrity. People seemed to regard him as if he were a romantic figure, like a character out of a novel, imbuing him with God only knew what heroic attributes. According to Blackie, they'd woven fancies around him, some saying that he was a secret Jacobite and others that he was a patriot. He was a victim, that was all he knew for certain, but whose victim remained to be seen.

One of the first things he had done on arriving in London had been to call on his good friend, Constable Loukas. Loukas was looking into the matter for him. If anybody could find anything out, it would be Loukas. He had connections and sources unavailable to the ordinary citizen. He also had an uncanny knack for gleaning the significance of inconsequential details and facts. Even though he was retired, his services were still in demand by former colleagues when difficult cases came their way.

This wasn't a particularly difficult case. It had to be Serena who was behind it all. What he wanted were the names of her accomplices. It shouldn't be too difficult to persuade her to give him their names. He held all the cards, including the trump. He was the one who had the certificate of marriage, and Serena was desperate to get her hands on it.

His erstwhile wife had already sent Flynn to him, requesting that he meet with her at a time and place to suit himself. It suited him to let her wait and stew. He wasn't vicious; he wasn't devious; but this time around he was resolved that the shoe was going to be on the other foot.

Tonight, according to Flynn, Serena was engaged to go with a party of friends, including her suitor, to Ranelagh Gardens in Chelsea. She wasn't expecting her husband to put in an appearance. Her brother, Sir Jeremy, had reserved a box close by the Rotunda where they would sit down to supper after the fireworks display. Julian meant to run into her quite by "accident," if only to gauge her unguarded reaction to him. Perhaps he was devious after all. His next thought had him laughing. A husband and a suitor? He wondered if she was equal to it.

In the marble entrance hall, Lady Amelia's coachman was already waiting for him. Quickening his pace, oblivious to the girls and croupiers who were hovering about, eyeing him covertly, Julian quit the premises.

The front doors had hardly closed before a bevy of girls, all employees of the house, made as one for the cloakroom, a small anteroom off the front entrance. Here they crowded around the long sash windows, trying to get a better view of Julian. There was nothing new in this. They'd watched his comings and goings for nearly a week.

Anastasia, the new girl, was the first to break the silence. "What has Lady Amelia Lawrence got that I haven't got?"

The girls tittered. Emerald, the most senior girl there, answered the question. "I presume you mean in addition to ravishing good looks, impeccable bloodlines, and more money than she knows what to do with?"

"No need to say more," drawled Anastasia, pretending to be crestfallen.

Emerald smiled. "Oh, that's not it," she said, "at least, not all of it." Her voice dropped to a confiding whisper. "Lady Amelia sets no store in her virtue."

Anastasia's eyes went round. "Is that all? For *him*, I'd be willing to make the sacrifice."

More laughter.

Emerald said, "You wouldn't be the first to try. And it wouldn't do you a bit of good. Julian Raynor has a cardinal rule about the girls who work for him. He is our employer, and he never steps outside that role."

Anastasia's nose wrinkled. "Rules can always be broken."

As the carriage outside the window moved off, the girls began to file out of the anteroom.

"Well?" said Anastasia. "What do you say to that?"

Emerald answered with a question. "What do you know of Lady Amelia?"

"Not very much. Why?"

"My advice to you is don't tangle with her. She may have the face of an angel, but she has the disposition of a cobra, as more than one poor lady has discovered to her cost."

"Who, for instance?"

"Oh, Mary Harvey, for one, if you must know."

Anastasia was by now seething with curiosity. A bell rang, and the girls moved to various tables in the cardroom. "Lord Harvey's sister?" asked Anastasia in a soft undertone.

Emerald nodded. "It's a long story. I'll tell you about it later."

* * *

Inside Lady Amelia's well-sprung chaise, Julian was holding off the amorous attack of the worldly-wise widow.

"Shameless," he murmured, caught between amusement and exasperation. He wrenched Lady Amelia's roaming hand from his groin and straightened his clothes a moment before the coachman flung the door wide and let down the steps.

"Damnation," said the lady, her magnificent eyes glaring at the coachman. "Who told you to stop the carriage, Hawkins?"

"But ma'am," stammered Hawkins, looking about him helplessly, "we've arrived."

Tipping her head back, with eyes narrowed on Julian, and her lips curved in a frankly salacious smile, she said, "Now that, Hawkins, is where you are in error. I haven't arrived. And I warrant that Major Raynor hasn't arrived either." Her eyes dropped deliberately to Julian's bulging groin.

"Baggage," admonished Julian, chuckling. He quickly brushed by the blushing coachman to descend to the pavement.

As he made to assist Lady Amelia from the coach, she hung back for a moment. Her eyes holding his, she said softly, "I say to blazes with Ranelagh Gardens and its boring walks and entertainments. The pleasure to be had at my house is more to my taste and yours, if I have not misread you, Julian. It's not too late to turn the coach around. What do you say? Is it to be Ranelagh for your delectation this evening or, quite simply, me?"

Julian was tempted. He had yet to break the period of celibacy that the long sea voyage had enforced upon him. But after a moment of consideration he shook his head. "Patience isn't one of your virtues, is it, my sweet?"

Resigning herself to the inevitable, she descended the

steps. "I have no virtue," she whispered huskily, her lips almost brushing his ear. "No more than you do. Don't try to persuade me that you wish to change me, Julian?"

No. He didn't wish to change her, and it showed in the sensual slant of his mouth. He'd had many women in his time, and for sheer sensual pleasuring, there wasn't a woman to match her. She was unashamedly carnal as well as insatiable, and that suited Julian just fine. Just watching the swift rise and fall of her breasts and the way her eyelids drooped in arousal sent powerful messages thundering through his blood.

Julian took a small breath, and let it out carefully. He was here for a purpose. Serena Ward. A cold gust of air seemed to blow through him, cooling his ardor. Serena. One day he would tell her that the thought of her was the perfect antidote to a man's passion. As his equilibrium returned, he gave a light laugh. Taking Amelia by the arm, shaking his head, he started forward.

As she nibbled on stale cake and looked out at the lights of the Rotunda from the booth that was reserved for their party, Serena reflected that her hopes for the evening had not been realized. What she'd had in mind was a small intimate family gathering where her beau, Mr. Hadley, would have a chance to shine. Well, perhaps not "shine" exactly. Trevor was not one to put himself forward in company, but in a small group of people, he could hold his own. She'd wanted her family to see that their opinion of Trevor was grossly unjust. He wasn't stodgy and as dull as ditch-water. He was as straight as a die.

No sooner had they arrived, however, than Jeremy had excused himself to go and speak to acquaintances he had caught sight of in the hordes of people who strolled the tree-lined walks. Shortly after, Clive had followed his example, leaving the three Ward ladies and Mr. Hadley alone in the box. But not for long. Catherine's most constant admirer had come calling, and Lord Charles had carried Catherine off on his arm. Only three people remained in the booth, Serena, Letty, and Trevor Hadley, and since Letty and Trevor could never see eye to eye on any subject under the sun, Serena was racking her brains for some neutral topic she might introduce to ease the silence that had fallen.

"I do hope the rain holds off," was what she finally hit upon.

Letty wasn't listening. She was leaning over the box, studying the crowd below, giving back stare for stare to the passing bucks who ogled her.

Mr. Hadley clicked his tongue. "I advise you, Miss Ward, not to encourage these impertinent young fops, or before you know it, they will have invited themselves into our box. One can't be too careful in this sort of crowd, you know."

"Stuff and nonsense," derided Letty, her eyes snapping. "I happen to be acquainted with some of those gentlemen whom you are pleased to call fops."

"All the same," went on Mr. Hadley, unperturbed, "it were better if you followed your sister's example and sat well back in the box."

The color was high in Letty's cheeks. "I thought the whole point of coming here was to see and be seen?"

Before Mr. Hadley could make matters worse, Serena quickly intervened. "Perhaps we could all sit forward a little? I know that Phoebe Cole will be here this evening, and we promised to look out for each other. It has only just occurred to me that if I am sitting at the back of the box, we may miss each other."

The compromise was accepted with good grace and the

chairs were duly arranged. From the Rotunda came the strains of an orchestra tuning up.

"Dancing," said Letty rapturously. She jiggled in her place and waved to someone below.

Lord Harry Egremont, Lord Kirkland's heir, called out, "Letty, come down and dance with me."

"Young unmarried ladies of breeding," said Mr. Hadley, "do not make a spectacle of themselves by dancing in public pleasure gardens."

Green fire flashed from Letty's eyes, but her smile was dulcet. "How old are you, Trev?"

Though he winced at the familiarity, he answered readily, "Thirty. Why?"

"To hear you speak, one would think you had one foot in the grave. Serena, may I dance with Lord Harry?"

Serena's annoyance was profound though she did not know whether she was annoyed with her beau, or her sister, or even herself for having arranged tonight's debacle.

"I can't see any harm in it," she temporized, and before she could say one more word, Letty was out of the box in a flounce of petticoats.

" 'Pon my soul!" Mr. Hadley stared at the door that was still vibrating after Letty's precipitous exit. "What did I say to bring that on?"

Floundering, Serena answered, "She is at a difficult age. Try to be patient with her, all right?"

She couldn't tell him the truth, that Letty was reacting to Jeremy's hopes for a brilliant match for her. Letty had a young girl's dreams of marrying for love, and had steadfastly turned up her nose at the several eligible gentlemen her brother had thrown her way. In this, Serena was her staunchest ally. Letty was young with her whole life before her. She shouldn't be made to accept second best; she shouldn't be made to give up her dreams of love and fulfillment. She should have her chance at happiness. She should be free to accept a man who loved her, whether or not he came with title and fortune.

She swallowed a small lump in her throat. Her own case was not the same as Letty's. She was older, more worldly-wise. Love held no allure for her. Her ambitions were more modest, more suited to her years and experience. Affection and children to love her—that was the most she could hope for.

For a girl with no dowry to speak of, she really was very fortunate. Trevor Hadley was not precisely wealthy, but he was no pauper either. His square face was pleasant to look upon; his hazel eyes held intelligence. It was a comfortable face, a nice face, and one that would not be forever turning to the next breathtaking beauty who came into his line of vision. He wasn't like Allardyce or Julian Raynor. He was more like Stephen. She could count herself the most fortunate of women.

Sighing, she turned to look out over the fashionables who were promenading about.

"Would you look at that!" exclaimed Mr. Hadley.

"What?" Serena obediently peered down at the couples who were milling about the Rotunda.

"Letty and Lord Harry! They've gone off by themselves! Look, over there, down one of those walks! Never fear, I shall bring her back to you."

"But—"

Trevor did not wait for whatever it was Serena was about to say. One moment he was there, the next moment she was talking to thin air. She couldn't remain in the box by herself. Grinding her teeth together, she went after him.

As the group of gentlemen vying for her attention crowded around her, Amelia sent Julian a coy, sideways glance. Relinquishing the lady with smiling grace, Julian turned aside to watch the fireworks display until Lady Amelia should grow bored with her little court.

It amused him to see that it was Lady Amelia and not the fireworks that was the cynosure of all masculine eyes. She drew men to her like moths to a flame. He wasn't jealous. He understood her allure only too well. She was a born coquette, a creature of the senses who appealed unashamedly to a man's carnal nature. This was not to say that she was any man's for the taking. Many men had made that mistake only to discover that they had been toyed with as a cat toys with a mouse. Amelia could be cruel when she had a mind to be, and never more so than when a gentleman truly lost his heart to her.

Chuckling, Julian wandered over to one of the small treed arbors which were set out at regular intervals around the man-made lake. Finding the arbor unoccupied, he paused for a moment to take snuff. Out on the lake, young bucks in punts were using their poles to try to knock each other into the water. His eyes lifted as a rocket flared over the lake and burst into a thousand stars. Pocketing his snuffbox, he leaned one hand against the twisted trunk of an old rhododendron which was just coming into bloom. When a woman's voice carried to him from the other side of the arbor, he dropped his hand and straightened. There was a rustling sound as her skirts brushed against the hedge of rhododendron, then she was there before him.

"Letty? Harry? Where . . . ?"

Serena paused at the entrance to the arbor. The light from the overhead lantern filtered through the dense screen of vines and branches like dappled moonlight, casting an unearthly glow. She took a small step forward, then another, before coming to a halt. The man in the shadows might have been anyone, broad shoulders tapering to a narrow waist, one hand on the hilt of his small-sword. Even if she had been blindfolded, she would have recognized him. The air between them was charged.

"Julian."

"So, it is you," he said.

Chapter Nineteen

❧

From the moment she knew he had landed on English soil, she had rehearsed in her mind how she would act and what she would say when they finally came face-to-face. Flynn had convinced her that there was no point now in demanding explanations and apportioning blame for something that no longer mattered to either of them, and Flynn was right. Julian had a new life in America. She had her life in England. Only one thing was important. They must forgive and forget. Then they could destroy the evidence of their brief union and they would be free of each other forever.

She had not foreseen that Julian Raynor in the flesh would have such a profound effect on her. Her heart was thundering against her ribs. Her mouth was dry. The pat little speech she had rehearsed so religiously skirted the edges of her mind, then quietly slipped into oblivion.

Clearing her throat, she said, "I'm glad everything worked out so well for you, Julian."

Whatever he said in reply was lost in the deafening report of exploding fireworks. Light streaked across the sky and for the space of a few seconds, inside the shelter of rhododendrons, there was enough light to see by.

He looked leaner to her, his face harsher, and there were new lines etched around his eyes. She'd always thought of him as a force to be reckoned with. Now she sensed a different kind of strength in him. Julian Raynor was a man who knew who he was and where he was going. America had done this for him. Then the light faded, and the darkness pressed in on them, seeming to draw them closer together.

In that interval of blinding illumination, Julian also had taken her impression. She was exactly as he remembered her—delicately molded features as pure as a cameo; finely spun gold hair that framed her face in clusters of waves. Her gown was just what he would have expected of Serena, nothing too much, nothing too showy. But even that unrevealing gown could not conceal her high-breasted womanly form, the graceful sweep of her throat, the tiny waist that was no more than a man's handspan. As the escort of Lady Amelia, the most desirable woman in London, he knew he was the envy of his peers. He also knew that if it weren't for the past, there was no woman he would rather have escorted than the one standing before him.

Smiling a little, he said, "You are looking well, Serena."

Encouraged by his cordial tone, she edged closer. "As you are, Julian. I think America must agree with you."

What he had not remembered was the perfume she always wore. He inhaled the fresh fragrance of wild poppies, and the recollections her scent stirred in him slipped through his defenses as easily as a fog invading an impregnable fortress. Within him, he felt some of the ice begin to melt.

As he watched the play of light across her lovely face, it seemed to him that he wasn't the only one who regretted the past. When her dander was up, she was a termagant. Had she struck out at him in that rash way of hers only to come to her senses when it was too late? Or had she come to see in retrospect that he had never been a threat to her precious escape route?

She stood there as docile as he had ever seen her, her

eyes huge in her white face, her breathing shallow as she waited for him to speak.

"Are you happy, Serena?"

She let out a pent-up breath. For no reason that she could think of, moisture pooled in her eyes. She had a sudden, irresistible impulse to try and make everything right between them. "I'm happier for seeing you, Julian. I'm sorry for the way things turned out, truly I am. I don't want us to remember each other with loathing. Life is too short for that. Can't we forgive and forget?"

Her appeal worked on him powerfully. And really, she was doing no more than voicing his own sentiments. The time had come to put the past behind them. "Yes," he said, extending his hands palm up. "Let's forgive and forget, shall we? As you say, life is too short for anything less."

She slipped her hands into his. He squeezed gently, and for one timeless moment, the harmony between them was consummate.

He smiled.

She smiled.

Drawing her hands away, but naturally, so as not to disturb this newfound harmony between them, she said, "I really shouldn't be here, you know. I'm supposed to be looking for my sister. Letty is at a bad age, if you see what I mean."

"You mean she slipped her leash to go gallivanting with her beau?"

She nodded and they both laughed.

"You should have written to me," she said, "to tell me you were coming to England."

"I wanted to surprise you."

He had certainly done that, but she wouldn't think now about the chagrin she'd endured, knowing that he was in London and had made no move to come to her.

Forgive and forget. That was the course Flynn had advised her to follow.

There was a burst of applause from the spectators on the lawns outside their shelter. "I must go," said Serena, "before Letty does something outrageous."

"No, don't run away." He blocked her exit by stepping in front of her. "Tell me about yourself, Serena."

The last thing she wanted to do was argue with him, especially over something as inconsequential as searching for her sister. There had been enough discord between Julian Raynor and herself to last her a lifetime, *ten* lifetimes. For once, Letty could look out for herself.

"I suppose," she said, feeling a little nervous to think that they were having a normal conversation, like any two normal people, "that the most important thing that has happened to me is that I am engaged to be married."

"Are you engaged? I understood that you were holding off until things were settled between us?"

This was a jarring note, and her eyes flew to his face. The flash of his teeth as he smiled at her was vastly reassuring. "Naturally," she said, "there will be no announcement until our marriage certificate is consigned to the fire." She laughed, and he laughed along with her.

"Do you have it, Julian?"

"Let me reassure you on that point. It is in a very safe place."

"You sound like a cautious man."

"In some things."

She didn't know how to answer this without stirring up old quarrels. "Well then," she said, "how soon may I expect to hear that it has been destroyed?"

He smiled at her eager tone. "Your suitor, Trevor Hadley, is it not? He must be a remarkably patient fellow?"

"Trevor is a very fine, upstanding man," she agreed amicably.

There was an interval of silence, then he said, "How have you managed to hold him off?"

"Hold him off?"

"Come now, Serena, I think you understand the question well enough. Your suitor must have pressed you for a reason for the delay in making your engagement public knowledge. Does he know about us?"

"Good God, no! No one knows about us, except for Flynn."

"Then how have you managed to persuade the inestimable Mr. Hadley to contain his impatience? You are not getting any younger in years. He must wonder why you have not snapped him up while you still have the chance."

He meant it as a joke. She knew he meant it as a joke. And even if he didn't, she couldn't afford to get his back up. And what did it matter if he alluded to her advanced years? At five and twenty, she *was* practically a confirmed spinster, wasn't she? He was saying no more than everybody else was thinking. Evidently, he thought she was at her last prayers.

Even if she was at her last prayers, she would never admit it to him.

"Serena, I—"

"Trevor isn't like you, Julian. He is devoted to me. My welfare always comes first with him. He respects my reluctance to take that final, irrevocable step. And this time around, there can be no destroying the evidence of the marriage if one's husband turns out to be a faithless libertine."

"A faithless libertine? Would you care to explain that remark?"

She detected the temper in him, and that made her smile. "Oh, I think you can explain it better than I can."

The finale of the fireworks display burst around them like an exploding sun. The earth trembled beneath their feet and the applause from the spectators rose to swell the unearthly racket of a multitude of detonating rockets and Catherine wheels. The silence of the two inside the arbor remained inviolate.

At length, Julian said, "You sound like a wronged wife. Jealous, Serena?"

"Jealous?" She sent him a look that would have reduced him to a smoldering cinder if he had been able to see it. "I would want my head examined if I were jealous of the sort of women you take up with."

He was truly amused now. "What do you know of the sort of women I take up with?"

She almost managed to hold on to her temper, then he laughed softly, and caution was thrown to the winds. "The whole of London is agog with your bedroom exploits in Charles Town."

"And here I thought I was the soul of discretion."

"Do you call it discreet to fight three duels in one night over three different women?"

"You will have to refresh my memory. I have no recollection of such a thing."

She gasped, swung away from him, then returned until they were toe to toe. "I suppose fighting duels over women is such a commonplace with you that you can't even remember the names and faces of the women involved?"

Even in that dim light, she could see that he was grinning from ear to ear. Stung, she went on hotly, "The actress, Mary Donovan? The madam of that bawdy house, Mrs. Carla What's-her-name? And last but not least, oh no, by no means least, that Indian girl whom you won in a game of cards? Does that refresh your memory?"

He didn't try to contain his laughter. Between chuckles and chortles, he got out, "Serena, you amaze me. Your memory is far better than mine. What I can't understand is why you should take on so? Those women can mean nothing to you."

"They mean less than nothing to me, except perhaps to convince me that the society of loose women is your proper element."

As soon as the words were out, she knew what he was thinking. He'd confided in her once that when he was a young boy, he had been practically raised by whores and prostitutes. That thought had not entered her head when she'd uttered her vile taunt.

"Julian, I didn't mean anything by it."

His teeth were clenched. "You have the disposition of a shrew and the mouth of a fishwife. But I have told you this before."

Her face flushed scarlet under his contempt. With great dignity, every inch the grande dame, she picked up her skirts and marched around him, making a beeline for the gap in the hedge. He came after her, shouldering his way through the crush of dispersing spectators. At one of the fountains, he caught up with her.

His voice was hissing with the force of his anger. "What makes you think you are different from those loose women you so obviously despise?"

When she stuck her nose in the air, ignoring him as she quickened her pace, he reached for her. Swinging her to face him, he administered a rough shake. "You shared my bed," he sneered, "believing that our marriage was a sham, then you betrayed me. What does that make you?"

"Betrayed you?" she cried out. "I never betrayed you! My God, I thought I was in love with you! But no longer! All I want from you, Julian Raynor, is an assurance that certificate has been destroyed. Then we shall both be free to go with our own kind."

"You'll have that assurance when it suits me, and not a moment before."

"What does that mean?"

"It means that when there is a pressing reason for me to have done with our marriage, I'll let you know about it."

Stunned, she stared up at him. Suddenly catching her breath, she shrilled, "You poisonous snake! I should have expected this from you, a gamester!"

"And I should have known better than to trust a deceiving, conniving light-skirts."

She reared back and swung at him with her clenched fist. Julian ducked, and her momentum carried her to the edge of the fountain. When he reached for her, she flung off his hands and went tottering back.

"Serena, no!"

His warning cry came too late. She took a belated step to the side, then staggered backward into the lily pond. Hooped skirts billowed out around her like a ship in full sail. Serena sat there in watery splendor, knees drawn up to her chin, water from the fountain cascading over her head and shoulders, and flowing in unending rivulets into the gaping bodice of her gown. When she looked up, she gasped in horror. In the heat of battle, while they had been deaf and blind to everything but themselves, a circle of grinning spectators had formed around them and were observing the little drama with avid interest. Their laughter and titters were more easily borne than the suppressed chuckles that issued from Julian's mouth.

"Serena!"

"Julian!"

The two voices coming simultaneously had Serena groaning in mortification. Trevor would never understand how she could come to be in this predicament. It was the other voice, however, that gave her her worst moment. Of all the people who must witness her humiliation, it would have to be Lady Amelia Lawrence.

Julian was the first to recover his wits. Speaking in a

carrying voice for the benefit of the curious bystanders, he said, "My dear Miss Ward, I do beg your pardon. It was most clumsy of me. Allow me to help you." Then he spoiled it with a snicker.

Though she wanted to scratch out his dancing eyes, there was nothing for it but to accept the hands he reached out to her. When she came out of the water, the spectators burst into a spontaneous round of applause.

"Aphrodite, rising from the water," Julian's amused voice whispered in her ear. "Tsk, tsk, Victoria. What a wanton exhibition."

Pulling away from him, smiling dulcetly for the benefit of the spectators, she said pleasantly, "My brothers will wish to thank you in person for all you have done for me, Major Raynor." Preferably with pistols at twenty paces.

His brows climbed at the implied threat. "I look forward to meeting them."

His words deflated her. Jeremy and Clive would be no match for this villain in a duel, nor had she seriously contemplated such a thing. The less she had to do with Julian Raynor, the better it would be for all concerned.

"Serena, what the deuce is going on here?" demanded Trevor Hadley, coming up at that moment. "If this gentleman has insulted—"

"Oh no, Trevor," Serena got out quickly. "I took a fall, and Major Raynor was helping me. Oh, I don't believe you are acquainted?" And ignoring the sodden state of her ruined frock, as well as the puddle of water forming at her feet, she made the introductions. Nor did her smile falter when the elegant brunette sidled up to Julian to lay a proprietary hand on his sleeve.

Lady Amelia Lawrence possessed an arresting beauty. She was slightly taller than Serena and far more generously endowed. Her dark good looks and exquisite figure were set off by an elaborate confection of silver tissue and dark-blue silk. Seeing her, Serena was made excruciatingly aware not only that she had the look of a scuttled sailboat, but also that her modest gown of green sarcenet had been made over from one of Catherine's ballgowns that was already three seasons out-of-date. Resolutely ignoring the grin on Julian's face, she held herself a little straighter; her chin lifted a fraction. Her one thought was to retreat with as much dignity as was left to her.

"Are you two ladies acquainted?" began Julian.

Lady Amelia answered with a little laugh. "Oh, Miss Ward and I have known each other these many years. But I don't believe I've had the pleasure of making this gentleman's acquaintance." Her dark eyes smiled alluringly into Mr. Hadley's.

As Mr. Hadley stuttered his name and made an awkward bow to London's reigning belle, Julian slipped out of his coat and draped it around Serena's shoulders. Truth to tell, she was glad that someone was aware of her discomfort but, perversely, she wished it had been anyone but Julian Raynor.

"A fine, upstanding man," he whispered, squeezing her shoulders consolingly. "Devoted, faithful, always puts your interests first?"

She flung him a look of smoldering reproach. Her lower lip trembled.

The smile died out of his eyes. "Victoria," he said softly, "you are magnificent."

Suddenly, it was all too much for her—Julian's mockery, Mr. Hadley's defection, Lady Amelia's perfection, and the goggle-eyed spectators who had yet to disperse. Turning on her heel, she stalked off, without a word of explanation, without a pretense of an apology. Mr. Hadley broke off in the middle of a sentence, uttered a surprised exclamation, and took off after her.

A muscle clenched in Julian's cheek as he watched their progress through the crowd.

Serena felt as if the weight of the world was balanced on the crown of her head. The coat draped around her shoulders smelled distressingly of Julian's cologne. Water squished in her shoes. In her present discomfort, to answer the barrage of questions that came at her from the five other occupants of Mr. Hadley's hired coach was almost more than she could manage.

"We were not quarreling. How should we be? I scarcely know the man. It's just as I told you. I was pushed from behind and went sprawling. I may have uttered a few choice words, but those were not directed at Mr. Raynor particularly. As I said, he came to my assistance. That's all there was to it."

"We could hear your raised voices as we came up to you," said Mr. Hadley.

Clive was laughing. "It sounded more like a lovers' tiff."

"Clive!" reproved Catherine, sending him a quelling glance.

"Well, it did. Oh, not that it was. I know that. But you could hear them practically all the way to the Rotunda. When I finally came up to them and discovered it was Serena and Raynor who were making all that racket, you could have knocked me down with a feather. I'll wager that Serena's name and Raynor's will be all around the gentlemen's clubs and coffeehouses by tomorrow morning."

"How vulgar!" exclaimed Catherine.

"Yes, isn't it?" replied Clive cheerfully.

Letty sniffed. "Not to mention Mr. Hadley's name and Lady Amelia's. That was the spectacle that sent me into hoots of laughter."

Mr. Hadley rounded on her. "None of this would have occurred if you had behaved with a modicum of propriety."

"Stuff and nonsense!" retorted Letty. "Lord Harry is practically a member of the family. There is nothing unusual in our going off together."

"Well, there ought to be."

"Jeremy, what's to be done?" Catherine Ward reached a hand to her husband as if to shake him from his reveries.

"It will all blow over," he said. "It's not as though Raynor is one of our intimates. We are not likely to cross paths very often. And when we do, if the world sees that we Wards are on terms of civility with the gentleman, the little contretemps will soon be forgotten. My advice to you all is to act as if nothing had happened."

"Sound advice," said Mr. Hadley.

Serena said nothing. She was thinking of Julian and Lady Amelia, wondering where they were and what they were doing. Sniffing, she pulled the folds of his velvet coat more securely around her.

Serena Ward was the perfect antidote to a man's passion. This was the thought that possessed Julian's mind as he climbed the private staircase to his rooms in his gaming house. He had not even attempted to bed the delectable Lady Amelia. How could he when his mind was full of another woman? Serena Ward. He'd burned with the thought of laying his hands on her and shaking the life out of her. He'd pleaded a headache, a *headache,* for God's sake. As an excuse, it was so absurd that Amelia had actually believed it.

It wasn't necessary to shake the life out of her. He had the means to bring her to her knees. She could moon over the inestimable Mr. Hadley till her hair turned silver before he would release her from their marriage bond, and she had only herself to thank for it.

Throwing off his smallsword, then his waistcoat, he stretched full length on top of the bed. He wasn't being precisely fair to Serena. Though it irked him to admit it, he was the one who had set things off on the wrong foot. One moment he had been all reasonableness, and the next moment, he'd been bristling like a sullen schoolboy.

Trevor is a very fine upstanding man. As soon as the words were spoken, he had remembered a different conversation, a different set of words. *I would no more think of taking up with your kind than I would with thieves and murderers.*

She must know how well he had done for himself. The whole of London knew it. In Charles Town, he wasn't a man of dubious origins who was kept on the periphery of society life as he had once been in England. He was a man of wealth, property, and considerable influence. His favor was curried by those in government circles as well as by society matrons who had young daughters to wed. Did Serena comment on any of his accomplishments? Of course she didn't! She flung in his teeth her baseless accusations about his women and his dueling.

Not entirely baseless. Mary Donovan, he would allow —was that her name? He took issue with Mrs. Carla What's-her-name. The only Carla he knew was the madam of a bawdy house and was old enough to be his grandmother. As for the Indian girl, he had merely rescued her from a brutal husband. There had never been anything between them.

Faithless. Now that was going too far. He understood about fidelity in marriage. His own father had been an example to him, which was more than could be said of Serena's father if rumor was to be believed. If Serena had been any kind of a wife to him, she would have had more fidelity than she knew what to do with. He would have given her fidelity every night of the week, and twice on Sundays. Maybe thrice.

If anyone was faithless, it was that beau of hers. He had stood there gawking like a half-wit when Amelia turned the full force of her charm upon him, and all the while Serena's teeth were chattering like castanets. Hadley hadn't had the presence of mind even to throw his coat over the shivering girl. Julian had wanted to throttle the man. And this was the paragon Serena had held up to him?

Good lord, in Trevor Hadley, she had nothing to crow about. Julian had done a little investigation of the gentleman. Mr. Hadley made his money from the sheep he farmed in the wilds of Wales. He hated society life and had only been persuaded by his dragon of a mother to come to town to find himself a wife—a docile, biddable wife who would breed the next generation of Hadleys just as his prize ewes produced his next crop of lambs. How Hadley had been taken in by Serena was beyond his comprehension. Docile? Biddable? He could almost feel sorry for the poor misguided poltroon.

His mouth twisted in a humorless smile. The things he admired in Serena would make poor Mr. Hadley take to his heels. He couldn't believe that she meant to waste herself on such a man. What would she find to do on a sheep farm in Wales? Englishwomen of gentle birth, when they were not producing the next generation of their replicas, were mere ornaments to be displayed. Hadley would hardly let her take a hand in his business enterprises. In the New World, things were different. Husbands and wives worked together to tame the vast wilderness and carve out a place for themselves. South Carolina was a young, vigorous colony. Women of Serena's stamp were its life-blood. And if anyone could prevail in the New World, Serena could. A lady, no, a woman capable of risking her life in the stinking sewers of London would not cavil at a few mosquitoes or the sweltering heat of a Carolina summer.

It wasn't all work, of course. When the harvests were in, planters and their families repaired to Charles Town. In Charles Town, Serena would—

Suddenly recognizing the direction his thoughts were taking, he flung himself from the bed and went to stand by the window. Jaw clenched, he stared out blindly, only vaguely aware of the press of vehicles below as patrons came and went through the front doors of his club. In Serena's eyes, he would always be the gamester who could never aspire to kiss the hem of her gown. Which was just as well, he told himself savagely, because the day he kissed the hem of any woman's gown was the day he would admit himself to an insane asylum.

I thought I was in love with you. I thought I was in love with you. Her words drummed inside his head. If he had believed that . . . He squelched the thought before it was complete. Past tense! He and Serena were past tense, and an ocean of regret could not wash out his mistrust of her.

Chapter Twenty

✦❧✦

Jeremy Ward's comforting prediction that the scene between Julian and Serena would be soon forgotten proved too optimistic. Within twenty-four hours, not only was the tale told a hundred times over—in gentlemen's clubs, in coffeehouses, in drawing rooms, in ballrooms—but with each telling the story became juicier and much more lurid.

Catherine Ward heard it first at her levee. She was feeling rather gratified at the crush of people who filled her little boudoir that particular Thursday afternoon. Lady Kirkland was present, as was her ladyship's bosom friend, Lady Trenton, and other notable members of the ton. This was something of a triumph for Catherine, and she wondered why she was being suddenly taken up by so many fashionables of the first rank. Before the room had emptied of all but her most constant admirer, Lord Charles, she had received a spate of invitations to routs, ridottos, balls and, most splendid of all, to a house party at the Kirklands' place in Kent.

"Charles," she exclaimed, clapping her hands, "this is like a dream come true. You see what this means, don't you?"

"Oh yes, I see what this means. Do you?"

For a moment, Catherine faltered beneath that somnolent stare. Then she shook her head and crowed with delight. "What this means is that Serena and Letty may enlarge their circle of acquaintances, you know, meet more eligible gentlemen." Catherine never put a guard on her tongue when she was with Lord Charles. They had known each other since they were children and she was as comfortable with him as she would have been with her own brother. "Then perhaps we shall see the last of Mr. Hadley. Oh, not that there is anything wrong with Mr. Hadley, you understand. It's simply that he is wrong for Serena."

Lord Charles rose to his feet and Catherine stared up at him as he came to tower over her. He wasn't as handsome as her own husband, but he was very pleasant to look upon. At one time, she had tried to play matchmaker, hoping his eye would alight on Serena or Letty. He was a most eligible bachelor, well breeched and heir to his father, the Marquess of Danham. Lord Charles evaded all her efforts to marry him off, and she knew why. He was an incorrigible rake, devoted to a succession of mistresses, and he had never bothered to hide it from her. Nor did she like him any the less for it.

"What is it, Charles? What did I say to amuse you?"

"How set are you on frustrating this match between Serena and Mr. Hadley?"

She dimpled. "You won't tell Jeremy?"

"He would be the last person in whom I would confide."

She glanced up at him quickly, but there was nothing to be read in his expression. Smiling confidingly, she said, "I'm utterly opposed to it. Mr. Hadley is very nice in his own way, but he won't do for Serena. That girl needs to be taken out of herself, you know, live a little more recklessly. I would be far happier if she found someone . . . well . . . someone like you, Charles."

"How fascinating," he drawled. "Then your happiness should be complete."

For one irrational moment, she thought he was implying he had offered for Serena, and her heart did the oddest flip-flop inside her chest. It was the satirical smile that brought her to her senses. "All right, out with it," she said, laughing up at him. "What is it you know that I don't know?"

"Julian Raynor," he replied gently. "I had it from my valet that Raynor's mistress came upon him last night as he was—shall we say, 'embracing' Serena?—and Lady Amelia toppled the poor girl into the lily pond in a fit of jealousy."

"Oh no!"

His eyes searched her face. "Do I detect a note of pique?"

"What?"

"You and Raynor. At one time, as I remember, he paid you assiduous court."

He sounded jealous, and she looked at him with an arch smile. Flirting with him, she said, "Julian is very hard to resist when he decides to charm a lady." Her smile faded before the sudden ferocity in his expression.

"I'm warning you, Catherine, I won't let you go to him. If you leave Jeremy for any man, that man will be me. I've invested too much in you to lose you now."

For a moment or two, she could not make sense of what he was saying. When his meaning registered, her face flushed scarlet and she sprang to her feet. "Invested in me?" She threw the words back at him. "I thought you helped me, helped us, because you were our friend."

"I'm not talking about money. I'm talking about us. There is something between us. There always has been. You know it too."

There had been something between them once, but that was a long time ago. As a young girl, she had been infatuated with him, not that he had known of it. Even then, he'd had an eye for loose women. When he had gone off to university and Jeremy Ward had come into her life, she had got over her infatuation.

When he made to take her in his arms, she backed away from him. "I love my husband," she said desperately. "I thought you knew it."

She thought for a moment that he would disregard her words, but he swung away from her and stood gazing out the window. When he turned back to face her, she saw with some relief that his habitual satirical smile was in place.

"Sooner or later," he said, "something like this was bound to happen. I am, am I not, an unconscionable rake, and you are a beautiful, desirable woman?"

His expression, his whole demeanor invited her to laugh with him. She laughed uncertainly. "And I should have expected it," she said.

"Friends?" He said the word whimsically.

"Always," she responded, trying to control her breathing.

His recovery was more rapid than hers. As if there had been nothing between them, he returned to their former topic of conversation. "It's not surprising that all of London is beating a path to your door. They hope to be in their boxes when the curtain goes up on the next act between Serena and Raynor. It's better than a cockfight, don't you know, and it would not surprise me if wagers were being laid all over town, right at this moment, on the outcome."

Lord Charles was correct. In the Cocoa-Tree Chocolate Shop, the odds were ten to one in favor of Lady Amelia establishing herself as Raynor's next flirt. In White's Coffee Shop, where a different version of the night's events was circulating, the odds were three to one that Serena Ward would give Mr. Hadley his congé, having surprised him in *flagrante delicto* with the worldly widow. In the St. James Coffee House, where the rumor was closer to the truth, the odds were even on Julian offering Serena Ward the position of wife before a fortnight was out.

Clive Ward thought it all a huge joke and, knowing his sister better than most, judiciously put down his blunt with every confidence that he would collect a packet.

At first, Mr. Hadley was flattered. The story he heard was that Lady Amelia and Serena Ward had come to blows over none other than himself. Further reflection sobered him. If the story ever got back to his mother, there would be no containing her tongue. The lady he married must be above reproach, or he would never hear the end of it. Serena had better tread carefully, and so he would tell her, tactfully, diplomatically, but indisputably the first chance he got.

Jeremy Ward was not so tolerant as his younger brother. When the rumors reached his ears, he cut short his business with Lord Choate and made directly for Julian's gaming house. Major Raynor, he was told, was not at home, but had gone off to Kensington on some unspecified business.

Meanwhile, ignorant of all this rampant speculation, Serena was spending the afternoon with Letty and her two young nephews on a fishing expedition. Now that Riverview was rented, the boys were missing some of their former pastimes and Serena made it a point to do interesting things with them. This was no sacrifice since she enjoyed her young nephews. Today, she was especially glad to be with them for she knew they would allow her little time for brooding.

They did not go far from home, but walked the banks of the Thames, downstream, till they came to the grounds of the old Savoy Palace. Here, under Flynn's instructions, they set up their fishing poles and laid out their picnic.

"You'll never catch no fish 'ere," Flynn said in an aside to Serena. He gestured to the many small sailing boats that bobbed on the river. "It's too bleeding busy and we're too late in the day."

"That's not the point. It's an outing. We are here to enjoy ourselves."

As anticipated, the fishing was uneventful, but no one was disappointed, least of all the boys. Flynn's resourcefulness was unending. Before Robert and Francis had tired of one game, he was onto the next. His knowledge of local history was inexhaustible, and after they had eaten he went off with the boys to explore the nearby ruins. Meanwhile Serena and Letty had been assigned, much to their nephews' glee, to women's work.

They were packing the picnic things, and had stopped to admire a particularly fine yacht out in the middle of the river. They did not hear the approach of horses along the bridle path. It was only when they heard voices raised in salute that they realized they were not alone.

Serena was the first to recognize the two young bucks. She had caught sight of their grinning faces at the scene of her humiliation the night before, when Julian had dragged her from the lily pond.

"You are the chit from Ranelagh," one mocked.

"So that's the filly on which my blunt is riding," said the other.

Serena felt a stab of fear. Rising slowly, never taking her eyes from them, she spoke in an undertone to Letty. "Don't run. Walk. Find Flynn and bring him here."

All the color ran out of Letty's face. She had taken only a step or two, when one of the riders dug in his spurs and came forward, cutting off her retreat.

"Why the haste, sweeting? Aren't Dick and I good enough for you?"

The one named Dick let out a whoop. "God love you, Salty, your eye has deceived you this time around. 'Tis the other little dove who is Raynor's piece."

Salty's head jerked round, and he eyed Serena askance. "You're hoaxing me, Dick! That ain't no fancy piece, leastways, I don't reckon she is. She's as stiff as starch. No, no, she's a schoolmarm or a governess or some such thing."

Both men snickered. "Why don't we ask her?" said the one called Dick.

Serena choked down her fear and glared at them with burning hostility. "You've had your jest. Now get yourselves gone before my brothers return and thrash you to within an inch of your lives."

Ignoring her threats, the two riders walked their mounts in a circle, hedging the girls in.

"I don't see any brothers, do you, Dick?"

Dick laughed suggestively. "Lud no! I don't see a single soul."

There was a wildness about them that turned Serena cold with fright, though she instinctively concealed it. Letty's fear was obvious as she clung, trembling, to Serena and that seemed to excite their assailants all the more.

Standing stiffly, head thrown back, Serena glared at them. "Our brother is Sir Jeremy Ward," she flung at them. "We are not playthings for your amusement."

"She don't half give herself airs. What the devil does Raynor see in her, that's what I can't understand."

"I aim to find out."

"Good. I'll take the other one. She's a dainty morsel and more to my taste."

As one rider made to dismount, Serena reached into the picnic basket and came up with a stone jar of Cook's homemade pickles. Throwing Letty off, she reared back and took aim as she had been taught to do when playing cricket with her young nephews. Her projectile caught Salty's horse a thunking blow on its flank. Rearing in terror, almost dislodging its rider, the horse bolted along the bridle path.

With a look of murderous determination, the other rider reached down and made a grab for Serena. She ducked under his horse's head and raced along the shore. He was on her almost at once. Flinging himself from his horse, wrestling her to the ground, he shoved up her skirts.

She opened her mouth to scream and his mouth came down hard on hers, forcing her breath back into her throat. It was Letty who screamed. Serena heard an answering shout. A shadow fell over her an instant before her attacker jerked back, releasing her. Letty stood over him, arm upraised, ready to strike him again with the stone jar. Flynn, arms waving, came racing down the rise toward them.

With a snarl and a curse, her assailant rolled to his feet. Mounting up, he sneered down at Serena. "Puffed-up bitch! You'll lower your crest soon enough once Raynor has had his fill of you. Then you'll be any man's for the taking." And digging in his spurs, he took off along the bridle path to catch up with his friend.

When Flynn reached them, Letty immediately began on a long, tearful explanation. Serena, still shaken, went to meet the boys as they bounded down the incline. They knew nothing of what had transpired, and no one enlightened them.

Flynn's eyes were troubled as they rested on Serena. He was thinking that it was time he had a man-to-man talk with Major Raynor.

The atmosphere inside that dingy little cottage in the village of Kensington was so dense that it gave the impression of a pea-soup fog that had blown in from the North Sea.

"Would you mind?" said Julian, indicating that he wished to open the window.

Constable Loukas drew on his long clay pipe and emitted another cloud of smoke into the choking interior. "What? Oh, I see what you mean. You are just like my Kate, God rest her soul. She never could abide the smell of smoke in the house either. When she was alive, I did my smoking in the garden."

Interpreting this as permission to open the window, Julian undid the catch and threw the window wide. After inhaling several long invigorating breaths, he said, "Smoking is going out of fashion, did you know? Snuff is becoming all the rage. Even society ladies are taking it up."

"As is young Harry. I cannot abide the stuff. Filthy habit."

"What is Harry getting up to these days?"

Loukas chuckled. "Can you believe it? He's hired himself on as an assistant to Thomas Burdus."

"The justice of the peace who has his offices in Bow Street?"

Loukas nodded. "It seems that the law is in our blood."

"I'm happy for him. I always thought Harry would go far."

"He'll want to see you, of course. You should look him up. His lodgings are in the Strand."

When Julian remained by the open window, Loukas frowned. Enlightenment dawning, he tapped his clay pipe into the empty grate and set it aside, saying gruffly, "Come and sit down, why don't you, so that I can make my report?"

Grinning, Julian accepted the invitation, not at all put off by his companion's fierce expression. Loukas and he went back a number of years, to the time Julian had arrived in London as a young stripling and had his first brush with the law. It was Loukas who had hauled him before Justice De Veil on a charge of breaking the peace, and it was Loukas who had persuaded the justice to go easy with him. Julian had come to know that behind the fierce exterior, Loukas had all the instincts of a true reformer. There was nothing that gave him greater satisfaction than setting a young man on the right road. With Loukas, that usually meant encouraging him to do a stint with the British army. He was a great believer in discipline as a builder of character.

Over the years, they'd kept up a correspondence. When on leave, Julian had spent many evenings supping with the Loukases in this very cottage. It was the nearest thing he had known to home since he had been left an orphan.

There were few people in whom Julian confided. Loukas was the exception, up to a point. Julian had glossed over his early years, mentioning only that he had been orphaned at a tender age. Loukas, however, was the only one who knew the details about his abduction and transportation to Maryland, and that only because Julian had enlisted his aid in trying to solve the mystery behind it.

"I'm listening," said Julian. "What, if anything, have you discovered?"

Loukas scratched at his wig, dislodging it in the process. "Not very much, I'm sorry to say. Lord Kirkland was telling you the truth when he said there is no record of any magistrate signing a warrant for your arrest. So it would seem that the militia who arrested you that night were rank impostors. You have made enemies, my boy, but I suppose that is to be expected in your profession."

Julian shook his head. "This has nothing to do with my profession. Promissory notes belong to the house, not to me personally. And even if I were dead, they would still have to be redeemed. My death would not profit any of my patrons."

Loukas reached for his pipe, recollected himself, and replaced it on the grate. "I suppose your next of kin would be the one to profit?"

Julian frowned. "What am I to make of that?"

"Your wife."

"You suspect Serena?"

"Hardly. You were not murdered, were you? No, you were transported to America, so whoever is behind it did not wish your death, only your absence."

Julian made a joke of it. "Perhaps Serena only wished to punish me, you know, for forcing her into marriage?"

Loukas laughed. "And risk your wrath when you finally returned to England? I think not. However, I shall certainly take that into consideration."

"Fine. Then what do you make of it?"

Loukas hesitated. "I say, Julian, you're not a government spy, are you?"

Julian cursed long and fluently. "If I had been a government agent, I would not be here now. I would have friends in high places who could help solve the mystery for me."

"Yet Lord Kirkland, the archenemy of all Jacobites, is your friend."

"And Serena Ward, the arch-Jacobite, is my wife."

"I see what you mean. Well then, perhaps your abductors were under the misapprehension that you were working for the other side. That still does not tell us who they are."

"What about the man who was in charge that night, the one I call Pretty?" he asked.

"Now, I may be onto something there. No, I won't say anything just yet. But you know, even if I find your 'Pretty,' I'm not sure what it will reveal."

They spent the next half hour speculating on first one

possibility then another, even going so far as to make a list of suspects. It was a long list.

When Julian rose to take his leave, Loukas walked him to the front door. "Do you know what I think, my boy?" The question was rhetorical, and after an interval, Loukas went on, "I think your best course is to complete your business here just as quickly as you are able and set sail for America. Yes, the sooner you leave England, the safer you will be. That's my considered opinion."

"No one," said Julian emphatically, "is going to chase me out of England. I'll go when I am ready and not a minute before."

Loukas smiled and clapped him on the shoulder. "Somehow, I just knew you would take that tack. In that case, if you are determined to unmask the culprits, there is only one thing to be done. We must flush them out."

"I'll think about it," said Julian. "There is something else I have been meaning to say to you." He looked around the small interior before bringing his eyes back to Loukas. "As things stand, I would feel more comfortable if I had someone I could trust working in my gaming house, you know, someone who could spot anything or anyone unusual. I don't think I stand in any real danger, but I'd be a fool to take unnecessary risks. Besides, I may want to confer with you, and it's a bloody nuisance having to come all the way out to Kensington."

"You are just saying that because you know I am bored with my retirement. It's very kind of you, my boy, but—"

"Fine," said Julian, "I shall find someone else."

"Oh, no you won't. If you really mean it, I'd be glad to do it."

"Then be there tomorrow morning sharp."

Loukas's list of suspects was still occupying Julian's mind when he entered his gaming house. It would never occur to Loukas to seriously suspect Serena. He admired her pluck, and had almost from the first, when he, Julian, had inveigled Loukas and his grandson, Harry, into helping him bring off their Fleet marriage. Julian had convinced them by describing Serena as a green girl whose heart was in the right place but whose politics were abominable. She was her own worst enemy, he told them, and it would take something extraordinary to make her give up the escape route. If she were married to him, he would put a stop to it.

Like himself, Loukas had been touched by the girl's efforts to save the lives of Jacobite fugitives. At the same time, he'd been horrified that she, a mere female, would run such risks. As for the law that Loukas was sworn to uphold, he took the broad view—the fewer Jacobites there were in England, the less likelihood there was of another Rebellion. If Serena had been involved in agitation and conspiracies, he would have taken a different view.

But he had not seen eye to eye with Julian on his solution to the problem. Marriage was too extreme a step. It was then that Julian had been forced to admit that there was another, more compelling reason for the marriage to go forward. Loukas had looked at him in astonishment, and Julian had flushed to the roots of his hair, stammering out something about Serena being blameless, that he had mistaken her character, that he had been overcome with his emotions and had taken advantage of her. Just thinking about the expression on Loukas's face that night still had the power to make him blush.

Scowling, he thundered up the stairs and burst into his rooms, kicking the door behind him. His manservant nervously stepped forward to inform Julian that he had a caller who had elected to wait for him in the bookroom.

Flynn rose at Julian's entrance. "I 'ave brought back

your coat," he said, "all cleaned and pressed," and he indicated the velvet coat which was folded over the back of a chair, the coat which Julian had last seen draped around Serena's shoulders.

"I'm obliged to you," said Julian curtly. He strode to the sideboard and poured himself a healthy dose of brandy. Raising the glass to his lips, he took a long swallow before turning to face Flynn. *Here,* he thought cynically, *is another specimen who is blind to Serena's true character.*

"Serena," said Flynn, drawing closer, "asked me to deliver a message to you."

Julian's expression darkened. "I have no interest in anything Serena Ward might have to say."

"This won't take long."

"Well? I'm listening. Out with it, man."

Flynn smiled, and gave it to him, right on the chin, with a blow that sent Julian reeling backward. Glass and brandy went toppling as he landed on the floor, his back coming to rest against the side of his desk. Shaking off the effects of that stunning blow, Julian roared, "Have you taken leave of your senses?"

Panting, feet splayed, Flynn crouched over his victim. "That's the message you deserve. Now, you and me is going to 'ave a little conversation, see, even if I 'as to beat some sense into that thick 'ead of yours. Well, what's it to be?" He raised his fists threateningly.

Now this was the language that Julian understood. Still, he didn't want to take advantage of Flynn. Though the boy had broadened and put on some weight in the last two years, he was still a boy. "I wouldn't want to hurt you, Flynn."

"Craven!" Flynn flung at him with unconcealed contempt.

Julian grinned. "Don't say I didn't warn you," he said,

and with a lightning movement of one leg, he sent Flynn flying.

Downstairs, in the crowded card room, patrons called out and girls screamed as chandeliers began to swing alarmingly. From the room above came the sounds of smashing crockery and falling furniture. A piece of ornate plaster fell from the ceiling and landed with a thud on the carpeted floor.

"Earthquake," said Colonel Mowbray, viewing the shaking walls with some interest. "This reminds me of Egypt. Did I ever tell you about the time I—"

"Yes!" said several voices simultaneously, heading him off before he could begin on another of his boring reminiscences.

The walls and ceiling stopped shaking; the chandeliers gradually stilled. There was the sound of muted laughter, then that, too, died away.

Chapter Twenty-One

"Was that really Serena's message?" asked Julian. He held out his hand and helped Flynn to his feet.

Flynn took a moment to work his sore jaw and feel his nose for broken bones. Satisfied that his beauty was unimpaired, he answered, "She told me to thank you for the use of your coat. It was her tone of voice that suggested the beating."

Julian couldn't help laughing. "Bloodthirsty wench!"

"Yes, well, she 'as good reason to wish to see you 'ung, drawn, and quartered, as I'm sure you'll agree."

As they spoke, they righted tables and chairs that had been knocked over in the course of their brawl.

"What about this mess 'ere?" asked Flynn, pushing at the fragments of a broken vase with the toe of his shoe.

"My man will take care of it."

Flynn chortled. "After the way you raved at 'im when 'e burst in 'ere, you'll be lucky if the poor devil ain't already 'anded in 'is notice. Barbarians, that's what we are." He looked at the porcelain fragments at his feet. "Ugly old thing, wasn't it? What was it—a present from your old auntie that you was afeared to part with?"

Julian looked from Flynn to the remains of what had once been a collector's piece, a Meissen urn that was worth more than Flynn could earn in a lifetime. "It was in payment of a gaming debt," he said.

"Oh well," said Flynn grandly, "tell me what the damages amount to and I'll be 'appy to settle them."

Julian turned away to hide a smile. "That won't be

necessary. I never liked it. You've done me a favor, truly. Now, what's your tipple, Flynn?"

"Whatever you've got."

Julian poured out two glasses of brandy and brought one to Flynn. Settling themselves in armchairs on either side of the hearth, they sipped at their drinks, grinning occasionally like mischievous schoolboys.

Breaking the silence, Julian said, "You said something about Serena having good reason to wish to see me hung, drawn, and quartered. I presume you are referring to our quarrel at Ranelagh and my refusal to destroy the record of our Fleet marriage?"

The mellow expression on Flynn's face evaporated to be replaced by something resembling belligerence. "If you don't wants 'er, you should let 'er go. I thought it was all settled?"

"And so it was. And so it will be. You may believe, Flynn, that I have no more wish to be married to Serena than she has to me."

"Then why did you mislead 'er?"

"Because," said Julian, more vicious than he meant to be, "she got my dander up."

Flynn scratched his head. When Julian did not explain himself, he said, "I don't know why you should take on so. You was the one who wronged her, gallivanting off to America with nary a word to let 'er know if you was alive and well."

"She knew."

"What did she know?"

Julian bolted the dregs of his glass. His smile became twisted. In that moment, he decided he'd had a bellyful of swallowing the praises of his erstwhile wife. Flynn had set Serena on a pedestal. It was time someone showed him that she had feet of clay.

"She arranged for my abduction," he said. "I was transported to the colonies as a convicted felon, oh, under an assumed name, you understand. I tried to explain who I was and why I should be set free. For my pains, my masters tried to beat the defiance out of me. In due course, I escaped. As you see, it all worked out for the best. You will not be surprised, however, if I do not fall on my knees and thank Serena for the favor she did me."

Flynn's expression was gratifyingly shocked. His mouth opened and closed like that of a fish out of water.

"I see from your face," said Julian, "that this has all been a great shock to you. That's something, I suppose. I had wondered if you and Serena were in this together. Now I have my answer."

Finding his voice, Flynn stuttered, "And you think . . . but why would . . . she said that you blamed her for something, but I never thought . . ." Then, in gathering volume as his senses came back to him, "What in blazes made you think that Serena was capable of such a thing?"

Julian reached for the brandy decanter and replenished his glass. "She told me she would, when she found out that I'd tricked her into marriage."

"What did she tell you?"

"That she would find a way to punish me. And she succeeded."

Flynn emitted a snort of disbelief. "And you thought that a girl of Serena's character could play such a mean-spirited trick?"

"Not at the time, no. I thought it was just temper speaking. Oh, you need not look daggers at me. Don't you think I've gone over it in my mind a hundred times over, a thousand times? Who else could it have been? And in case you should ask—no, I was never a spy for His Majesty or for any secret Jacobite sect either, so don't go looking for scapegoats, Flynn, because it won't wash."

Julian had told himself time out of mind that he'd closed the door on that chapter of his life and that Serena's betrayal no longer had the power to affect him. He was coming to see that he had been deceiving himself. In South Carolina, he hadn't allowed himself the time to think about her. He'd been like a man demented, working as hard as any field hand in his determination to drive her from his mind and heart. Work and other women had proved the perfect panacea to Serena Ward, or so he'd thought at the time.

It had been a mistake to come back to England, a mistake to see her again and resurrect all the old anger, all the old pain. He'd buried it so deep inside him that he hadn't been aware of its existence until now. He wished he had buried it deeper. At the same time, now that he had finally voiced a small part of his bitterness, he experienced an odd sense of relief.

He hadn't wanted to confide his suspicions to Constable Loukas, because of some twisted sense of loyalty to Serena. Looking at Flynn, he knew that there was nothing he could say, no argument, no proof he could make that could shake this young man's faith in her. Instead of goading him, that knowledge acted like a lance to draw off the poison that had been building to a head.

"Mean-spirited?" said Julian. "I never said that Serena was mean-spirited, never thought such a thing. In point of fact, she has more spirit than is good for her. That's the trouble with Serena, as I should know. I was her victim. God, have I not been her victim!" He made an abrupt motion with one hand to silence Flynn as he made to answer him.

"Flynn, you *know* what she is like when she is in a temper. Her wrath cannot be contained. She acts first and repents at leisure. You know I speak the truth."

Flynn leaned back, studying Julian with an unsettling

shrewdness. "And you think that she plotted your abduction in a fit of temper, then came to regret it almost at once?"

"It's the kind of thing she would do."

"If you can say that, you never knew 'er."

A chill crept into Julian's voice. "And you do, I suppose?"

Flynn nodded, then grinned, not with humor, but in a taunting way. "I *should* know 'er. I became 'er page when I was six years old. You wants to know about Serena? I'll tell you. Serena is as straight as a plumb line. She could never do what you 'as described because that would be like stabbing a man in the back. That's not 'er style. If Serena was to best you at your own game, she'd want you to know it, not let someone else take the credit for it. Ask that beau of 'ers who she jilted at the altar."

Julian's brows snapped together. "Serena jilted someone?"

"In a manner of speaking. She was only a girl of seventeen at the time. Captain Allardyce 'e called 'imself, but if 'e ever served in 'Is Majesty's cavalry, my name ain't Richard Flynn."

Satisfied with the intent look in his companion's eyes, Flynn went on, " 'E was a rake of the first magnitude, as well as penniless. I tried to tell her, but she wouldn't listen. In those days, Serena 'ad a dowry."

"What happened to the dowry?" cut in Julian.

"What? Oh, she gave it to her bleeding father when she came of age, you knows, to 'elp him with 'is political ambitions." Flynn snorted. " 'E squandered the lot of it on guns for them there Jacobites of 'is."

"And Letty? Did she lose her dowry too?"

"Oh no. Letty and Mr. Clive was underage. Sir Robert couldn't put 'is greedy paws on their moneys. It was left to them in trust, by their grandmother, you see."

"Yes, I do see. Poor Serena. Go on."

"Well, as I was saying, anyone with a lick 'o sense could see that all Allardyce was after was 'er dowry. 'E told 'er that 'e loved 'er and 'ad become a reformed character. 'Course, Sir Robert would never 'ave entertained such a match. So they was going to elope. I don't mind telling you, I was at my wits' end." He paused to take a swallow from his glass.

"Then what happened?"

"Then Serena discovered that all the time 'e was courting 'er, 'er loving suitor was 'aving an affair with that Lawrence woman."

"Lady Amelia?"

"I see you knows 'er," said Flynn dryly.

"Never mind that now. Get on with your story."

Flynn grinned as the recollection came back to him. "On the night they was to elope, guess who climbed down the ladder and into 'er lover's arms?" Flynn nodded. "Yes, your 'umble servant, Richard Flynn. You must remember, in those days, I was a smooth-faced boy of fourteen summers, and all dolled up in Serena's finery, with a veil to cover my face, even my own mother would not 'ave recognized me."

"Good God!" exclaimed Julian. "You and Serena were incorrigible even then!"

"Yes, well, to get on with my story. 'E took me to that chapel in Mayfair, you knows the one, where 'is friends was all waiting for us. At the altar, when I threw back my veil and 'e saw 'ow Serena 'ad tricked 'im, I thought 'e would kill me. 'Is friends, on the other 'and, was all laughing their 'eads off."

So was Julian, and the tears ran down his cheeks. Mopping at them with a large linen handkerchief, he choked out, "Flynn, what possessed you to do such a thing? You were fortunate that the scoundrel did not run you through on the spot."

"Serena made it worth my while. She gave me the ring the villain 'ad given 'er to plight their troth. At least *it* was genuine even if 'e was not. 'Course, I didn't 'ave no use for no ring, so . . ." He touched his finger to the emerald in his left earlobe.

"I always wondered about that earring," said Julian.

"Well, now you knows. 'Course, I told Serena that anyone could see from the ring Allardyce 'ad given 'er, that 'is affections were not worth a tinker's damn. Well, look at it! This emerald 'ere could fit on the 'ead of a pin. 'Serena,' I said, 'you'll know when a man loves you, 'cos 'e'll give you an emerald that's worth a king's ransom.' "

They both fell silent, remembering that the wedding band Julian had given Serena had been fashioned from a curtain ring.

At length, Julian said, "Whatever happened to the suitor?"

" 'E was laughed out of London and we never seen 'is face again. But the point I am trying to make is this— even if no one else knew it, 'e knew that Serena 'ad given 'im his just deserts."

There was a long, thoughtful silence as Flynn's words hung between them. Julian breathed deeply as though inhaling the clean scent of them. When he realized that Flynn's account of Serena's aborted elopement was having the very effect that Flynn intended, he shook his head at his own gullibility.

Gullible or no, he felt as if a great weight had been lifted from his shoulders. Becoming aware of Flynn's searching look, he said, "Point taken. But how did you manage to keep Serena's name out of it?"

"Oh, we let on that 'er brother 'ad engineered the 'ole

thing. And Allardyce was too ashamed to let the world know that 'e 'ad been bested by a mere girl."

"Bold little hussy!" said Julian, laughing, and there was a trace of pride in his voice.

"Not so bold as you would think," corrected Flynn.

"No?"

Flynn sighed. "Well, you must 'ave formed an opinion of the sort of men she takes up with? Stephen 'Oward? Mr. 'Adley? Tame, predictable specimens, and that's the best you can say about them."

"And you think that's Allardyce's doing?"

"She loved 'im," said Flynn simply, then he went on, " 'Er own father was no 'elp to 'er. Sir Robert was no saint and that's the truth of it. Even when 'er mother was dying, 'e was off with one of his light-skirts and no one could find 'im. It was a long time before Serena could bring 'erself to forgive 'im for that."

When Julian offered the decanter, Flynn held out his empty glass. "Tell me about Serena's mother," said Julian, filling Flynn's glass to the brim.

"What about 'er mother?"

"I saw her portrait once. Serena's resemblance to her is remarkable."

"Poor Lady Ward," said Flynn. "I 'ardly remember 'er. She died when Serena was sixteen, poor thing. Sir Robert only married 'er for 'er money, leastways, for 'er father's money. 'E was rich, see, and Sir Robert's debts were astronomical. What more can I tell you? She never made no impression on me. I will say one thing, though. Serena was close to 'er mother. You might say that Serena was 'er mother's champion. Poor Lady Ward didn't 'ave it in 'er to say boo to a goose."

Flynn's description raised all kinds of speculations in Julian's mind. He could not help wondering at the closeness between mother and daughter which Flynn had mentioned. What kind of confidences had passed between them—a woman who was humiliated by her husband's unending infidelities and a young girl who was on the threshold of womanhood? If he was right in what he was thinking, it explained why Serena had fought against the irresistible attraction that had leapt between them almost from the moment they had set eyes on each other. Did Serena think that he was cast from the same mold as her father? Did she really believe that he would turn out to be another Allardyce?

Of course she did! He had seduced her and offered her the position of mistress. What else could she think of him? *I would no more think of taking up with your kind than I would with thieves and murderers.* Your kind. She wasn't disparaging his humble beginnings. *Libertine! Faithless libertine!* Those were the words she most frequently employed when her hackles were raised. It was his reputation with women which galled her. Even at Ranelagh, it was his women that she had flung in his teeth. Good God, didn't she realize that if he had had her, there would be no women now to regret?

He thought of something else. At Ranelagh, he had been with Lady Amelia, and Serena must have known what to make of that. She had given him such a look, then had slunk away like a whipped cur. He swallowed, remembering the look she had thrown him.

I thought I loved you. I thought I loved you. God, what had he thrown away?

"At any rate," said Flynn, breaking into his thoughts, "that's all beside the bridge, now, ain't it? You've got your life in America and Serena is 'appy with 'er Mr. 'Adley, or she will be once you do the 'onorable thing and burn that certificate of marriage."

Whatever response Flynn had hoped to hear was dashed with Julian's next words. "You're right, of course, and the sooner it's done, the better. I suppose we should both be present when I destroy the evidence, otherwise Serena will always wonder whether or not her marriage to Hadley is genuine?"

With those unfeeling words, the marriage of Serena and Mr. Hadley seemed to take a giant step forward in Flynn's mind, and he sipped his brandy in glum silence.

"You'll arrange it, Flynn?"

"What?"

"A meeting between Serena and myself so that we can both be present when I destroy the evidence of our Fleet marriage?"

"That may be impossible to arrange the way things stand."

"The way things stand?"

"The wagers in all the coffee'ouses, the rumors and speculation—you knows what I mean."

When it was evident that Julian did not have the faintest idea to what he was referring, Flynn enlightened him.

"It will soon blow over," was Julian's callous response to what Flynn told him.

Flynn regarded him in pent-up silence before bursting out, "That's easy enough for you to say. Nobody thinks any the less of a gentleman for 'is peccadilloes, yes, and that piece what you 'as been taking up with. You and Lady Amelia 'as nothing to lose. It's Serena's virtue that is being questioned; it's 'er reputation that is tarnished."

Julian was genuinely amused. "No one who knows Serena," he said, "would ever take her for a woman of easy virtue."

"Is that so?" retorted Flynn scathingly. "As I remember, you did once. And 'ow do you account for those two rogues who accosted 'er this very afternoon, when my back was turned, yes, and did their best to ravish 'er?"

For the first time since planting his fist in Julian's face, Flynn had the satisfaction of seeing the expression he wanted to see. Julian's nostrils were flared. His brows were down. His gray eyes had lightened to an arctic transparency. Under Flynn's fascinated gaze, a hot tide of color rose from throat to hairline. The voice that addressed Flynn put him in mind of distant thunder.

"If anyone has laid a finger on my wife," said Julian, "he will answer to me for it."

It was no great feat to discover the identities and lodgings of Dick Montrose and Salty Saltcoat. They were young provincials who had come up to town to acquire a little polish by mixing in polite society. When they became bored with polite society, they had attached themselves to the young dandy set who devoted their energies to drinking, gaming, and wenching. Julian and Flynn found them in the Magpie and Stump, their regular haunt, absorbed in a game of cribbage. The ladies who hung on their shoulders were not precisely ladies.

At sight of Julian, the gentlemen went parchment-white, but they recovered a little when Julian greeted them pleasantly and made no move to unsheathe his smallsword. Flynn had insisted to Julian that this could not be settled with pistols or foils, lest Serena's name attract even more scandal than it already had.

There was a quarrel. Julian did not like the way Mr. Montrose tied his cravat. Flynn took exception to the sneer on Mr. Saltcoat's handsome face.

"My advice to you pretty boys," said Julian amicably, looking from one to the other, "is to leave London on the first available stage. Gentlemen, if I find you here tomorrow, I may be a little out of humor, which would not bode well for you. Tell them, Flynn."

"Castrati," said Flynn gleefully. "Then your pretty voices would match your pretty faces."

Hands reached for the hilts of weapons, but before they could be unsheathed, both Julian and Flynn, fists flying, had launched themselves simultaneously at their respective targets. It was over so quickly that Julian felt thoroughly cheated.

But fortune smiled on him. Some of the regulars, grossly put out by the way these swaggering fops were forever throwing their weight about and walking off with the choicest women, decided they'd had enough of it. Jeers and catcalls quickly degenerated into shoves and pushes. Someone smashed a chair against a table and raised it threateningly. There was a silence, then a roar. A tankard went flying and the battle was joined.

It was a grand dustup and the major was a grand gentleman, as all readily agreed when, honor satisfied, the combatants retired to the bar to enjoy several rounds of drinks that Julian generously sponsored. Only Dick and Salty did not join in the celebration. When they came to themselves, they slunk away as Julian's back was turned, and booked seats on the first stage that was leaving London.

Some time later, accompanied by a band of well-wishers, Julian and Flynn staggered their tuneful way toward St. Dunstan's Court. At the side door to Julian's house, the procession halted. Julian squinted down at Flynn. He was swaying alarmingly, Flynn noted and put out a hand to steady him.

"I have been meaning to ask you," said Julian, his speech more precise than Flynn had ever heard it, "why you are still attached to the Ward household? A young man of your abilities, Flynn, could do so much better for himself."

"And so I shall, when the time is right."

"Why not today? I could use a good man like you."

Flynn fingered the emerald at his earlobe. He shifted restlessly. "You'll never 'ear me say it," he said, "so don't go setting no traps for me."

Julian smiled. "I thought as much. Poor Flynn. Poor me. Poor Mr. Hadley, and all buggers like us."

Doffing his hat, he executed a long and courtly bow to his boon companions. The effect was somewhat spoiled when, finally straightening, he mistook his direction and entered the wrong house. With one last cheery wave, he shut the door.

The procession of men stared dumbly at that closed door. Their eyes lifted when a light flared to life at an upstairs window. Suddenly, several piercing shrieks in quick succession ripped the silence, followed almost instantaneously by the blast of a blunderbuss. A moment later the front door was wrenched back on its hinges and Julian came rocketing down the steps, coattails flying, pursued by the wronged husband.

It was just one more lurid tale to increase Serena's disgust of him was Julian's last woeful thought before he pitched on his face at Flynn's feet.

When Flynn returned to Buckingham Street, he discovered that Serena had waited up for him.

"What are you doing here?" he asked, making an angry motion with one hand to encompass his small bedchamber.

Noting inwardly that Flynn was forgetting to drop his aspirates, a sure sign that he was foxed, Serena said coolly, "I wanted to talk to you. What has happened to your face?"

Flynn glowered at her. "Do you know what time it is? What will people think if they find you here, alone with me, in my room?"

"What will people think?" Her brows knit together in perplexity. "Flynn, this is Serena. No one will think anything."

As he advanced into the room and she had a closer view of the several marks and bruises on his face, she gasped and ran to him. "Flynn, who did this to you? Was it Julian?"

He slapped her hands away as she made to touch him. "Didn't you hear me? You shouldn't be here alone with me. We shall talk in the morning, in the breakfast parlor."

"You, Flynn, are in your cups," she said.

He laughed without humor. "I was never more sober in my life." Swinging away from her, he moved to the washstand and poured water from the china pitcher into the basin. Wringing out a cloth, he dabbed at his face before turning to face her.

"Look at yourself!" he said, snarling at her. "In your night rail! Serena, this is not decent. Haven't you heard of footmen seducing their mistresses?"

She gave a crow of incredulous laughter. "Flynn, don't be ridiculous. I'm too old for you. Who on earth has been putting these notions into your head?"

"There is only three years' difference in our ages." He was deadly serious, and her smile faded. "It happens all the time. Don't we both know of ladies of your own rank who have eloped with their footmen? Do you want to elope with me, Serena? Is that it?"

She moved quickly to the door. "I wish you would tell me," she snapped, "why you are trying to spoil our friendship."

"When we were children, we could be friends. We are not children now."

"Fine, if that's the way you want it."

She hesitated and he growled, "Get out of here before I finish what those two bastards started this afternoon."

The door banged behind her. Flynn remained frozen for a long time, then suddenly groaning, he flung himself on top of the bed.

In the morning, when he entered the breakfast parlor, Serena eyed him warily. Flynn was all smiles.

"I 'as a faint recollection," he said, "that you was waiting up for me last night, but I was so foxed I 'ardly knows if I imagined it or not."

The wariness gradually left her eyes. "You were like a bear with a sore paw," she said.

"And now I feels like a bear with a sore 'ead."

Everything was going to be all right between them. Serena let out a relieved breath. When the door opened to admit Catherine, she picked up her cup and drank from it. She and Flynn had yet to have their talk. Not in his bedchamber, nor in hers, she decided. Those days were gone forever. Flynn was right. It wasn't decent.

She glanced at him covertly over the rim of her cup. It was evident to her that Flynn did not remember a word of what had passed between them the night before. She didn't want him to remember, or she would never be able to be natural with him again.

"I think I shall go for a walk," she said.

"Be sure to take Flynn or one of the maids with you," said Catherine absently.

"Flynn?"

They left the breakfast parlor together.

Chapter Twenty-Two

꧁꧂

The problem with summer was that the sun never set before ten o'clock and, even then, twilight lingered for a long while after. For those who were intent on pursuing some clandestine end, such as highwaymen and burglars or ladies who had a secret assignation to keep, the long summer nights could prove extremely awkward.

Such were Serena's thoughts as she glanced at the clock on the mantel, noting that a whole minute had passed since she had last taken stock of the hour. Outside her window, the gloom was deepening. The only sounds in the house were clocks ticking and odd groans and creaks as both house and servants settled themselves for sleep. Through the open window, she could hear watermen calling to each other across the river and the occasional tolling of a bell.

She was nervous, naturally. When the clock chimed, it would be time to leave the safety of her bedchamber and set off for her rendezvous with Julian. Even now, the boatmen would be waiting for her, only a stone's throw away from Ward House, at the York Water Gate. They would row her downstream to Blackfriars Stairs, whence Julian's sedan, with an escort to protect her, would convey her to his gaming house.

Pacing restlessly, she paused to examine her reflection in the looking glass. Pride had dictated that tonight she not disgrace herself. The ladies in Julian's gaming house, as she well remembered, were no frumps, but rather dazzlers of the first order. Though her own blue silk was remade to bring it into vogue—tight-fitting bodice and waist, moderate hoops, and yards of silver lace ruffles at her elbows and throat, Julian would never know it. Her fair hair was undressed and curling loosely to her shoulders, not from preference, but because a lady who had taken to her bed feigning a headache could hardly ask her maid to dress her hair as though she were engaged to go out for the evening. It was bravado that had prompted her to affix a black silk patch at one corner of her mouth, and sheer vanity that had persuaded her to rouge her lips and cheeks.

She pinned the girl in the looking glass with a hard stare. "What do you hope to gain by all this?" she demanded, making a motion with one hand to take in her finery. The girl in the looking glass, far from returning glare for glare, looked to be crushed, as though she might burst into a fit of weeping if someone looked at her the wrong way. Hardening herself against that look, Serena stomped to a straight-backed chair and plumped herself into it.

She did not know why she was beset by so many uncertainties. Everything was working out just as she had wished. It wasn't as though Julian were coercing her into keeping this appointment. There was good reason why they should both be present when the evidence of their Fleet marriage was finally consigned to the flames. She, as much as Julian, would never feel secure if she did not witness the deed with her own eyes. Once it was accomplished, they would both be free to go on with their own lives.

For her part, that meant marriage to Trevor Hadley. Though it was many months since they had talked of marriage, she knew that she had only to drop the hint and Trevor would pay her his addresses. Until now, he had deferred to her wish that they prolong the courtship so that they could come to know each other before taking that irrevocable step. It had certainly been a long courtship. Patience, she supposed, was Mr. Hadley's most notable virtue.

Delving into her pocket, she pulled out a lace-edged handkerchief and proceeded to blow her nose. It was absurd, she scolded herself, to find fault with Mr. Hadley for his lack of ardor when she was the one who held him off. She didn't want an ardent suitor. She wanted someone who was steady and dependable, and that was exactly what she had got. She should be happy, not moping like some silly schoolgirl who didn't know what she wanted.

She felt guilty, of course. Now that the one obstacle to their marriage would soon be removed, she wondered if she dared go through with it. It was taken for granted that she, an unmarried lady, would be coming to her husband untouched. She had wrestled with her conscience long and hard over that particular wrinkle, and had decided that she should not be made to suffer for the rest of her life for something that wasn't her fault. It was easy to make that decision when their marriage had seemed so far in the future. Now that it was at hand, her logic had lost some of its force.

Trevor was so moral. He would never understand how she had come to be involved with someone like Julian. As it was, he was deeply distressed with all the rumors and speculation after the debacle at Ranelagh. In this instance, he knew she was blameless. If he ever suspected . . .

When the clock struck the hour, she started. Eleven o'clock. Rising to her feet, she moved to her dressing table and studied her reflection as she set her silver lace mask in place. Taking up her stole of matching silver lace, she threw it carelessly over her shoulders, and after dousing the candles, she stole from the room.

There was no Flynn waiting for her on the other side of

the door, not this time, and she felt his absence keenly. Tonight, Flynn's services had been appropriated by Jeremy for Lady Kirkland's assembly. Nevertheless, it was Flynn who had arranged tonight's meeting, Flynn who had persuaded her that Julian's anger had abated and he was as eager as she to have matters settled between them. They only needed to be in each other's company long enough to burn their marriage certificate and she could be home in her bed long before the other members of her family returned from Lady Kirkland's do.

A few steps took her to the York Water Gate. It wasn't a boatman, however, who came out of the archway to meet her. It was Julian himself. She drew away to look up at him, studying him by the light from the lantern on the wall.

In his black cape and mask, he had the look of a highwayman. She gave a shivery, soundless laugh. In that moment, as she absorbed everything about him—his virile beauty, his arrogant, uncompromising masculinity—she no longer wondered why she had once been so susceptible to him, was still susceptible to him. Few women would be able to resist that appeal. The thought that few *had* resisted him settled the little flutters in the pit of her stomach.

"Don't be alarmed," he said. Taking her hand, he led her to the water's edge. "I took it upon myself to escort you in person. I'll not chance your safety to mere lackeys, not when Flynn could not be here to take you to me."

For some absurd reason, tears stung her eyes. "Thank you," she managed in a choked voice, and was saved from the necessity of saying more when he swept her into his arms and sprang lightly into the boat.

As the boatmen dipped their oars into the water, a silence fell, but it was a silence that held no undercurrents of hostility, at least, not as far as Serena could tell. Ever since Flynn had told her of Julian's abduction and all that he had suffered as a convicted felon, she had been overcome by a piercing sadness. Julian hadn't seduced her then deliberately abandoned her. What had happened was nobody's fault. They had been the victims of circumstance and their own prejudice.

No. They had been the victims of some monstrous plot to remove Julian from England. She and Flynn had racked their brains, trying to solve the mystery of who might have been behind it. No solution came to them, or rather, so many solutions that they were no further ahead.

It hurt her, of course, to think that Julian could have believed that she was capable of arranging his abduction. Flynn wasn't clear on this point, but he thought, hoped, that he had persuaded Julian that she had been innocent of plotting against him. Soon, they would part forever. She wished desperately that at least they could part as friends. In the future, when she thought of Julian, there would be no bitterness to taint her memories. She wanted his memories of her, supposing he ever gave her a passing thought, to be equally as untainted.

At the Blackfriars Stairs, when Julian handed her out of the boat, a young man came forward to assist her. It took a moment before Serena recognized him. In her mind, she would always think of him as "Lord Alistair."

"All's well," said Harry Loukas, looking at Julian.

When they came to the head of the stairs, it was a hackney that was waiting for them, and not the sedan that Serena had anticipated. For a moment, she hung back, her eyes darting from Julian to his companion. It was all so reminiscent of another time, when Julian had forced her into his carriage and had carried her off to Twickenham.

He made no move to coerce her, not even to hint her into the waiting carriage. "Either you trust me or you don't," said Julian. "Which is it to be?"

He had made up his mind that this time around, Serena must be allowed to make her own choices. She must come to him freely and without demur. And if she did, it would be forever; there would be no going back. There must be no misunderstanding on that point. But it would be her choice.

Good God, who was he trying to hoax? It was in his nature to use every weapon in his arsenal to persuade her to his will. He wanted to be fair, he wanted to be sensitive to her feminine scruples, but it was difficult when she was under such misapprehensions about him. He wasn't like her father; he wasn't like Allardyce; and if he couldn't persuade her of that fact, so much the worse for her.

He was doing it again, condoning conduct that in another man he would condemn as thoroughly reprehensible. Nevertheless he had made up his mind that Serena should determine their future. Whatever her decision, he would abide by it. So be it.

She entered the carriage unassisted, mentally chastising herself as every kind of a fool. That other time, their circumstances had been entirely different. Julian had been suffering a guilty conscience, thinking that he had ruined an innocent young girl. Having learned that she had a suitor, he had no reason to feel responsible for her, no reason to carry her off.

Now that there were no boatmen to inhibit conversation between them, she racked her brains for something innocuous to say. "That was young Mr. Loukas, was it not? What is he doing here?"

Julian indicated that she should look out the window. "He's arranged an escort for us."

Serena looked out the window and counted three outriders. "Are you expecting an attack?" she asked incredulously.

"You can ask that after what happened to you the other day?"

She experienced a small ripple of resentment at the hard tone he had employed, followed almost immediately by a flood of remorse. Flynn had told her how he and Julian had exacted their own form of retribution on the men who had attacked her, and though the finer part of her nature was shocked by Julian's uncivilized conduct, there was another side of her which relished the punishment he had meted out in defense of her honor.

"Why did you do it?" she asked, voicing a stray thought aloud. Recovering quickly, fearing that he might think that she was fishing for some sort of declaration, she plunged on. "Flynn should not have told you about the attack on me. All the same, I can't say I am sorry that those two came by their just deserts. Thank you, Julian. I mean that sincerely."

"They didn't meet with their just deserts, and they can thank Flynn that they got off so lightly. And who else should Flynn confide in? Mr. Hadley? He would not have lifted a finger against them. Your brothers? Their gentlemen's code of honor would have demanded satisfaction with pistols or foils, and all London would have got to hear of it. Yes, and the reason for it. No one will lift an eyebrow if they hear that I, a gamester and a commoner, resorted to fisticuffs to settle a dispute."

She was, as ever, confused by his sudden shifts in mood. Just once in her life, she would like to know exactly where she stood with him! On second thought, she decided she didn't wish to know. Better not to open that Pandora's box.

When the carriage stopped at the side door to his house, Julian alighted first. He insisted that Serena wait until some pedestrians had passed before he reached in to help her down. The humor in the situation began to work on her.

"Really, Julian, is all this caution necessary? Whose reputation are you trying to protect? Yours or mine?"

He was smiling when he answered. "Since I have nothing to lose, as you and Flynn have been at some pains to convince me, it must be yours."

"According to Flynn, I don't have much of a reputation to lose either." She was making conversation, hardly aware of what she was saying, relieved and pleased that his mood had lightened. "They are making wagers in all the coffee shops, but you will know all about that. Jeremy is fit to be tied."

"Yes, he came to me to see what, if anything, could be done to put a stop to it."

As they conversed, they mounted the stairs to his rooms. "Jeremy came to see you?" Serena's brows met in a frown. "He said nothing to me."

"He will, in his own good time."

"And . . . and what did you decide?"

"Nothing untoward. You know the sort of thing—that we should meet in public places, ostensibly by chance, and let the world see that we are merely polite and distant acquaintances."

"And neither you nor Jeremy thought to consult my wishes?"

"I'm consulting you now. What do you think we should do?"

No inspiration striking her, she said lamely, "I don't know. But I do know that I like to be consulted about things that concern me."

"That is exactly what I told Sir Jeremy. He assured me that nothing would be done without your consent."

She wasn't sure that she liked the sound of that, but

noting the grin on his face, she picked up her skirts and swept by him as he held the door for her.

Just inside the bookroom, she halted. There were vases of massed poppies on every available surface, making a vivid impression, and in front of the empty grate, a table with a pristine white damask cloth had been set for two. Along the sideboard were laid out a plethora of gleaming silver servers as well as crystal decanters and glasses.

"It's only a cold collation, I'm afraid," he said, removing her stole and throwing it over the back of a chair. Before she could divine his purpose, he had removed her mask and tossed it aside also. "In the interests of privacy, I gave my man the night off."

"But . . . I didn't think . . . I didn't expect . . ."

His expression altered; his voice became less animated. "I see. Then, if you cannot bear to be in my presence for more than a few minutes, by all means let us proceed to the one thing that is of any real interest to you. I shall only be a moment."

She started to put out a hand, then snatched it back before he could see it. Once the door had closed behind him, however, she wished she *had* stopped him. He had gone to so much trouble for her, not just tonight, but in avenging her honor and in consulting her brother about her welfare. She could not believe how ungenerous she was. Surely there could be no harm in sharing a bite of supper with him? She had wished with her whole heart that they could part as friends. Evidently, so did he. Then why was she suddenly acting like a silly schoolgirl?

She was acting like a silly schoolgirl because Julian Raynor, quite unconsciously, was putting ideas into her head, and that was nothing compared to what he was doing to the rest of her anatomy. Her breasts were heavy and bursting the confines of her tight bodice; her pulse

was racing; deep inside, she detected the quickening of
her womb and the melting that anticipated the hard in-
trusion of his body. There was no point upbraiding herself
for what was beyond her control. A woman in her dotage
would fare no better than she. Julian had this effect on
many women, as she should know.

Somewhat sobered by that thought, she marched to the
sideboard and began to inspect what was under the lids of
the various servers.

This was how Julian found her a moment later when he
stepped into the room. Since she was unaware of his presence, he allowed himself the pleasure of feasting his eyes
on her. In her blue silk gown with the silver lace, she was
unquestionably beautiful, and the soft glow of the candlelight gilded her hair and skin, making him want to reach
out and touch. He had always known she was a graceful
girl. He watched her movements as she investigated the
supper his chef had laid on for them. She was every inch
the lady, and that made him smile.

When he made love to her, she didn't look like a lady.
She was loose-limbed and wanton, and everything a man
could wish for in his woman. His smile faded as the need
rose in him, not to pleasure her, not to take his pleasure of
her, but to be intimate with her in the fullest sense of that
word. He did not think he would ever be able to get close
enough to her.

Shutting the door, he moved to join her at the sideboard.

"Does this mean that you have changed your mind?"

At the sound of his voice, she swung round, then
gasped when she saw his face. He had removed his mask,
and bruises and scrapes stood out grotesquely against the
tanned skin. She was startled into a giggle.

"You look as though you had walked into a stone wall.

Did . . . did you receive those injuries on my behalf, Julian?"

He answered her easily. "Not entirely. Didn't Flynn tell you? No matter, you'll hear soon enough. I was surprised by a jealous husband when I was climbing into bed with his wife. He let fly with a blunderbuss. Naturally, I took off as though a rocket had been lit under me. Unfortunately, I fell headlong as I sprinted out the front door."

The emotions that chased across her face at these blunt words tickled his fancy. She looked as though she wanted to hit him. "Of course," he said, "it was all a misunderstanding."

"Oh, with you, it always is," she retorted, and slapped some fishy concoction onto her plate before moving to the next server.

"No, really. Flynn will tell you. I was highly inebriated and entered the wrong house, the one next door to be exact. I wasn't there above a minute or two. It was an innocent mistake, but you may be sure the tattle-mongers are already embellishing the story. They always do."

She subjected him to a searching stare. "Why are you telling me this?"

He answered her seriously. "You said something at Ranelagh about my reputation with women. I wanted you to know that it has been highly exaggerated."

"But not entirely without foundation?"

His eyes bored into hers. "Not entirely."

Flustered by that look, she quickly made her selections and crossed to the table at the hearth. Julian held her chair as she seated herself and carefully adjusted her hooped skirts.

Taking the other chair, which was set at right angles to hers, he pulled a rolled-up parchment from his pocket and tossed it into her lap. "Our marriage certificate," he said.

"Shall we eat first, and decide afterward how best to bring the thing to a satisfactory conclusion?"

She nodded absently, her eyes downcast as she unrolled the parchment. "Do you know, it was when I read the names on this document that my memory came back to me, that day at Twickenham?"

He poured out some wine and cajoled her into drinking some of it. "Did you really suffer from a concussion? I was never sure after . . . later, I was never sure later."

Edging forward, she stared at him with huge, appealing eyes. "Julian, you cannot believe that I had anything to do with your abduction? The only thing I wanted was to escape from you. If I had known you were going to be set upon, why would I have run from you?"

He set down his knife and fork. "Why did you run from me, Serena? Was marriage to a gamester so horrifying to you?"

A slow flush crept across her cheekbones, but she kept her eyes level with his. "If I said something to offend you, I'm sorry for it. But Julian, you must admit, the profession of gamester is not an entirely respectable one."

"Oh? What do you think of when you think of gamesters?"

The words came to her automatically. "Wild. Dangerous. Reckless. That sort of thing."

"Good God! Those are the words that come to mind when I think of you! But I digress. Tell me why you ran from me that night of the storm."

She did not know how to take him in this humor. Rubbing at her puckered brow with one finger, she cast her mind back to the time in question. "I don't know what I thought," she said. "I was so confused. It seemed to me that there must have been some sinister reason that you duped me into marriage, something to do with the escape route."

"You thought I was a government agent?"

"I wasn't sure. But later, when Flynn told me that you really had helped to smuggle the real Lord Alistair out of England, I knew that could not be true."

"I was never an agent. My reasons for marrying you were entirely honorable. I had taken your innocence. Naturally I wanted to give you the protection of my name. It was you who made things difficult, Serena."

She flared up at this. "And did you suppose that I would tamely accept a husband whose only reason for marrying me was his conscience? You didn't want me as your wife. Nor," she hastened to add, "did I want you as my husband."

He grinned. "Because I was a gamester and libertine?"

"Yes! And later, when you disappeared without a word, and eventually turned up in America, it seemed to me that you had seduced me and abandoned me."

"In the manner of a true libertine?"

"Yes."

He studied her as the silence lengthened. Finally, he said softly, "How can someone as beautiful and as clever as you have so little confidence in her power to hold a man? A real man is what I mean."

For a moment, she thought that he was taunting her, but the light in his eyes was so tender, so compassionate, that the sting in his words was instantly disarmed.

His smile was dazzling. "Drink your wine, Victoria," he said, and diverted her train of thought by inviting her, on the next breath, to tell him about her future plans.

She had to search her mind for something to say. Aside from marrying Mr. Hadley so that she would no longer be a financial burden to her brother, she had no clear idea of what her future would be like. Ashamed at this entirely mercenary view of her suitor, a gentleman who was worthy of her utmost esteem and respect, she launched into a catalogue of his virtues. One thing led to another, and before long she was telling Julian about all her former beaux, and was surprised to find herself relating the tale of Captain Allardyce in a humorous vein, as though it had made no impression on her, and not blighted her young life.

He was an excellent listener, leading her gently when she faltered. For some reason, she found herself telling him about her mother and all that she had been made to suffer by a husband's indifference.

"And even knowing this," said Julian gently, "not long after your mother's death, you were willing to trust yourself to Allardyce, a man who must have seemed to you to be made in the image of your father?"

"He swore that he had reformed. But, of course, he lied. They always do."

His voice was very low, very grave. "There have been no women in my life since before I left Charles Town, and after you, certainly no one of any significance."

Tingles shivered along her spine, and her throat went parchment-dry. To her great distress, all the discomfort of her former arousal came back to plague her. She reached for her wine glass and took a long, fortifying gulp.

"Enough of me," she said. "I want to hear about your life in America. Are you really a farmer, Julian? Somehow, I just can't see it."

He laughed, and said yes, he really was a farmer, and went on to enthrall her with his description of his plantation and life in the colonies.

"The house is fine for a bachelor," he said, "but when I have a wife, I shall want something grander, as befits a family man."

A family man? Julian?

His smile conveyed his complete knowledge of her

doubts. "I suppose someone like myself, who was raised with all the benefits of a happy childhood, will want the same for his own children. But I told you this before, in Twickenham, don't you remember?"

She did, but what she remembered most vividly was his harrowing description of life in the workhouse and his boyhood years in the brothels of Manchester.

Perhaps it was the wine, perhaps it was the intimacy of the moment, but for whatever reason she reached out impulsively and clasped both his hands in hers, bringing them to her breast. Tears blurred her vision. "I'm sorry, Julian," she whispered, "so sorry, sorry, sorry, sorry."

He moved closer, and disengaging one of his hands, stretched his arm along the back of her chair. "Are you, my love? What are you sorry for?"

"For *everything*," she said comprehensively. For all that he had lost as a young boy, for the caprice of an awful fate that had savaged his life twice over, for not being the right woman for him, for the children they would never share. She had a fleeting impression of Julian surrounded by a brood of gray-eyed, dark-haired infants, and she wanted to cry her eyes out.

He kissed her tears away, but there was nothing comforting in those openmouthed kisses.

And most of all, she was sorry that he was a rake and she was what she was, and practically promised to another gentleman. She drew away gently and offered a teary smile. Looking regretfully at the parchment in her lap she picked it up and passed it to him. "We have dined," she said. "It's time to bring everything to that satisfactory conclusion you promised."

"So it is." He gazed at that parchment for an inordinate length of time. "I suppose," he said, "that the best thing to do is to put the candle to it, then throw it in the grate when it catches fire?"

That seemed reasonable. She nodded.

"Fine. You don't mind if I close my eyes while you do the deed? I don't think I can bear to watch." And so saying, he curled her fingers around the parchment and thereupon covered his own eyes with his cupped hands. "Tell me when to open my eyes," he said.

Serena looked at the parchment in her hand, then up at Julian. Her mouth worked.

"Is it done?" he asked. "Have you finished?"

When she was silent, he opened his eyes to see the parchment still clutched tightly in her hand. Tisking, he said, "Didn't you understand? Here is the candle," and he indicated the candelabra which was set to one side of the table, "and here is our certificate of marriage; and here is the empty grate. All you need do is this," and as if she were a half-wit, he pantomimed the motions of putting the flame to the parchment and throwing it in the grate.

This time, when he covered his eyes, Serena said, "Julian, surely it is your place to burn the evidence of our marriage? You are the male."

"Now that doesn't sound like the Serena I know," he said.

It didn't sound like the Serena she knew either. Steeling herself, she leaned across the table and put the parchment to the flame of one candle. As the parchment heated, and a brown scorch mark curled one corner, she gave a little cry and quickly withdrew her hand before the thing could catch fire.

"Serena, this will never do," said Julian.

"Please, Julian, won't you do it?" she pleaded.

He did not take the proffered parchment. "No," he said, "I won't do it because I want our marriage to stand. I shall give you one more chance. But understand this,

Serena. You either burn that certificate or you make up your mind to become my wife in every sense of that word. No. I don't want an argument. Burn the parchment, Serena, or face the consequences. This time, the choice is yours."

Chapter Twenty-Three

❧

S he lurched to her feet, throwing the parchment on the table.

He rose at a more leisurely pace. "Why won't you destroy our marriage certificate, Serena?"

"Why? Because of religious scruples, because it goes against everything my mother ever taught me, because it is distasteful to me. But you can have no such objections. It's your duty to burn it."

He was holding out the parchment, and she had flung back as if he were offering her a snake.

"That's not the reason," he said, and his eyes gleamed brilliantly. "Look at you! I've never seen you rigged out in such finery! And that beauty patch! Rouge, too, Serena? You have taken a great many pains with your appearance tonight, have you not? You wanted to seduce me, and by God you have succeeded."

Her teeth were grinding together. "You conceited oaf! No such thought ever crossed my mind."

"Didn't it, Serena? *Didn't* it?"

She glared at him.

He lifted the hand which held the parchment, bringing it closer to her. "Last chance, Serena. Destroy our marriage certificate, or make up your mind to what this means."

She stuck her nose in the air and folded her arms across her breasts. "I don't know what game you are playing, Julian Raynor, but you don't frighten me."

He laughed recklessly, and with a flick of his wrist sent

the parchment flying in an arc to the top ledge of one of the bookcases.

Serena raised her brows. "That changes nothing."

He threw his arms wide. "Come here, little wife, and I'll show you what it changes."

When he lunged for her, she retreated quickly to the other side of a plum-colored sofa. "I was right about you," she said, baring her teeth at him. "Wild. Reckless. Dangerous. I thought so from the moment I clapped eyes on you."

He grinned and shook his head. "If you could only see yourself, Victoria."

"Don't call me that."

"Why not? It's how I think of you. With you it must always be a battle, and you must be the one who carries off the victory."

"Naturally," she taunted, and bobbed him an insulting curtsy.

He threw back his head and laughed. Eyes narrowing, he came after her. "Only a real man would ever be able to take you on. You may count yourself fortunate that you fell in my way. Who else would be willing to put up with your temper tantrums?"

Arms akimbo, she stamped her little foot. "For your information, Julian Raynor, allow me to point out that Mr. Hadley and I have never exchanged *one . . . cross . . . word.*" She shrilled this last at him.

"No! Really? Poor Victoria! What a bore for you."

This was so close to the truth that she was stung into justifying herself. "I like men who are civilized. I like men who are nice."

"Then you've got your work cut out for you, for I refuse to run tame at a woman's skirts. No. Don't misunderstand me. I aim to be a faithful husband. But I'll allow no woman to mold me to her whim, not even you. Admit

t, Victoria. Only a man like me would ever do for a
woman like you."

Her brows were drawn; her eyes were smoldering. "To
hear you speak, anyone would think I was a virago."

When he began to stalk her, she kept pace with him,
carefully preserving the width of the sofa between them.

"Virago!" he tossed out.

"Gamester!" she flung back.

He halted and braced his weight with both hands on
the sofa back. "There's a sparkle in your eyes. Your lips
are turning up. Your color is high. You are enjoying this
as much as I am. Admit it, Serena."

"If you think that, then you have mistaken my character, Julian Raynor. I hate quarreling with people."

"Quarreling? Who said anything about quarreling? We
are like thunder and lightning. For us, it could never be
any other way. But when the storm has spent itself, we'll
find our calm. Until the next time, of course."

Before he had finished speaking, he was vaulting the
sofa. She let out a shriek that was not quite a cry of terror,
not quite a laugh. Launching herself at the door, she
twisted the brass knob. His hands lashed out and
slammed against the door, preventing her from opening
it. Wrenching her by the shoulders, he spun her to face
him. Her head arched back. Hearts pounding in tempo,
breath mingling, they fought the battle with their eyes.

His fingers speared through her hair, and he jerked her
head up. Her hands splayed across his shoulders, digging
in to him as she steadied herself. He brushed his lips
across hers then nipped at them with enough force to
make her cry out. Not to be outdone, she retaliated in like
manner.

Drawing away, he searched her expression. "*This* is
what I have missed!" he said fiercely. "This is what I have
wanted from you! My God, Serena, there's none can com-

pare with you," and he swooped down, crushing her mouth beneath his, claiming her completely.

Her nails dug into his shoulders, and a low moan caught in her throat. She had never felt more alive in her life. Her blood was singing; she felt as though she were floating on air. Her heart was beating so hard that breathing was becoming difficult. She was free and wanton, and she reveled in it.

Her arms wrapped around him and she kissed him with all the passion that had been locked inside her since he had gone away. It was almost too much. Tears slid from beneath her lashes. Her knees buckled and she would have slipped to the floor if he had not caught her. Lifting her effortlessly, he carried her to the sofa and set her down.

With one arm bent above her head, she watched him strip out of his clothes. When he was down to his satin breeches, he bent to her. He dealt with her petticoats first, deftly collapsing the hoops and sliding her undergarments away with a practiced skill that told her far more than she wanted to know. So he knew his way around women's clothing. What difference did it make?

There was no game now, only a curious earnestness about them, the dark man with the burningly intent look, and the fair, blue-eyed girl. They looked at each other as though they were strangers, yet not strangers, but actors in some drama that had yet to be performed. Everything was new to them and unrehearsed. Everything was as familiar as the sun rising with each new dawn.

She had forgotten that beneath the rich fabrics he generally wore, he was uncompromisingly male, arrogantly so. His shoulders were broad and well muscled; dark hair was crisp upon his chest. He was sleek and hard, and as powerless to resist as a ravenous, prowling jungle cat.

The picture that formed in her mind sent shivers dancng along her skin. His eyes flared at the betraying tremor.

He buried his face against her hair. "No," he said. "Don't look like that. I may have the brute strength, but your power over me has no limits. Don't you know that yet?"

She shook her head.

Holding her eyes in his fiercely possessive stare, he pulled her forward to sit on the edge of the sofa. He was on his knees, almost in an attitude of supplication.

"Let me show you what I mean," he said. "Put your arms around my neck."

When she obeyed him, he closed his eyes then opened them wide. With agonizing slowness, he began to unfasten the hooks that fastened the front closure of her bodice. The laces on her corset were similarly dealt with. When she was down to nothing but her thin lawn chemise, the tremors began anew, deep in her body.

His voice was thick and low. "This is what you wanted when you came here tonight. You wanted me to make love to you. Admit it, Serena."

She was so tortured with wanting that nothing seemed to matter, especially not her pride. "Yes."

"It's been like this between us since the night we met. Look at me!" His hand lifted her chin, forcing her eyes to meet his. "Tell me! I want to hear you say it."

She moistened her lips. "Yes. It's always been like this."

His chest rose and fell, and for a long moment, he was silent. Then he smiled. "So much wasted time; so many wasted recriminations! Well, no longer. You, my sweet, are going to make it all up to me."

Impatient hands slipped the straps of her chemise over her shoulders, down to her waist. She saw the fierce heat of passion burning in his eyes as he stared at her quivering flesh.

"I have dreamed of this," he said, and gently touched a finger to one distended nipple.

Serena felt that touch all the way to her loins. Gasping, she squirmed involuntarily, clamping her legs together.

His hands drifted to her calves, then to her knees, and in one wrenching movement, her chemise went floating to the floor. In only her white silk stockings and garters, she felt utterly decadent.

"Open your legs for me," he said, coaxing her, and applying very little pressure, he spread her legs and planted himself solidly between them.

Reaching for her, he brought her head down, kissing her relentlessly as though to quell any lingering resistance. When they broke apart, they were both trembling violently. Their breath rushed in and out of their lungs; their lips were wet and bruised from the kisses they had shared. When he sat back on his heels, she murmured a protest and reached for him.

Shifting to keep her at arm's length, he removed first one silk stocking then the other. Every brush of his hands was sheer torture, every random kiss, and there were many of those as he swept her stockings away, drove her pulse frantic. In her nakedness, she felt vulnerable.

He watched her face as he cupped her breasts, massaging the nipples to hard erect points. Her eyes glazed over and she shook her head. This merely encouraged him to add to her torment. Bending his head, he gave suckle, using teeth and lips to drive her pleasure higher. When her breath came in short, hard gasps, he smiled and moved on, trailing one hand over the flat of her stomach, lingering at the soft thatch between her thighs. He entered her gently, and found the hot slickness that was infinitely reassuring. She was wet and ready for him. Excitement swept through him in a wild, uncontrollable flood.

It was too much; the pleasure was too fierce; she couldn't bear it. When she tried to close her legs against him, he blocked her movement with his body. Though his words were soft and soothing, he increased her anguish, sliding his fingers in and out of her, flexing them, driving her to the edge of insanity.

She was writhing and twisting, half crazy with the torment of his touch. Suddenly launching herself at him, she tumbled him to the floor. On her knees, she reared over him. His look of shock gradually gave way to one of unmitigated delight.

For a moment, she hesitated.

"Oh no," he said. "I won't allow you to turn craven on me now. You wanted to exercise your power over me. Well, now's your chance."

He captured her hands and brought them to the closure of his breeches. She made no move to assist him, but that did not deter him. Cupping her hands with his, he showed her how easily buttons could be slipped from their buttonholes.

"It will get easier with practice," he told her, and his eyes danced with wicked enjoyment. "And I aim to ensure that you get plenty of practice." Deciding that it would take forever if he waited for Serena to undress him, he quickly peeled out of his garments till he was down to bare skin.

She didn't move, didn't even breathe, but knelt there like a lifeless statue, her eyes fastened on the huge, swollen sex that seemed to spring out at her from the thicket of dark hair at his groin.

He had gone too far to draw back now. "Never say you are conceding defeat, Victoria?" he said in a teasing, mocking whisper.

A breath shivered through her and her eyes locked on his. Tossing her head, she boldly straddled him. When he made to cup her breasts, she shifted position, slapping his hands away.

"Yield," she told him, "or face the consequences."

His eyebrows climbed and his lips quirked. Then, reclining with unconcerned masculine grace, he folded his arms behind his neck and dared her to do her worst.

Now what was she supposed to do? With his example to guide her, she touched a finger to the little nipples that were half hidden in the whorls of crisp black chest hair. The teasing light went out of his eyes when she rubbed her knuckles over the hardened nubs, playing with them, plucking at them, making love to them the way he had made love to her.

With growing confidence, she moved on, trailing her hands along the flat of his stomach, slowly, slowly, building his anticipation with ruthless determination, until he was writhing and moaning with need. When she came to his swollen sex, she hesitated.

Julian pulled himself up in one smooth movement. "Courage, Victoria," he gritted between clenched teeth, and taking her hand, he wrapped it around his hard length. When she squeezed involuntarily, he gasped, then groaned like an animal in pain. She squeezed again, deliberately, fascinated by the expressions that chased across his face. Something electrifying and entirely feminine swept through her. If she really wanted to, she could make this man her slave.

He raised his eyes to look at her. "It works both ways," he said, as if reading her mind, and hooking one powerful arm around her waist, he held her while he explored her with his fingers, stretching her, then rotating his wet thumb against a pleasure point that had her bucking and heaving in an agony of suspense.

Abandoned, desperate, they rolled together on the floor. Wild, reckless, dangerous—she gloried in the feelings he aroused in her. When he thrust into her, she ground her hips against his groin, forcing him to make his penetration as deep as he could make it. Plunging wildly, they came together in a shattering, explosive climax that went on and on and on.

He knew he was grinning like the proverbial cat that had swallowed the cream. There was something exhilarating in knowing that one's lovemaking could make a woman oblivious of her surroundings. A wife had a right to expect that her husband would take her in bed, with all the restraint and delicacy of which he was capable. Yet, here they were, on the floor of his bookroom without a stitch of clothing between them, like two shameless pagans from the mists of time. And it was glorious.

She was curled on her side, away from him, and he could tell from the sound of her breathing that she was drifting into sleep. Something sweet and ineffably tender moved in him, and he reached for her, hooking one arm around her waist. Serena squirmed, not shaking him off, but trying to get close to him. Her bottom was wriggling against his groin. The result was inevitable.

He mustn't. He shouldn't. It would be uncouth and ungentlemanly to initiate her into too much too soon. Besides, knowing Serena, she wouldn't take kindly to the notion that he was the teacher and she was the novice who had much to learn. Then she wriggled her bottom once too often and the struggle with his conscience was lost.

He nuzzled her neck. She sighed languorously. He cupped her breasts, bringing her spine hard against his chest. His fingers teased, arousing her. She squirmed and moaned as she slowly came to herself.

Shifting her body, lifting her, he entered her from behind. Serena gasped and looked back over her shoulder. She saw the pulse of desire in his eyes and hectic color ran across her cheekbones. Her jaw gaped and her mouth worked.

"Julian! What . . . ?"

"I want you, I need you," he crooned. "Let me love you, Serena. Yes, love, like this."

He gentled her with soothing, persuasive words, and aroused her to fever pitch by sinking into her in smooth, rhythmic strokes. Resisting her when she begged to turn into him, locking her body to his, he quickened his pace. When her head arched back on his shoulder, and he felt the convulsions deep in her belly, he loosed his own control. Pounding into her, in hard violent thrusts, he exploded in a flood of passion.

They lay for long minutes, laboring to even their breath. Reaching for her, he rolled her on her back so that he could gauge her expression. Relief swamped him. She didn't look angry or disgusted or even reproachful. Not only did she have the love-dazed look of a woman who had been well and truly pleasured, but she looked at him with something like awe.

He couldn't resist that look. Bending to her, he covered her face with moist, tender kisses. "Did I shock you, love?"

Her eyes slid away from his and she blushed furiously.

He smiled, a look of pure masculine arrogance. "I think I'm going to enjoy shocking you." When her eyes flew to his, he nodded. "Oh yes, that was only a foretaste of things to come. You have much to learn, Serena, my love, and I aim to be a patient, devoted teacher."

"Rake," she said, but her lips were twitching.

Grinning, he nodded. "And you are going to be the beneficiary of all my extensive experience."

She struggled to her elbows. Eyes dancing, she retorted, "There may be a thing or two I can teach you, Julian Raynor!"

His brows wiggled suggestively. "From what I could tell, Mr. Hadley hasn't done much more than steal the odd kiss, if he dared even that."

Mr. Hadley. The light in her eyes faded away. Horror-struck, she covered her cheeks with her hands. "Oh God," she moaned. "I really am without shame! How could I betray him like this, with you?" Reaching for her clothes, she began to dress herself.

Julian was stupefied. "Betray him?" he roared. "I'm your damned husband! How can you betray him by allowing me my conjugal rights?"

Her throat ached, and shame and misery washed over her. How could she have forgotten about Trevor Hadley? She might not love him, but he did not deserve this from her.

Julian reached for his own clothes, and began to jerk them on. "I did not do anything you did not want me to do," he said quietly, when it was evident that she was not going to answer him. "I gave you a chance to destroy our marriage certificate, and you refused it."

"What difference does it make? It's done now."

She was on her hands and knees, hunting for her garters. Her chemise came down to mid-thigh. Though he was furious with her, he couldn't help admiring the soft contours of her bottom. He remembered how she had wriggled against his groin only moments before, and he was tempted to lay his hand to her bare backside.

He yanked his shirt over his head, then his arms, and thrust the tails into the waistband of his breeches. "You are right in this. The thing is done, and whatever our wishes in the matter, there's no going back now. You might well be pregnant with my child."

"Don't you think I know that? Oh God, how can I face

him? What can I say? Don't just stand there. Dress yourself before someone walks in and finds us together."

Julian's face was like thunder. "A few moments ago, you didn't care who walked in and found us."

She pressed a hand to her eyes. "I know. I know. You don't have to gloat about it."

He wasn't gloating, he was bewildered and hurt. For the next several minutes, they dressed in silence. Julian's eyes went frequently to Serena but her attention was studiously focused on doing up the hooks and buttons on her gown.

When they were ready to leave, he spoke to her. "I shall call on Sir Jeremy tomorrow and lay the whole matter of our Fleet marriage before him."

She was aghast. "You'll do no such thing! How could I explain it to Trevor? He will think that I have been amusing myself at his expense. I need more time."

He was done arguing, done trying to convince her to take a chance on him. Jaw set, he escorted her from the room.

They were halfway down the stairs when the sound of revelers in the gaming house wafted to them down the well of the staircase. Julian halted and turned to look up, and the noise suddenly abated.

"What is it?" asked Serena.

"Someone must have opened the door to the gaming house."

"Is that so odd?"

"It is if you consider that I locked the door from the inside, and we are the only two people in this section of the house. You go on down. Don't wait for me. On the other side of the door, you will find Harry waiting for you. Tell him to see that you get home at once."

He ascended the stairs quickly and silently. When he came onto the landing that led to the gaming house, his attention was drawn to the door to his office. It was ajar. Lifting a candle from a wall sconce, he cautiously pushed into the room. His eyes were instantly drawn to the doors to the dumbwaiter. They stood open. Crossing to them, Julian depressed the lift and opened the safe. Everything was there, everything was exactly as he had left it when he had extracted his marriage certificate not an hour before. The same could not be said for the rest of the room. Every drawer in his desk gaped open; papers littered the floor; pictures were askew.

Setting down the candle, he quickly turned on his heel and strode to the door to the gaming house. It was unlocked.

When he stepped through that door, he came out onto the gallery. People were milling about, laughing and conversing as they idled from one room to another. Julian stood with his hands curled around the balustrade, his eyes scanning the throng below searching for he didn't know what.

Someone hailed him, and several faces turned to look up. Julian's eyes moved over them, then suddenly jerked back. Eyes blazed out at him from one of his own liveried footmen whose handsome face was marred by a long white scar that ran across one cheekbone. Then the face was averted as the footman began to shoulder his way toward the exit. Anticipation shivered through Julian as recognition struck. *Pretty,* he murmured under his breath, and started after him.

He had not counted on the press of people who were eager to exchange a few words with him. He was rude, he was abrupt, and it made no difference. He was a person of celebrity, and every man and his lady wanted to shake his hand. In mounting exasperation, concentrating only on his quarry, he shook people off and broke into a run. Pretty was well aware that he was being pursued. From time to time, he looked back over his shoulder. As he approached the front doors, Julian shouted a command to the footmen who were stationed there. Misunderstanding him, they left their posts and came forward to meet him, passing Pretty on his way out.

Julian swore. Fortunately at that moment Loukas came out from one of the cardrooms, immediately grasped what was afoot, and gave chase.

Out on the street, Julian was hampered by a crush of sedans and pedestrians.

"Halt! Thief!"

At the familiar voice, Julian's head whipped round. Constable Loukas, arms waving frantically, was in hot pursuit. Julian sprinted after him. He heard the cries of alarm and the terrified scream of horses rearing and plunging as their driver tried to bring them under control. Then there was nothing but a deathly hush.

He was panting for breath by the time he caught up with Loukas. The constable was bent over the prone figure of a man.

"It was an accident," the driver of the coach told the bystanders who were crowding round. "He darted across the road in front of me. There was nothing I could do."

Julian kneeled beside Loukas. Pretty's eyes were staring blankly. The constable closed them.

"Damn!" said Julian.

"He did not deserve this," said Loukas. "Nellie Bloggs was merely a petty criminal."

"Nellie?"

"Nelson. Go back to the house. I'll take care of things here."

"But—"

"We'll talk later. It's best if you do as I say."

Julian reluctantly followed his friend's advice. Once in his private office, he looked over the disorder with a perplexed frown. One thing he soon discovered was that Bloggs had entered his private suite of rooms by climbing the shaft of the dumbwaiter. What he could not understand was that Bloggs had been hoping to find. Had he been intent on stealing his ledgers and the bills and vowels of his patrons? Or was he after something else? Until an hour ago, the only other document of any interest in the safe was his marriage certificate.

His hands clenched into fists and his whole body went rigid. Slamming the doors to the dumbwaiter with a resounding crash, he stormed out of the room and along the corridor to his bookroom. A swift, comprehensive glance told him that the marriage certificate was gone.

He was furious with disbelief. Sloshing brandy into a glass, he drank it back in one go, then poured himself another. He could not have been so mistaken in her. She could not have prostituted her body so that her accomplice would have time to do her bidding.

He was on his third glass of brandy before he calmed down enough to remember that the certificate of marriage could hardly profit Serena, not when he had already given her the chance to destroy it.

His thoughts shifted, and finally settled on the man with the scar. It hardly seemed possible that Bloggs did not have some connection to Serena. The more he thought about it, the more convinced he became that there could be no peace for him until he got to the bottom of this. He had to know how deeply Serena was involved and how far she would go. Loukas was right. They must flush out his enemies and bring them into the light.

Chapter Twenty-Four

E sther, Countess of Kirkland, surveyed her handiwork with pleasure. A mound of gilt-edged cards lay strewn around her desk, invitations to her "informal" house party to be held later in the week at Bagley, their country place. She did not anticipate one refusal, considering that her guest of honor was the most celebrated man in London. Julian Raynor was, without doubt, the man of the hour.

She longed to share her triumph with someone, but that was impossible. Her husband, the earl, was not at all interested in what he considered domestic trivia, and even if he were, these days he was preoccupied with matters of state. Nor would she confide in her bosom friend, Lady Trenton, for fear Dorothea would steal a march on her.

She reached for a silver bell on her escritoire and shook it delicately, summoning the footman who was stationed on the other side of her boudoir door. When he entered, she indicated the cards on her desk.

"See that these are delivered today," she told him.

The footman's response was, as ever, neutral. Inside his head, he was calculating how long it would take five footmen to hand deliver her ladyship's invitations. More than one day, he decided, and he wondered if he dared set aside a portion of them for the morrow. The countess would never know it.

"And Thomas," said the countess, pinning him with a shrewd eye, "tell the footmen to wait for replies. I shall expect you to report back to me at"—she glanced at the clock on the mantel—"shall we say shortly after the dinner hour?" And smiling, she left him to it.

Lady Amelia was one of the first to receive her invitation. Her answer was an unequivocal affirmative. Julian had already told her what to expect. He was attempting to scotch all the unpleasant rumors that were circulating respecting Serena Ward that had got started at Ranelagh. Her own reputation hardly mattered to her. Nor did she care one way or the other how things turned out for Serena Ward. Lady Amelia had her own plans. A house party in the country would be the ideal setting. Smiling, she called for her maid to begin the morning's toilette.

Trevor Hadley was another who had anticipated the invitation. It was Serena's brother, Sir Jeremy, who had warned him that he was counting on his support to see Serena through what must be a very difficult time for her. Mr. Hadley gazed at the gilt-edged invitation reflectively. The house party could not come too soon for his liking, and when it was over . . . his lips curved in a smile. When it was over, he would be free of all obligation.

"You may tell her ladyship that I accept with pleasure," he said, and pressed a coin into the footman's palm.

On receiving his invitation, Clive Ward let fly with a vicious profanity. "Beg pardon," he said, grinning sheepishly. He was in his rooms where he and some of his cronies, his Jacobite cronies, had whiled the night away in drinking and gaming.

Lord Roderick took the card from his hand and read it with interest before passing it on. From the remarks that followed it was obvious that Clive's friends envied him his good fortune. In their eyes, Julian Raynor was a figure of glamour.

"What's got into you?" asked Lord Roderick, noting his friend's chalk-white complexion.

"Don't be an idiot," drawled Quentin Page. "You

know perfectly well that Lord Kirkland is the archenemy of Jacobites. No self-respecting Jacobite would care to dine with him." A thought occurred to him. "I say, do you suppose that there is any truth to the rumor that Raynor was once a government agent?"

"Now why would you say such a thing?" demanded Clive.

"It was only a thought."

Lord Roderick tried to cover the awkward moment. "Thank God we are small fry and need not concern ourselves about such things. We are not agitators. We are not conspirators." He smiled benignly. "We are merely drunken sots who know every Jacobite toast ever invented."

He raised his glass of ruby-red wine. "Gentlemen," he said, "To His Majesty across the water."

Those who were awake and still reasonably sober obligingly raised their glasses and followed the ritual of passing them over a bowl of water which was set in the center of the table. "To His Majesty," they said, and every man there knew that they were not referring to the king who sat on the throne of England.

Jeremy Ward was sharing a very late breakfast with his wife, when Lady Kirkland's footman begged a few minutes of his time. On returning to the dining room, he passed Lady Kirkland's card to Catherine without comment.

After reading it she made a moue of distaste. "I suppose we must go?"

"Now that's an odd thing to say when you know that Raynor and I have been expecting the invitation."

"Julian has certainly risen in the world if the Kirklands are taking him up. Or perhaps you are responsible for the invitation, Jeremy?"

"No. I think we may say that the countess was seized

by the notion all on her own and immediately acted upon it. She likes to be first in everything."

"And you and Julian decided to make use of her?"

"Precisely."

"I hope you know what you are doing."

This was said with so much feeling that Jeremy set down his teacup before she could replenish it for him. "Now what might you mean by that?"

"I don't know what I mean, not really. I just hate the thought of being on display. You know, of course, that everyone will be hoping for the worst?" To his questioning look, she replied, "You know what I mean. More of what happened at Ranelagh, scenes, duels, that kind of thing."

"Then they shall be disappointed." He reached for her hand and grasped it in a comforting clasp. "Look, nothing will go wrong. The world will see that we Wards are all on amiable terms with Raynor, and the gossip will die a natural death. Then, perhaps, things will return to normal and we can take up our own lives."

"You don't suppose there's any truth to the gossip, do you, Jeremy? It always seemed to me that Serena was partial to Julian, yes, and vice versa."

Smiling, he shook his head. "Even if that were so, Raynor is committed to his life in America. He'll be gone before we know it—thank God!"

She did not return his smile. "That's not what Lord Charles says."

His expression altered. "Oh? What does Charles say?"

"He says that Julian has had a change of heart, that he intends to settle in England."

There was a long silence. Coming to himself, Jeremy shook his head. "It makes no odds. By the by, the footman was most anxious to locate Lord Charles. I took it upon myself to give him the direction of that little house of his in Chelsea. I hope I did the right thing?"

A small frown pleated Catherine's brow. "What little house in Chelsea?" she asked, and Jeremy told her.

In his house in Chelsea, Lord Charles received his invitation to Lady Kirkland's house party in unsmiling hauteur. "Damned impertinence!" he told the lady whose bed he had risen from only moments before. "And how the devil did Jeremy know where to send the footman—that's what I should like to know?"

Lily Danvers, his mistress of two years, a former actress whom he had rescued from a life of prostitution, came to herself slowly, then more rapidly as she sensed the rage in him. "Jeremy?" she repeated carefully. "Would that be Sir Jeremy Ward?"

Preoccupied with his own thoughts, he did not hear her question. "If Jeremy knows," he said savagely, "you may be sure that she knows also."

"Lady Catherine? And why shouldn't she know?"

He turned his head to look at her. "Does it matter?"

Her breathing quickened and she hauled herself up to a sitting position. "What is it, Charles?" She couldn't keep her bitterness from showing. "Are you afraid that if Lady Catherine finds out about this house, finds out about me, she will be jealous?"

"Jealous?" He laughed shortly. "I haven't the vaguest idea of what you mean."

"I think you do. I think you are in love with her. She thinks you flit from one woman to the next, doesn't she? It's what you want her to think. But there are no others, are there, Charles? There is only me, and you don't want her to know it, because you are afraid she will see it as a betrayal."

When he was silent, she went on heedlessly, "Why, she

might even run away with the idea that I was important to you, and we both know that is laughable."

For a long, long moment, he stared at her. Then, cursing softly, he began to dress himself.

Serena and Letty found Lady Kirkland's invitation on the mantelpiece when they returned from an outing to Dawes' bookshop in Piccadilly. Serena looked at the card indifferently, handed it to Letty, then went upstairs to change out of her outdoor things.

Letty was thrilled. House parties, especially for young people her age, were something to look forward to. Unmarried girls had their own quarters, usually in the attics, and they had a glorious time exchanging confidences till all hours of the night, and sometimes getting up to tricks and all sorts of naughtiness that would scandalize their elders if they only knew of it.

She was eagerly counting the days off on the calendar when Mr. Hadley walked in. "Look," she said, and her eyes danced with excitement, "the invitation to the Kirklands' house party has arrived," and she waved the gilt-edged invitation under his nose.

Mr. Hadley took it from her. "Yes, I received my invitation an hour ago."

At his somber look, which in Letty's mind was always tinged with censure, some of the excitement began to drain out of her. "There's no need to look so grave," she said. "You may not credit it, Trevor, but house parties are supposed to be fun."

He frowned. "That may be so, but I have been given to understand by Sir Jeremy that our purpose in going there is a serious one."

"Pooh!" said Letty, tossing her dark curls. "I care nothing for that! You are the one who made a fool of yourself at Ranelagh over Lady Amelia, grinning at her like a love-struck schoolboy. You are the one the gossips will be watching, not me." Tilting her head defiantly, she said, taunting him, "I intend to have a glorious time."

At the mention of Lady Amelia, his color had heightened. "You are a fine one to talk to me of Lady Amelia," he said scathingly, "when your own conduct does not bear examining. You are an out-and-out flirt! If I had the schooling of you, my girl, I'd make you run a very different course." His hands clenched and unclenched at his sides.

She flounced toward him, hand raised to strike him. When she was within arm's reach, he grabbed her wrist and held on. Her throat worked. Tears gathered in her eyes, but she stared up at him doggedly, refusing to give way.

He groaned, and hauled her into his arms, kissing her fiercely, possessively, experiencing emotions he had never experienced for any woman. And she kissed him back! She kissed him back! When they pulled apart, they looked at each other with horror.

"I can't love you," she sobbed. "I can't! I have hated you forever."

Mr. Hadley groaned again, and dragged her into his embrace, kissing her even more feverishly than before, if that were possible.

Neither was aware of the door opening. Serena took one look at the couple locked in a passionate embrace, and quickly whipped herself out of the room before they could see her.

"You don't love me," said Letty brokenly. "You can't." She was groping in her pocket for a handkerchief. "I am a hoyden. I have no manners. It's what you are always telling me." She looked at him hopefully.

Mr. Hadley tenderly mopped her wet cheeks with his own handkerchief. "You are all of that, my girl, and I *love* you for it."

She rewarded him with a teary smile. "We would not suit. You are straitlaced and I am a tear-away."

He smiled at her innocence. "We shall suit perfectly. When I am with you, I don't feel the least bit straitlaced. In fact, I feel like a ravenous tiger."

She looked at him doubtfully. "You are always finding fault with me."

"How else was I going to preserve my honor? I *love* you, I tell you, and I can't go on pretending that I don't."

Letty was very pale. "Oh, Trev, what are we going to tell Serena?"

His mind had already been working on those lines. His face hardened. "The truth, of course. It's the only way, but not yet. She is counting on our support, and we must give it to her. After the Kirklands' house party, I shall break it to her as gently as I can."

"Oh, I do love you, Trev," said Letty, and she rested her head on his broad chest.

Not far from Ward House, in Pall Mall, where London's most exclusive coffeehouses were to be found, there was a sedan stand directly outside the famed Cocoa-Tree Chocolate House. In an upstairs private parlor, Julian sat at a table overlooking the street, occasionally raising his head from the periodical he was perusing to watch the comings and goings of the various sedans.

One in particular caught his interest. Stepping down from it was an aging dandy, an exquisite complete with powdered wig, sequined waistcoat, and an excess of Michelin lace at throat and wrists. As Julian watched, the exquisite began arguing with the chairmen over the price they were charging. Other chairmen were joining in the argument and calling on passersby to settle it for them.

A rap on the door momentarily distracted Julian's attention. "Yes, what is it?" he called out.

A waiter entered. "Are you ready to order, sir?"

"No," replied Julian, "I'm waiting for—" He broke off and swiveled sharply when he heard the unmistakable cocking of a pistol. "What the devil? Loukas?"

A smiling Constable Loukas locked the door carefully before advancing into the room. "A seasoned soldier such as yourself," he said, "should know better than to allow his attention to be distracted. If this were loaded"—Loukas tapped the pistol in his hand—"and I were your enemy, you might be a dead man by now."

Julian glanced out the window. "The fop is Harry, I suppose?" When Loukas shook his head, Julian frowned, and returned his gaze to the scene below, studying it more intently.

"Harry," said Loukas, "is a passenger in one of the other chairs."

"Now I've got him. And the fop?"

"Oh, he's my man all right, a regular actor, as you can see. Parker is a man of many masks. There isn't an accent he cannot mimic. He's a useful man to know for someone in my profession."

"Shall they be joining us for breakfast?"

"That would not be wise, not when they shall meet us later this evening, at Lady Kirkland's house party. It would not do if someone were to see us together before then. It might put ideas in their heads. Take a good look at Parker, Julian, so that you will know whom you can count on if things start to go wrong."

Julian laughed. "I could hardly miss him." He shook his head. "Don't you think we are carrying things too far? The more I think about it, the more farfetched my suspicions appear to be."

As he seated himself on the other side of the table, Loukas eyed Julian speculatively. "Do you know what I think?" he said.

"You are going to tell me whatever I say. I remember that look of old, you see."

"I think," said Loukas, "that you don't wish to unmask your enemy for fear that he or she turns out to be someone you don't wish it to be."

The amusement was wiped from Julian's face. Abruptly changing the subject, he asked, "What did you find out about Pretty?"

Loukas shrugged. "Nothing that helps us. As I told you, Nellie was a petty criminal. Sometimes he worked for himself. Sometimes he hired himself out to others. There were short stretches when he seemed to be living a more settled existence."

"You knew him?"

"He passed through my hands from time to time. I always recommended leniency. I had hopes, you see, that he would make something of himself. Well, he'd had a hard life, abandoned as a child, abused, you know the sort of thing I mean. No one came forward to claim his body."

Julian's face darkened.

Loukas looked at him closely. "Are you blaming yourself? Nellie made his own choices. He had only himself to blame."

"That's not it. What I think is that his fate could so easily have been mine."

"I don't believe in fate," said Loukas. "Now, do you have our invitations to this house party?"

"What?"

"Our invitations to Lady Kirkland's house party. Do you have them with you?"

Julian fished in his pocket and produced the gilt-edged cards. "As instructed, I gave Parker's name as Mr. Giles Bowring."

"Good," said Loukas. "Parker is very sensitive about using his real name. Harry and I, of course, have led blameless lives, and have nothing to hide." His eyes twinkled.

"However," said Julian, "I also told our hostess that he was lately arrived from the West Indies." To Loukas's blank look, he answered, "She asked me about his background, and it was the best I could come up with on the spur of the moment."

"I don't think Parker knows the first thing about the West Indies."

"Then," said Julian, "he had better acquire a little knowledge before we begin this charade." He paused. "I'm still not convinced this will work. It's only a house party after all."

"Yes, but all our suspects will be there, watching you, watching each other, putting two and two together. And of course, we shall do our part to stir things up."

"There will be scores of people there. Only a fool would show his hand among so many witnesses."

"Perhaps. But a clever man or woman might recognize that in the midst of so many suspects with something to hide, he or she might never be given a better chance to escape detection. Besides, our villain may not show his hand till later, you know, when we play out the last scene in the act."

Julian leaned back in his chair and subjected his companion to a searching look. "Do all the suspects have something to hide?"

"My dear Julian, everyone has something to hide, even you. Especially you."

Julian shook his head and laughed. "But what exactly do you suppose might happen to me?"

"Another abduction, perhaps, though I don't put much stock in that notion." Loukas scratched his head. "No, this time around, I think our villain will want to make sure that you are removed from the scene permanently."

"Charming!"

"Yes, isn't it? All the players will be there, I presume?"

"According to Lady Kirkland they will."

"Good. Good. Remember what I said. Don't let yourself become distracted. Be alert at all times. In my experience, danger often comes when we least expect it."

Julian couldn't help smiling. "And where will you be in all of this?"

"Oh, I shall be around, never fear. In the meantime . . ."

"Yes, yes, I know. Keep my head down and stay out of trouble."

Hearing his disgruntled tone, Loukas said, "Just look at it this way, my boy. By staying out of the public eye this last sennight, you have given your poor bruised face a chance to return to its former beauty."

Julian worked his jaw.

"Is it still tender?" asked Loukas in a commiserating tone.

"A trifle," admitted Julian.

Loukas beamed. "I think I am ready for that breakfast you promised me. Oh, and don't stint yourself on account of your sore jaw. I have enough appetite for the two of us."

"You are too kind," said Julian.

Chapter Twenty-Five

❦

The Wards, *en famille*, with Mr. Hadley in tow,
were among the last of Lady Kirkland's guests to
arrive at Bagley. There was just enough time for a
hasty toilette before they were summoned to the great
salon where the guests were assembling before going into
dinner.

Serena was tense the moment she joined her family to
begin the long descent of the cantilevered staircase. She
knew, of course, that Julian would be there accompanied
undoubtedly by Lady Amelia, just as he knew that she
would be there with Mr. Hadley making up one of their
party. It was all part of an elaborate charade concocted by
Julian and Jeremy to scotch the rumors over that horrid
fiasco at Ranelagh.

Under the interested eye of polite society, the principals in the affair were to meet as affable though distant
acquaintances, and generally conduct themselves like the
well-bred ladies and gentlemen that they were. Then her
spotless reputation would be reestablished. That was the
whole point of the exercise, according to Jeremy.

It was a worthy ambition, she supposed, only it wasn't
her ambition. She was here because Julian Raynor—damn
him!—had suddenly turned skittish on her. And elusive.
No, not elusive, precisely. *Truant* was the word she
wanted. It was as though he were deliberately avoiding
her. Since that night in his gaming house, he had not
come near her. He really was the most perverse specimen
of masculinity ever to have fallen in her way, and that was
saying something. And now, she was reduced to chasing

him down so that she could tell him that the way was clear to announce their marriage.

He had won. She was willing to admit it. Let him publish the nuptials. She wanted the whole world, including Lady Amelia Lawrence, *especially* Lady Amelia, to know about it. She was Mrs. Julian Raynor, and had her precious certificate of marriage to prove it. It's what he said he wanted. So why the devil had he taken himself off this last week, without giving anyone his direction?

She had not come to her decision without a great deal of soul-searching. Julian wasn't the sort of man she had ever thought to marry. She had wanted someone nice and civilized. Julian was too wild, too reckless, too . . . What it came down to was he wasn't the sort of man a woman could manage very easily. But she was willing to give it a try. She couldn't say fairer than that.

Good Lord! Who was she trying to convince? She didn't want to manage him, no more than she wanted *him* to manage *her*. She wanted to make a home with him, mate with him, bear his children, be with him. When she was with him she felt more alive, more herself than she had ever felt in her life. Julian had fostered these feelings in her, and he had done it deliberately. She was in love with him and she believed, hoped, that he loved her too.

She wasn't afraid that history was repeating itself. Her feelings for Captain Allardyce had been based on a sham. Allardyce had flattered her, pandered to her vanity, skillfully manipulated her until he had her just where he wanted her. And all the time it was her dowry he had coveted.

Julian wasn't like Allardyce. He had nothing to gain by allowing their Fleet marriage to stand. He could look much higher for a wife. He was the one with the fortune. He was the one whose star was rising. Marriage to her brought him nothing but her own person. He must love her. Nothing else made sense.

When they reached the doors to the great salon, Jeremy cast a glance over the members of the Ward party. "For God's sake, smile!" he barked out, and everyone dutifully bared a set of pearly white porcelains the moment before their host and hostess came forward to receive them.

Lord Kirkland, as ever, hung back behind his wife's skirts, and Serena remembered the great wit Horace Walpole remarking that while all the company was afraid of the countess, the earl was afraid of all the company. Serena made it a point to greet his lordship with as much warmth as she could muster, especially since she, too, was afraid of all the company.

Lady Kirkland, on the other hand, was in her element. If the Prince of Wales, himself, had deigned to put in an appearance, she could not have been more gratified. The flower of English nobility was represented here, as well as those fashionables accepted in polite society because of their own merits—wits, playwrights, and personages of some celebrity, such as Julian Raynor. Her house party, she knew, would be an event that would be long remembered.

Julian's eyes fastened on Serena the moment she stepped into the salon, and it took every ounce of his willpower not to go to her and claim her openly as his wife. Never had she looked more beautiful to him. With her finely molded features and powdered blond ringlets caught back and entwined with a string of small seed pearls, she was the epitome of an English rose. By the prevailing standards, he supposed her gown was rather plain. In his view, the simple cream silk over moderate hoops made every woman present appear vulgarly ostentatious.

Breeding. Grace. Poise. As he watched her progress

toward him, with Lady Kirkland subtly edging Serena closer to the group which surrounded him, he felt the admiration swell in his chest. Serena must be aware of the avidly interested glances of the oh-so-casual bystanders. Yet she appeared sublimely unaware that everyone in that room was anticipating the moment when they would come face-to-face.

"The consummate actress," whispered Lady Amelia at his elbow. Her eyes were trained on Serena.

Though the words conveyed a grudging respect, they launched Julian's mind on an unpleasant course. *The consummate actress.* A muscle in his jaw clenched and his eyes went blank.

Serena was painfully aware of the suspense which seemed to charge the atmosphere. Though she tried to appear natural, she was sure everyone must know that her knees were knocking together, and that her fingers were clutched in a death grip around her fan. Only Jeremy remained by her side, like a faithful hound. The other members of their party, as was to be expected, had been waylaid by various acquaintances to become absorbed in the crush.

Bystanders fell back, opening up a path that led directly to Julian and Lady Amelia, and suddenly Serena came face-to-face with them.

"I believe, Lady Amelia," said the countess in a voice that reminded Serena of melting treacle, "that you are acquainted with Miss Ward?"

Both ladies inclined their heads gravely while uttering the usual pleasantries.

Though Serena longed to look at Julian for reassurance, she could not tear her eyes from the woman at his side. Lady Amelia was an incomparable. There was no other way to describe her. She knew for a fact that the lady was on the wrong side of thirty, yet her flawless, timeless beauty cast every woman there into the shade.

She braced herself for the familiar feelings of inferiority to sweep over her. They were there, but muted, and she was overcome with the oddest sensation, as though a ghost that had long haunted her had suddenly been exorcised. Even the woman's perfume no longer irritated her.

But how was this? It came to her then that there was nothing to fuel a woman's confidence so much as the knowledge that she was truly loved for her own self. If Julian had wanted Lady Amelia, he would have destroyed the proof of their marriage. He had chosen her, Serena, not because she had a dowry, not because she could ease his way in society, but because he preferred her. It was as simple as that.

And Lady Amelia knew that this time she had lost. Serena could see it in her eyes. It wasn't a hostile expression. It was closer to perplexity, as if she were trying to fathom what Julian could possibly see in a girl with no claim to beauty or style.

With that thought, the tension drained out of Serena. "A long time ago," she told Lady Kirkland, "Lady Amelia did me a very great service." Her eyes met Lady Amelia's. "I don't believe I ever thanked you for it?"

"What service?" asked Jeremy.

Lady Amelia smiled provocatively. "It was of no moment," she murmured. "I merely removed a . . . a splinter that had become embedded in Miss Ward's . . . em . . . thumb. I take it there were no lasting effects from the wound?"

"None whatsoever," conceded Serena airily, and she turned her sparkling gaze upon Julian.

She could see at a glance that he was going to be difficult. His face was lean and hard and almost inscrutable. But Serena sensed the fierceness in him, and she wondered if it was because the last time they'd been together, she'd had the presence of mind to go back for her marriage certificate. There had been nothing devious or cunning in her thinking. It was simply that she'd feared he might take it upon himself to consign it to the fire, believing that was what she wanted him to do. Of course, it was the last thing she had wanted, and so she would tell him the first chance she got.

A wave of tenderness washed over her. She was the guilty party here. She was the one who had provoked that daunting look by hesitating to commit herself to him, as was natural for any woman in her position. She would make him understand.

Though her words were bland, the melting look in her eyes weighted them with meaning. "Mr. Raynor . . . Julian . . . I wish I knew how to thank you for . . . for Ranelagh, and everything. Your kindness was . . . is . . . deeply appreciated."

His words were equally bland, equally weighted with meaning. "Put it out of your mind, Miss Ward. I assure you, I have already done so."

Serena was still mulling over this oblique dismissal when the stately butler rapped out a tattoo on the parquet floor with his gilded staff to announce that dinner was served.

As the guests began to idle their way toward the gallery which served as the dining room on formal occasions, Jeremy regarded Serena with an assessing eye. "What was all that about?" he asked.

Now was not the time to enlighten him, not when Julian was keeping her at arm's length. She managed to look vague. "Beg pardon?"

"You and Raynor. Catherine thinks there may be something between you?"

Serena's eyes were trailing Julian and Lady Amelia.

They made an extraordinarily handsome couple, as indeed one elderly gentleman remarked to his companion in Serena's hearing.

She gave what she hoped was a convincing laugh. "Raynor and I? Are you serious, Jeremy?"

A slow grin tugged at the corners of his mouth. He patted her gloved hand. "I knew I could count on your good sense," he said.

When they came to the man-made lake, Lady Amelia slowed her steps and gazed quizzically at Julian. "I must have been blind not to see it," she said.

He did not pretend to misunderstand her. "Is it so obvious?"

She shook her head, sending her dark ringlets dancing. "Not to anyone who does not know you. I tell you, Julian, I feared I would be burned to a cinder in the current that passed between you, in there, when you and she came face-to-face."

They both laughed, and Julian looked at her appreciatively. Amelia was a woman after his own heart. Not only was she the most beautiful and sensual woman of his acquaintance, but she was not jealous, nor was she vindictive.

He brought himself up short. Damn this game he was playing! He must suspect everyone, and play his part accordingly.

"You do realize," said Lady Amelia, "that you will never have her without benefit of marriage?"

Julian pulled a long face. "It had occurred to me." He was wondering what the devil Serena had done with their marriage certificate. But he would get to that later.

"I'm . . . surprised, to say the least," said Lady Amelia.

"Surprised that a man of my station should reach so high as Serena Ward?"

By tacit consent, they had resumed their walk. Occasionally, they nodded to other strollers who, like themselves, had come out for a breath of fresh air in the interval between dinner and the ball that was to follow. From the corner of his eye, Julian spied his watchdogs—three gentlemen who had ostensibly left the house to enjoy a quiet smoke together.

"Your station?" She laughed. "Julian, these days you are considered a matrimonial prize. You are a man of property, are you not? You have friends in high places. Why, you are getting to be boringly respectable. No. What surprises me is that your interest should fix on someone like Miss Ward. I've always thought of her as a cold sort of girl." She emitted a small laugh. "I suppose you will say I have only myself to blame for that."

Julian halted, and catching her by the wrist, turned her to face him. Pale moonlight played across her features, sculpting bones and flesh into something of incredible beauty. Very quietly, he said, "What happened, Amelia? Didn't you know she was in love with Allardyce?"

"I knew it."

"And?"

Carefully disengaging her wrist from his clasp, she took a step back. "What are you implying, Julian? That I was some sort of monster?"

He answered her gently. "No. What I think is that you loved Allardyce too."

"With my whole heart," she whispered.

"And hated Serena?"

She shook her head. "No. I pitied her, as I pitied myself. He used us both. Me, he abandoned. Serena had the good sense to abandon him."

They walked on in silence until they came to the rotunda. Behind them, the great Palladian mansion blazed with lights. In front of them, the sweep of lawns merged with the riverbank. They paused to savor the scent of wild honeysuckle.

Turning to him at length, she said softly, "Why did you bring me out here, Julian?"

"To say good-bye," he said simply.

"Strange."

"What is?"

"It reminds me of the last time we said good-bye, you remember, shortly before you sailed for America? I have a distinct impression of déjà vu."

He remembered very well. It was on the occasion of his marriage to Serena, when he'd tactfully severed his connection to Amelia, among others. And he hadn't sailed for America. He'd been transported against his will. Amelia could not know that, unless she had been a party to his abduction. Her artless words appeared to exonerate her. Or was she trying to throw him off the scent? God, he hated the role he was playing.

"Yes," said Julian. "I feel it too."

They made the return walk to the house in almost complete silence.

The evening was well advanced when Lord Kirkland came upon Julian on the terrace. Her ladyship was not pleased that the guest of honor seemed to have vanished into thin air, and the earl had been given the task of tracking him down. Kirkland hung back when he saw that Julian was in conversation with a foppish gentleman whose name he could not remember but who had bored him insensate in the billiard room with tales of his sugar plantation in the West Indies. He was on the point of slipping away unnoticed when Julian himself came toward him, leaving the bore at the stone balustrade.

"I've been sent to f-fetch you," said his lordship in his diffident way. "Her ladyship thought you, um, might wish to join her in the c-card room."

Julian had no intention of allowing the countess to monopolize his time any more than she already had that evening. He'd had his work cut out for him, giving the performance that he and Loukas had decided upon, approaching all the principals in the affair (or "suspects," as Loukas called them) and duplicating, as far as possible, the conversations that had taken place two years ago, just before he was abducted. This was the first chance he'd had to have a few words alone with the earl.

"Frankly, my lord," he said, smiling easily, "I was hoping to have a respite from gambling for the next day or two. What would please me is a moment or two of your time."

The earl cast one quick look over his shoulder, then fell into step beside Julian. He gave a low, conspiratorial chuckle. "What Esther can't see won't m-matter to her, I suppose. Oh, don't think I'm finding fault. You know how women are. When she sets her heart on things, no one can gainsay her."

"She is very devoted to you, I've been told."

"Very, and I to her."

This was going nowhere, thought Julian, and plunged in. "Lady Kirkland tells me that she does not see much of you these days, that there is something big going on at the War Office?"

Occasionally, Lord Kirkland had a sly look about him. This was one of those occasions. "Something b-big? Like what, for instance?"

"Oh, I don't know. There are always rumors of Jacobite conspiracies."

They spoke in generalities, going in circles, arriving at nowhere. This was no more than Julian had expected. At the same time, as he and the earl strolled in the garden, he could almost feel the eyes that were following them. At one point on the path, they came face-to-face with Lord Charles Tremayne. Since he had flirted with Catherine Ward earlier in the evening, right under Lord Charles's nose, Julian was not surprised at the smoldering look he received.

There was only one act left in the drama, and it was to open with Serena.

Chapter Twenty-Six

The burst of song from the floor above shook Serena from her reveries, and the hand dragging the brush through her hair stilled, then fell away. Her bedchamber was directly beneath the "barracks"—the communal dormitory where all the young single men were housed. Evidently, the young bucks were serenading their female counterparts in the chambers across the hall. As she remembered from her salad days, the fun was likely to go on till the wee hours of the morning unless it became so rowdy that his lordship was called from his bed to read the riot act. On second thought, she rather suspected that the servants would summon her ladyship. Kirkland was so inoffensive as to be almost a nonentity. No one would pay him the least heed. Poor man.

She heard the sound of doors slamming and girls giggling. Oh, to be young and carefree, like Clive and Letty! Ladies of her advanced years were considered above such goings-on and were given their own bedchamber. The young people would have been aghast if anyone had suggested that they be confined to their own families. House parties were supposed to be fun.

Shaking her head, smiling a little, she went back to brushing her hair, wielding the brush vigorously until she was satisfied that every particle of powder had been removed. Usually a maid would have done this, but with so many guests, maids were in short supply, and Serena did not have the patience to wait for one to become available.

Setting the brush aside, she rose from the dressing table and slipped into a brocade robe. Though it was close to two of the clock, she was far from ready to retire to her bed. For one thing, the racket overhead was increasing by the minute. From the foot-stamping and clapping, she deduced that the young men in the barracks had embarked on a riotous country dance. Good grief, what next?

There was another reason for her wakefulness. All evening long she had sensed a sinister undercurrent. She climbed on top of the bed and braced her back against the headboard. Staring into space, she tried to recall the exact moment she had sensed that all was not as it seemed to be. It was at the dinner table, now that she remembered it. The conversation had focused on Julian. Someone remarked that he'd heard Raynor had decided to settle in England. A hush had fallen. By sheer coincidence, her glance had been resting on Clive, who sat across the table from her. His hand had jerked, scattering droplets of ruby-red wine on the pristine white tablecloth.

She dwelled on that thought before moving on. There was very little to go on, only fragments and impressions that added to her confusion—Lord Charles and Jeremy, and their voices raised in anger; Catherine with a haunted look about her; silences, and covert looks; and long unexplained absences of those who should have known better. She wasn't thinking only of Letty and Mr. Hadley. Jeremy had scarcely put in an appearance all evening, and when he did return to the ballroom, just as the dancing was drawing to a close, he looked very thoughtful.

As for Julian, she had scarcely exchanged more than two words with him all evening. He'd been everywhere at once and as impossible to reach as a distant star.

There were other unconnected things that bothered her. There was the bore from the West Indies who had monopolized her attention just as Julian had slipped into the gardens with Lady Amelia; and the little footman with the wig that sat slightly askew atop his head. She had only caught a glimpse of him from the back, but there was something vaguely familiar about him, something that hovered at the edges of her mind.

She was startled by a sudden thundering of footsteps descending the stairs, followed by an uproar of slamming doors and irate masculine voices demanding to be granted a little peace and quiet so that ancient relics such as themselves could catch their damned beauty sleep. The young men from the barracks responded with laughter and rude catcalls. From what Serena could make out, they had decided on impulse to go swan hunting in his lordship's man-made lake. More doors slammed, and as the thunder of the stampede died away, the house seemed to exhale a long, pent-up breath before settling into an uneasy silence.

The poor girls in the attics would be desolate to lose their beaux. There could be no adventures for females in the middle of the night. What they had yet to learn was that young men could be very inventive. She well remembered a house party she had attended as a young girl, where the boys had gone off gallivanting and later, much later, had tried to reenter the house by climbing the ivy outside the girls' dormitory windows.

She couldn't help giggling. On that occasion, the girls had been caught in their underthings, and in their confusion they had overturned the *pot-de-chambre,* much to the amusement of the boys. They had practically raised the roof with their shouts of laughter. She hoped Letty and Clive were enjoying themselves. Life of late had become very dreary in their household. Clive was hardly ever there and Letty was very subdued.

No. This was not precisely true. Letty was only giving the appearance of being subdued. When Mr. Hadley came calling, a blush crept into her cheeks and her eyes sparkled. Serena could still scarcely credit the way things had turned out. Letty and Trevor Hadley? They were as different as a frothy syllabub and plum pudding. She hoped Letty knew what she was doing. Poor Trevor. The thought made her smile. He might think that Letty was young and impressionable. It was Serena's opinion that Letty would lead him a merry dance.

Sighing, settling herself more comfortably, she turned her thoughts to Julian. He was keeping her at arm's length, and it was her own fault. If she could only have a few minutes alone with him, she was sure she could make him understand.

That thought inevitably led her to speculate on why he had slipped away with Lady Amelia, and whether or not he had arranged with Mr. Bowring to waylay her in case she went after him. How could she have gone after him when she was hedged about all evening by Clive or some other member of the Ward party? Besides, she had too much pride.

In any case, her woman's intuition told her that Julian simply wasn't interested in Lady Amelia. Smiling, she held on to that thought, examining it from all angles, sifting through it, then the thought slipped away as she slipped into sleep.

She came awake on a scream. A hand was cupped to her mouth, smothering her cry against her lips. Her assailant had straddled her, and the press of his weight made movement impossible. Rigid with terror, she stared up at him. As recognition dawned, her body went limp. Julian!

As soon as he saw that she wasn't going to struggle or make an outcry, he removed his hand from her mouth and rolled to his side. Serena immediately dragged herself to a sitting position so that their eyes were on the same level.

"I suppose you climbed the ivy outside my window," she said humorously, trying to relieve some of the tension between them. "If anyone had seen you, so much for our little charade to repair my reputation!" She looked at him hopefully, but could detect no softening in him.

"No one saw me. Rest assured, your reputation is still intact. Serena, there is something I must tell you, something that is going to come as a great shock." He paused, letting her digest his words.

He was going to break things off with her. She read it in every line of that hard face. She couldn't allow him to do it. She simply couldn't. She damn well wouldn't.

Grabbing for his hands, she brought them to her bosom. Her heart was in her eyes. "Julian," she whispered, "I love you."

His eyes flared and he made a sound that was not quite a gasp, not quite a groan. "You love me?"

Disregarding the sarcastic tone, which she thought he might be entitled to, she nodded vigorously. "I always have. I always did. You see, Julian—"

He shook her off. "Don't start that now. I haven't got the time for it. Or is this an attempt to entrap me?" He broke off as it came to him that by that last incautious remark, he had almost betrayed himself. It was no part of his plan to take Serena into his confidence. She was pivotal to the whole scheme, but if she ever suspected that he was using her, there was no saying what she might do.

"Entrap you? Is that all our Fleet marriage means to you?" Indignation was beginning to stir in her.

This was not the time to go into this. Breathing deeply, he started over. "Serena, listen to me. There is something I must say to you."

She could have wept in frustration. After all her soul-searching, and after all she had endured by agreeing to attend this horrid house party, he didn't want her anymore, just like that. Lady Amelia, no doubt, had helped make up his mind for him. Pain and temper sizzled through her. So, that's what they had got up to when they had slipped away to the gardens. So much for womanly intuition!

Launching herself at him, she toppled him on his back, then quickly straddled him. "Have you been making love to that Lawrence woman?" The sound of her teeth grinding together was clearly audible.

Julian was beginning to feel slightly disoriented, as though he had imbibed one glass of champagne too many. "I pity that poor woman, as you should, Serena." His voice rose to a muted roar. "How dare you accuse me of such a thing after everything that has passed between us?"

This answer evidently found favor with her for she planted a moist kiss directly on his mouth. After a moment or two of pleasurable activity, Julian tore his lips away. "Now will you listen to me?"

"I don't want to talk."

"Then just listen, dammit!"

"I don't want to listen."

"Serena," he warned.

When she laughed recklessly, Julian groaned. Before his eyes, she was turning into Victoria, and Victoria was the last person he wanted at this precise moment. "Victoria, be reasonable," he pleaded, but already she was tearing at his clothes, trying to get at him.

"This is what I want," she crooned.

He grabbed for her shoulders and shook her with enough force to get her attention. "I am trying to act the gentleman, you wanton little hussy."

She loved it when he teased her like this. "Gentleman!" she scoffed. "Then how do you explain this?" and she caressed the hard bulge that was threatening to burst his breeches.

As control began to slip away from him, with one last

heroic effort he tried to recall himself to his purpose in being there.

Loukas had used his influence to have a real warrant sworn out for his arrest. Those were genuine soldiers who would be coming for him, and a genuine justice of the peace. They must make his subsequent flight look convincing.

"Victoria, don't do this. You may come to regret it." Even as he spoke, his eyes were traveling the room, searching for the clock, trying to gauge how much time was left to him. They could just manage it.

"I could never regret this," she said lovingly, and she covered his face with moist, openmouthed kisses.

"Oh Jesus," said Julian, "I must be insane. Victoria, I yield. Take me. But for the love of God, do it quickly."

She didn't know that he had one eye on the clock. She only knew he was a hot and lusty lover whose appetite was sometimes so voracious that only a quick coupling could satisfy it. Losing no time, she eagerly began on the buttons of his shirt.

"We haven't got time for that," he said. "Take me now, Victoria. I want to be inside you *now*."

The words were so passionate that her own senses leapt in response. Her fingers quickly undid the buttons on his breeches, and she captured his hot, silky shaft in her cupped hand.

Though she reveled in the knowledge that she could so easily demolish his control, she couldn't help wanting to prolong the moment. Julian was having none of it. His hands were everywhere at once, and before she could understand his intent, he had horsed her on the saddle of his loins, impaling her relentlessly on his hard length.

Gritting his teeth against the excruciating pleasure of the snug fit of her sheath, he tried to hint her into motion.

She was about to rebuke him for going too fast for her, when she became aware of the advantage of her position. She was the one who was on top.

He watched as her eyes widened in feminine appreciation. When she flashed him a smile of bare-faced triumph, he grinned. "Yes," he said. "You are the jockey. But the trick is to keep up with your mount. Do you think you can keep up with me, Victoria?"

She accepted his challenge instantly. When he began to move, so did she. He quickened his rhythm. She kept pace with him. Neck and neck, hell-for-leather, they raced like lightning for the finishing line. He could still feel little after-shocks deep inside her when he reluctantly pulled from her body and rolled from beneath her. At least he had managed to deprive her of speech for a few minutes.

He readjusted his clothes before shaking her awake. "Serena, I must go."

"Go? Where?" She tried to pull him down to her.

His voice grew more desperate as the minutes ticked by. "Time is of the essence. You must listen to me."

The urgency behind his words finally penetrated her sensual inertia. "What is it, Julian?"

"They've come for me, the militia, just like the last time. It's what I came to tell you. I had not expected them to arrive so soon. Can you hear them?"

In a moment, she was as alert as he. Pulling herself up, she stared at him in horror. "You must be mistaken. How . . . ?"

"Listen!"

Doors were slamming. Voices were calling out. "It's only the boys from the barracks out for a little sport," she said, but her voice was uncertain.

"No. I don't think so. This time I've been forewarned. They're coming for me tonight."

"Who warned you?"

"A friend. I can't say more than that."

"But . . . what have you done?" she cried out.

"They say I murdered a man. Nelson Bloggs. Do you know of him?" He was watching her intently.

She shook her head.

"I'm innocent, of course. Once again, it's a trumped-up charge. They'll never be satisfied until they finish me off."

"But I don't understand. Who is 'they'?"

"I wish I knew. Look, Serena, I've got to go into hiding, get away from them somehow. I hate to involve you in this, but there is no one else I can turn to. Will you help me, Serena? Can I ask that much of you?"

All her vague premonitions of disaster rushed back in a flood. Every pore, every fine hair on her body was tuned to his danger. This was what she had feared. This was what she had sensed beneath the gaiety and merriment. There were sinister forces at work in this house that boded no good for Julian Raynor.

She threw herself into his arms. "Julian, I would do anything for you. Anything. You must know it."

"Then you'll help me?"

"Only tell me what you want me to do."

Chapter Twenty~Seven

❦

Serena's eyes flicked from table to table in the common room of The Thatched Tavern, and she experienced an overpowering sensation of déjà vu. Everything had come full circle. It was as though she had been flung back in time to the night she had first met Julian. Even the cardplayers had a familiar look about them, these young actors and actresses from nearby theaters. And there was Flynn, across the table from her, looking a good ten years older with those wire-rimmed spectacles, gazing attentively at the cards he had just been dealt

Her own costume was far more subdued than the getup she had worn on that other occasion. This time, she had learned her lesson. She wasn't passing herself off as an actress, but as a very prim and proper lady's maid, an abigail, and if anyone were to ask her name, it was there on the tip of her tongue. Abigail Straitlace, she would tell them, and she was resolved to live up to her name.

Her fingers trembled alarmingly when she picked up her own cards. That other time, she had been overwrought, but nothing like this. This time it was Julian who must be got away, *Julian,* not some fugitive Jacobite whom she did not know.

Oh God, if only it was a nightmare, if only she could awaken and find everything as it was before the militia had descended on the Kirklands' place with a warrant for Julian's arrest. Would she ever forget that assembly of stony-faced guests in the great salon, and Lord Kirkland grimly advising them that if anyone knew of Julian's whereabouts, he or she must come forward with that information. Not to do so was a criminal offense and would be severely punished.

She hadn't known where Julian was. She still did not know. All she knew was that he had given her a week to set things in motion, a week to reopen the escape route and arrange passage for him out of England.

"We shall rendezvous at dusk, a week from tonight, at The Thatched Tavern," were his last words to her before he had slipped over the windowsill to become swallowed up in the night.

He had given her other instructions before that, admonishing her to trust as few people as possible, that his own name must not be mentioned, that his life depended on her discretion.

Oh God, who were "they"? Who were these nameless, faceless enemies who wished him harm? And what had he ever done to provoke such hatred? Was he keeping secrets from her? Was he involved in plots and counterplots that she knew nothing about? Her brain was reeling from all her wild conjecturing, and she was still no nearer to finding answers to her questions.

"Your trick, I believe."

Flynn's voice recalled her to the present. Had she actually won that hand when her mind was miles away? Apparently she had.

Flynn, of course, had guessed from the outset that the person who must be got away was Julian. Not that it mattered. She trusted Flynn implicitly. If it had been possible, they would have contrived things without taking anyone else into their confidence. But they had no connections, no means of arranging passage out of England for Julian. They had to take Clive into their confidence, up to a point. They could not tell him, however, the identity of their "passenger" for fear he would refuse outright to help them. In Clive's code, Jacobites were men of honor. Murderers were beyond the pale. But Julian wasn't a murderer, and if she could have been sure of convincing Clive of it, she would have pleaded his case.

It was Flynn who had found a way around their dilemma. He was the one who had approached Clive, saying that he was calling in all the favors Clive owed him for all those Jacobites he had helped in the past. This time, he, Flynn, was the one with the mate who must be got out of England.

Clive had been reluctant, but in the end, Flynn had persuaded him. When they delivered Julian to the safe house tonight, Clive would know that they had duped him, but by that time, it would be too late to draw back. She would make sure that Clive understood that, even if it meant threatening him with exposure. He must help Julian. He must.

When the door to the taproom opened, her heart leapt to her throat, but it was only a couple of liveried footmen who were taking refuge from the weather. Outside, a thick, pea-soup fog had brought the city to a standstill. There were few sedans about and even fewer carriages. So much the better. In the event that something went wrong, the fog would make pursuit that much harder. On the other hand, time was wasting, and she was beginning to wonder if Julian had become lost in the fog. Oh God, now what were they supposed to do?

She was on the point of signaling her distress to Flynn, when one of the patrons called to the landlord that he was ready to pay his shot. Heart pounding, she half turned in her chair to get a better look at him. Julian! Though his table was in a dimly lit alcove, she could see at a glance that it was he. He had taken no pains to disguise himself. Either the man needed his head examined or he was reck-

...ess beyond redemption. Dangerous. Reckless. Wild. Hadn't she always known it? Then why was she smiling?

He had got here before them, and while she had been watching the door, waiting on tenterhooks for him to appear, he had been watching *them*. From the looks of things, he had done so in comfort, consuming a leisurely, substantial supper. He must have nerves of steel. Her own nerves were shot to pieces.

A quick look at Flynn convinced her that he was well aware of Julian's presence. The card game was coming to a close, and he was letting it be known that he and his "intended" must take a reluctant leave of their newfound friends. Serena took the hint, and with many regretful looks and promises to return another evening, she allowed Flynn to escort her from the premises. On the pavement, they dallied, as though they were not quite sure of their direction in that impenetrable fog. A few minutes later, they were joined by Julian.

"Well," said Flynn, "I think we timed that to a nicety."

"Yes, we did, didn't we?" said Julian. "Well, what's the next step, Flynn?"

"Now, we go underground, to them Roman ruins."

Serena was too choked to speak. Now that Julian was with her, now that she could reach out and touch him, all the dread and panic she had suppressed this last week came rushing to the fore. She felt as shivery as a jelly.

"I did not recognize you at first," he said. "I was expecting a dark-haired lady." He touched a finger to her blond curls. "You know who I mean. Victoria Noble."

"No," said Serena. "Tonight, I am Abigail Straitlace."

"Coward," he said, and laughed.

Flynn looked from one to the other. "I 'ates to interrupt, but I thinks we should be moving along."

Julian extended his hand to Serena. She clung to it,

trying to take comfort from the pressure he exerted. There was so much to say, and so little time left to them. She did not know how she could bear it

"I had no notion," said Julian, "that these underground passages were so extensive." He held up the lantern in his hand to look back the way they had come. "Are these all Roman ruins?"

They were waiting at the bottom of a flight of broken-down stone stairs for Flynn to give them the signal that it was safe to come out of hiding.

"Flynn would say so, but I doubt it. They're old but more than that I cannot say."

He nodded. "Nor had I expected to meet so many people coming and going. It's almost like a thoroughfare."

"Hardly that. And no one hangs around to greet his neighbor. Everyone here has something to hide."

She didn't know why they were having this inane conversation when there were so many important things that needed to be said. And even if what they felt was too deep for words, at the very least, he could take her in his arms and kiss her.

"Julian, I—"

He spoke at the same moment. "Do you know, Serena, it never ceases to amaze me that you can come and go as you please."

"What?"

"You seem to enjoy more freedoms than most ladies of my acquaintance. Yet, you are unmarried and of gentle birth. What on earth is your brother thinking of to allow you so much latitude?"

"For heaven's sake, Julian, I am no green girl! I am five-and-twenty, well beyond needing a chaperon." Her tone was sharp, not so much because of Julian's censure, but because he had referred to her as "unmarried" without

ualifying that statement. "As for Jeremy, he has enough
o do just keeping our heads above water. My father left a
norass of debts! Do you know what my brother is doing
t this moment?"

"Serena, I'm sorry I mentioned it, all right?"

She tried to check the emotion in her voice, but it was
nore than she could manage. She was overwrought, and
he least thing would have set her off. "Jeremy is at Riv-
rview, showing the estate to a prospective tenant. That
vill be the third tenant this year. If he could find a buyer
or our house in Buckingham Street, he would gladly let
t go. His own wife and children hardly ever see him. And
ou accuse him of neglecting a sister who has long since
een her own mistress?"

When she paused to draw breath, he shrugged help-
essly. "I had not known that things were so bad with
ou," he said.

"Why should you? We Wards are very good at putting
. face on things. No one knows, not really."

"I'm sorry, Serena, truly I am."

"Apology accepted."

There was a silence, then Julian said in a lighter vein,
"This isn't exactly ideal weather to show an estate."

She forced a smile. "I expect Jeremy is cursing the fog.
Jntil it clears, he'll be marooned at Riverview."

"The same might be said of me. Until the fog clears, I
hall be marooned in port."

"We've found a safe house. No, really, we know what
ve are doing. You'll be perfectly safe until we can get you
way."

The scrape of stone on stone brought their heads up.
"All clear," came Flynn's whisper, and they picked their
vay up the stone stairs with Serena in the lead.

The house where Clive had rented rooms was indistinguishable from other houses they had used in the past.

Though shabby, it was fairly respectable, and only a stone's throw from the docks. Flynn remained outside the building, acting as lookout, while Julian and Serena ascended to the second floor.

"Where does the money come from to rent these safe houses?" asked Julian.

He wasn't talking for the sake of making conversation, leastways, Serena did not think so. He was cautious, and he had every right to be. "There's a group in Oxford, Jacobite sympathizers, who cover Clive's expenses. That's all I know."

When she saw that her answer had satisfied him, she knocked on the door with the secret code. It wasn't very elaborate, only three pairs of short raps, but Julian's eyebrows climbed all the same.

The door was opened almost at once, and Serena swept into a dark corridor, with Julian in her wake.

There was a moment of awkwardness when Clive seemed at a loss for words. Then he smiled and took Julian's cloak from him. "I was almost sure it would be you, sir," he said. "I don't know why Serena and Flynn thought that all this secrecy was necessary."

"That was my doing," said Julian, "though I was not thinking of you when I swore Serena to secrecy. You'll still help me, then?"

"What, after the service you rendered my friend? I count it an honor. Come this way, sir."

He led them to a small parlor that boasted a table and two chairs, and an odd assortment of shabby upholstered pieces. Serena moved to one of the upright chairs.

"No, don't sit down," said Julian. "You're not staying." Then, addressing Clive, "Your friend? Ah yes, that would be Lord Alistair? Now that I think of it, you and Sir Jeremy were in France at the time. A sad business. I expect Lord Alistair met up with you there?"

Clive cleared his throat. "Yes. As a matter of fact, he did."

"What do you mean I'm not staying?" asked Serena. "I thought I would take a glass of wine with you." She indicated an opened bottle of wine and glasses on the table. "It's almost a ritual. We always share a glass of wine before Flynn and I go on our way."

"I think not. Your part in this is over. I, for one, shall be happier knowing that you are home safe in your bed. Would you excuse us, Clive? This will only take a moment."

As each word fell from his lips, the pressure on Serena's heart seemed to weigh the more heavily till she thought it would shatter. This was the moment she had been dreading. He was sending her away, and there was no saying when they would meet again.

In the corridor, he turned her to face him. She was so frozen with despair that it took a moment or two before his words registered.

". . . stay there. Do you understand? I don't want you trying to solve any mysteries. I don't want you to put yourself at risk. Whatever happens, I want you to be safe. If it's possible, I shall send for you. If not, then I want you to forget me. Promise me something?"

She gave a choked little sob and nodded.

"Don't let Victoria slip away from you. Don't lock her away. She is a part of you, Serena. Trust her. She knows what's best for you. Together, you are irresistible—leastways, you are to me."

Her eyes were burning. The tears were brimming over.

"Promise me!" he said fiercely.

"I . . . I promise."

His kiss was whisper soft. She wanted to deepen it, she wanted to taste him, know him, take his impression so that she would never forget him, never. When he released her, she clung to him.

"Softly, softly," he said. "Don't make this hard for both of us."

He moved so quickly that before she could prevent it, she was on the other side of the door and it was Flynn's arms that were holding her.

"Get her away from here," said Julian, and he shut the door in her face.

"Oh Julian," she said, staring at that closed door. "Oh Julian."

When Julian returned to the parlor, Clive had already poured out two glasses of wine. Though he had prepared himself for this, there was something in Julian that balked at going like a lamb to the slaughter. Telling himself that it was too late to turn back now, he accepted the proffered glass before seating himself in one of the upholstered chairs. If he was going to be drugged, he didn't want to do himself an injury by falling on his face or hitting his head against a sharp corner of some piece of furniture.

Praying that everything was going according to plan, and that the deuced fog would not throw Loukas and his "militia" into confusion, he took a careful sip of his wine.

"What happens now?" he asked.

"I have to get you away from here."

"I'm aware of that."

"No." Clive bolted his wine in two long swallows, and poured himself another. "You don't understand. I have to get you away from this house tonight."

Julian imbibed slowly. "Indeed? I understood that this was a safe house."

"It may be, then again, it may not be. There are too many people about for a prolonged stay. And in the fog, there's no saying when ships will be allowed out of the harbor."

"You are going to take me to another house?"

Clive nodded.

Curious, thought Julian, the boy was getting edgier by the minute. "I suppose," he said, "that your Oxford friends are directing things?"

Clive gave a start of surprise. "Oh, Serena told you, I suppose?"

"She did."

"There are no Oxford friends."

"No?"

"That was merely a blind. God, I can't believe—" He broke off, and one hand pulled roughly at his cravat, as though it were choking him. "I'm not permitted to tell you anything."

"Ah, so there are others involved?"

"I'm to take you to them. Oh, there's nothing to fear. I won't let you out of my sight. They mean you no harm. I'm sure they mean no harm. It's just that . . . well, they are being cautious, especially at a time like this."

Perhaps the wine wasn't drugged. Julian took a long swallow. "You have relieved my mind," he said.

"God, it's hot in here." Clive rose to his feet and staggered to the window. Opening it wide, he breathed deeply. A moment later he returned to his chair. "Don't you feel the heat?" He loosened his cravat.

"Now that you mention it, I do. Tell me, what is it we are waiting for?"

"A carriage. They are going to send a carriage."

"I see. And who are 'they'?"

Upending his wine glass, Clive drank deeply. "This must be cheap wine," he said. "It leaves a bitter aftertaste." And he passed a hand over his eyes.

"How much of that wine did you consume before we arrived?" asked Julian.

"A glass or two. Why?" Clive looked at his wine glass, then looked at Julian. A look of horror crossed his face. "It's the wine, isn't it? You put something in it!"

"Not I," said Julian.

Clive closed his eyes. "Then . . . No! They wouldn't! They wouldn't!" He lurched to his feet, took a few staggering paces, then sank to the floor unconscious.

With every step that took her away from Julian, her feet became more leaden. A great void seemed to be opening up in front of her, and there was nothing she could do to halt the momentum that was propelling her into it.

"Don't dawdle," said Flynn. He held up the lantern and retraced his steps when he saw that Serena wasn't keeping up with him. "We 'as a long way to go yet."

Serena nodded, and forced herself to go on. A moment later, she halted.

"Serena! What is it now?"

"Flynn," she said, keeping her voice to a whisper in that dark, unholy passage, "I want to go back."

"Now what's brought this on?"

She clutched at his arm. "It was something Julian said. He seems to think he may not come out of this alive."

Flynn's voice gentled. "We ain't lost a 'passenger' yet. You knows that as well as I do."

"I know but—"

"But what?"

For one moment more, she hesitated, then she seemed to come to a decision. "I want to go with him."

"*What?* Oh, no you don't, my girl. I 'as my orders. I aim to take you 'ome and keep you out of trouble till this is all over."

"I know you mean well, Flynn, and so does Julian, but

don't you see, I can't face the future without him." Her words were tripping off her tongue in her haste to convince him. "I've lived through this before, and I simply can't go through it again, wondering where he is, not knowing whether he is alive or dead. Even this past week has been sheer hell.

"And there's nothing to keep me in England, is there? Mr. Hadley doesn't love me. Letty and Clive don't need me. I'm a maiden aunt, Flynn, and without Julian, that's all I'll ever be. Is that what you want me to be for the rest of my life?"

As though by rote, Flynn replied, "The major will send for you. 'E told me so. And even if what you say is true, you'll never persuade 'im to take you with 'im."

"Perhaps not, but I have to try. Do you know, he hasn't even told me yet that he loves me. At the very least, I want to have those words from him. If I'm to die an old maid, I want to know that once in my life I was truly loved."

"Serena! Wait!" Flynn cursed in frustration as he watched her retreating back. It wasn't going to do her a bit of good. The major would never allow Serena to put her own life at risk. Now what was he supposed to do?

He had only two choices. He could either throw her over his shoulder and carry her off by force, or he could go with her.

Invoking the gods against all women in general, and Serena in particular, he started after her.

"What the devil?" Constable Loukas peered through the window of the stationary hackney of which he was a passenger. "Confound it! This wasn't supposed to happen."

His two companions followed the path of his eyes.

Harry Loukas was the first to catch on. "You think it's

Flynn and the girl? I don't see how you can tell in this blasted fog. All I can see is a man and a woman."

"You must be mistaken," said Parker. "Their part is over. Why would they return now?"

"I don't know," replied Loukas testily. "Unless they are in it up to their necks. No, no! I don't really believe that. As for recognizing them, I would know Flynn's swagger anywhere."

Harry whistled. "Now what do we do?"

"The only thing we can do," said Loukas. "We must get them out of there before the real villains arrive on the scene."

"I think," said Parker, "it may be too late for that."

The three gentlemen fell silent as the sound of carriage wheels rattling over cobblestones drew nearer. The carriage passed them and turned the corner before drawing to a stop.

"Now what?" asked Parker.

Loukas drew in a long breath. "We give them five minutes, ten at the most, then we go in after them."

"And Flynn and the girl?"

"Like Julian, they will simply have to take their chances."

While Flynn stood watch, Serena ran up the stairs to the rooms Clive had rented. In her agitation, she forgot about the secret code she had invented, and rapped smartly on the door. It was a door on the landing above that opened. The man who descended the stairs, regarding her with open suspicion, was dressed in the coarse garments of a dock worker.

"I . . . I misplaced my key," she told him, and she pounded on the door as fear rose in her. "Clive!" she cried out. "Clive! Open the door, do you hear me? It's Serena."

She heard a curse from behind the door. The neighbor

took a step toward her just as the key turned in the lock. Throwing herself over the threshold, she slammed the door behind her.

There was no candle in the corridor to see by. Brushing past her brother, she made for the parlor. "There's been a change of plan," she said. "By the way, I don't like the look of your neighbor. He seemed . . . out of place, suspicious—"

Her words died away as she took in the scene in the parlor. Julian, eyes closed, was gagged and his arms were tied behind his back. Clive was slumped in one of the chairs. Clive!

She spun to face the man who had let her into the house.

"Why didn't you drink the wine?" he said. "You always do."

She was so frozen with shock that he had her gagged and bound before she could do more than put up a pathetic resistance.

Chapter Twenty-Eight

❧

It was Serena's voice, now raised in anger, now reduced to teary sobs, that roused Julian from his stupor. He must have made some sound for she broke off her harangue and came to kneel in front of the chair he occupied.

"Here, drink this," she said, and pressed the rim of a cup to his lips.

His head felt too heavy for his neck. His legs felt like water. At least he wasn't gagged. He flexed his wrists. The bonds, too, had been removed. They must feel very sure that he posed no threat to them. Hell! He didn't pose any threat. The way he was feeling, he could not have fought his way out of his own coat.

Opening his eyes slowly, he took in his surroundings. Two men were silhouetted against a French window that gave onto what he supposed was a terrace. Though it was light outside, the fog had not lifted, and several candles around the room had been lit. He saw a desk and shelves of books. Then he saw Serena.

"Drink," she said.

He took the cup from her hands and gingerly tasted the contents. Water, sweet and pure. He drank it to the last drop. The two gentlemen had come to tower over him. He recognized one. The other was unknown to him, but he knew, deep down, he knew his identity.

"Sir Robert Ward," he said, "or his ghost. How do you do, sir? Jeremy, this is a surprise! I say, is that wicked-looking pistol you are holding loaded? Because if it is, I'd be much obliged if you would lower it. Thank you. And this must be"—his eyes traveled the room—"this must be Riverview."

His captors exchanged a long look.

"Do you know," said Julian, straightening in his chair, "I never expected this? I was almost sure that Lord Charles was directing things, or even Lord Kirkland."

"Julian," said Serena, "I am as shocked as you. When I entered this room, not five minutes ago, I could not believe my eyes. That my own father, my own brother, would perpetrate such a trick on me! I truly believed Papa was dead. I swear it, Julian."

Though Serena's words registered on one level of Julian's consciousness, and he felt a surge of elation, knowing now that she was innocent, for the most part he was absorbed in taking stock of the man whom he had once sworn to bring to ruin. Sir Robert was a virile figure of a man, not unlike his son, Jeremy, but where Jeremy exuded a natural graciousness, Sir Robert had a hardened look about him, like a military man. His face was hawk-like, his eyes were razor-sharp and watchful. There was not a shadow of doubt in Julian's mind that this man was in control, had always been in control, and that he would pursue his ends with single-minded purpose.

"So you are Raynor," said Sir Robert. "You should have remained in America. You were a fool to return."

"Will someone please tell me what is going on?" demanded Serena. Her voice was rising in her agitation.

"Why is she here?" asked Julian.

It was Jeremy who answered him. "I had to bring her. She caught me in the act of abducting you."

Julian let that thought revolve in his mind. "And Clive and Flynn?"

"You need not trouble yourself about them. They have not been harmed."

Serena elaborated on this curt statement. "Clive is upstairs, under guard, and Flynn," she steeled herself to tell the lie, "well, I sent Flynn home last night. I had decided to see the thing through to its end, you see."

Sir Robert made a sound of derision and Serena's eyes moved to him. She was still stunned, still grappling with the discovery that her father was not only alive, but that for two years he had also callously and deliberately allowed her to believe that he was dead. "Why, Papa? Why was it necessary to falsify your death? You had received a pardon from the Crown. You could have returned to England openly. This does not make sense."

"It makes perfect sense," said Julian, "if you consider that Sir Robert Ward, that most fanatical of all Jacobites, would always come under surveillance." He spoke his thoughts aloud as they occurred to him. "What better way to allay suspicion than to obtain a pardon and, shortly after, succumb to a fever? How unfortunate! How tragic! How brilliant! And all the time, Sir Robert was here at Riverview, directing things from the grave, so to speak. No one, of course, would question Jeremy's frequent trips out here. To all intents and purposes, he was merely protecting his investment, or showing the property to prospective tenants. Now that I think of it, this place is the perfect setting for conspirators. It's close to London and at the same time, it's on the river with direct access to the sea, and France."

"But Jeremy has no interest in advancing the Jacobite cause," Serena cried out. "Clive and I could never take him into our confidence, he was so adamantly opposed to helping Jacobites."

"That's what he wanted you to believe," said Julian. "Don't you see, he was playing a role? If you had known the truth, you might have inadvertently betrayed him. He could not take that chance. He is too important to the Cause. You and Clive were small-fry. All you were doing was helping a group of wretched fugitives escape to freedom. Your brother, Jeremy, was involved in treason up to his neck."

She was staring at her brother. "Jeremy, it can't be true! Tell me it isn't true?"

"Think about it, Serena," said Julian. "Who passed these Jacobite fugitives on to you? No, there was no group at Oxford. It was Jeremy. All the time, it was Jeremy, and behind Jeremy stood your father. Oh, there may have been a go-between, but they were the ones who were directing things."

Jeremy said, "I did what was necessary to promote the Cause."

Her face was ashen. She was remembering conversations round the dinner table, and Jeremy warning them all, especially Clive, to steer clear of his Jacobite friends. "Then why did you warn us not to become involved? If we had listened to you, the escape route would have ceased to exist."

Jeremy looked a question at his father. "Tell her," said Sir Robert.

"Clive is a hothead," said Jeremy. "I knew that he and that wild set of his were members of one of those so-called Jacobite societies. If they had started something, and if Clive were part of it, it might have proved disastrous for our plans. He was calling attention to us Wards, and that is the last thing we wanted. It was necessary to warn him off.

"As for the escape route, almost as soon as our man recruited Clive, I came to regret it. You and Clive are too rash; you run too many needless risks. Lord Alistair is an example. No one gave Clive permission to help that young man escape to France. Clive did that on his own initiative. I even forced him to accompany me to France so that in my absence he could not get up to mischief.

Much good it did! That debacle with Lord Alistair was the final straw. After that, I made damn sure that you and Clive were out of it. Others took your place, so you see, the escape route was still open."

"And all the time, Clive knew about you, knew about Papa?" she asked incredulously.

Jeremy made a gesture of impatience. "Of course he did not know. Do you think we are such fools? Do you think we would trust our lives to children who only play at being grown-up? This is not a game, Serena. This is war."

"But . . . but Clive must know." She looked helplessly from Jeremy to her father. "He reactivated the escape route to get Julian away."

Sir Robert answered, "I deemed it expedient at this point to lay all the facts before him. He is no longer a boy. He must put his youthful enthusiasms behind him and learn to act the man. He is a Ward, and it is inconceivable that a son of mine would not have a part to play in our plans to restore the Stuarts."

Julian scoffed, "You mean your *plots* to overthrow the anointed king of England! And that's what it is, isn't it, Sir Robert? Insurrection?"

Into the silence, Sir Robert said, "You are remarkably well informed, Major Raynor."

Julian's eyes narrowed. "Let's just say that I can put two and two together as well as the next man. You drugged Clive, did you not? That tells me that he isn't really with you on this. You don't trust him, and he knows it. He said something . . ." Julian's eyes went wide. "My God! There is something big going on, isn't there? Or there soon will be? That's why Jeremy has been so preoccupied of late. That's why it suddenly became necessary to take Clive into your confidence? That's why you took fright when I let it be known that I was fixed in

England for a long time to come? What is it, Sir Robert? Is this the moment when Charles Edward Stuart, your Messiah, returns to England in glory to reclaim the crown for his father?" He made a scoffing sound. "You are insane if you think that Englishmen will look upon that catastrophe with favor."

"Enough!" roared Sir Robert. "Enough, I say!"

In the moment or two that passed as Sir Robert struggled with his temper, Julian's impression of the man came more sharply into focus. A profusion of unrelated images and snatches of conversation flashed through his brain. He wasn't dealing with an ordinary man, he was dealing with a fanatic. To Sir Robert Ward, Jacobitism was a religion, and nothing came before it. Those who opposed him were heretics, and must be dealt with accordingly.

His own father must have known his man, and knowing him, he had chosen to go into hiding with his family. Clive may have suspected it. Serena? No. He did not think that Serena had even begun to plumb the complexity of her father's character. And Jeremy Ward? Julian's eyes came to rest on Serena's elder brother.

Jeremy Ward, the man he knew, seemed to change before his eyes. The very things he admired in Jeremy— his moderate political persuasions, his efforts to stave off the financial ruin his father had brought on him, his open and friendly manner, all these things were based on a misconception. Like everyone else, Serena included, he had believed what Jeremy had wished him to believe. It was not Serena who was the consummate actress. It was her brother who was the consummate actor.

He should have remembered that Serena was no slouch at putting two and two together either. Before he could head her off, she went on the attack.

"It's true, isn't it? Everything that Julian says is true! I think I could forgive you both your loyalty to the Stuarts. What I cannot forgive is your rank deceitfulness." Anguish and outrage made her voice tremble. "I *mourned* for you! Do you understand, Papa? I *mourned* for you! No. You wouldn't understand, would you? You've never mourned for anyone in your life."

Jeremy said, "That's enough, Serena. It was necessary to convince you that Father's death was genuine so that your grief could not be questioned by our enemies. And it worked."

In an instant, her anger found a new target and she rounded on her brother. "You fraud!" she said, advancing upon him, halting suddenly when he brought his pistol up, pointing it directly at her. "Who was it," she went on, anger making her heedless, "who was it found fault with Father and the misery his allegiance to the Stuarts had brought upon our family? You blamed our financial woes on him—the loss of my dowry, the loss of this house —your wife's house, not yours—the stringent economies we've been forced to practice, and let's not forget your earnest desire to get Letty and me married off so that we would no longer be a burden to you. You've been raising money for the Stuarts, paying bribes, buying arms, equipping men. I remember from the last time how it's done, you see. That's why we are on the verge of financial ruin, isn't it, Jeremy?"

"You are a woman. You do not understand these things," said Jeremy. "What we are suffering now is only a minor inconvenience compared to the honors and wealth that will be heaped upon us when the Stuarts are restored."

"How dare you speak of honor," she yelled, "you . . . you snake!"

"Calm yourself, Serena," said Sir Robert, "or I shall be

orced to gag you and tie you to that chair. I mean it.
Now sit down."

She looked as though she might argue the point, but
fter exhaling a soft protest, she obediently seated herself.
Only then did Sir Robert take his place behind the great,
lat-topped desk. Jeremy stationed himself to one side of
ir Robert, where he remained standing, the pistol cra-
led in the crook of one arm. There was another pistol on
he desk by Sir Robert's right hand. Julian glanced at it,
hen looked away. He began to flex his muscles, and by
heer dint of will, forced the haze in his brain to recede to
nanageable proportions.

Sir Robert addressed himself to Julian. "We did not
oring you here so that we could answer your questions,
out so that you could answer ours. This is in the nature of
. court-martial, Major Raynor. As a soldier, you should be
amiliar with what that signifies. We are not outlaws. We
re not barbarians. Even in times of war, such as this, we
abide by the codes of the civilized world."

"You have no right to try me," said Julian. "I do not
ecognize your authority."

"Nevertheless, we shall proceed."

Serena half rose from her chair. "If you harm one hair of
Julian's head, I shall expose the lot of you. I mean what I
ay."

"And I mean what I say," snapped Sir Robert. "If you
nsist on acting like a child, Serena, you will be punished
ike one. It is not by my wish that you are here. Now that
ou are, however, I expect you to remember that you are a
Ward. No, hear me out. If you think that your brother
nd I were heartless in our treatment of you, you will
:ome to see that this man has behaved toward you like a
nonster."

"That's a lie!" Softening his voice, Julian turned to
Serena. "He lies, Serena, I swear it."

She nodded in acknowledgment of his words, but it was evident to Julian that a small seed of doubt had been planted in her mind. Folding her hands, she stared intently at her father, waiting for him to begin.

It was becoming clear to Julian that something had gone seriously awry with his friends. They had not anticipated that he would be moved from the safe house. Even so, Loukas was no fool. He would have been prepared for anything. His eyes strayed to the window. Except, perhaps, for the fog.

With the realization that he could no longer rely on Loukas to rescue him, Julian began to think of the logistics of escape. He must take Serena with him. He could not depend on her father's charity, not even to his own flesh and blood. If she opposed Sir Robert, there was no saying what he might do. He did not think it would come to physical harm, but there were other methods of restraining a rebellious daughter.

A thought occurring to him, he said abruptly, "What are you going to do with Clive?"

A look passed between father and son. "That need not concern you," said Sir Robert.

"I'm right, aren't I?" said Julian. "You don't trust him. He has no stomach for your Cause. That's it, isn't it?"

Jeremy took a threatening step toward him, but Sir Robert stayed him with a gesture. "Clive is a young man," he said. "He has yet to learn that war is not child's play. He will remain loyal to the Cause for he knows how we deal with traitors."

The silence which followed these words was so profound it was like the deathly aftermath of a forest fire. Julian felt the fine hairs on the back of his neck begin to rise. He was no longer sure how far Sir Robert would go if Serena proved recalcitrant. He did not dare look at her

ut hoped, sensed, that she was aware of her own danger
s well as his.

"Shall we begin?" said Sir Robert. "You, sir, are a spy
n the employ of an unlawful government. The evidence
gainst you is incontrovertible."

He motioned, and Jeremy Ward took over. "We first
uspected you when you appeared at one of our rendez-
ous points, The Thatched Tavern. You do remember The
hatched Tavern, Major Raynor?"

"I was there by chance," said Julian. "It had nothing to
lo with your blasted rendezvous."

"Nevertheless," said Jeremy, "it was a close call, not
nly for the 'passenger' whom Clive was to get away that
ight, but also for two of our agents who were watching.
Though they were taken into custody, fortunately they
vere later released."

Because her fingers were trembling uncontrollably, Se-
ena hid them in the folds of her skirts. Trying to appear
natural, trying to disguise the revulsion and panic that
nad taken hold of her, she forced herself to speak calmly.
"Are you saying, Jeremy, that you had me watched?"

"No, not you particularly. It was always our practice to
nave other agents in place in case of trouble."

"I never knew it."

"It was these same agents who first mentioned Raynor's
nterest in you at The Thatched Tavern."

Serena's stomach clenched as she waited for Jeremy to
eveal that she had spent the night with Julian. When he
lid speak, however, it became clear to her that he knew
nothing of it, and she let out a careful breath.

"From that moment on," said Jeremy, "Raynor courted
you assiduously. What were we to think?"

Julian retorted scathingly, "What any sane man would
think—that I was taken with her, captivated by her, that
I loved her if you want the unvarnished truth."

"You and Serena? It seemed to us, then, farfetched. However, we were willing to give you the benefit of the doubt, though we kept a watchful eye on you. And then, when we were in France, we were joined by Lord Alistair and it became clear to us that you had infiltrated our network."

"That was my doing," said Serena.

"Yes, that, too, became clear to us, which is why we were forced to make other arrangements when our messengers had to be got in and out of France."

"Messengers?" said Serena, as in a daze. "I thought they were fugitives?"

"Not latterly, no," said Jeremy, "except for Lord Alistair. As I said, that was Clive's doing, and it was quite unauthorized. However, it showed us how far Raynor had advanced in your confidence, how close he was to unmasking us."

"Raynor was never in love with you," said Sir Robert. "Surely you must have realized it when it became known that he kept his mistress at that house of his in Twickenham. What was her name, Jeremy?"

"Victoria Noble."

They didn't know about her Fleet marriage, didn't know that she and Victoria Noble were one and the same person, didn't know just how far in her confidence Julian had advanced. And she never wanted them to know. Of that, she was very, very certain. Inhaling a shallow breath, she said, "I did know it, and after I found out, you may be sure I put a guard on my heart."

Sir Robert brought his fist down hard on the flat of the desk. "Do you expect us to believe you when you persuaded Clive to open the escape route to get this man away? Have you no sense? Do you really believe he has murdered a man and is fleeing from the law? I tell you, Serena, he is playing a dangerous game. Think how much harm such a spy would do to our Cause if we passed him along to our agents. He would know names and faces, as he now knows ours. What did you think, that only you, Flynn, and Clive were involved? I tell you, this man could have done irreparable harm to our friends. If I'd had my way, this would never have happened. We should have rid ourselves of him a long time ago. It was a mistake to spare his life, as I told the prince."

"You were the one who was behind my abduction," said Julian. He had to grit his teeth against the rage which boiled in him.

Sir Robert's face remained impassive. "I was, though was in favor of the death penalty."

"And I presume some higher authority commuted my sentence?"

"It was the prince who took a hand in things. Since you were not there to defend yourself, he counseled clemency."

"I'm obliged to the prince. And I suppose he is the reason we are going through this farce?"

"In cases such as this, the prince insists that offenders be tried by a military court."

"So, you dare not get rid of me without due process for fear the prince—" Julian broke off as a startling revelation clicked into place. "There were two attacks on me that night. The first was your doing, wasn't it? Whatever the prince may have counseled, you were determined to see me dead. You sent those highwaymen to kill me before my abduction could take place. The one was sanctioned, the other was unsanctioned."

Serena's breath came hard and fast as she tried to take everything in. "No," she said. "No. That cannot be right. They were in France, Julian. How could they be in two places at once?"

"They sent their minions to arrange things while they

played out their little charade far from the scene of the crime. It was one of their cutthroats I recognized when he broke into my gaming house. What was he doing there? What was he looking for?"

Jeremy answered him. "He was searching for evidence against you."

"What evidence? There is no evidence, because I am innocent."

Jeremy shook his head. "Then how do you explain how you came to have my bills and mortgages? I warn you, I know full well that they did not fall into your hands by chance. You deliberately set out to acquire them. What did you think, that you could use them to force Serena into betraying her friends?"

Julian checked himself as he tried to marshal his thoughts. It was Lord Charles who had redeemed the vowels and mortgages when he was already a prisoner aboard the transport ship.

"You put Lord Charles up to redeeming those bills?" he said.

Jeremy inclined his head. "I did, though not directly. There is nothing Charles will not do for my wife, Catherine. He holds them still, and would not dream of asking me to redeem them."

"And so you laid another false trail. You are diabolical, do you know that?"

"Answer the question," said Sir Robert. "What was your purpose in gaining possession of those bills and mortgages?"

Julian looked into those cold, pitiless eyes and he understood for the first time how his gentle, forbearing father had chosen flight rather than battle.

He wasn't like his father. He had no wife and children to protect. He had never run from a fight in his life.

He leaned forward in his chair, hands clasped in front

of him. "Yes, I deliberately set out to acquire your bills and mortgages, but not for the reason you think. It had nothing to do with Serena or trying to infiltrate your precious escape route."

He had to draw a breath, a long, steadying breath before continuing. "Don't you know me, Sir Robert? Have you not guessed my identity? Look at me, really look at me, and see if I do not remind you of someone."

At these strange words, Sir Robert came away from the back of his chair. His eyes were very sharp as they carefully assessed Julian. Finally, he said, "I never saw you in my life before today."

"I am William Renney's son," said Julian. "Surely you remember my father? He was tutor to Lord Kirkland at one time, the present Lord Kirkland is whom I mean. My father eloped with the girl you had hoped to marry. Yes, I see that you do remember him."

"Father?" said Jeremy.

Sir Robert silenced him by holding up one hand. "If you are Renney's son," he said, "it does not surprise me that you are a government agent. Like father, like son, I've no doubt."

Julian had to clench his hands to restrain them from wrapping themselves around the man's throat and choking the life out of him. "I'm proud to be my father's son. He was a man of honor and integrity. You know it too. There never was a letter betraying you to the authorities, was there? You made that up."

"And why should I do that?"

"So that you could ruin my father's good name. You hated him for depriving you of the woman you loved, my mother, Lady Harriet Egremont."

Sir Robert smiled, a thin disdainful curving of the lips. "If you knew me better, you would know that women play a very insignificant part in my life. Your mother meant nothing to me. I would not have troubled myself over a woman. No. Your father wrote that letter, and I punished him for it."

The ring of truth stamped Sir Robert's words. For a moment, Julian faltered, then another blinding revelation clicked into place.

"My father was not the author of that letter," he said. "Lord Kirkland wrote the letter, but that is not important now. What is important is that I was determined to ruin you for all the misery you had brought to my family. You hounded my father from pillar to post till he died a broken man in a debtors' prison. Do you deny it?"

Sir Robert's face twisted in a sneer. "He brought it on himself. The man was a weakling and a coward, though we did not know it at the time. By betraying us, he won my implacable enmity."

"And so you destroyed his good name and made it impossible for him to find employment in his chosen profession. Naturally, my father wasn't the only one to suffer from these reprisals. He had a wife and children. What do you suppose became of them?"

"He should have thought of that before he betrayed us."

"My mother and younger brother and sister died in the workhouse. I was the only one of my family to survive."

He heard Serena's voice whisper something brokenly, but his eyes never wavered from Sir Robert's face.

"If you think that will sway me," said Sir Robert, "you don't know me."

"Sway you?" Julian laughed. "I think I know you better than that. There isn't a drop of the milk of human kindness in you. All I am doing is proving that I had good reason to . . ."

His words died as a sound, a thrumming, reached them from outside the house. Jeremy strode to the window and opened it wide. Serena joined him. The thrumming grew louder, took shape, and formed itself into the rhythmic beat of a hundred drums. It seemed as though an army was on the move.

"Soldiers," said Jeremy.

Julian laughed recklessly. "If I am not mistaken, Lord Kirkland has called out the militia. Can't you feel it in your bones, Sir Robert? Can't you smell it in the air? Unseen powers are at work here, bringing everything to a sublime consummation."

He had risen to his feet and was supporting himself with both hands on the flat of the desk. "I am no government agent. I knew nothing of your Jacobite conspiracies. Yet I, William Renney's son, am the one who has brought your ambitions to ruin. Cosmic justice! Think about it, Sir Robert."

With one lunge, he grabbed for the pistol on the desk and sent it clattering to the floor. Rolling, he came up with it in his hand. Sir Robert backed away from him.

"Julian, run for it!"

His head whipped round. Serena was struggling with Jeremy, trying to get the gun away from him.

"Serena, no!" He leapt for her, and even as he reached her the gun went off. Air was stripped from his lungs. His heart stopped beating.

A look of surprise crossed Jeremy's face, then he sank to his knees and rolled to the floor.

Julian closed his eyes. "Thank God," he said.

Doors were slamming. Men were calling for him by name. Lord Kirkland's voice. Loukas's voice. Julian hesitated. Serena was bent over her brother's inert form, using the hem of her gown to wipe the trickle of blood that dribbled from the corner of his mouth. When she saw that his eyes were staring, she gathered his head in her lap, and crooning his name, began to rock with him.

"Serena?" said Julian.

She gave no sign that she heard him. The voices outside the door became more strident. With one last look at Serena, Julian went to answer them.

Tears were clouding her vision when she finally looked at her father. "Jeremy is dead," she said. Her father seemed to be in a state of shock. She couldn't think of rights and wrongs at this moment. That would come later. But she knew that whatever happened, whatever came to light, she could never hate her father or her brother.

"Papa, save yourself," she whispered brokenly. "Go now, through that window, before it's too late."

Her words seemed to bring him to his senses. He pressed a hand to his temples. "This has ruined everything. Without me, without Jeremy, the prince will never set foot in England. There can be no uprising now."

Even now, with his firstborn son lying dead at his feet, he could think of nothing but the Cause. Serena began to weep in earnest. "Forgive me, Jeremy," she said, and she brought one of his hands to her cheek.

She wasn't aware when her father quit the room or of how much time had elapsed before Julian returned and kneeled beside her on the bloodstained carpet. His touch on her shoulder was whisper soft. Unsure.

"Your father . . . Serena . . . I don't know how to tell you this."

"He's dead, isn't he?"

"He shot himself. He might have escaped. There was a boat, a yacht. When we heard the report of the shot, we . . . we found him in the cabin. Serena, I'm sorry."

She recoiled wildly when he reached for her. "You're sorry!" The words exploded from her. "Why should you be sorry? This is what you wanted, isn't it? You wanted to hurt my family. You wanted to pay off old scores." She as weeping uncontrollably, in great wrenching sobs. You plotted this in meticulous detail. And I was your pawn. God help me, I was your pawn. Without me, none of this could have happened. I trusted you! Oh God, I trusted you. I wish we had never met."

"Serena, you don't know what you are saying. I love you."

She screamed at him. "Don't talk to me of love! You re responsible for this. Deny it if you dare!"

Julian rose to his feet.

"Serena?" Clive stood in the doorway, his face tortured with remorse.

She held out her arms to him, and he quickly crossed to her. As they kneeled together over Jeremy's body, Julian quietly left the room.

Chapter Twenty-Nine

❦

Night had almost fallen when the caravan of carriages and riders made the return trip to town. After Serena, Flynn, and Clive were dropped off at Ward House, the other gentlemen repaired to Julian's gaming club. Harry and Parker diplomatically decided to try their luck at the gaming tables, leaving Julian, Lord Kirkland, and Constable Loukas to talk things over in the privacy of Julian's bookroom.

"So," said Julian at one point, "the story is that Sir Jeremy died tragically while cleaning his pistol. As for Sir Robert, it will be as though he were never there. Well, he never was there. I had this from Clive—Sir Robert was known to the few people who saw him as Mr. Smith, the tenant of Riverview."

"It's best this w-way," said Lord Kirkland. "I see no point in revealing the truth, not with Sir Robert d-dead. It would only stir up a great d-deal of unpleasantness for the Wards as well as create disquiet among the general p-population. The less said about the threat of a Jacobite uprising, the better it will be all round."

"I take it," said Julian, "that your colleagues at the War Office have agreed to what you propose?"

"They will," said Lord Kirkland. "They always d-do."

At this expression of confidence, Julian and Loukas exchanged a quick glance. "And Clive?" said Julian. "What will become of him?"

"Since he was a p-prisoner when we arrived at the house, we must assume that h-he was not part of Sir Robert's insane plot."

"That's very generous of you," said Julian.

His lordship shrugged. "He is only a boy, after all, and I think he h-has learned his lesson. As for Jeremy Ward's accomplices, they did not appear to be Jacobites to m-me."

"Indeed, no," said Loukas. "I recognized a few of them. Petty criminals who would sell their own mothers for a shilling."

Having poured out three glasses of brandy, Julian handed them round. "And now," he said, seating himself, "would someone please explain to me how I was rescued? And in particular"—he pinned Constable Loukas with a steely eye—"how you allowed Jeremy Ward to carry me off in his carriage?"

Loukas cleared his throat. "To put it bluntly, we were taken off guard. That is to say, while we were waiting in our carriage for the villain to arrive, he had got there before us, only we didn't know it. He must have been biding his time in another part of the house. And just to complicate matters, who should return to the scene of the crime but Serena and Flynn. It was the last thing we expected."

"Why did she return? She never explained that to me."

"Perhaps she left her hatpin behind."

Julian allowed Loukas's sarcasm to wash over him and merely smiled.

Loukas took a swallow of brandy. "Lucky for us, and you, Flynn has a very suspicious nature. He was on watch, outside the house, when he heard a carriage and came to investigate. That's when we grabbed him. You'll find this hilarious, my boy. Flynn thought that *we* were the villains, can you believe it, and was on the point of yelling 'murder most foul,' when the real villains came out the front door."

"Flynn? Serena said she had sent him home."

"I expect she was trying to throw her father and brother off the scent."

Julian let that thought sink into his mind. "So, Flynn was with you all the time?"

"He was."

"And when the villains came out the front door, you recognized Jeremy Ward?"

"No. All we saw in that fog were three men with what looked to be an equal number of inebriated companions. We might have closed with them then, but my instincts told me to hold off, that there was more to come."

"Your instincts? A pox on your instincts! We agreed that you would take no chances, that you would pounce on the villain as soon as he showed his face."

"Did I say that?"

"You know you did."

Loukas grinned unrepentantly. "If I had not followed my instincts, we would never have caught up with Sir Robert. Think about it."

Julian did, and took a long swallow of brandy. He was coming to believe that he should have let sleeping dogs lie. He couldn't tell Loukas that. "You did the right thing," he said. "Then what happened?"

"After that, we simply followed your carriage. We lost it a time or two, but Flynn was invaluable to us. You see, he recognized the road we were traveling as the road to Riverview. Once he told me that, everything fell into place, that is, everything but Sir Robert. It never occurred to me that he was alive and behind it all."

Julian addressed Lord Kirkland. "And you, sir? Did you suspect Sir Robert?"

"Lord, n-no! Nor even Jeremy Ward, until the last m-moment."

"Then, I don't understand. How did you come to be at Riverview?"

His lordship laughed nervously. "I was determined that this time around, nothing was going to h-happen to you if I c-could prevent it. I've had you watched, Julian, for a long time now, yes, even before you went to America. You s-see, I thought you were a Jacobite. No, don't look so shaken. What w-was I to think when you practically told me, yourself, that you were supplying the m-money for Sir Robert's pardon?"

"I told you that?" asked Julian blankly.

"You did, don't you remember, in the reading room downstairs? You asked me if I thought Jeremy Ward would ever be in a position to redeem the vowels you held. I got the impression the s-sum involved was quite s-substantial. What else was I t-to think but that you were lending him the money for his father's pardon?"

"Yes, now I remember," said Julian.

"Not only that," said Kirkland, "but it s-seemed to me, then, that you were trying to use your influence with me to pave the way for Sir Robert's return to England."

"Well, I was," said Julian, "but not for the reasons you think. And supposing me to be a Jacobite, you had me watched?"

"I did. One of my agents was a gardener at your house in Twickenham. It was he who brought me the report that s-soldiers had arrested you. I knew they m-must be impostors, and immediately called out the m-militia to investigate."

"So that's why you were so quick off the mark. Because your agent was there when I was arrested."

His lordship nodded. Julian wondered what else the agent had discovered. Leaving that for the present, he said, "And did you still suspect that I was a Jacobite when I returned to England?"

"Not latterly, no. By this time m-my agent was one of

your trusted familiars. He knew you were s-setting a trap for the men who had abducted you."

"Who is this agent?" demanded Julian wrathfully.

"Parker," said his lordship, "though I must say, even I did not recognize him at Bagley."

"Parker!" exclaimed Julian and Loukas in unison. They looked at each other and began to laugh.

"Y-yes, Parker," said his lordship, joining in the laughter. "He kept me informed of your comings and goings."

"So," said Loukas, "while we were following Jeremy Ward's coach, you were following ours?"

"I was," admitted the earl.

"Damn it all—I beg your pardon, your lordship—but Parker was supposed to be watching in case we were followed."

"And so he did, I think you will find."

"And the militia?" said Julian. "Where did they come from?"

"The barracks at Gravesend. It's the last stop before Riverview. Like Loukas, once I recognized the r-road I was traveling, things began to fall into place, and I decided that reinforcements might be a good idea. However, I never s-suspected Sir Robert. That took me completely by surprise."

After that, they talked in circles, clarifying one point, then another. Presently, Loukas, sensing something unfinished between his companions, took his leave of them.

For some time after this, nothing was said. Then Julian took the bull by the horns. "You know who I am, don't you, sir?"

The earl's eyes flickered, but he did not look away. "Oh yes," he said softly. "You are my sister's son. When you l-looked at your mother's portrait, that day in my office, I knew it then. You loved her very much. I could see it in your face."

"And you loved her also?" This was more of a state-ment than a question.

"I would have done anything f-for her. But you know that too."

"Yes," said Julian, then very gently, "You wrote the letter betraying your brother and Sir Robert. There *was* a letter. I had that from Sir Robert. And no one but you or my father could have written it. It was you, was it not?"

The earl nodded. "Do you know, it c-comes as a great relief to be able, finally, to confess to it? My g-guardian would never permit me to mention the events of that night to anyone. Oh yes, he knew. But he would not tolerate the scandal that must come to our f-family's name if my part in it came to light."

Taking a moment to compose himself, breathing deeply, the earl began. "Everything went wrong that night. Nothing turned out as I m-meant it to. My brother and Sir Robert were supposed to be gone before the soldiers arrived. They decided to stay until the f-fog lifted."

His voice was very soft, very halting as he began to relate the events that had been the cause of so much ha-tred, so much heartbreak. He loved his sister, and knew how she feared Sir Robert Ward. William Renney, his tutor, knew it too. He loved Harriet, but would never have aspired to marry her if it had not been for Sir Robert. He could not see her go to a stern, unfeeling man who cared nothing for her happiness. No one had told young James any of this directly. It came to him in servants' gossip, and snatches of conversation which died whenever he entered a room. But he had eyes to see. His tutor and his sister were deeply in love. He made up his mind to help them.

"I w-watched and waited my chance. The details don't matter. Suffice it to s-say, I discovered the n-night and the hour they were to elope. I h-had convinced myself that my one aim was to p-prevent my father putting a stop to it. In retrospect, I see that I was c-carried away by my sense of the d-dramatic. I saw myself as my s-sister's savior."

After a long pause, he went on, "It seemed so simple at the t-time. Because my brother, Hugo, was a fugitive, soldiers frequently came by the house to question my f-father. Sometimes he was escorted to the local m-magistrates. I n-never understood, n-never realized how d-dangerous it all was. The s-soldiers were always so respectful. We knew them and they knew us. They were l-local men. I even knew s-some of them by name. So, without telling anyone, I wrote the l-letter, and disguised as a stableboy, delivered it to the h-house of our l-local magistrate. I was sure that they w-would come for my f-father and take him away for questioning. And that's all I thought w-would happen. By the time he returned, I hoped Harriet and Mr. Renney would have a h-head start."

Julian said quietly, "What did the letter say?"

Lord Kirkland looked intently at the glass in his hand. "To the best of my r-recollection, I wrote, 'If you want to know where two Jacobite fugitives are to be f-found, ask Lord Kirkland.' I did not sign it, not did I p-put your father's name to it. I swear it, Julian."

In the same hushed tones, Julian said, "And Lord Hugo and Sir Robert were hiding in the house?"

"In the b-boathouse. But you s-see, I thought they had gone. They were not s-supposed to be there. It was the f-fog. They c-could not get away because of the f-fog."

"I see. Then what happened?"

Lord Kirkland closed his eyes as the horrifying events of that night came back to him. Visibly shaking, he forced himself to go on. "It was l-like something out of a nightmare. There was a new garrison, and a new c-captain, a vicious m-man who hated Jacobites. Y-your parents were gone, thank God, before they arrived. Sir Robert g-got away, but the soldiers turned on my f-father and m-me, and H-Hugo came back to h-help us." His voice cracked and he shook his head. "He should h-have left us to our fate. I, at least, d-deserved it. You know the rest."

Julian looked down at his clasped hands. The thought that was going through his mind was that later, when his father knew Sir Robert was hounding him, knew about the letter, he must have guessed that the only person who could have written it was young Lord James. Yet, William Renney had kept that knowledge to himself. His father had been a far greater man than he had realized, a far greater man than he.

Clearing his throat, Lord Kirkland said, "Later, much later, I confessed my part in it to my g-guardian. He b-beat me to within an inch of my life." And beat him, and beat him, and beat him until he was of an age to strike out on his own. By that time, the beatings had become necessary to him. It was the only way to purge him of his sins.

"I was afraid to l-let it be known that I was the author of that l-letter, afraid of Sir Robert and what he would do to me. And by the time I overcame my f-fear, it was too late. Can you ever f-forgive me?"

Julian, who was still staring in rapt attention at his clasped hands, jerked up his head. "I have nothing to forgive. You were not the one who hounded my father to his grave. I don't hold you responsible for what happened to my family."

"Still, if I h-had not written that l-letter . . ."

"You were only a boy of twelve. What would you have me say? That you should be punished for it? I am not

God, but the God my mother preached to me would be more forgiving, I think, than you have been to that boy of twelve."

Suddenly conscious of his fierce tone, Julian immediately moderated it. "I beg your pardon. Do I sound angry to you? I'm not, you know. I was thinking of Clive Ward, and Serena, thinking of the part I played in Sir Robert's downfall. Unlike you, I am not a boy of twelve."

"But, you can't blame yourself for what h-happened."

"No, and neither should you blame yourself. I wish, though . . ." He shook his head in frustration. "I wish I had not tried to play God."

There was a long silence after this, as each gentleman became lost in his own thoughts. Finally, Lord Kirkland said, "This is not the time or place, but one day, I should l-like you to tell me about your parents."

"I should like that," said Julian, and even as he said the words, he knew that he could never tell Lord Kirkland about the workhouse, never tell him about his mother's fate and the twins. The old boy had suffered enough. "And I should like to hear about the Egremonts," he said.

After his lordship had taken his leave of him, with drink in hand, Julian wandered over to the window. He had much to reflect on. His thoughts roamed far and wide, and came full circle. He was thinking that it were better if he had not tried to play God. The thought weighed on him, possessed him, tormented him. He should not have tried to play God. He wondered if Serena would ever forgive him.

He was glad that Flynn and Clive were with her now. He supposed that they would be going over the night's events, in much the same manner as they had done here. He'd told Flynn to make sure she had a few drops of laudanum to help her sleep. She would need all her strength for the morrow, when officers of the law arrived at the house to break the "news" of her brother's "accident." Yes, he was glad that Flynn and Clive were there to comfort her. Especially Flynn.

He drained the glass in his hand and stared moodily at the lights reflected in it. Without volition, his arm jerked and he hurled the glass against the wall where it shattered into a thousand pieces.

Once outside, Lord Kirkland breathed deeply of the cool night air. The fog had dissipated, blown to smithereens by a fresh westerly breeze. He had the doorman hail a hackney for him. It was Saturday night and he was, after all, a creature of habit.

The hackney let him down at a coffeehouse in St. James. His lordship did not linger in the coffeehouse, but after a suitable interval, he slipped out through a side door and made the short walk to the Temple of Venus in King's Place.

He stared at that unprepossessing little house as if he could not remember what had brought him there. When the doorman spoke to him, coming to himself, the earl turned aside. Hailing a sedan, he gave the chairman the direction to his house in Hanover Square.

Chapter Thirty

❦

Outside Ward House, servants were bustling around following Lord Charles's instructions for stowing the baggage in his carriage. Clive was mounted on a bay, as was Mr. Hadley. Letty, with a nephew's hand firmly clasped in each of her own, was waiting patiently for the servants to be done so that she could enter the coach. A week had passed since Jeremy's funeral and the Wards were going to Lord Charles's place near Henley to recuperate. Serena had chosen to remain at home.

Inside Ward House, Catherine and Serena were saying their farewells.

"Won't you reconsider and join us at Stanworth?" said Catherine. "I don't like the thought of leaving you in this house alone."

"I won't be alone," said Serena. "Flynn will be with me. And if I change my mind, Henley isn't so very far away. I can be there in a few hours."

Catherine made no further argument, and Serena felt a small twinge of conscience, knowing that she had deliberately misled her sister-in-law into thinking that Mr. Hadley and Letty were the reason she was declining Lord Charles's invitation. Though they hadn't announced their betrothal, there was no doubt in anyone's mind now which sister Mr. Hadley preferred. On hearing the news of Jeremy's "accident," he'd come straight round to Ward House, and it was Letty who had thrown herself into his arms.

Serena's real reason for declining Lord Charles's invitation was something she preferred to keep to herself. She wanted peace and quiet away from them all. She couldn't talk about Jeremy, couldn't forget that she had been wrestling with him for possession of the pistol when it had gone off. She was consumed with guilt and remorse, and that guilt became unbearable every time she looked at Catherine and her two fatherless nephews.

As a footman edged past her with one of Catherine's boxes, Serena moved aside. The front doors stood open, and the excited chatter of young Robert and Francis as they admired Lord Charles's equipage was a welcome sound to her ears. In the week since Jeremy's funeral, this was the first time the boys had raised their voices above a whisper.

Catherine's eyes filled with tears. "They are so young," she said. "They don't understand about their father, not really. Perhaps I shouldn't be going to Stanworth. But Charles thought that it would do the boys a world of good to get out of the city, and I could not bear to take them to Riverview."

"It *will* do them a world of good," said Serena, striving to hang on to her own composure. "And you too." Linking arms with Catherine, she walked her to the front doors.

Catherine dabbed at her eyes. "Do you know, I still can't believe it? At any moment, I think I am going to waken and discover that this has all been a bad dream, and that there never was an accident. How could it have happened? Jeremy was always so careful around guns." Her voice broke, and she pressed her handkerchief to her lips.

There were some lies that simply had to be maintained. "We shall never know," said Serena. "It's best not to think about it."

As they came out to the front steps, Lord Charles came

forward to meet them. Serena relinquished Catherine's arm and watched as he helped her sister-in-law into the coach. He was very matter-of-fact, very much the old family friend, and his pose did not fool Serena for one moment.

When he made to follow Catherine into the coach, he hesitated, then turned back to speak with Serena.

"Is there nothing I can say to make you change your mind?" His voice was guarded, as was his expression.

"Nothing, thank you," said Serena. She had already said her farewells to the rest of the family, but her throat clogged with tears as she waved to her nephews. She was thinking that Jeremy had never really got to know his children. In that respect, he was like their father, and now she knew why. They were always too busy drumming up support for the Stuart cause.

Lord Charles's mouth flattened. "Surely, for Catherine's sake, we can set aside our differences? I know you have never liked me, or perhaps it would be more accurate to say that you have always mistrusted my motives. What can I say, what can I do to reassure you?"

She gazed at him with a mixture of remorse and reserve. "I never knew . . . never understood." She paused, faltering a little. "May I speak frankly?"

"Please do."

"I never knew how much my family owed you, never realized that you were always there to help us when my brother Jeremy got into . . . financial difficulties."

He stiffened. "You were never meant to know. And as I have already explained to Clive, I regard all debts canceled with Jeremy's death, so you need not fear I will set duns on you."

"You misunderstand. I never thought that for a moment."

His expression was still wary, and she could not blame

him. She had never tried to conceal her dislike of him when he came to the house, had never understood his devotion to Catherine. She'd summed him up as a rake, with nothing on his mind but making another conquest, and she had wanted to protect Catherine from him. How could she have been so blind? If anyone had Catherine's best interests at heart, it was this man.

She put out her hand. His surprise was evident, but he accepted her hand just the same, squeezing her fingers gently before releasing them.

There was a catch in her voice. "I know it's too soon to say this, but I want you to know that I am glad Catherine has you to lean on. I know you will take good care of her and the boys. You always have." She smiled, blinking away the threatening tears. "And from now on, Charles, you may count me among your most devoted friends."

His eyes searched her face, then he smiled. Saluting her, he turned on his heel and entered the carriage.

Catherine's look was questioning.

"I was trying to persuade Serena to join us," he said.

"Uncle Charles, are you really going to take us fishing at Stanworth?" piped up young Francis. "And . . . and teach us to ride, and everything?"

"Of course. I said I would, did I not?"

"Yes, but, I mean . . . will you come with us, sir, or will you be too busy?"

"You promised you would come with us," said Robert.

"Robert! Francis!" said their mother, embarrassed, exasperated. "Lord Charles has more to do than look after two rambunctious boys."

"What does he have to do?" asked Robert.

Catherine did not know where to look. She was thinking of the house in Chelsea and what Jeremy had told her about the lady Charles had installed there. Charles was devoted to his mistress, and though many women had tried to displace her, his interest was fleeting. He always returned to Mrs. Danvers. It was mortifying to think that she had once believed she held a special place in his heart.

Lord Charles said, "You are quite wrong, Catherine. I have nothing better to do than look after two, um, lively boys."

"Really, Uncle Charles?"

"Really," he replied.

Catherine raised her eyes. "Charles," she said, "I don't wish you to . . . to put yourself out for us. I know that there are things in town . . ." Her glance slid to Letty. Having assured herself that Letty was deep in conversation with Mr. Hadley through the open window, she went on a little desperately, "You will want to keep up with your friends, and . . . and so on. We understand that. We won't feel neglected if you leave us for a day or two . . . or . . . or whatever."

"There is nothing to take me to London," he said, then added softly, "Not now."

For a moment, she saw something in his eyes that made her catch her breath, then the look was gone, and he put his head out the window, giving his coachmen the signal to get under way.

Serena remained on the front step until the carriage and riders had turned the corner of Buckingham Street into the Strand. In the hall, she came upon Flynn. In his black livery relieved with white lace and silver waistcoat, he looked very handsome, very distinguished. Her own unrelieved blacks made her feel like a crow.

"There is something I wish to say to you," he said.

"Flynn, if this has anything to do with Julian Raynor—"

"It has nothing to do with the major, leastways, not the way you mean."

"Good grief, this must be serious! You are forgetting to drop your aspirates."

There was no returning smile. "It is serious, Serena."

Nodding, she led the way into the breakfast room. "The coffee may be tepid," she said, indicating the silver coffeepot.

"It will do."

She poured out two cups and handed one to Flynn. "Sit down, Flynn. No need to stand on ceremony with me."

She didn't know why she was trembling, didn't know why she sensed that another blow was coming, but sensing it, she braced herself.

"Major Raynor has made me an offer I'd be a fool to refuse," said Flynn.

She didn't flinch. She didn't breathe. Not a muscle betrayed her. "I see," she said. Then, like an animated doll, she came to life. "A lucrative offer, Flynn? Yes, of course it must be. So you are giving notice, is that it? Is that what you are trying to tell me, that Raynor has stolen you away from me?"

He shook his head. "Serena, he isn't stealing me away from you."

"No? Then why don't you explain it to me so that I can understand. How long have you been with me now, Flynn? It must be all of sixteen years. I suppose it is time to move on. Oh, if it's a character reference you want, I'll vouch for you. Heavens, I look upon you as my dearest friend."

If he had not known how she was suffering, he might have been tempted to turn her over his knee and spank some sense into her. There was no reasoning with her in this mood, but he had to try.

"Major Raynor has offered me a share in his gaming house. He takes ship for America at the end of the month, did you know? At any rate, he wants someone running things in his absence, someone he can trust. He has made the same offer to Mr. Black—I think you may know of him?—so I won't be working on my own. I know I have a lot to learn, and Blackie is willing to teach me all I need to know. This is a chance in a lifetime for me. You must see that, Serena."

When she said nothing, he went on in the same level tone. "You always knew that I wanted to make something of myself, that I wanted more than this." He gestured with one hand, encompassing far more than that small room.

"And I applaud your ambition, I mean that sincerely, Flynn. It will be a great step up for you. I suppose you will take up residence in Raynor's rooms when he vacates them?" When he nodded, she went on brightly, "You'll be quite the gentleman, and you can do it too. Your language is as cultured as mine when you want it to be. Well, I suppose there is nothing more to be said. In lieu of notice, I shall give you a month's wages. I'm not sure how we are fixed, but I know that Clive will want to do right by you. There should be a generous annuity, and somehow, I know we shall manage it. Sixteen years is a long—" She couldn't go on, couldn't pretend that her heart wasn't breaking. This was one betrayal she had never, never expected. Abruptly rising, she moved to the sideboard, where she fiddled with servers and plates.

Flynn rose slowly. "I'm not leaving you in the lurch," he said quietly. "I told the major that I would serve out my notice. By that time, Lady Ward should have returned. I wouldn't dream of leaving you alone at a time like this."

She spun to face him. "You and Raynor should deal well together," she said. Her voice was cracking. "You both know how to use people to your own advantage."

"That is uncalled for, Serena, and you know it." In

contrast to her heated tones, his were gentle. "I'm not thinking only of the slur to my own character. The major has done nothing to deserve this."

Through a haze of tears, she stared at him. "Flynn," she said, appealing to him, "how can you choose him over me? You know what he did to me."

"He did nothing to you! You are being totally unreasonable, Serena. If you would only think about it, you would see that the major acted for the best."

"You dare to defend him to me?" In a rustle of skirts, she returned to the table. Her voice rose hysterically. "He used me to set a trap for my own father and brother. He admitted it. If I had not trusted him, they might still be alive today. How do you suppose I feel when Catherine turns to me for comfort? What words can I offer her? What should I say to my nephews? That I allowed love to blind me to the nature of that . . . that creature?" Her voice broke but she went on regardless. "I trusted him, Flynn, and my reward was the destruction of my own family. Do you know how far I was willing to go? Even knowing that he had used me, tricked me, I took his part against my own brother."

Flynn was as white-faced as she. "And if you could relive that moment, would you change things so that your precious brother and father could prevail? Oh yes, they would be alive, but you may be sure that the major would be in his grave. Would that please you? They were villains, Serena. Major Raynor did not know that they were involved. No one suspected them. But it is not that which riles you so much as the thought that your love was not returned. If you would only think about it—"

With a violence that stunned them both, she hurled her cup at him. "Get out!" she screamed. "I never want to see your face again. Do you hear me? Get out!"

Flynn used a handkerchief to wipe the coffee from his

face. Without a word of farewell, he turned on his heel and left her.

Serena heard the front door slam. Dazed, disbelieving, she flung herself into a chair. Arms extended on the table, head down, she let the bitter tears flow.

She was in her bedchamber when she heard Flynn's voice in the corridor. He sounded as though he had spent the whole day and half the night carousing. Without a word to her maid, she darted through the door.

"Flynn!" she called out. "Flynn!"

He had one foot on the stairs to the attics where his chamber was located. Turning to face her, he made a courtly though somewhat unsteady bow. "Fair Cyrene," he said, and his speech was slurred. "I am helpless to resist your spell, as you see."

Serena sped along the corridor. Her feet were bare. She was attired in a lace negligee, but she cared nothing for that. Coming to a sudden halt, she extended one hand toward him. "Flynn," she whispered. "Oh Flynn, I could not bear it if I lost your friendship. That means more to me than anything. Tell me we are still friends."

Her small hand was lost in his larger one. He looked at it for a long moment, then smiled into her eyes. So unaware, he thought, so damnably unaware of him as a man.

"Say you forgive me, Flynn. Please say you forgive me."

"There is nothing to forgive."

Whatever she saw in his eyes reassured her. With a little sigh, she walked into his arms. "Don't leave me, Flynn, not yet. This is a wonderful opportunity for you. I see that now. Please, please, just give me a little time to get used to the idea. All right?"

He held her in a loose, comforting clasp. "Oh Serena," he whispered, "what am I going to do with you? What am I going to do with you?"

* * *

In the weeks that followed, Serena did not put a foot outside the door of Ward House. A good part of the time, she moved through the rooms like a wraith, halting in her tracks as memories came back to her, as clear and as vivid as though the events had happened yesterday. There had been laughter in these rooms, there had been times, many times, when she was sublimely happy, but that was when she had been a child. Somewhere, somehow, as she had grown to womanhood, the joy had slipped away from her. She supposed it was the difference between being a girl and being a woman.

She tried hard not to think of Riverview, and the frightful events that had taken place there. But no matter how hard she tried, she could not wipe out the painful memories.

Flynn did not understand. There had never been any doubt in her mind that when it came down to it she would do whatever was necessary to save Julian. She had chosen him over her own father and brother, and if she had to relive that moment, she would do exactly the same again. What filled her with self-loathing and anguish was that Julian had made her his dupe, had used her for his own purposes. There was a horrible, horrible logic to things she had never understood before—his pursuit of her, their Fleet marriage, his determination to make it a real one. He had made her part of his vendetta, and that was unforgivable.

By his lights, she supposed Julian had just cause. She wasn't blind to her father's sins. What he had done to Julian and his family was iniquitous, beyond the pale. She would never understand it, never condone such unconscionable conduct. He deserved to be punished for what he had done. But why, oh why, had Julian chosen *her* to be his pawn in his deadly game of revenge?

She would never know the answer to that question. She never wanted to see him again, and if he had called at the house, he would have been turned away. She need not have worried about meeting up with him again. Julian had no more wish to see her than she had to see him.

Serena might not wish to meet up with Julian again, but she could not help hearing about him. In the weeks following her family's departure, friends and acquaintances called at the house to offer their condolences. In the general flow of small talk, Julian's name frequently came up.

It seemed that Lord Kirkland had acknowledged him as a long-lost nephew. He and his countess were fêting Julian, and introducing him to their own exalted circles. There was to be a ball at Hanover Square on a scale that had never been seen before, just prior to Major Raynor's departure for America. It was the oddest thing, and no one had explained it adequately, but it turned out that his name was Renney, not Raynor, though he was quite happy to answer to both names.

One such caller who took Serena completely by surprise was Lady Amelia Lawrence. It was Flynn's voice that she heard first. He was turning someone away at the door, intimating that Serena was resting and was not up to receiving visitors. There was something in what he said. The peace and quiet she had hoped to achieve by remaining in town was proving to be elusive, not least because of the steady stream of visitors. She was on the point of slipping away unnoticed when she recognized Lady Amelia's voice. Flynn's reluctance to allow the caller admittance to the house was now explained. He knew how much she had always detested the woman.

It was curiosity that prompted her to intervene. Lady Amelia was no friend to her. She could not think what purpose there could be to this visit, but she was curious to find out.

Descending the stairs, she said, "I am quite rested now, thank you, Flynn. Lady Amelia, how kind of you to call."

They spoke in commonplaces as Serena led the way to the upstairs drawing room. When Flynn dispensed the sherry, then stationed himself by the door, Serena almost smiled. He was acting as her watchdog again, ready to defend her if Lady Amelia said one wrong word.

That wasn't going to happen. The old animosity, for whatever reason, had vanished. They were simply acquaintances and could meet and converse like two polite strangers.

"That will be all, Flynn, thank you," said Serena and pointedly ignored the warning look he darted at her before he left the room.

For the first few minutes, the conversation was of the recent tragedy, and how the Ward family members were bearing up in their sorrow. Lady Amelia was on her second glass of sherry before she broached what was on her mind.

"I never expected such kindness in you," she said. "I know I don't deserve it."

Lady Amelia's expression was so serious, her voice so earnest that Serena checked the polite and meaningless reply she was on the point of uttering. Not knowing what to say, she remained silent.

"I have resented you for a long, long time," said Lady Amelia. "All of eight years, is it not?"

Eight years ago, she and Lady Amelia had been rivals for Allardyce's affections. Since that time, they had treated each other like lepers. "Eight years," said Serena. "That was a long time ago." It seemed so far away, so insignificant, she could hardly remember it.

Lady Amelia sighed and looked away. "I have always

regretted the way things turned out—you know what I mean. We have behaved abominably to each other over the years. How could we have allowed someone like Allardyce to have such a profound effect on us? You became a shadow of your former self, and I . . ." Her voice cracked, and she coughed into a lace handkerchief.

Serena hardly knew what to say. She looked at that breathtakingly beautiful woman who could have any man she wanted, a woman whom she had envied quite desperately at one time, yes, and for more years than she cared to remember, and it was like seeing her for the first time. It came to her then that Lady Amelia had loved Allardyce far better than she, and for far longer.

I pity her, Julian had said, *as you should pity her, Serena.*

Swallowing, Serena put out a hand, and awkwardly patted Lady Amelia on the shoulder. "We have behaved like silly schoolgirls," she said, and they both laughed.

"We won't make that mistake again."

"Beg pardon?" said Serena.

"What I mean to say is, this time, you won't accuse me of stealing Julian away from you? There is nothing between you two, is there? Oh, I admit that for a time there I thought there was. The way he looked at you! The way you looked at him! I was quite envious, really. No one has ever looked at me in quite that way. I see now, however, that you were only playing a part, you know, as we all were, to scotch the ugly rumors that were circulating."

The warm, friendly feelings that had begun to kindle in Serena's breast were rapidly cooling. Julian and Lady Amelia? She must have misunderstood. "What exactly are you saying?"

Lady Amelia gathered her things together, and Serena rose with her, walking her to the door. "I thought that would be obvious," said Lady Amelia. "I'm fond of Julian, more than fond of him. If there is a chance for me, I intend to pursue it. Is there a chance for me, do you think?"

Serena managed to hold on to her smile, though she could not prevent the chill in her voice. "Julian is the one you should be asking, not me," and ushering Lady Amelia through the door, she shut it with a snap.

Flynn had stationed himself on the landing. As Lady Amelia came up to him, he moved in front of her, escorting her to the front door in his most impeccable footman's manner. Nothing was said till they came to the front hall.

"How did it go in there?" he asked in a quiet undertone.

With a quick look about her, Lady Amelia whispered, "Quite well, I think. But Flynn, explain to me, if you please, why you almost turned me away at the door, and why all the speaking looks to Serena?"

Flynn grinned. "Oh, that's just Serena's way. If you try to get her to do something, you can be sure she'll do the opposite, and vice versa. Besides, we wouldn't want her to suspect what we are up to, now would we?"

"I see," said Lady Amelia, not seeing at all.

On the other side of the drawing-room door, Serena took several breaths in quick succession. It was one thing to give Julian up, it was quite another to see him go to another woman, especially to someone as beautiful and desirable as Lady Amelia. This was not on a par with losing Allardyce. Allardyce had been a silly, schoolgirl infatuation. She was coming to see that losing Julian was on a par with dying a slow, painful death.

Her future stretched out in front of her, a future without Julian, without joy, and with her luck she might even live to be a hundred. The thought was intolerable. And it wasn't as though she hated Julian. She still loved him.

That could never change. But she couldn't forgive him, that could never change either.

When Flynn entered, he took one look at her and alarm coursed through him. Arms folded across her stomach, she was hugging herself, shivering uncontrollably. "Serena, what is it?" he said, and quickly crossed to her. "What did Lady Amelia say to bring this on?"

Her voice was shaking as badly as the rest of her. "Oh Flynn, say something, anything, to convince me that Julian wasn't merely using me as an instrument of revenge."

"Revenge? Against whom?"

"My father, of course!"

"Now how did that maggot get into your brain?"

"Don't tease me, not now! You know the whole story as well as I do. He hated my father, and with good reason."

"That is true." Flynn's smile was grim. "But you are forgetting one small point. Like the rest of us, the major believed that your father was dead and buried these two years." He gave her a moment to think about it.

She touched a hand to her throat and a light leapt in her eyes. Then the light faded, and she shook her head. "That's easy to say, but how can I believe it? You didn't hear him, Flynn. His one purpose in life was to see my father ruined and shamed. I think he suspected my father was alive and used me to get to him."

He made a small sound of impatience. "There is something else you should know, something I had not wished to tell you for fear you would put the wrong interpretation on it. Serena, we could easily have taken your father prisoner. The major stopped us. We knew that Sir Robert was making for that boat. We assumed he would make his escape, as he could have done if he had wanted to. When we heard the report of that shot, can you imagine how the major felt, how we all felt?"

She stared at him for a full minute, then her face crumpled and she said achingly, "Oh Flynn, if only you had told me! Why didn't you?"

"Because I thought you would say that Raynor is such a monster that he guessed that your father would take his own life, and that he was merely saving himself the trouble of doing it for him."

"Please, Flynn, no more." She was trying, unsuccessfully, to brush away the torrent of tears that coursed down her cheeks. One part of her was overjoyed. Julian would have spared her father if it had been possible, and she knew with unshakable conviction that he would have done so only for her sake. Another part of her was wallowing in self-pity. Her faith in him had come to her too late. No man wanted a woman who was forever mistrusting his motives. She had lost him, and it was her own fault.

Flynn was pitiless. "Since you are determined to mistrust the man, I'm sure if we put our minds together, we can come up with other good reasons for you to hate him."

She stared at that stony face, hoping for some sign of softening, but there was nothing but unrelenting contempt. "I have been such a fool," she whispered brokenly.

"There's no denying it."

She sniffed. "He won't have me, you know. Not now. He must despise me."

"That would not surprise me."

She looked away. "Lady Amelia . . . Lady Amelia wants him for herself."

"He could do worse." He could see that her hackles were beginning to rise, and he decided to add one more faggot to the flames. "In fact, I think they would do very well together. She is a beautiful, accomplished woman. Adventurous too, by all accounts. Well, she would need to be if she is going to accompany him to America. She'll be an asset to him, don't you think? I mean, they say he is thinking of standing for their Houses of Parliament, or whatever they call it over there."

Her eyes glinted up at him. "Lady Amelia," she said, "would be an asset to any man. But there is one small thing neither she nor you has taken into account."

"What's that?" asked Flynn.

"Julian already has a wife."

She left him in a flounce of skirts and with the door vibrating so alarmingly that Flynn expected to see it fall off its hinges.

"Now you're talking," he told the empty room.

Chapter Thirty-One

❧

W hen the carriage stopped, Flynn jumped down and helped her to alight. Now that they were here, now that she was about to beard the lion in his den, her courage began to ebb.

Flynn led the way to the side door to Julian's house. As she shook out her skirts, she heard the key grate in the lock, and was reminded that as part proprietor, Flynn now had keys to every door in Julian's gaming establishment.

"Don't dawdle, Serena," he said. "I told you that Julian is engaged to attend an assembly at the Stows' this evening. You have only a few minutes to say what you have to say. Time is of the essence."

Nervous as she was, she could still smile. Flynn was spending so much time at the gaming house these days that he was now on Christian-name terms with Julian. His speech and manners had also undergone a change. In short, Flynn was quite the gentleman. It seemed incredible to her and rather wonderful that he had advanced so far. In his pocket was a gilt-edged invitation to the same do that Julian had been invited to attend. Her family had never aspired so high as the Duke and Duchess of Stow, nor had they once crossed the threshold of their magnificent house in St. James Square.

"Perhaps we should have told Julian I was coming," she whispered. Though she had yet to take a step inside the door that Flynn held for her, her eyes were traveling up the length of that candle-lit staircase, and it seemed like a long, long way to the top. "Or I should have sent round a note asking him to call on me?"

Flynn clicked his tongue. "If you were to follow that route, you would never be given the opportunity to come within a mile of him. You are not exactly his favorite person at present. Frankly, Serena, I dare not breathe your name in his hearing for fear of setting off an explosion."

"That . . . that sounds encouraging, don't you think, Flynn?"

He said nothing, but his look robbed her of the little courage she had left.

"Perhaps," she said, "this isn't such a good idea."

"Suit yourself. It's your idea, not mine."

There was something about Flynn's indifference that brought out the stubborn streak in her. With a swish of skirts, she stepped over the threshold and planted her foot firmly on the bottom stair.

"I'll wait in the carriage," said Flynn.

Her head whipped round. "What? Aren't you coming with me?"

"Oh no, Serena. I know better than to put myself in the middle of a cat-and-dog fight. Oh, good luck!" And with these cheering words he shut the door on her.

Before ascending the stairs, she took a moment or two to shore up her courage. A lady who had been a prime mover in a Jacobite escape route need not fear a few cross words. Now who had put that idea in her head? Flynn, of course, but Flynn had never seen Julian in a temper.

She started over. Julian had once told her that she must never forget that she was Victoria as much as she was Serena. "Victoria," she whispered as though invoking the help of her guardian angel. Victoria was brave, confident, honorable, charming, vivacious . . . She groaned. It was too bad Victoria wasn't here. Well, she would just have to make do with Serena.

It *was* a long staircase, far longer than she remembered. With each faltering step, her skirts rustled and the boards creaked. At any moment, she expected to see Julian at the top of the stairs, demanding to know why she was sneaking into his establishment, or what was worse, perhaps mistaking her for a burglar. Either way, it was quite possible that he would throw her bodily off the premises.

It's what she deserved. But he wasn't without his share of the blame for what had happened either. Guilt. Innocence. None of that mattered. They loved each other. That was the important thing, and that's what she would try to impress upon him. Unless, of course, he threw her out first.

When she took that last step and came out onto the corridor, she saw that all the doors were closed bar one, the door to Julian's bedchamber. It stood open. She heard voices, Julian's voice, and one she couldn't identify, but at least it was masculine. If she had heard a female's voice, she would have gone on the rampage.

At the door to Julian's chamber, she halted. His valet was helping him into a pale green satin coat with silver embroidery. His hair had already been powdered, but lightly, as was his custom. Though his back was to her, she looked at his reflection in the mirror. He looked so handsome, so arrogantly masculine, that her heart clenched as if from a blow. If it had been possible, she would have decked herself out in her finest. She was in her blacks, as was proper for a lady in mourning. It was hardly the effect she wanted to achieve when she had half a mind to seduce him.

Without her being aware of it, she had taken several steps into the room. Julian's head suddenly came up, and their eyes locked in the looking glass. His expression was so icy, so chilling, that she froze in mid-step.

"That will be all, Tibbets," he said.

Even the valet seemed to feel the arctic temperature.

Suppressing a shiver, with a long pitying look at Serena, he beat a hasty retreat.

"What the hell are you doing here?" asked Julian. He didn't even turn to face her, but hunted on top of the dresser for odds and ends which he stuffed in his pockets.

Her rehearsed speech went clean out of her head. "I . . . I have decided to give you another chance," she said.

He came at her with such terrifying speed that she fell over herself in her haste to get away from him. He went right by her and reached for his dress smallsword which lay on top of the bed. Buckling it on, he said, "Now why would I want another chance?"

"Because we love each other? Because we both made mistakes? Because . . . Julian, you are not making this easy for me."

"I have no interest in making anything easy for you. But I should like to know what made you change your mind."

She looked down at her clasped hands. "Flynn told me that you would have allowed my father to escape. I knew, then, that I was more important to you than your revenge."

"I see."

This was no time to be craven. "That's not it, Julian. I love you, and that's all there is to it."

Without warning, he blew out the candle. For one joyous, thrilling moment, she thought she had won, that he was going to make love to her, but he stepped into the corridor and made for the stairs. Surprise held her captive for one moment, then she raced to catch up with him.

"Julian, this is absurd!"

"It certainly is." He spoke over his shoulder. "Why are you dogging my footsteps?"

"Because I am determined to make you listen to me, determined to make you forgive me."

When they came out onto the pavement, he made straight for the hackney, the hackney she had hired with her *own* money, and he stepped inside without reaching a hand to help her into it. Lifting her skirts, glowering at him, she hoisted herself on board.

"Good of you to call for me, Flynn," said Julian.

As Serena came in one door, Flynn went out the other. "I think," he said, in some alarm, "that I shall be more comfortable riding on the box with the coachman."

Serena settled herself on the banquette opposite Julian. By now, she was getting desperate. "Julian," she said, trying to sound sincere, going as close to groveling as she would permit herself to go, "just tell me what to do to make it up to you, and I promise I shall do it."

"What can you do?" he asked indifferently.

Before she could frame an answer, he flicked his eyelashes, dismissing her, and he turned to stare fixedly out the window.

As the hackney rattled over cobblestones, Serena sank into a morass of despair. *Too late, too late, too late!* Even the carriage wheels were mocking her. The dismal prospect of life without Julian passed before her eyes. "Oh God," she whispered fervently, "don't let me live to be a hundred."

"What did you say?" asked Julian.

"We are turning into the square."

When the carriage pulled up outside Stow House and Julian lightly jumped down, Serena hesitated for one moment then flung herself after him. She couldn't give up now.

On the pavement, however, she began to have second thoughts. Throngs of people dressed in every shade of the rainbow were milling about. She was in mourning. It wasn't seemly for a lady so recently bereaved to attend parties. Besides, she didn't have an invitation.

"Come along, Victoria," said Julian. "Oh, did I tell you that you look magnificent in black? Every lady here is going to wish she were in mourning."

The words electrified her. It was all the encouragement she needed. Flanked by Julian and Flynn, she entered the house. No one challenged her. No one asked to see her card. Her escorts were two of the most celebrated men in London, glamorous figures, gamesters both, touched with danger, wildness, recklessness. In short, her perfect complements.

"Tarnation!" exclaimed Flynn, " 'Ow a man is supposed to keep 'is balance with these 'ateful smallswords dangling between 'is legs is more than I can comprehend. I could do myself an 'einous injury." With a little help from Julian, he adjusted the smallsword till it hung at just the right angle.

"You are a pair of lambs in tigers' clothing, did you know?" said Serena.

Laughing together, they joined the queue which was wending its way to the reception line in the great drawing room. As each guest came up to the majordomo, he beat his ornamental cane on the tiled floor and called out the appropriate name.

When it was Flynn's turn, the majordomo beat out a fancy tatoo, not unlike one of Serena's secret codes. He did it to honor one of his own. In his eyes, Flynn's meteoric rise was a cause for national rejoicing.

"Mr. Richard Flynn," he called out at the top of his lungs, and just to make sure that no one missed Flynn's big entrance, he called his name again.

Serena's eyes rested on Flynn, and she thought him the picture of elegance. His fair hair was tied back by a green velvet ribbon that matched his velvet coat. At his left ear winked the green emerald, adding a touch of recklessness. She felt her heart swell with pride as he flashed her a smile, sharing this precious moment with her. He had broken the barriers of his class. Nothing could hold him back now. And Julian had made it possible.

It was her turn.

Tell me what to do to make it up to you, she'd said.

What can you do?

Julian was on the point of giving their names to the majordomo.

"Wait!" she cried out. And suddenly, she knew what to do, knew what Victoria would do if she were in her place. Victoria wasn't afraid to take risks. Victoria wouldn't let the man she loved slip away from her under any circumstance. Just thinking like Victoria made her feel that she *was* Victoria.

Looking at Julian with all the love she could muster, which was fathomless, she said slowly and distinctly, "My name is Mrs. Julian Raynor, yes, that's what it is, Mrs. Julian Raynor."

A sudden silence gripped the bystanders and they turned to stare. Some raised their eyebrows. There were a few titters.

Before the majordomo could do more than raise his cane, Julian stopped him with a chilling, "No!"

Everything inside Serena shriveled. He didn't love her, didn't want her. She had ruined everything and he was going to shame her in front of all these people. She had gambled and lost.

The silence was so long that she was forced to look at Julian, and what she saw in his eyes made her breath catch and her heart contract. Love and joy blazed out at her. No one had ever looked at her in that way before.

"No?" she asked, and her voice was not quite steady.

He put his hand out for hers, and she grasped it. He was trembling almost as badly as she.

"The name is Renney," said Julian, "not Raynor."

The majordomo looked to Serena for confirmation. She didn't see him. She was staring openmouthed at the ring her husband had just slipped on her finger. An emerald as big as a robin's egg, set in a cluster of amethysts and diamonds, winked up at her. And when she was still in shock, still trying to catch her breath, Julian shocked her even more. Dropping to one knee, he quickly kissed the hem of her gown.

Reading the lady correctly, the majordomo went through the ceremonial ritual. "Mr. Julian Renney," he called out, "and Mrs. Renney."

In the great drawing room, Flynn raised his glass of champagne in silent tribute. A moment later, he turned away and became lost in the crush of onlookers.

She wakened to such a sense of well-being, such a sense of harmony, that she knew this moment in time would be forever locked in her memory as something to cherish. No two people had ever loved like this; there had never been such joy.

It was more than his lovemaking, more than the embraces they had shared when he had taken her to his bed last night. Long into the night, they had talked their hearts out, saying everything that needed to be said.

She would always honor the memory of her father and brother. Though she knew that they would have shown no mercy to Julian, she loved them still. Julian understood this, just as she understood why he had been driven to do what he had done. It seemed incredible that in the midst of so much ugliness, with everything against them, they had been drawn to each other from the very first. As Julian had told her, it was as though the Deity, or the

owers that be, had singled them out for the final con-
ummation of what had been a sad and tragic story. Julian
nd she were the happy ending, as well as the beginning
f something rare and beautiful.

She couldn't help looking at the ring Julian had given
er. Never, in her whole life, had she ever possessed any-
ing so beautiful or costly. It was a ring fit for a queen.
he held her hand up to the light and examined the ring
om all angles. It was a ring to treasure, not because it
as beautiful, not because it was costly, but because it
as the symbol of a love that had triumphed against all
dds.

"What are you thinking?" Julian's arms tightened
round her, bringing her more securely into the shelter of
is body. Though the passion between them always
unned him, he found a different kind of joy in the after-
ath of their lovemaking, something sweet and infinitely
umbling.

She wrapped one arm around his waist, and exhaled a
oft sigh. "I was admiring the ring you gave me."

He captured her hand, glanced at the ring, then gave
er a searching look. "You don't think it's a . . .
m . . . tad ostentatious?"

Actually, that thought had occurred to her, but think-
ng it disloyal, she had crushed it. "Certainly not!" she
aid, managing to look affronted. "I shall wear your ring
vith joy and pride."

He smiled. "I wanted to give you something extraordi-
ary to show how much I love you."

Her eyes filled with tears. His smile died. "What is it,
erena?"

"I almost lost you," she whispered. "If I had not forced
our hand, I would have lost you."

Laughing, he slapped her on the bare backside and
ame up and off their bed in one lithe movement. "Not a

chance," he replied. "Everything worked out exactly as
planned it. Now get dressed, woman. The last thing w
want is for some stranger to carry the report of our mar
riage to your family." He glanced at the clock on th
table by the bed.

"We're running late, but . . ."—he flashed her a sala
cious grin—"that's to be expected after the night w
shared." Bending to her, he pressed a quick kiss on he
open lips. "My poor love, did I quite wear you out? Neve
mind. You can sleep in the carriage on the way to Henley
What's the name of Lord Charles's place, by the by? I ca
never remember it.

"Stanworth," Serena replied automatically.

As she hauled herself up to a sitting position, h
stretched, arms above his head, quite oblivious to his na
kedness.

"What do you mean," said Serena, eyeing him appre
ciatively, "that everything worked out just as you planne
it?"

"Hmm?" He was at the washbasin, pouring a pitche
of cold water into a basin. "You're here, are you not? Yo
finally acknowledged that you are my wife, not only t
me, but publicly."

He laughed to himself as the recollection of the Stows
assembly came back to him. He and Serena had caused
sensation. How proud he had been to have her by his side
unquestionably his wife, his woman, as well-wishers had
mobbed them. How touched and humbled he had beer
when the Kirklands had come to stand beside them, add
ing not only their exalted presence but also making
silent though unmistakable declaration to the world tha
Serena and he were members of their family. And through
it all, Serena had been magnificent—gracious, charming
a warm and vibrant woman, and a great lady. He was the
luckiest man in the world.

"Julian?"

He turned to look at her. "Aren't you up yet? Oh, I ould have told you. My man should have delivered a tcher of hot water to the dressing room by now, rough that door there." When she made no move to get t of bed, he added pointedly, "for your convenience, rena."

"But . . ." She was gazing at her wedding ring in me perplexity.

"But what?"

"It can't be true!"

He turned to face her. "I assure you, Tibbets would not re forget my express orders. Through that door you will d everything to make a lady feel more comfortable."

"Julian!" she said with so much feeling that he looked her more closely. "Tell me the truth! Did you plan is?" and she held up a hand to display her wedding ng.

The smile left his eyes. Padding back to the bed, he lged down beside her. "Does it matter?" he asked seri- sly.

"Yes, it matters."

"Damn! I should have kept my mouth shut! Serena, is is absurd! What difference does it make if I took a and in things? You love me. I love you. You said so ourself. At last we are together. Don't spoil things for us, ot now."

"Tell me!"

He took her hands in his, and brought them to his lips. I sent Lady Amelia to you," he said quietly. "Flynn did e rest."

His eyes were wary, unsure. Hers were dazed as en- ghtenment dawned. With a great shriek of laughter, she ddenly launched herself at him, and Julian let out a lieved breath.

"I couldn't lose you. I couldn't," he said.

"There never was any fear of that, my love." She planted a lingering kiss on his mouth.

"At the same time, I wanted you to come to me willingly. It was a test, if you like, and you passed it with flying colors."

She shifted slightly to get a better look at his face. "Is that why you kissed the hem of my gown?"

He looked strangely embarrassed. "I did it on impulse, because you surpassed all expectations." To her unspoken question, he replied, "I was about to give the majordomo our names as Mr. Julian Renney and Mrs. Renney, when you forestalled me. You may imagine how I felt."

"But Julian! To kiss the hem of my gown! I distinctly remember that you scorned all such romantic gestures!"

Color crept over his cheekbones. "It was an impulse, and one I am not likely to repeat, no, not even if I live to be a hundred. So don't ask it of me."

"And the ring?" she said softly. "Julian, you must have been very sure of me."

"Yes," he said, and cleared his throat. "Flynn . . . um . . . told me that you kept our marriage certificate in your dresser. Since you had not destroyed it, even after the tragic events at Riverview, I knew there was still hope for me."

"Flynn told you? I can't believe Flynn went through my things!"

"He did it as a favor to me."

Serena was scandalized. Victoria thought it was rather touching, and Victoria carried the day. "That was very naughty," she said, and smiled.

"There was something else Flynn found that gave me hope." His eyes were soft with love. "He found my fifty-pound promissory note and a curtain ring."

"And . . . and that gave you hope?"

"I knew you must love me, else why would you trea-
re them?"

"Treasure them?" She looked at him blankly, then sud-
nly rolled on the bed and convulsed in whoops of
ughter. The harder she laughed, the deeper Julian
owned. The deeper Julian frowned, the harder she
ughed.

"I wish you would tell me," he said, "what I have done
rouse you to such hilarity."

She tried to answer him, but it was almost impossible
r the laughter that kept bubbling over. "That fifty . . .
und note? I was saving it . . . to stuff up your—"

"Serena!" said Julian sternly.

"—nose! And as for the . . . curtain ring, oh
ar . . . no . . ."—she was watching his face—"no, I
n't think I dare tell you what use I was going to make
it. But I shall give you a clue, shall I? I was reserving it
r another part of your anatomy. Then your days as a rake
ould be over."

He reached for her and administered a playful shake.
pitfire!"

She came up on her knees and draped her arms around
s neck. "Rake!" she said lovingly, and kissed him.
hen they drew apart, her voice was choked, her eyes
ere brimming. "I swear, Julian, you will never have to
it me to the test again."

He smiled and wrapped her in a bear hug. "No?"

"No. I love you, Julian Renney, and I am going to
end the rest of my life proving it to you." As an after-
ought, she added, "and I hope we both live to be a
ndred."

ABOUT THE AUTHOR

Elizabeth Thornton holds a diploma in education and a degree in Classics. Before writing women's fiction she was a school teacher and a lay minister in the Presbyterian Church. Ms. Thornton has been nominated for and received numerous awards, among them the Romantic Times Trophy Award for Best New Historical Regency Author, and Best Historical Regency. She has been a finalist in the Romance Writers of America Rita Contest for Best Historical Romance of the year. Though she was born and educated in Scotland, she now lives in Canada with her husband. They have three sons and two granddaughters.

Ms. Thornton enjoys hearing from her readers. Her e-mail address is <thornton@pangea.ca> or visit her at her home page:

http://www.pangea.ca/~thornton

If you loved *DANGEROUS TO LOVE,*
don't miss

ONLY IN HER DREAMS

by award-winning author
Elizabeth Thornton

On sale in spring 1998

Read on for a preview of this spectacular
new historical romance . . .

She came awake on a cry of terror, momentarily disoriented, as if she had been flung back in time to another house, another place. As awareness seeped into her, her heartbeat gradually slowed. She was safe. No one was hunting her. No one knew who or where she was.

The hiss of the rain lashing against the windowpanes had almost soothed her into sleep when lightning flashed and thunder exploded overhead. She raised herself on her elbows in anticipation of Quentin flinging himself into her room. He wouldn't admit that he was afraid of thunderstorms, of course. At eight years old, Quentin was beyond admitting that he was afraid of anything. It would be an amusing charade. Having discovered that his governess was terrified of storms, he would pretend that he had come to comfort *her*. She, none better, understood his bravado.

When the storm increased in ferocity, and still her young charge had not appeared at her door, Deborah felt for the candle on the table by her bed. After several unsuccessful attempts to get it lit, she gave it up, and slipping from the bed, reached for her wrapper. It took her only a moment or two to traverse the corridor to Quentin's room, and a moment after that to ascertain that the boy's bed was empty.

She hesitated, debating whether her employer, Lord Barrington, could have got there before her and carried his son off to his own chamber, or whether Quentin was playing tricks on her again. Deciding the latter, she groped her way into the corridor, her hand trailing along the handrail, till she came to the bannister at the head of the stairs. In that darkly shadowed interior, the light spilling from under the oor to his lordship's library on the floor below shone like a eacon.

She hesitated when she came to the turn in the stairs. "Quentin?" she called out. "Quentin?" There was no answer.

With a small sound of annoyance, she went to investigate, her mind already jumping ahead to the possible consequences of Quentin's rash prank. His health was not obust. He was just getting over a fever. If he had not donned his robe and slippers, she would give him the ough edge of her tongue.

As she approached the door to the library, she heard oices, and her steps slowed. She couldn't make out what vas being said, but she knew that one of those voices belonged to her employer, and he sounded distraught. The hought that something awful had befallen Quentin leapt nto her mind. Her hand reached for the doorknob, then roze in mid-air as Lord Barrington's voice rendered the ilence.

"Let the boy go," he pleaded. "For God's sake, have pity. He is only a boy. You of all people. Kendal, Lord Kendal . . Don't harm him!" The timbre of his voice thickened as his anguish increased. "Quentin, run for it!"

There was a thud, and Deborah was galvanized into motion. A gun went off as she flung the door wide and Quentin came bounding into her arms. The picture of her employer slumped on the floor with a shadowy figure standing over him flashed through her brain, but beyond that she registered nothing. Instinct had already taken over. She slammed the door shut and grabbed for Quentin's hand.

Then they were off and running, running, running, running.

Deborah ends up disguised as a dowdy teacher at Miss Hare's School of Deportment for Young Ladies in Bath, England. Here she hopes she can keep Quentin safe from the man she heard her employer identify as "Kendal"—before he was killed. Now a new employer has arrived to offer Deborah an idyllic-sounding position as companion to his young sister. But Deborah doesn't know that the charismatic "Mr. Gray" is known to his friends as John Grayson, the Earl of Kendal . . .

In the pink and white drawing room of Miss Hare's school of Deportment for Young Ladies, the ritual of taking tea was in progress. This was no empty ritual as was to be found in legions of drawing rooms throughout England in almost any day of the week. This was an exercise in deportment, a way of putting the girls through their paces, testing their competence in the social graces. That was the theory.

In practice, thought Deborah dismally, it was sheer torture, not least because the guest of honor on this particular afternoon happened to be a handsome, personable gentleman whom Miss Hare had vaguely introduced before abandoning him to his fate. It was he, of course, Mr. Gray, the gentleman who was seeking a mentor for his young sister, and Deborah could have wept in frustration. Of all the times to be caught unawares, this was unquestionably the worst. She could do nothing with the girls. They did not give a straw about learning the rudiments of drawing room conversation. They were all man-mad, and were flirting outrageously. Miss Hare frequently arranged for gentlemen guests to be present when the girls took tea, but no one of Mr. Gray's attributes had ever visited them. It was inevitable that these brazen hussies would be thrown into a twitter.

He was certainly handsome. In her experience, most men with his looks had the conceit to go with them. They fed on feminine adulation and knew how to charm a female into doing whatever they wanted. Mr. Gray wasn't like that. It had taken her only a few minutes to sum him up. She could see at a glance that he wasn't used to being the center of attention. He was ill-at-ease and seemed more than happy to allow her to do most of the talking. His modesty, his ineptness around females, was quite touching.

As her gaze lingered, his head turned, and eyes as blue and clear as a mountain stream caught and held her stare before the gentleman looked away. She had a flash of unease, a quick impression of a cat among the pigeons, then sanity returned. She was overwrought. She was imagining things. If Lord Kendal's minions ever caught up with her, they wouldn't waste time by taking tea. They would swoop down like vultures and carry her off in pieces. This quiet, unassuming gentleman was exactly what he appeared to be. She had nothing to fear here. Then why was he smiling? What was he thinking?

Gray was congratulating himself on the approach he had decided to take with the girl. His first inclination had been to swoop down and carry her off by force. His interview with Miss Hare had persuaded him to a more subtle course of action. There was no doubt in his mind that Miss Hare would raise Cain if her protégé were to be mishandled. Not only would she call in the constables, but she would pursue the matter with the tenacity of a British bulldog. The last thing he wanted was to involve others in how he meant to proceed with Miss Weyman.

The more he observed her, the more the conviction grew that he was not dealing with an enemy agent but a guileless innocent who had somehow got in over her head. It would be no great feat to terrify her into submission. He had every confidence that in a matter of days, if not sooner, she would be willing to tell him all that he wished to know. Yet, a small part of him regretted that he must be so hard on her. It was not his way to make war on defenseless women. He dismissed this thought almost as soon as it occurred to him. He could not be sure that she was as innocent as she appeared, and even if she were, she had abducted Quentin, and Quentin's safety took precedence over everything.

Deborah touched a finger to the furrow on her brow, willing an incipient headache to retreat, and she did her best to ignore the fluttering eyelashes and simpers that emanated from her charges. When, however, Millicent Dench rose to offer Mr. Gray another cucumber sandwich, Deborah sat bolt upright in her chair. One never knew quite what to expect from Millicent. It wasn't that the girl was wicked. It was simply that she could not refuse a dare. One quick look around at the girls' faces convinced Deborah that mischief, in bold letters, was brewing.

She was on the point of rising to head the girl off when Mr. Gray's voice arrested her. "Thank you, Miss Dench," he said, "but I prefer something sweeter. Miss Moir, I'll have a slice of that cake, if you would be so kind."

The hush that descended eddied with hidden currents. Deborah knew that she had missed something, but could not begin to guess what it was. She was aware that Millicent had received a snub—the girl's blushes attested to that fact—but there was more to it than that. Something had happened and she was the only person present who had missed it. She was aware of something else. The balance of power had shifted to Mr. Gray, and his innocuous words were responsible for it.

She looked at him curiously, and saw things about him that she had missed before—the breadth of his shoulders, the powerful masculine physique, and now that she came to think of it, that pleasantly modulated voice had carried an edge of steel. Had she mistaken his character? If so, it hardly mattered. The gentleman could be as masterful as Jupiter, just so long as he did not try to master her. There was no fear of that. His business would take him to London almost at once, and she and Miss Gray would be left to their own devices in the seclusion of his country estate. It was perfect, if only she could manage it.

When he turned to look at her, she saw that his eyes were smiling, and an unspoken message flashed between them. There was a joke in this somewhere, and later he would share it with her. When she nodded imperceptibly, Mr. Gray gave his attention to the cup and saucer in his hand. The smile on Deborah's face lingered.

She hadn't been mistaken in him. He really was a nice man, the sort of man a woman could make a friend of, up to a point. The only other men she had ever befriended had all been elderly, with the exception of Lord Barrington. Her thoughts drifted and a wistful expression came over her face, an expression that was not lost on the gentleman who was assiduously drinking his tea.

She came to herself with a start to discover that the girls had taken advantage of her preoccupation and were firing off questions like English archers releasing their arrows at the Battle of Agincourt. Was Mr. Gray married? Betrothed? How old was he? What was his profession? Where did he live? Why had he come into Bath? As the only mistress present, it was Deborah's duty to give the girls a push in the right direction when conversation flagged, or restrain them when they got the bit between their teeth. Though she was curious to know more of Mr. Gray, experience had taught her that if she gave the girls an inch they would take a mile, and there was no saying what they would come up with next.

"Girls," she said, and got no further. A gong sounded, loud and clear, and Deborah tried not to let her relief show. A lady who earned her bread by caring for other people's children must always appear in command of every situation.

"Study hall," said Deborah brightly, addressing Mr. Gray, and all the girls groaned.

With a few muttered protests and a great deal of snickering, the girls began to file out of the room. Deborah assisted their progress by holding the door for them, reminding them cheerfully that on the morrow they would be reviewing irregular French verbs and she expected them to have mastered their conjugations. As the last girl slipped by her, Deborah shut the door with a snap, then rested her back against it, taking a moment or two to collect herself.

Suddenly aware that Mr. Gray had risen at their exit and was standing awkwardly by the window, she politely invited him to be seated. "You'll have a glass of sherry?" she inquired. At Miss Hare's, the guests were invariably treated to a glass of sherry when the ordeal of taking tea was over. At his nod, Deborah moved to the sideboard against the wall. The glasses and decanter were concealed behind a locked door, and she had to stoop to retrieve them from their hiding place.

As he seated himself, Gray's gaze wandered over the lush curves of her bottom. There was an appreciative glint in his eye. The thought that was going through his head was that Deborah Weyman bore no resemblance to the descriptions he had been given of her. Spinsterish? Straitlaced? Dull and uninteresting? That's what she wanted people to think. She had certainly dressed for the part with her high-necked, long-sleeved blue kerseymere and the ubiquitous white mob cap pulled down to cover her hair. An untrained eye would look no further. Unhappily for the lady, not only was he a trained observer, but he was also an acknowledged connoisseur of women. Advantage to him.

Since her attention was riveted on the two glasses of sherry on the tray she was carrying, he took the liberty of studying her at leisure. Her complexion was tinged with gray—powder, he presumed—in an attempt to add years and dignity to sculpted bones that accredited beauties of the *ton* would kill for. The shapeless gown served her no better than the gray face powder. She had the kind of figure that would look good in the current high-waisted diaphanous gauzes or in sack-cloth and ashes. Soft, curvaceous, womanly. When she handed him his sherry, he kept his expression blank. Behind the wire-rimmed spectacles her lustrous green eyes were framed by—he blinked and looked again. Damned if she had not snipped at her eyelashes to shorten them! Had the woman no vanity?

"I missed something, didn't I?" said Deborah. "That's why you are smiling that secret smile to yourself."

"Beg pardon?" Gray's thick veil of lashes lowered to diffuse the intentness of her look.

Deborah seated herself. "I missed something when Millicent offered you a cucumber sandwich. What was it?"

If he had the dressing of her, the first thing he would do was banish the mob cap. There wasn't a curl or stray tendril of hair to be seen. "A note."

"A note?"

"Mmm." Red hair or blond. It had to be one or the other. Unless she had dyed it, of course. He wouldn't put it past her. If this were a tavern and she were not a lady, he would offer her fifty, no, a hundred gold guineas if only she would remove that blasted cap.

"Are you saying that Millicent passed you a note?"

Her voice had returned to its prim and proper mode. He was beginning to understand why she had kept out of the public eye. She couldn't sustain a part.

"The note," Deborah reminded him gently.

"The note? Ah, yes, the note. It was in the cucumber sandwich." She was trying to suppress a smile, and her dimples fascinated him. No one had mentioned that she had dimples.

"Oh dear, I suppose I should show it to Miss Hare. That girl is incorrigible."

"I'm afraid that won't be possible."

"Why won't it?"

"On her way out, she snatched it back. I believe she ate it."

When she laughed, he relaxed against the back of his chair, well pleased with himself. That wary, watchful look that had hovered at the back of her eyes had completely dissipated. He was beginning to take her measure. The more he erased his masculinity, the more trustful she became. Unhappily for him, there was something about Debrah Weyman that stirred the softer side of his nature. Advantage to her.

Deborah sipped at her sherry, trying to contain her impatience. As her prospective employer, it was up to him to begin the interview. He lacked the social graces. She wasn't finding fault with him. On the contrary, his inexperience appealed to her. It made him seem awkward, boyish, harmless. Besides, she had enough social graces for the two of them.

"Miss Hare mentioned that you were seeking a governess for your young sister?" she said.

He was reluctant to get down to business. All too soon, things would change. That trustful look would be gone from her eyes, and Miss Weyman would never trust him again. Pity, but that was almost inevitable. Still, he wasn't going to make things difficult for her at this stage of the game. That would come later.

Deborah shifted restlessly. "You will wish to know about references from former employers," she said, trying to lead him gently.

"References?" He relaxed a little more comfortably against the back of his chair. Smiling crookedly, he said, "Oh, Miss Hare explained your circumstances to me. Having resided in Ireland with your late husband for a goodly number of years, you allowed your acquaintance with former employers to lapse."

"That is correct."

"I quite understand. Besides Miss Hare's recommendation carries more weight with me."

"Thank you." She'd got over the first hurdle. Really, it was as easy as taking sweetmeats from a babe. Mr. Gray was more gullible than she could have hoped. The thought shamed her, and her eyes slid away from his.

"Forgive me for asking," he said, "Miss Hare did not make this clear to me. She mentioned that in addition to teaching my sister the correct forms and addresses, you would also impart a little gloss. How do you propose to do that?"

There was an awkward pause, then Mr. Gray brought his glass to his lips, and Deborah shrank involuntarily. She knew that she looked like the last person on earth who could impart gloss to anyone.

For a long, introspective moment, she stared at her clasped hands. Seeing that look, Gray asked quietly, "What is it? What have I said?" and leaning over, he drew one finger lightly across her wrist.

The touch of his finger on her bare skin sent a shock of awareness to all the pulse points in her body. She trembled, stammered, then fell silent. When she raised her eyes to his, she had herself well in hand. "I know what you are thinking," she said.

"Do you? I doubt it." He, too, had felt the shock of awareness as bare skin slid over bare skin. The pull on his senses astonished him.

His eyes were as soft as his smile. Disregarding both, she said earnestly, "You must understand, Mr. Gray, that governesses and schoolteachers are not paid to be fashionable. Indeed, employers have a decided preference for governesses who know their place. Servants wear livery. We governesses wear a livery of sorts, too. Well, you must have noticed that the schoolteachers at Miss Hare's are almost indistinguishable, one from the other."

"You are mistaken. I would know you anywhere."

The compliment was unexpected and thrilled her until she remembered that he saw her as an aging dowd. She'd seen his kind in action before. She'd wager her last groat that he was quite the gallant in the presence of elderly ladies. In another moment, he would be pinching her cheek and swearing that, in her salad days, she must have been a breaker of hearts. It was too mortifying to be borne.

"The thing is . . ." she began.

"Were you happy as a governess?"

"Beg pardon?"

"It could not have been easy, submerging your own personality to fit someone else's preconceived notions of what you should be."

She didn't mind being a governess. It was the necessity for her elaborate disguise that was hard to bear. In some ways it was like a prison sentence, but she couldn't tell him that. Behind the spectacles, her lashes flickered. She didn't want his sympathy, she wanted his respect. She had to convince him that she was the right candidate for the position.

"Mr. Gray, the point I am trying to make is this." Conscious that her tone verged on the tart side, she tried to sweeten it with a smile. "You may not think it to look at me, but I have knowledge of court life; I know what it is to prepare a girl for her first season; I am well versed in the modes and manners that prevail in the upper echelons of court circles. I don't have the credentials to prove it, but I am quite willing to be put to the test. Ask me something, anything you like, and I shall endeavor to answer you."

He could almost taste the desperation behind her words. She would know, of course, that he was after her. Did she fear him? If so, that was all to the good. One thing was certain. She did not fear Mr. Gray.

He had her in the palm of his hand. The thing to do now was to bring the interview to a speedy conclusion and arrange a time convenient to them both to convey her to the "villa" Nick had rented outside Wells. He did not wish to bring the interview to a close, not yet. There was something about Miss Deborah Weyman, a sadness, a wistfulness, and yes, a heart-tugging bravado that drew him like a magnet. If only for a few moments, he wanted to prolong the pleasure of her company. It might well be the only time she would look upon him with favor. Once again, he felt the sting of regret, and was taken by surprise.

"I don't know what to ask," he said, throwing her a helpless look.

"Think of your sister. What is it you wish for her?"

That was easy to answer. The real Margaret was quite [a] handful, and likely to give him a crop of silver hair befor[e] he had safely married her off. "Well . . . ," he began warming to his part.

"Nothing you can say will embarrass me, I promis[e] you."

His lashes lowered to half mast. If the lady was eager t[o] play games, he was willing to indulge her. "As Miss Har[e] may have told you," he said, "my sister, Margaret, is quit[e] an . . . um . . . heiress. Oh don't mistake me. Margare[t] is no fool. She knows about fortune hunters and men o[f] that ilk. It is experience in turning them off that she lacks. What advice would you give her?"

"Nothing could be simpler," said Deborah, bringing t[o] the question the same directness she would bring to a prob-lem that one of the girls had raised in class. "Avoid suc[h] men as if they were poison."

And that's exactly what he had told Meg, not that she'[d] listened to him. For all her paucity of years, she though[t] she knew how to handle men. He'd wager that Meg kne[w] more than Miss Weyman did.

Her bright eyes were watching him. Making a steeple with his fingers, he said, "With some gentlemen, that only makes them more persistent. They see it as a challenge. What if . . . what if she were caught unawares, like . . like you, for instance, alone, with me, behind close[d] doors?"

Deborah's eyes flicked nervously to the closed door, the[n] back to Gray. Cautiously inching forward in her chair, sh[e] looked with alarm at his left shoulder.

"What is it?" asked Gray, frowning.

"Don't move," she whispered. "There's a wasp crawling inside your collar."

"What?!"

While Gray lurched to his feet and batted ineffectually with his hands, Deborah darted to the door. With her hand on the knob, she turned back to laugh at him. "It's all right, Mr. Gray," she said. "There was no wasp."

By degrees, his glare gave way to a sheepish grin. Shaking his head, he said, "That was diabolical!" and he strolled toward her. When he came to the door, he negligently propped one shoulder against it. "You have convinced me that Margaret could do no better," he said. "In the interests of harmony, though, I think we should avoid the word 'governess' and substitute 'companion.' What do you say, Mrs. Mornay?"

Deborah's eyes were brilliant. Her voice wavered. "You won't regret it, Mr. Gray. I promise you."

"No, I daresay I won't. Then it only remains to arrange the day and the hour when I may convey you to my sister."

"I must speak with Miss Hare first."

"Naturally."

Deborah pulled on the doorknob to no avail. "Would you mind, Mr. Gray?" she said, indicating that the door would not budge because he was still propped against it.

In one smooth, unthreatening movement, he caught her by the wrist and held her fast. There was no fear in Deborah's eyes, only a question.

"And what if, my dear Mrs. Mornay," he said, "my sister should find herself in this predicament?" He raised her wrist and resisted her feeble struggles when she tried to free herself. "What advice would you offer then?"

Deborah dimpled up at him. "Assuming the girl has lungs, I would advise her to use them. Scream, Mr. Gray. She should scream, and when she is rescued, as she is sure to be, she should give out that a wasp crawled inside *her* collar."

"You have an answer for everything," he said in a slow, sleepy voice, and he edged closer. "I know how to prevent a scream. What if . . . what if the gentleman in question were to kiss her?" His eyes dropped to Deborah's mouth.

He was close, so very close, and she could feel his warm breath on her cool cheek. It wasn't fear or curiosity that held her captive, nor yet the restraining grasp on her wrist. A strange yearning uncurled inside her, then spread out in ripples, till she was shivering in anticipation. Slowly, inexorably, he tugged on her wrist, bringing her closer. Her lips parted and she forgot to breathe. His head descended. Hers lifted.

A gong sounded, just outside the door. Gray's eyes flared. Deborah blinked rapidly, then she looked about her as though she had no recollection of how she had got there.

When she gasped, he released her and took a quick step back. She was still gazing up at him, horror-struck, when he opened the door with a flourish and motioned her to precede him.

"If I'm not mistaken," he said, "study hall is over."

Her cheeks flooded with color and her eyes anxiously searched his. "Mr. Gray, I don't know what . . ."

He spoke at the same moment. "You were going to stamp on my foot. That's it, isn't it?"

"What?"

"You were playing up to me. Then, when I was distracted, you were going to stamp on my foot?"

She fastened on his words as if he had thrown her a lifeline. "Y-yes," then more emphatically, "Yes. That's exactly what was in my mind."

When they came into the corridor, they were caught up in the rush of girls who were coming and going to their various classes. Deborah was glad of the confusion, and embarked on a disjointed flow of small talk that lasted till Mr. Gray had taken his leave of her. As soon as the door closed upon him, she spun on her heel and made for the long pier glass in the teachers' common room.

Her reflection was vastly reassuring, she told herself. Mr. Gray could not possibly have been flirting with her. It was all in her head. Her steps were slow and heavy as she made her way to Miss Hare's office.